AN AMERICAN RECKONING

JOHN STONEHOUSE

Copyright © by John Stonehouse 2022
All rights reserved.

John Stonehouse has asserted his right under the Copyright, Designs and Patents Act 1988 to be identified as the author of this work.

All rights reserved. No part of this publication may be reproduced or transmitted in any form or by any means without permission of the author.

This book is a work of fiction. Names, characters, places and incidents are either a product of the author's imagination or are used fictitiously. Any resemblance to actual people, living or dead, events or locales, is entirely coincidental.

Cover Design by Books Covered
Interior Layout by Polgarus Studio

ISBN: 9798412999586

Chapter One

Shelby County, Tennessee
2014

4 a.m. Sweating in a new, ill-fitting T-shirt—heart racing, lights dim.

The lock on the door is wadded with cardboard—with paper, with pieces of green, state-issue soap.

The man behind him holds out a single shoelace between tattooed fingers. "Travis…"

The man named Travis takes it. Looks in the man's wild eyes, sees his nostrils flare above the short-trimmed beard.

He turns to the door. Works the lace into the housing around the lock, pushing it in behind the half-stuck latch, threading it behind an exposed, steel block.

Feeling for an edge, he tensions the lace. He steadies his hand. Pulls slowly.

The latch moves back—fully back into its housing.

Holding his breath he takes a half-step away.

The bearded man stares. "You get it? You pop it?"

The man named Travis eases open the door a quarter-inch.

Silence.

No sound.

No shriek, no pierce of alarm.

Static silence.

Heart hammering, Travis takes a breath, eyes the slit window—sees only black sky.

He pulls the door, turns to the bearded man; "Ready?"

The man looks at him, nods.

Stepping out, scanning the corridor—the bubble is empty.

No guard.

No face behind the glass in the observation cubicle.

A fresh bloom of sweat breaks on Travis's brow. "Let's go, let's move…" His voice a low whisper.

Padding down the corridor, ceiling lights glow as he reaches the turn on the wing.

He steps around.

Stops. Stands dead still.

The bearded man stops beside him.

Looking along the short length of corridor Travis sees the sally port—two hardened steel doors, a void between them. He strains his ears in the silence. "Reed?"

The bearded man looks at him.

"You hear anything?"

The man named Reed shakes his head.

A faint hum pervades the corridor, from overhead lighting.

Travis stares at a box-like feature, three feet wide—running floor-to-ceiling up one wall.

A shaft.

A pipe-chase shaft.

"Keep listening...." Stepping to the shaft he crouches at an access door spanning the full three feet of the vertical chase. No exterior handle. Only a small indent within it; a hole for a key.

From the back pocket of a pair of brand-new jeans he slides out a plastic toothbrush filed thin.

He lines up with the gap around the door. Steadies himself, eases the toothbrush in, starts to pry.

It won't be locked, he tells himself.

He hears a sound—a snap—feels adrenaline—his breath catches in his throat.

The man named Reed spins around—stares at the sally port, eyes locking onto the steel outer door. "The hell's that?"

"This. It broke. It snapped off." Travis feels the toothbrush handle limp between his fingers.

"Son of a bitch…"

Leaning in, alarm rising, he hooks the fingernails of one hand into the wooden edge of the door, pressing back with the toothbrush, levering.

It *has* to be unlocked.

Pressing harder, he feels the thin plastic yield.

Heart in his mouth he feels the door move—start to open.

Travis grabs at it, yanks it wide.

Reed grunts, "Alright, man, let's go, let's go…"

Water pipes and power lines plus an AC vent disappear into the ceiling.

Travis squeezes in, reaches up between the pipes and the vent.

Flattening against the wall he starts to climb.

The man named Reed squats, guides Travis's feet onto the tops of his shoulders, pushes him up.

Feeling over the lip of the pipe-chase, Travis thrusts his hands into the space above the ceiling. He pulls with well-honed arms, drags his body into the darkness of the void.

Turning around, he reaches down, grips Reed's outstretched arm.

He braces, pulls him up, hauls him over the lip of the shaft into the roof space. Lies panting, sweating. In the dark, still, dryness. Hearing nothing, sensing nothing.

Reed gasps, "Come on, keep moving…"

Turning onto his belly, Travis follows the AC vent; feeling for its metal sides in the pitch black.

Twenty yards in, his hand is at a concrete block wall.

The AC vent turns ninety degrees, runs vertical. "Right here…" his voice a whisper. "*Reed*, right here…"

On all fours now, pushing head and shoulders into the next shaft leading up. Pressing against the sides of the chase. Climbing.

Sensing something.

The air in the shaft cooling.

As the muscles in his legs and back and arms start to burn.

Sensing dim shapes—pipes, the aluminum vent.

The shaft above him turning again—through ninety degrees—horizontal.

He can hear Reed, hear him climbing, laboring.

He pushes up, struggles through the turn.

Crawls out onto the flat surface of a roof. Eyes blinking in the cold night air. Lights around the site of the prison dazzling—adrenaline pumping in his veins.

Reed scrambles from the opening of the shaft.

Both men lie flat against the roof. A fine mist of rain in the air.

Travis watches it swirl around the pole lights, around the guard towers—four of them.

He can make out officers inside two—a single figure in each one.

Fanning out from a hub in the center of the roof he sees the spot at the far end of an adjacent wing—the perimeter fence running close to the prison building.

He points to it for Reed.

The bearded man grunts.

Crawling toward the hub the sound of a vehicle is in the night air—somewhere over to the far side of the prison, the main entrance, a motor slowing—the first of the day shift showing up.

The first count of the morning less than an hour away.

Tracking onto the roof of the next wing Travis stares at its end—out over the perimeter fence—to the ground beyond.

Stomach twisting, he thinks of the drop. But the ground is raised, more than at any other point around the prison.

The fence passing close to the building—a fault, design fault, a weakness he'd searched out, and found.

Reed stares at him. "So, we going?"

Travis gets up on his haunches. "I'm going."

"How far down you think it is?"

"Fifteen feet, maybe. Twenty."

Reed rubs at his beard.

"What do you have to lose?"

"Both my legs," Reed answers.

Travis stares at the fence. Squats, stretches, touching the toes of his shoes. Stretching out, thinking of faux gymnastics in the prison yard—practice, jumping from boxes, rolling, conditioning their bodies for the fall. "Won't need your legs if your back gets broke."

Scanning the roofline, he checks the guard towers, the line of the perimeter fence. Heart racing. Blowing air from his lungs.

Focusing his mind he takes in the top of the fence wire, the grass of the landing site beyond it. Scrub vegetation, trees leading off into the dark. "Pick your spot, remember..."

"I know, man."

"Pick your spot to land, focus on it. Keep stable in the air."

Pacing back from the edge, he turns, counts down in his mind, the way he's rehearsed it a hundred times.

He takes a breath, runs—leaps from the side of the building. Tucks his chin to his neck, elbows in, knees bent. Eyes fixed on the landing spot. Holding stance to hit the ground with the balls of both feet.

The seconds stretch out.
In the black, hurtling.
Rush of cold air and sharp light.
And the whip choke of fear.

Chapter Two

Hudspeth County, Texas

Beneath the spreading branches of a Mexican white oak the German Shepherd at the edge of the neighboring property snarls through mesh wire fencing at the end of its chain.

Through the open window of his Chevy Silverado, Deputy US Marshal John Whicher eyes the dog, its body rigid, teeth bared.

He checks the address.

Scans the property alongside of the truck—a one-floor house, run-down, ranch style, with wood sides, painted green.

Around the house is a dirt yard. Patches of burnt dry grass and long weeds. A twenty-year-old sedan is on the driveway—a Nissan, its body panels marked up, hub caps missing.

He checks his watch.

Eleven thirty-five.

In the rear-view of the Silverado, a vehicle is rolling in behind.

He stares at it—a new-looking Buick SUV.

Straightening his necktie, he reaches for the tan, felt Resistol hat on the passenger seat beside him. He places it on his head, squares it. Steps out beneath a cloudless sky. On a rural lane, a November morning, temperature in the low seventies. The edge of a far West Texas town.

Fewer than a thousand souls. A town of small houses on scorched plots. Trucks and lean-tos among the live oak and prickly pear. Dirt blowing over aging asphalt roads.

The marshal buttons the jacket of his charcoal gray suit. Stands by his truck.

The Buick signals, pulls over.

Whicher smoothes the bulge beneath his left arm—the fabric of his jacket curving over the large-frame Ruger revolver in a leather shoulder holster.

A black woman behind the wheel of the Buick shuts off the motor.

She steps out.

She's in her forties, her face handsome, her body lean in slacks and a short-sleeve shirt. "Marshal?"

Whicher nods. "Ms Eastman?"

"Georgia Eastman." The woman steps toward him, offers her hand.

Whicher takes it.

"West Texas Juvenile Liaison Service," she says. "I hope I didn't keep you waiting."

"I was early, ma'am."

Behind the neighbor's fence, the German Shepherd growls, pacing back and forth on its length of chain.

Georgia Eastman reaches inside the SUV for a folder. "I came out from Fort Stockton." She swings the door of the car shut. "There anybody home?"

The marshal answers, "I thought to wait on you."

Eastman casts a look at the little green-sided house, at the car in the yard. She holds up the folder. "You get a look at any of this?"

Whicher shakes his head. "The call came into USMS first thing this morning. My boss told me to haul ass. That's about it."

Eastman looks at him. "Alright. Well, we have Bella McConnell, twelve years old—nobody's seen her since yesterday afternoon."

"Little over twenty hours," the marshal says.

Eastman nods. "She's currently the subject of a congregate care order in Fort Stockton. Living in a residential child care community. Secure, hostel accommodation."

"How come she's in there?"

"Bella has a history of truancy, drug taking and assault," Eastman says. "With this type of care order, we'll look for a hostel—typically, with a half-dozen or more kids. With close support till their behavior is stabilized. Fort Stockton was the nearest."

"Even though it's two hours away?"

"She also has a potential charge of felony burglary pending."

The marshal makes a question with his face.

"She denies it. Along with everything else," Eastman says. "The juvenile court is awaiting reports."

"Any idea what might've happened?" Whicher says.

"The hostel staff called yesterday when she didn't show up."

"What time?"

"A little after five thirty," Eastman says. "If a minor disappears from residential care the staff are obliged to call me—and I'm obliged to call law enforcement, let the police department and the county sheriff know. Bella's classed as high risk, marshal. She's vulnerable. She'd be prey to traffickers, child prostitution, to narcotics, you name it, it's a risk to her."

Whicher nods, looks over at the house.

"I called the mother last night," Eastman says. "Two times. I spoke with her. Told her to call me if she heard from Bella. I spoke to her again this morning."

"She know anything?"

Georgia Eastman arches an eyebrow. "Let's go ask her again."

The marshal follows Eastman up the dirt yard to the front door.

The German Shepherd watching, eyes shining.

Eastman knocks.

Whicher hears footsteps inside.

The front door opens.

A woman stands in the doorway—a striking woman—her hair long, thick, dark, almost black.

Her eyes are luminous—gray-blue in an alabaster face. Flawless skin over high cheekbones. Whicher takes in the full mouth, the poise. And a strangeness in her bearing.

Georgia Eastman nods a greeting. "Jessica."

The young woman folds her arms.

"This is Deputy US Marshal Whicher."

"Ma'am." Whicher holds out his badge and ID.

"Jessica McConnell," Eastman says to the marshal, "Bella's mother."

The young woman looks at him, coolly—takes in the suit, the hat, the six-one frame of the man in front of her.

She puts her hands on her hips—a black, cotton top hugging the curves of her figure. She leans her head on one side.

"Can we come in?" Eastman says.

"She's not here…"

Behind the show of calm, Whicher senses tension.

"We need to speak with you," Eastman says, "the marshal and I."

The woman turns from the door. Waves them in, into a cluttered hallway.

Whicher takes off his hat, passes a chipped mirror hanging from a hook on the wall. Wide-set hazel eyes look back at him above a broken nose. He smooths down his short, brown hair.

Jessica McConnell leads the way into a living room.

Whicher notices the faint smell of cigarettes.

A window is open letting in a light breeze.

Nothing about the house and the woman seem a fit—not the house—old, tired, untended—not the décor; faded walls and pictures, thrift-store furniture.

Jessica McConnell indicates a pair of hard-backed chairs.

Georgia Eastman sits, puts the folder on top of her lap.

The marshal takes the second seat, places the Resistol onto one knee.

The young woman sits on the arm of a sagging couch. Skintight jeans ripped at the knees, toe-nails of her bare feet painted a dark red. "I haven't heard from her."

"Bella is officially missing," Eastman says.

"Is that why he's here?" Tossing back a hank of black hair Jessica McConnell glances in Whicher's direction.

The marshal tries to read the look in the young woman's face. Surprise. Distress. Alarm, maybe. Something he can't quite place.

"Bella's listed as missing," Eastman says. "Local law enforcement don't have the resources to mount an extensive search."

"*Missing…*" Jessica says.

"She's not where she's legally meant to be."

"She'll be perfectly fine."

"Nobody knows where she is," Eastman says.

The young woman colors. "She just objects to being in that god-awful place."

"The Marshals Service have the resources to go out and find her."

"Ma'am," Whicher says. "You have any idea where your daughter might be? Who she might be with? Friends? Acquaintances? People she trusts?"

"No."

Whicher looks across the room to the window—to a threadbare green drape blowing in the breeze—then back again. He pins her with a look.

She spreads her hands. "I mean, I've called everybody. Everybody I could think of. But she probably just skipped out someplace, I don't think she's run off."

"You're not worried?"

"Of course I'm worried." The woman's eyes widen.

Whicher looks to Georgia Eastman. "How about people she might have come in contact with since she's been at the hostel?"

"I've spoken with some of them," Eastman answers.

"They're supposed to be looking after her," Jessica says, her voice tight, "aren't they?"

"Bella's not confined," Eastman says, "she's allowed an amount of freedom to come and go. She knows she has to be there at set times…"

"She never ran away from here. From me." Jessica McConnell gnaws lightly at her lower lip. "She shouldn't be in there—none of this should even be happening."

"You have a recent photograph of your daughter?" Whicher says.

The young woman stands, walks to a table at the side of the room. Picks up her phone, starts to scroll. Holds it out, shows its screen. "This. This was taken two weeks ago."

The marshal studies the photograph—a young girl, striking-looking, like her mother—the same eyes, the same near-black hair. Same look of self-containment. A hint of makeup, lipstick—she's older-looking than her twelve years.

He takes out his own phone. "I take a shot for the record?"

The woman nods.

Whicher takes a photograph of Bella McConnell—framed on the screen of her mother's phone.

"She shouldn't be in there. She knows it. That's why she's gone."

Georgia Eastman inclines her head at the folder on her lap. "Bella has a history of drug abuse, of truancy…"

"She smoked a joint a couple of times with friends. She skipped school now and then, so what?"

Whicher looks at her.

The young woman returns his stare. "You have kids?"

He nods.

"A daughter?"

He nods again.

"How old?"

"Ten," the marshal answers.

She sighs. "Well. Then you'll see."

Georgia Eastman raises the folder an inch. "There was an assault, at the school."

"A girl-fight. Bullshit."

"More importantly, possible indictment for felony burglary."

Jessica McConnell pulls a turquoise pack of American Spirit cigarettes from the pocket of her jeans. She lights up. Takes a drag. "You people are stressing me the hell out." She steps to the open window, shakes her head, blows out smoke. "Bella had nothing whatever to do with that so-called 'burglary.' She was just around, you know? Around a bunch of people—two idiot boys that went in a house…"

"The homeowner made a complaint," Eastman says.

Jessica looks to Whicher. "She was with a bunch of friends, plus these two boys. The boys went in some neighborhood house, Bella was with a bunch of girls, they were just with them. They didn't break in, the house was open, it was just some stupid stunt."

"The homeowner called the police?" Whicher says.

"It's just nothing. Just a misguided prank—a misdemeanor at worst."

The marshal takes in the evenness in the woman's voice.

She takes a pull on the cigarette. "They're not going to take her to court."

"The court will make its own decision," Eastman says.

"We need to think on where she's at right now," Whicher says, "get her back where she belongs."

"She doesn't belong in that damn place."

"You're not concerned for her safety?" the marshal says.

"No. Yes. I mean, of course I'm concerned. I just don't think she ran off anyplace, I think she'll be around, she'll be with someone. She'll probably just show up. She's got an attitude, I admit, but I don't think she needs cops searching for her, freaking out, freaking her out, turning the whole thing into some kind of circus."

"The first few hours when a child goes missing can be critical," Eastman says.

Whicher taps the hat on his knee. "If she's with the wrong people, that's not a good thing, ma'am."

The young woman clamps the cigarette to her full mouth, pulls hard, draws the smoke down deep.

"We need to find her, real fast." The marshal looks to Georgia Eastman. "We need a list of family, friends."

Eastman lifts the folder. "We have all of that."

"You live here alone?" Whicher says.

Jessica McConnell blows her smoke out in a long stream. Nods.

"Does your daughter have any siblings?"

The young woman stubs out the cigarette before it's half finished. "She's an only."

"How about other family? Father? Grandparents?"

"Her father hasn't been around in a couple years. My family live back east."

"Any other acquaintances you can think of?" Whicher says. "She have a phone?"

Eastman cuts in, "Residents are not allowed phones so long as they're in care."

Whicher looks at Jessica. "She have a phone?"

"No," the young woman answers. "I have it. I took it from her."

"Jessica," Eastman says, "I wanted you to meet the marshal, you'll be hearing from him again. This is serious. We have to take it seriously. The main thing you can do to help is call if you hear anything."

"I will. I will."

Georgia Eastman stands. Her face softens. "Do you have someone? Anyone you want me to call?"

"I'm alright." The young woman looks away. "I'm okay."

Whicher stands. Regards her at the window. Distracted. Thoughts running behind her eyes.

"Marshal?" Eastman says. "Unless you have any other questions?"

"You have all the details?"

Eastman nods.

"Alright. Well, I guess I'm good."

"My daughter's not a runaway," Jessica says.

Eastman gestures for Whicher to follow her out of the room into the hall.

"You're overreacting." Jessica McConnell walks behind them to the door.

Whicher takes out a business card, hands it to her.

She glances at it.

"Call," he says. "If you hear anything, you call."

⋏

Scanning the scrub at the end of the lane, Whicher leans his arms on the roof of the Chevy. Behind a pickup moving in the far distance dust is rising. Bare mountain cuts the haze at the long horizon.

"Doesn't seem like she belongs here, somehow," the marshal says.

Behind the neighboring fence, the dog prowls, straining on its length of chain.

"I don't think she's lived here long," Eastman answers.

"Y'all worried about this?" Whicher cuts a look at her. "At the juvenile service?"

A shadow passes over the woman's face. "The last two missing minor cases we had ended badly. One was a girl that ended up trafficked for eighteen months. We found her out in California, held captive in a house in a suburban street—'servicing' Chinese businessmen. You'd never have believed it, unless you'd seen it. The other was a fatal overdose in a toilet stall—in the bus station in El Paso."

Whicher nods. Sees the pain behind the woman's eyes.

"Are you new to this?"

"Ma'am?"

"The Marshals Service missing child program? It's just that I haven't heard your name before."

"I'm not with the missing child program."

"Oh. Well, you have experience?"

"I'm a criminal investigator. USMS, Western District."

"Maybe the daughter just skated, like she says. Maybe she'll be back soon. Tonight. You know?"

"I'll find her." Whicher lets his eyes rest on Georgia Eastman's a moment.

"If it goes the wrong way…it stays with you…" Eastman's voice trails off.

Whicher takes the plastic folder from her. "I'll find her," he says.

CHAPTER THREE

Montgomery County, Tennessee

Sweat runs down his back.

He guns the twenty-year-old Grand Marquis off the highway into a parking lot in front of a Kroger store.

Accelerating, he scans for spaces—the supermarket busy—a few empty bays still showing among the stationary cars.

"Son of a bitch, Travis…"

"Keep it down, man."

"I swear to God…"

The man named Travis swerves, straightens, eyes a line of trees dividing one section of the lot from another. "Is he coming in?"

"I can't see."

"Reed. *Come on.*"

Turning around, the big man cranes his neck, holds the back of the passenger seat.

Five minutes.

Five minutes a state trooper has been behind them.

Despite exiting the highway on the southern edge of the city of Clarksville.

Despite two random turns into a commercial district.

"If that dumb bitch girlfriend of yours started singing…"

"She can't," Travis answers. "She's a hack, man, corrections officer, she says something, she's screwed, they'll lock her ass up."

"Whoa…that's him." Reed's chin juts. "That's him, he's turning in here."

Travis steers past two lines of cars, panic rising.

He turns in on a row of vehicles parked in the shade of a strip of trees.

"He's comin' in here, man."

Slowing the big sedan, he lines up on a bay in the middle of the row.

"We stop," Reed says, "we're a sitting target."

"We need to lose him."

"Like this?"

"Let him blow by, let him roll out."

"Keep driving," the man named Reed says.

Travis brakes, yanks at the wheel, buries the car between a pickup and a van.

Reed turns, looks at him.

"Keep watching," Travis says.

Anger flares in the big man's eyes. "This is bullshit…"

Scanning the lot in front of the car Travis leaves the motor running.

He sweeps the surrounds, looks for exit points, dead ends, signs of other cops.

The Highway Patrol cruiser is stationary a few hundred yards across the lot.

Only its front end shows.

Reed stares. "The hell's he doing?"

Travis strains to get a look at the driver. "If he's following the car, if they're looking for it, we have to ditch this."

"You said she wouldn't talk."

"I'm saying *if*." Travis studies the store entrance—shoppers milling around, people talking on phones. "Get your stuff."

"What? What for?"

"The guy's looking for an automobile…" Travis pushes back his dark brown hair. Glances at the partial view of the cruiser.

Reaching into the rear of the sedan he grabs a black, nylon backpack, a sheep-wool lined denim jacket.

He cuts the motor.

Reed turns around to face him. "What the hell're you doing?"

Travis takes the keys from the ignition. Pushes open the driver's door. "Come on. Get out. Get your stuff."

Stepping out, he swings the door hard.

Tracking across the lot he pauses by a half-ton truck, turns briefly—to see the big man coming after him—jeans ill-fitting, a limp from the prison roof fall. Jacket tight over his muscled torso, his bearded jaw clamped, eyes unnaturally bright.

He can see the back of the cruiser. The trooper at the

wheel—talking into a radio. He feels his heart beat faster.

Reed steps alongside. "We need to get back in the car."

Travis walks fast, moves across the roadway entrance, dodging incoming cars.

Stepping onto a sidewalk he slows, tries to loosen up, compose his face.

Fifty yards off, the trooper in the cruiser stares forward.

Travis shrugs off the backpack, takes a step beneath the shade of a walkway along the front of the store.

A girl in sweat pants eyes him.

Flicks her hair, flashes a smile.

Travis ignores her.

Reed crosses the road between two cars.

He steps up onto the sidewalk, "I said we need to get back in the goddamn car…"

"If the cop came here for something else," Travis says, beneath his breath, "we can get back in. Five minutes we'll be gone, we'll be on our way."

Reed glares, arms twitching at his sides.

"If he's trying to find the car…"

"You said he can't be…"

"If he *is*. If he somehow is…" Travis turns, gestures for Reed to follow to the store entrance—to stand in a wait-area, filled with vending machines and shopping carts and teenagers; folk standing with bags of groceries, store staff smoking on break.

The girl in the track pants watches from the sidewalk. Eying Travis. Recoiling slightly from the man at his side.

The cruiser waits, its brake lights flared red.

Reed steps in close. "So, what's he doing?"

Travis puts down the backpack. Makes a show of settling to wait.

The door opens on the cruiser, the trooper gets out.

A city police car rolls into view.

It pulls up by the cruiser.

The trooper leans into the squad car's open window—speaks to two black-uniformed officers. The exchange is short.

Travis only watches, feels the dryness in his throat.

The girl studies on him, curious, now.

The trooper gets back in his vehicle. Pulls out, drives the few yards to turn in on the nearest parking row. Light bar just visible above the roofs of the cars.

It reaches the end of a row, makes a turn into the next.

"What the hell, man?" Reed says.

Travis picks up the pack.

He moves beneath the covered walkway. "Come on. Don't look back."

"Whoa, this is going to shit…"

"Just walk with me. Just walk."

Reed falls in step beside him.

Fifty yards along at the end of the building is a Papa John's.

The cruiser turns to make the next row.

It swings in, drives a few yards.

Stops.

Where the Grand Marquis is parked between the pickup and the van.

"Son of a bitch."

"We need to go," Travis says, "right now. Don't stop. Don't look back."

⋏

Behind a Perspex screen dividing the cashier office from the front of the store, Kendrick Dupris pushes paperwork through a stainless-steel slot in the counter.

He studies the man on the other side, disheveled, sullen.

"You get to keep the car. Drive around in it."

The man nods.

"Still got your wheels." Dupris looks at him. "You don't have to take the deal, either."

The man scratches at a skinny arm, rubs the sallow skin of his face. His hand is scrolled with ink tattoos, fingernails bitten to the quick.

He studies the paperwork for five seconds. Takes in nothing. A hank of greasy hair flops over his face.

"You repay the full loan amount, plus the interest, title reverts back to you," Dupris tells him. "You only sign if that's what you want."

The man looks up from the paperwork, nods.

Kenny Dupris eyes him—knowing the look.

A trapped animal.

An animal seeing its way out.

Sly. Shifty. About ready. To jump headlong off the nearest cliff. "You don't want to sign for a title loan, we do payday loans, or you can pawn items of value instead, to secure a cash advance today."

The man stares at nothing, runs a finger beneath his nose.

"You want to go ahead or not?"

"Hell, you got my TV. Got my surround sound, got my speakers." An ugly grin cracks on the man's face. His teeth stained, gums receding.

Classic tweeker.

Methamphetamine freak.

Kenny Dupris makes no response.

He glances around the pawn store goods on display—little memory of the man's TV, or his speakers. "If you don't repay the loan amount, plus interest, the car legally becomes the property of this company."

The man grabs hold of the pen at the side of the counter. "I get it."

"Signature and today's date," Dupris says.

The man scrawls his name where the top sheet of paperwork is marked with an X.

Practiced, Dupris thinks.

A practiced loser.

Taking back the paperwork, he crosses to the cash drawer, takes out the agreed sum in used bills.

He puts the money into a business envelope.

Slides it through the scuffed hatch.

The look changes in the man's rat-like features—furtive pleasure, barely concealed haste to get out of the door.

A week, Dupris gives him.

A week to burn the money in a frenzy. Manic. Degraded. Paranoid and high.

The car will go to auction, he can have the boys go pick it up.

"Later," the man says, pocketing the wad.

Kenny Dupris nods, not bothering to reply.

There'll be no later.

Not until he sends the recovery truck.

He watches the man thread his skinny-ass frame between rows of pawned consumer items. Watches him head out. Cracks a dry laugh as the door closes behind him.

Have fun smoking your car, douchebag.

He checks his watch.

You know, you gotta laugh.

Unlocking the office door, he steps out into the store, walks down to the main door, locks it, flips over the sign from '*open*' to '*closed*.'

Passing back through the office, he slips a leather jacket off of a seat back, runs a hand over his shaved head. Stands a moment pumping the muscles in his arms, the same routine with his shoulders. Activating the biceps. The delts, the traps.

He picks up a workout bag—he can hit the gym for an hour. Then maybe head on up to Sunshine Smiles, hit the bar, maybe pick out one of the girlies, maybe drop a little green. Go a little extra.

Exiting the building at the rear door, he grins to himself. He locks up, sets the alarms.

Out in back he heads to a shined, detailed, black Mazda SUV.

A man is standing by one of three dumpsters in the back lot—the dumpsters filled with construction garbage from a renovation and refit on the next over unit.

His clothes are hanging off of him. A backpack is by the man's feet.

"Hey," Dupris calls out.

The man looks over.

"What're you doing? This is private property, here."

The man doesn't move, he just stares, says nothing.

Goddamn vagrants. "Get the hell out of here."

Across the road in the lot of the Kroger store Dupris sees flashing blue lights. Law enforcement vehicles. He shakes his head. Shoplifting. Scumbags boosting shit out of there again. Always stealing. Always hanging around outside the store. Stinking up the place, too.

He takes out the keys to his SUV, flips them over in his hand.

The man with the backpack is still by the dumpster.

Dupris puffs out his chest. "What're you doing?" He starts to walk across. "What's going on? You diving in that thing?"

The man cuts a look toward the Kroger store. His gaze comes back again. His face is edgy.

"You taking stuff out of that? Uh?" Dupris makes a show of pointing to the sign at the entrance in back of the store. "Private. This is private. This all here. You read that? *No Trespassing.* You can read that, right?"

No answer.

"You know it's illegal to take stuff from a dumpster on private property? What's even in there?" Approaching the man now, temper rising, having to deal with yet another goddamn douche.

But the man's not looking at him. He's looking at something—at Dupris' hand.

"Did you take something out of there? Uh? What's in that pack, there? Let me see."

Bully 'em. Got to bully 'em, they won't come back.

"Nothing," the man finally says.

"Get the hell out of here. Before I throw your ass out."

The man looks across the road again. "We're leaving," he says. "We're just leaving."

Dupris sees him glance sideways, at something out of sight behind the side of the overfilled dumpster.

"Is somebody else back there?" Dupris says. "What is this?" He walks fast to where he can see a second man, bigger, bearded. "What are you—jacking up? Or is this some kind of a queer deal?"

Something about the bearded man brings him up short, his voice trails away in his throat.

The bearded man lifts a piece of broken timber out of the dumpster.

"Look," Dupris says, "if you want trash timber, go ahead and take it. If you want it to make a fire…"

The big man's eyes are filled with a strange kind of light.

Kendrick Dupris swallows. "Or whatever, take it."

The man lifts up the length of timber, as if inspecting it. Gauging a bat in a practice cage.

Kenny Dupris sees it swing for only a split second.

Before searing pain explodes through the side of his head.

Into white. Into nothing.

Chapter Four

Reeves County, Tx

At the corner of Fifth and Cedar in the city of Pecos, John Whicher parks his Chevy Silverado at the side of a two-story courthouse building of pale brick and glass and red clay tile. The parking lot is mostly empty—he leaves his truck in a tree-shaded bay.

Stepping out into the bright glare of morning, he scans a blue and white streaked sky.

Squaring the Resistol, he enters the courthouse through a keypad-operated secure door.

He takes a set of stairs to the upper floor. Punches in an access code to the Marshals Service suite of offices.

A squat man in a suit and black Stetson is by the coffee machine—Deputy Marshal Booker Tillman.

Civilian support workers sit at the far side of the office, two women—both of them nod at his arrival, then turn back to the computer monitors at their desks.

"I get you a cup?" Tillman calls over.

"Thanks," Whicher answers.

"Black, no cream, no sugar?"

The marshal nods, takes off his jacket, slips off the Ruger revolver in the leather shoulder holster.

He carries the rig to a gun safe in the corner. Leaves the service-issue Glock and extra magazines clipped to the belt at his waist.

Booker Tillman places a white, china mug of coffee by the marshal's computer terminal.

"You're in early?" Whicher says.

"Court security," Tillman answers, "we have a full day today." A frown crosses his pugnacious features. "Expecting some trouble, too. Assault and battery case this morning. We had a hearing on it last week, they stopped a guy in the screening area trying to bring in a revolver and live rounds."

"Into court?"

"In his boot," Tillman says. "Man claimed he forgot it was in there. The same hearing the X-ray machine picked out three separate members of the upstanding public trying to bring in weapons—knuckles and knives."

"Who's the defendant?"

"Some biker," Tillman answers. "It's some biker beef—with another of their tribe. It's like stone-age folk coming in here."

Whicher grins. "You can handle it."

Tillman looks at him. His eyebrows arch. "We've got a mental health assessment set up this afternoon, the defendant's making threats to kill the judge." He runs a hand across a trimmed, mid-brown mustache. "Police department called me on it this morning—they say the guy's sister is threatening to blow up the courthouse on her social media page."

"Serious?"

"I mean it's out there," Tillman says. "They put it out, we have to do something about it."

"You got extra people coming in?"

"We'll get deputies from the sheriff's office. Maybe some K-9. You going to be here?"

"I doubt it."

"Too bad," Tillman says. "You could stand around. Look mean."

The marshal sits at his desk. "I have a new case."

"Oh?"

"Missing child."

Booker Tillman makes a face. "Never like a kid being in it…"

At the back of the room, the door to an office opens.

A woman in her mid-fifties steps out. Steel-gray hair. Tough-looking. Slim in a two-piece navy suit.

Whicher nods at his new boss—Chief Deputy Martha J Fairbanks. Two months in post, from out of the Houston office.

"Ma'am. Good morning."

The chief marshal nods back.

She carries an armful of forms to the civilian support staff. Sets down the paperwork. Exchanges a few words. Then calls over, "Did you hear anything yet?"

Whicher shakes his head.

"Nothing overnight?"

"So far, no," the marshal says.

She gestures toward her office. "I have news…"

Whicher takes a sip on the cup of coffee, sets it down, stands. Leaves his hat and jacket at his desk.

He follows his boss into a box-like office, the window blinds half-closed. Rows of file cabinets fill one wall, the desk is full but well-organized.

"Take a seat."

The marshal pulls out a steel frame chair.

Fairbanks settles behind her desk. She studies a notepad a moment, her face sharp. "Did you go talk with the mother?"

"Yes, ma'am. Over to Hudspeth County, yesterday. I met with her, met with a juvenile liaison officer—Georgia Eastman."

"How'd she seem?"

"Kind of strange. A little hard to read," Whicher says. "Pissed, maybe."

The chief marshal looks at him.

"She thinks her daughter will show up. Says she probably just went off with somebody."

"She's twelve. The mother wasn't alarmed?"

"Getting that way," Whicher says. "But maybe blaming it on us. Juvenile service is obliged to escalate it. Law enforcement get involved, she gets a marshal showing up at her door."

Fairbanks thinks it over. "Well there's been a development," she says. "I had a call. From USMS, Tennessee."

Whicher shifts in his seat. "Why's that?"

"Two people broke out of a prison facility back there. Just outside of Memphis. Yesterday. About four o'clock in the morning. Marshals Service are part of the effort to locate and return both inmates at the earliest opportunity. Standard protocol, you know, is we look to identify potential support networks—associates, family members any fugitive might have."

Whicher nods.

"One of the escapees has links to people living in Texas." Chief Marshal Fairbanks looks at him. "The escapee's name is Travis McConnell."

"McConnell?"

"His estranged wife is Jessica McConnell."

Whicher sits forward. Pictures the woman from the day before.

"McConnell also has a cousin, a Karyn Dennison living in the area. Not far from where Jessica McConnell lives."

"Is he related to the missing child?"

Fairbanks says, "He's the father."

Whicher studies the edge of the chief marshal's desk. "Do USMS Tennessee know this man's child is missing?"

"Not yet," Fairbanks says. "I haven't spoken with them, this just came in overnight. I wanted to talk with you first, get your thoughts."

"We know anything about the second fugitive?"

"His name is Reed Barbone. No connection with this area, as far as anybody knows."

Whicher blows out his cheeks. "We need to check for any connection between the two events."

"You have any feeling on that?"

"I need to talk with Jessica McConnell again."

Fairbanks nods. "I'll tell USMS Tennessee you'll go talk with her. I'll let the Juvenile Service know. How come the daughter's in care?"

"Long list of misdemeanors, according to Ms Eastman," Whicher says. "Plus possible involvement in a burglary."

"She have a history of going AWOL?"

"So they say."

"Tennessee's a long way from West Texas," Fairbanks says. Despite herself, tension shows in the set of her face. "Can you see Jessica McConnell this morning?"

Whicher pushes back his chair. "I'm on my way."

Fort Stockton, Tx

The Hispanic boy at the window fishes for a lighter in his low-slung jeans.

Across the room the girl on the dilapidated couch plays with threads of a cotton bracelet at her wrist.

She sits, cross-legged, her body folded forward. Her long black hair loose about her face.

The boy takes the lighter from his jeans, sparks up a fresh Marlboro. Checks the street again.

Wind rattles the tin roof of the derelict house. Pinpricks of light pierce the dim interior through holes in the walls.

"You want to eat?"

"No," the girl says.

He points to a bag of churros on a fire-blacked table.

She shakes her head.

Turning to the street, the boy sees a cut-down Camaro with trick paint turn in slow to cruise the row. Past run down houses and vacant lots. He feels for the switchblade in his back pocket, slips it out. Knocks ash against a broken window pane.

The Camaro rumbles along the street.

Four men inside, looking out, surveying the scene.

The boy listens to the beat thumping from the car's speakers, Chicano rap—a song he recognizes.

He opens out the blade of the knife.

The car rides low along the block, passing by in front of the house.

He feels his heart tick faster.

The Chevy continues along the street.

Turning back into the room, the boy stares at the girl on the couch. "You sick?"

Her eyes are on the knife in his hand. She looks up from it to him.

"You don't look right."

Her head moves. Her leg bounces against the side of the couch.

"What's the matter?"

"Nothing." She swallows, looks away.

He takes a long drag on the cigarette, blows smoke sideways from his mouth.

Turning back to the window, he sees an older model, white Toyota four-door.

It noses its way from the corner into the street. Waits at the turn a moment.

The boy watches.

"Hey…" He looks back at the girl. "Get up."

Her face blanches.

"I think this is him."

She looks away.

The boy turns back to stare at the sedan—moving slow now—inside, only the driver, only one man he can see. "Come on," he says, "get up, get moving."

He turns around—to the girl still folded in on herself on the couch.

He crosses to her, takes a hold of her wrist. Closes his grip as she tries to pull her arm away. "Come on…"

"Get off of me."

He braces his legs, yanks her from the couch to her feet.

"Get the hell off…" Her eyes burn him.

He pulls her across the room to where he can see out of the window.

The car slows to a stop outside.

The driver waits at the wheel, scanning, looking left to right. Then stares up into the car's rear-view mirror.

Seconds pass.

The faint sound of the motor dies.

The door of the car opens, the man steps out.

The boy sees the look in his face.

He studies the house. Crosses the fence line to the property—threads a path through piles of junk and trash timber and waist-high weeds.

"This is it," the boy says.

The girl flinches. Like a hunted animal.

She won't look at him.

A knock sounds at the front door.

"You know you have to do this?"

Chapter Five

The doors are locked and bolted, all the windows fastened tight. No lights show anywhere. The phone on the wall rings— a third straight time in a row.

A figure passes by the window at the side of the house— she sees its shadow on the opaque fabric of the blind in the hall.

From her place on the floor she hears the knock at the back door.

She hears the handle move, recoiling at the sound.

A wave of nausea sweeps through her.

Numbness.

Weight in her limbs.

She can hear the dog—snarling, growling, barking out over and over.

The ringing phone cuts abruptly.

Silence follows. She tries to fight down the fear.

The air around her flickers. Panic threatens to break like a wave.

Eyes wide, she strains her senses to hear—stares at the

blind on the hallway window.

Something is moving at the other side of the house.

She sits, knees drawn up in the hallway. Breath short in her chest.

Both hands clenched. Heart racing.

⋏

Window down in the Chevy Silverado, Whicher eyes the German Shepherd beyond the green-painted house.

The dirt yard is empty.

He takes the phone from its holder on the dash of the truck, scrolls a list of contacts—keys a number.

The call rings—picks up.

"West Texas Juvenile Liaison Service. Georgia Eastman speaking."

"Ms Eastman? This is Deputy Marshal Whicher—I'm out at Jessica McConnell's place. I'm trying to get a hold of her. She's not here, she's not around."

"Did you try her number?"

The marshal glances at the folder on the passenger seat. "The landline? I tried it, there's no reply. There's no one here at the house. Y'all have any other way to get in contact?"

"We have the child's usual place of residence," Eastman answers. "Apart from that…I can check, I don't think we have anything else on file."

"What do you know about Jessica McConnell?" Whicher says. "She have a job, she work someplace?"

"I think she works at a couple of restaurants, waiting tables. There may be a record here somewhere. I can take a look. Is this urgent? Did you need her right now?"

"I called this morning before I set out from Pecos. Left a message. She hasn't returned the call. I need to see her. We had a message to our office overnight," Whicher says, "from the Marshals Service in Tennessee."

"Oh?"

"Something happened. With the father."

"Regarding this?"

"Bella's father broke out of a prison back there."

"Good Lord."

"Him and another inmate. Yesterday."

Georgia Eastman is silent on the line.

"I don't know what this all has to do with Bella's disappearance," Whicher says. "It's a material change. I need to find the mother, talk to her." The marshal lifts a sheet of paper from the folder. "There's a family relation listed in the area—a Karyn Dennison?"

"She's just outside of Sierra Blanca," Eastman says. "We have a next of kin or a family member in case of emergencies. I've never spoken with her."

"Might as well go see her," Whicher says. "Long as I'm here."

"I'll double-check, marshal. Maybe I could find someone who could raise Jessica."

"I'd appreciate it, ma'am."

"What do you know about the prison breakout?"

"Nothing more at this time. I'll talk with the folk in Tennessee but I need to find Jessica McConnell. Are you back in Fort Stockton?"

"Yes, I am."

"Call the hostel," Whicher says, "see what they have. I get done here, I'll drive over there, speak with them." He catches his reflection in the driver mirror; sees a hardness in his face. He softens his voice. "Stay on it, stay with it…"

"I'll do what I can, marshal."

Whicher finishes up the call.

Firing up the motor in the truck, he shifts his gaze to the unfenced, empty dirt yard—the ground marked up with oil stains, imprinted with the tracks of tires.

He moves the shifter into drive, rolls forward—in line with the house on the neighboring lot. A tumbledown, clapboard building. Empty-looking. No vehicles parked.

No other houses are near on the rural lane.

Only the dog faces him, its body taut, straining at its chain.

Ridge high along the length of its back.

In its amber eyes a well of violence.

⋏

Logan County, Kentucky

The State Police cruiser is in his rear-view mirror—Travis McConnell eyes the silver dot, in traffic, a hundred yards back.

He glances down at the dash of the SUV. Keeps his speed beneath the posted limit.

Reed Barbone's eyes are on the side of his face.

He can feel them.

"He still there?"

"Yeah," Travis says.

"What's your big idea, now?" An edge is in Barbone's voice.

"We get off the road."

"We just got on it."

McConnell grips the wheel of the big Mazda.

Police cars are everywhere—both sides of the state line, Tennessee and Kentucky. Roadblocks, checkpoints. "I'm supposed to know what's going to be out here?" A green exit sign marks an off-ramp up ahead. "I got us out, right? I got us out…"

Checking in the rear-view, he lets the vehicle's speed bleed away. Considers whether to signal.

Go early, see what the cruiser does?

Go late, give him less time?

From the trunk space of the SUV the man named Kendrick Dupris gives a muffled groan.

Travis McConnell glances at Dupris' driver's license in the center well by twin cup holders.

License and a billfold—four hundred dollars. Hard cash.

A find. Good fortune. One good thing, against all the bad.

Money for gas, on top of what little they'd had. From the CO, from the dumb hack.

McConnell puts thoughts of the woman from his mind—thinks of Dupris; quiet, the last hours. A look he's seen after prison fights. Men battered senseless. Maybe dying. Life eking away.

He signals—maneuvers the big Mazda—switches to the exit lane.

Looking up in the rear-view, he sees the cruiser—not shifting.

At the far end of the off-ramp a stop light is on red.

McConnell keeps his eye on the interstate, slowing the car.

The cruiser draws level with the turn for the exit.

Barbone swivels in his seat.

"Don't look over."

"He staying on?" Barbone says.

McConnell sees the stop light flick from red to green, checks his mirror. "He's staying on."

Back on the gas he makes a left beneath a concrete overpass.

"We could've kept on," Barbone says.

"We take the back roads."

"Says you."

McConnell bites on his lip—knowing the interstate for a mistake.

Knowing that he shouldn't have relented.

"We need to make ground," Barbone says. "Fast. I keep telling you, we got to get the hell gone."

One night in the woods, McConnell tells himself.

One night.

Already out of patience; no long game.

No self-control, Barbone. Only now; here and now—everything right now.

"We could've drove all night," the big man says. "What

are we, three hundred miles from Memphis? We should be twice as far as that."

"We travel in daylight," McConnell tells him. "When folk are around. We can pass unnoticed. We travel at night, we make it too easy—cops at night want to know your business. We'll be an easy target."

Barbone stares at a Cracker Barrel restaurant and store at the side of the road. "Man, I got to eat."

McConnell shakes his head.

"Why not?"

Flicking his jaw toward his shoulder, McConnell answers; "We got a man in back there, in the trunk, you know? Uh? How you think that looks?"

Barbone sits silent a moment. "We need to fix that."

McConnell keeps his eyes focused ahead on the road. Smaller now—a country two-lane, flanked with light woods, with meadows, leaves half off of the trees.

Nothing else is on the road.

Not a single car ahead—nothing behind.

A familiar sensation is in his gut. The clenched knot feeling. The buzz in his brain. Part fear. Part surge in his blood—a search for release. Before the act. Robbing a store at gunpoint. Sailing off the roof of a prison. The same feeling.

From the same pressing need.

He lets his senses wake fully—taking in the unfamiliar road—the Kentucky fields, the thrum of tires, the interior of the SUV, its newness, its plastic-smell, the feel behind the wheel.

Fully aware.

Senses fully alert.

Mind turning.

He checks the rear-view.

His own dark eyes look back.

Nothing behind on the road.

Nothing out there ahead.

Woodland closes in now, replacing fields and meadows. He drives on under a gray, fall sky.

The will to do it.

Commitment.

Was what it took.

Striated light comes through the trees. And something glinting—light reflecting.

Staring into the woods he sees the surface of a body of water, a small lake.

A lake surrounded by woodland.

Lost in trees.

He sees a dirt track peeling from the road.

"Here," he says.

Barbone sits up. "What?"

McConnell brakes sharp. Turns the car onto the track.

"What the hell?"

"We'll do it here." He drives in fast.

Out of sight, between the trees he stops.

He shuts down the motor. Cracks the driver's door. Sits a moment to listen.

Only the sound of birds comes; faint wind moving in the trees.

Barbone looks at him, "So?"

"So, come on. Get out."

McConnell steps from the Mazda. Walks around to the rear.

He opens up the lift gate.

Dupris is lying on his side—knees drawn up. His eyes shut.

His mouth is open.

Dried blood is on the side of his face.

His skin is drained of color, flaccid. Barely signs of any breathing.

"You lift him?" McConnell says.

"Screw that."

"Alright, the both of us." McConnell reaches in, takes a hold of Dupris beneath an arm.

Yanking him out toward the lip of the trunk something registers in the man's face.

His eyes stay shut.

Barbone steps to the trunk, grabs Dupris beneath his other arm.

McConnell takes some weight, lifts Kendrick Dupris onto the ground.

Dupris makes a muffled sound, air escaping from him, incoherent.

Travis McConnell takes a look at the water through the trees—looming, flat and dark.

"Think anybody comes here?" Barbone says.

"No."

"Not ever?"

"Not any time soon." Bracing his back, McConnell starts to drag the man.

Barbone falls in step on the other side.

No song comes from the woodland birds, now.

From a dead limb of oak a single crow lifts into the sky.

Chapter Six

Hudspeth County, Tx

Sierra Blanca dominates the horizon beyond the old adobe house—a long, high, sloping ridge in the distance, pale in the sun, Lord of all other mountains.

Through the windshield of the Chevy, Whicher studies the house at the end of a winding lane of hard-packed sand. Its render worn, adobe bricks of mud and straw exposed in patches.

Along the edge of the property on a sagging fence, rags and hub caps and strips of fabric flutter in the wind.

An ancient Ford pickup sits beneath the shade of a desert willow.

The marshal checks the address. Pushes open the truck door, steps out.

The name tag on a battered mailbox reads—*VASQUEZ / DENNISON.*

He walks a beaten-earth path to the house, to a door of rough-sawn planks. Presses on a doorbell recessed into the wall. Takes in the dry mountain and arid ranch land stretching to an unbound distance—the Trans-Pecos—barely populated.

The door to the house opens.

A young woman with long red hair looks out. Wearing a striped cotton dress. Cigarette trailing from her hand.

"Karyn Dennison?"

She looks him up and down. "I do something for you?"

Whicher takes out his badge and ID. "With the US Marshal Service. Trying to locate the whereabouts of a missing girl, a minor. Bella McConnell."

"Bella?"

"Yes, ma'am."

"Is something wrong?"

Whicher says, "If I could come in?"

The woman frowns. "Alright. I guess."

She moves aside.

Whicher steps into a cool hallway. "There someplace we can talk?"

Karyn Dennison leads the way into a living room. Cluttered with sculpted wooden pieces, oil paintings hanging from the walls.

She waves a hand at a worn leather armchair by a cowhide couch. "Take a seat."

Whicher lowers himself into the armchair.

Dennison picks a ruby-red glass ashtray from a table, sits on an arm of the couch.

The house is silent, thick walls deadening the wind outside.

"You live here alone, ma'am?"

"No," she says. "With my boyfriend. Santiago."

Whicher makes a mental note.

"I paint," she says. "He sculpts, carves wood," she gestures about the room.

"Your name is listed as a contact, an emergency contact," Whicher says. "With the Juvenile Liaison Service—out of Fort Stockton."

"It is?" The young woman takes a drag on the cigarette.

The marshal studies her face—petite, pretty. Her eyes rounded. "Did you know that Bella's been living back there? Back in Fort Stockton?"

"Well, yes."

"You know why?"

"I know she's been running a little wild."

Whicher takes out a lined notepad. "She's under a court order, ma'am. You tell me how y'all are related?"

"I'm a cousin of Bella's father."

The marshal taps his pen against the notepad. "Of Travis McConnell?"

"Yes." The woman's face hardens.

Whicher scans the room, his gaze settling on a photograph of a Hispanic man. Arm draped around the woman looking at him. "I was over to Jessica McConnell's house just now," he says. "Nobody was home."

The young woman flicks her cigarette in the ashtray. "There rarely is."

"She work?"

"Let's just say if she was home more, maybe Bella would be too."

Whicher waits for her to go on.

"Is Bella alright? Has something happened to her?" Dennison looks at him.

"She's missing," Whicher says. "So far, that's all we know."

"You must be concerned. Or you wouldn't be here."

"She might have skipped out with a friend, it may be nothing."

Karyn Dennison takes another pull on the cigarette. "How long?"

"Day and a half."

"She's been gone a day and a half? Did you speak with Jessica?"

"Yesterday," Whicher says. "She thinks her daughter doesn't like where she is. The hostel."

"Who could blame her?"

"Ma'am, you say Jessica is out often? How would that be?"

Dennison sniffs. "I'm not her keeper. I don't know everything she does."

"What do you know?"

"She spends a bunch of time in church. In town. First Baptist."

"Here in town?"

"It's off the highway. Over by the railroad line."

The marshal writes in the notepad. "She a regular churchgoer?"

"She is now."

Whicher looks up.

Some thought passes behind Dennison's eyes.

"She wasn't always?"

"Look," the young woman says. "You need to ask her, you know? Not me."

The marshal nods. Glances at the view of the mountain through a set of double-wide glass sliders.

Dennison says, "I guess you know about Travis?"

Whicher's eyes come back on to her.

"I mean, that he's in prison? That she came here to get away from all that. So that Bella wouldn't have to be around it the whole time. Have to visit her father in prison, grow up with that." Dennison runs a hand up and down her forearm. "She's from back east, Tennessee. She moved out about two years gone. Her and Bella. She wanted a fresh start. I tried to help her out."

"She have some connection here, this area?"

"Only me," the woman says.

"You?"

"Right."

"Her husband's cousin."

"Travis's cousin, right. In prison back in Memphis. For armed robbery. Jessica wanted a new start—I moved out here ten years ago. She asked me to help. I did what I could. I found her a cheap place to rent; that house they have. Found a couple restaurant jobs, you know, little things, to get her a start."

"Are y'all close?"

"Me and her? No. I mean, she didn't come here for me." Dennison stubs the cigarette out in the ashtray. "She just wanted to be someplace else. Anyplace, I guess. She told

Travis she'd be near family, me being here. I told her—it's not for everyone, West Texas."

"She separated from her husband?"

"She said she needed space. But they're still married."

"What do you know about Bella?"

"I mean, she's a sweet kid. I don't think she ever wanted to be here, though, you know? It's not an easy thing, a young girl, moving someplace new."

"She get in any kind of trouble before she came out?"

"I don't know, I don't think. Jessica's not much for rules as such. You ask me, that's a good thing. But Bella. Maybe she has a little of her father's thing. She can be reckless. Get herself in trouble. But she's a good kid."

Whicher nods. "I'm sure you're right."

"I wish I never would've helped them come on out here."

"I just need to find her. Make sure she stays safe."

"I know Travis was pissed. I know he doesn't like it."

Whicher studies the young woman's face. "When's the last time you talked to him?"

"Not since they put him away," Dennison says. "But I hear things. You know? Through family."

"You heard he didn't like her coming here?"

"Would you?"

"You have any idea where I might try looking for her?"

The young woman shakes her head.

"Or who I might ask?"

"Ask Jessica," the young woman says. "Everybody gets on Bella, like it's all on her. Maybe they're looking in the wrong place. Is all I'm saying. Maybe it's not her. You know? Maybe she's not the guilty one."

⋏

Tarrant County, Tx

Grains of salt lie scattered across the red-topped table in the diner on the edge of Fort Worth. The girl watches as he sweeps them up, gathers them into his hand—to empty them into a paper napkin.

He eyes the room, eyes the counter, searching for the woman again, the waitress.

He can't see her.

He scans the booths all the way to the back.

Across the table, the girl picks at the burger, at the stack of fries on her plate.

His own plate is empty, the food consumed. "Can't you eat a little faster?"

She sits hunched forward in her purple, hooded top. Expression on her face unchanging.

Her eyes slide away. She barely nods.

Looking out of the picture window he watches a busy stream of traffic out on the road—cars and trucks, big rigs and semis.

Across the highway, low-rise residential units line the road, intercut with big-box stores, with franchise restaurants. The parking lot outside is half full—the diner brisk. Couples and families. Groups of working men.

He leans forward, checks his watch, glances out at

another car pulling in.

Across the tabletop the girl slurps milkshake through a straw.

Noisy.

Distracted.

He looks at her.

She lets her eyes rest on his a moment. Pushes a strand of long, dark hair behind her ear.

Turning away, he searches the counter area—a man is ringing up a check at the register—a woman putting on a coat by the door.

The waitress is there again—the waitress with the brass-colored hair. At the far end of the room, by a coffee machine—staring right over at their table.

Staring at the girl.

At him, now.

He shifts his gaze.

Turns around to the girl. "We need to go, now."

She stops chewing. Stays a french-fry in her hand.

Shifting weight on the bench seat, he pulls out a billfold. Takes out a brace of twenties.

"I'm not done eating."

"Take it with you." He pulls a handful of paper napkins from a stainless-steel dispenser. "Wrap it up."

A look passes across her face.

He angles his head, looks again for the waitress.

She's at a table—writing an order for an older couple. Looking over now—looking at him.

He breaks off.

Turns to the girl. "Wrap it up in that."

Her shoulders bunch beneath the hooded top.

From the corner of his eye he sees the waitress leave the table, pass the coffee machine, disappear through a doorway to the kitchen in back.

He pushes up from the booth, dumps the girl's half-eaten burger and fries into a napkin.

She looks at him.

He puts the food in her hand. "We have to go."

He grabs the milkshake.

Her face darkens. Her eyes glaze.

Trapping the cash for the check beneath the menu holder, he steps out.

The girl stands, steps away from the booth.

He hustles her out—close behind her, between tables, not too fast. The waitress still in the kitchen; they can be out before she gets back.

He opens the door, holds the girl's milkshake. Guides her out into the lot. Into a cold rain starting to fall.

At the white Toyota four-door he takes out his keys.

She stops. "We've been driving hours already." She holds the burger and the fries and the napkin in her hand. "*Jesus Christ…*"

Defiance.

Defiance in the set of her face, in her body.

"Get in the car." His voice harsh, grating, now.

She looks at him only a moment, before her eyes cut away.

He takes in the gray light above the rooftops and

warehouses, the dark sky, lowering. Opens up the passenger door. "You get on in."

He thrusts the milkshake into her hand.

She climbs inside.

Walking around to the driver's side he gets in, fires up the motor. Sees the shut-down look on her face.

He backs out of the parking bay.

Better to be gone from prying eyes. From folk, from questions. From people remembering a car.

"Can't we just…" she starts.

"No." He tightens his grip at the wheel.

A bunch of cars and pickups pass on the road—headlamps lit, as if emerging from out of a storm.

He knocks the shifter into drive.

At the last moment, twists around, cranes his neck, despite himself.

To double-check.

A face stares from the plate-glass diner window.

A face framed with brass colored hair.

And a notepad open.

And a pen in her hand.

Chapter Seven

Fort Stockton, Tx

Pulling in to the residential care facility, Whicher sees the Buick Enclave already parked beneath the shade of a sabal palm—Georgia Eastman's car. He parks his truck alongside it. Cuts the motor. Pushes back in the driver's seat. Two hours riding east on I-10—still no news on Bella McConnell.

The marshal steps out, crosses the lot to the door of a reception lobby.

Through an inset glass panel he sees Eastman—standing talking with a Hispanic woman. Her black hair long, unruly, streaked with gray.

He holds up his badge and ID.

The woman presses on a switch in a wall-mounted panel.

Whicher hears the latch in the lock slide open.

He pulls the door wide, steps in.

"Marshal," Georgia Eastman says. "This is Rafaela Salinas."

The woman regards him, weight on one leg. Her eyes dark, a hard edge in them. She's dressed in jeans and a sweat top, a lanyard and ID hanging from her neck.

She puts out a hand.

The marshal takes it. Notices the faded symbols on the backs of her hands—jail ink tattoos. "Ma'am."

"Ms Salinas is supervisor of the facility here," Eastman says. To the woman; "Marshal Whicher's lead on the effort to locate Bella."

Salinas nods.

She walks across the lobby to a small, cramped office.

Whicher and Georgia Eastman in tow.

Diplomas and photographs line the walls—framed letters in childish hands. Pictures of young adults, former residents.

"Take a seat," the supervisor says.

Eastman sits in a chair by the window.

Whicher sits in line with the desk.

Rafaela Salinas slides open a file cabinet, picks out a plastic jacket filled with printed papers.

She sits at her desk. Leans forward.

Georgia Eastman clears her throat. "I told Ms Salinas the police department have had no contact with Bella. The sheriff's office say the same."

"This morning I rode out to talk with the mother," Whicher says. "Nobody was home."

The supervisor eyes him.

"I can't raise her on the number I have. I called in at the home of a Karyn Dennison—a cousin of Bella's father. She's had no contact with either Jessica or Bella. Said she hasn't seen Bella since she was moved here, to Fort Stockton."

The supervisor glances at Eastman and back again.

"The cousin gave me a little background," Whicher says. "She told me she helped Jessica move out to Texas. From back in Tennessee. After Bella's father ended up in prison."

The supervisor's eyes are hooded. "Nobody can get a hold of Bella's mother?" she says.

Eastman frowns.

Whicher looks at Salinas. "How long has Bella been with y'all?"

"Six weeks," the woman answers.

"Could you tell me anything about her? About how she is?"

"She's disruptive. Self-centered. Self-destructive," the woman says. "Like most of them here. She's here to access behavioral support. Learn to recognize patterns, cycles she gets in. Learn to break that, control destructive impulses."

"Tell me about the day she disappeared?"

"Nothing out of the ordinary," the supervisor answers. "She attended group sessions, took the classes she was supposed to take. She had some free time later in the day. After four weeks, we let them have time out. Out of here. So she went out, the same as she has several times before, with no issue. This time she just never came back."

"She on her own?"

"No," Salinas says. "They have to be in pairs, buddy-up. Look out for one another."

"She was with another girl?"

"She was. But they split up. Bella wanted to go to a taco stand on the street. Gabriela, the other girl wanted to go get ice cream. So she went off. Gabriela went off. Bella didn't come back."

"I talk with this girl?"

Salinas nods. "They're not supposed to split up—I guess sometimes it happens when they're out."

"Does Bella have her own room here?"

"They all do."

"I see it?" Whicher says.

The supervisor pushes the plastic document jacket across the desktop. "I made a copy of her notes, assessments from counselors, progress reports. Nothing confidential."

"There were no red flags?" Georgia Eastman says.

The supervisor's eyes are flat. "Deceptive behavior is rife in this community."

Whicher takes the documents. "I'd like to see Bella's room."

Georgia Eastman stands.

Rafaela Salinas pushes up from the desk.

Whicher follows the two women from the office, back into the lobby, down a corridor to a communal living area—leading on to individual rooms.

Two girls sit at a table by a window overlooking an enclosed courtyard. Notepads and pens and books cover the table, both girls in their early teens, the marshal guesses.

Salinas stops at one of the doors—takes a card from her pocket, slides it into a reader to open the lock.

The room is small, with blinds on the window, wardrobe space built in, a couple of shelves.

There's a neat-made bed. Attached at one side, a bathroom.

The marshal takes in the clothes showing in the open wardrobe—tops and jeans not much bigger than his own daughter Lori's. Pairs of sneakers; flashier, less cute.

The beads and bangles and trinkets on the nightstand seem just as young as his daughter's.

Georgia Eastman scans the room. "It's pretty organized. For a twelve year old. I've seen worse."

"We make them clean up," Salinas says.

"Good for you."

"I ask you something?" Whicher says. "You think Bella McConnell needs to be in here?"

"She gets close support twenty-four seven," Salinas answers, "while her behavior is stabilized. Most of our young people are with us around six to eight months before they can go on back to parents or a foster family."

"It works," Georgia Eastman says, "the majority of cases. It's constructive. It's a way to avoid sanction by the court."

Whicher looks at Salinas. "Ma'am, what do you think? You know her a little."

The supervisor eyes him steadily.

"How about the staff, the counselors here? Are y'all worried for her?"

"We are now. I'm obliged to report a child failing to return," Salinas says. "But coming down right off the bat—bringing in law enforcement—can make a situation worse."

"You know the risks," Eastman says, "to any of these kids."

"Law enforcement ups the ante," the woman says. "We

bring down a heap more trouble on their heads. These people are young, vulnerable. Somebody comes along, tells them they can take them somewhere nice, get 'em nice stuff, somewhere to live, give 'em clothes, money, drugs—they're easy prey. Every trafficker and pimp and narc and pervert out there is all over them. Girls here don't want to go back where they came from—most of them already rejected that life. Or were rejected by it."

"What might she have done?" Whicher says. "Where might she go? Do you know what was on her mind?"

"Her whole life," Salinas says. "Her father."

"What do you know about her father?"

"She talks about him," Salinas says. "She has trouble dealing with his absence, processing it. Her mother threatened to take her out of here before."

Whicher looks at Georgia Eastman.

"I didn't know that," Eastman says.

"She's made comments—she says her daughter shouldn't be in here. She told more than one member of staff."

"Did you report it?" Eastman says.

"It's on record in the relevant file," the supervisor says. "If I reported everything I hear to law enforcement, they'd never be out of here. A lot of the young people here have anger issues. They're pretty disturbed, their families are disturbed, they're chaotic, dysfunctional…" She pauses. "Some of it, we just have to let go."

"You didn't take the threat seriously?" Eastman says.

"Jessica McConnell's born-again," Salinas says, "she

found God. She's chosen. She takes her orders straight from Him."

The marshal looks at her. "You think Jessica McConnell could have taken her daughter?"

"I'm only telling you what she said."

"You think it's possible?"

The supervisor doesn't reply.

⋏

In an outdoor courtyard at the back of the hostel building, Whicher sits at a table beneath Texas live oak—Rafaela Salinas and a young girl on a bench seat opposite.

Gabriela Marquez is in her early teens—heavy—her eyes defensive, deep-set.

"Tell me what happened that afternoon?" the marshal says.

"We didn't do nothing."

Whicher looks at the girl.

"Gabriela." Salinas speaks softly. "Just tell the marshal what you did, what you've told us. You're not in any trouble."

The girl nods. A grimace settles on her face. "We went out."

"What time?" Whicher says.

"They get a break around four in the afternoon," the supervisor says.

"She asked me did I want to go out?"

"Bella asked you?" Whicher says.

Gabriela shrugs. "She asked. I said, okay."

"So, you walked out someplace?"

"We went out, we went a couple of blocks."

"They get forty-five minutes," Salinas says.

Whicher nods. "Did she tell you what she wanted to do?"

"No. I said I'd go with her, that's it."

"What y'all talk about?"

Gabriela stares across the courtyard. "Nothing."

Salinas puts a hand on the girl's arm. "*Gabriela…*"

"We didn't do nothing. We didn't talk about nothing, we just went out."

"And you split up from her?" Whicher says.

"I wanted to go get ice cream. Bella wanted to go on down to the next street, to get a taco."

"You couldn't do both?"

Gabriela shakes her head. "We don't get enough time."

"So, you went different places," Whicher says. "You ever meet anyone when you're out?"

"No."

Salinas turns to Whicher. "Sometimes boys will come up, you know? If they're out on the street. Residents are not supposed to meet with anyone—unless they're also from here. But we're living in the real world—we can't control it all, who they run into."

Whicher keeps his eyes on Gabriela. "Did anybody meet up with Bella?"

The young girl looks grim. "Maybe."

"Maybe?"

She stares into the middle distance. "Sometimes."

"Boys?"

Gabriela pulls her arms around her sides.

"You been out with Bella a bunch of times?"

"I don't know, I guess."

"Is there someone she meets up with? Somebody she likes? Someone she sees?"

"This one boy, maybe."

The marshal leans forward. "You know his name?"

"I don't know. I've seen him, like, a couple times…"

"What's he look like?"

"He's just a guy."

"A guy? Or a boy?"

"A boy, I guess. He wears a bandana." She gestures, circling her forehead with her hand. "He wears a bandana, he plays a lot of music."

"What kind of age?"

"Sixteen? Seventeen?"

"There anybody else?"

"I don't know."

Whicher writes in his notepad.

The girl shifts her weight on the bench.

"Was there anything different that day—from any other day?" Whicher says. "Was she up? Down? Tense? Anything at all?"

"I don't know."

The marshal looks up from the notepad. "What y'all talk about?"

"I don't know—nothing, just *stuff*—this place, like, things we want, things we like, things we don't like…"

"Nothing out of the ordinary?"

"*No.*"

From inside the building, Georgia Eastman emerges, hunted-looking. "I called the sheriff's office and the city police."

The marshal turns to her.

"They've talked with people at the taco place, nobody remembers anything—they don't remember a girl like Bella. They say officers checked for CCTV in the area—anything that could have picked up Bella on the day. There's a single camera located by an ATM on the street, nothing else."

Whicher turns back to Gabriela Marquez. "You think she might've been meeting up with someone that day?"

"I told her I'd see her back here," Gabriela says. "I went to get ice cream. She went ahead to get a taco. That's all I know. I thought I'd see her back here."

The marshal eyes the girl, tries to read her.

She shrugs, a veil descending. "After that I didn't see her no more."

Chapter Eight

Pecos, Tx

The barbecue and burrito joint off of West Jefferson is busy with the lunch time crowd—oil and gas field crews and ranch hands, businessmen and nurses from the county hospital.

Whicher spots his boss, Chief Deputy Marshal Fairbanks, at a table by the window.

She raises a hand, beckons him over.

The marshal threads his way between tables, ceiling fans turning the air in the room, dim light shining off the rag-painted walls.

"Marshal Tillman told me you'd be in here."

"The courthouse is a circus today," Fairbanks says. "He tell you we had a woman threaten to blow us up?"

"So I heard."

"I was about to order," the chief marshal says, "will you join me?"

Whicher pulls out a hard-backed chair, sits. Unbuttons the jacket of his suit.

Fairbanks takes a sip from a glass of iced tea. "How'd it go this morning?"

"No sign of the mother," Whicher says. "She's not home, she's not answering her phone."

A Hispanic waitress in a tank top and jeans approaches with an order pad.

"Can I get the club salad?" Fairbanks says.

The woman nods, turns to Whicher.

"And I'll take the brisket fajita plate."

"Something to drink?" the waitress says.

"Just coffee," Whicher answers, "thanks."

The woman turns for the kitchen.

"I talked with the cousin of the husband," Whicher says. "Karyn Dennison. She helped Jessica move out from Tennessee with her daughter, after McConnell got himself sent to prison. She says Jessica spends a lot of time in church. Maybe not enough time around her daughter."

"Oh?"

"The hostel supervisor in Fort Stockton told me Jessica McConnell's born-again."

"You went over to the hostel?"

Whicher nods. "The day she went missing, Bella left with another girl. They split up, Bella was going to get a taco from a street stand. Local police checked, nobody remembers seeing her. They're checking for CCTV footage, so far nothing's come up."

"The girl just disappeared into thin air?"

"Hostel supervisor says Jessica's made threats," Whicher says. "About removing her daughter from care. But they're used to people running their mouths."

The chief marshal frowns. "Did she strike you as the kind of person who might do that?"

Whicher thinks about it, doesn't answer.

"I had a call from USMS, Tennessee," Fairbanks says, "the Memphis office. Things aren't going real well. They formed up a task force to locate both escaped felons. A vehicle they're known to have used to get away was found in a supermarket lot a couple hundred miles away—in the city of Clarksville."

"We know how they got out?"

"They had help," Fairbanks answers. "One of the corrections officers. It looks like she got in some kind of a relationship with McConnell. Evidently he can be quite the charmer. They say he's pretty smart. McConnell worked the CO, little by little. She supplied them with clothes, money, a car."

"The car they found?" Whicher says.

The chief marshal nods. "The CO there is in a world of trouble. But these were high-security prisoners in a medium-to-low secure facility. McConnell's serving time for robbery, he's known to be violent—the other inmate, Reed Barbone is a convicted murderer. They broke out of the cell they were sharing in the middle of the night."

"How was that?"

"The locking mechanisms on half the cell doors are known to have faults," Fairbanks says. "According to the Memphis field office they got themselves out of their cell, then used a pipe-chase exiting on the prison roof to get out.

They jumped from the roof right over the perimeter fence. They must've set it all up, figured everything out. The CO left the car close by."

"Does Memphis know about the situation with the child?" Whicher says.

"I told them. They're not sure what to make of it. But escapees need resources—they're asking for family members to be watched."

Whicher looks at his boss. "Surveillance?"

"I told them it's too early. The first couple of weeks, they're usually smart enough not to try family or friends, or associates."

"We don't know where Jessica McConnell is," Whicher says. "Or Bella." The marshal stares at the window, lets his gaze run out across the street. "All three of them suddenly disappear. The father. The mother. The daughter…"

The waitress brings the order, puts the plates down onto the table.

"Gracias," Whicher says.

"We have limited resources," Fairbanks says. "I told Memphis we can't station people to cover properties twenty-four hours a day. But you're already looking for Bella McConnell—as of now I want you looking for Jessica too. If she doesn't show up today, I'll have an arrest warrant drawn up."

"On what charge?"

"Felony kidnap of a child. Her daughter goes missing, she doesn't want to talk to us? She doesn't return our calls?"

Whicher takes a forkful of brisket, tries the corn-and-bean-salsa side. "She found God. According to the cousin, Karyn Dennison. Her daughter gets taken away, maybe she doesn't think the courts have the right. That only God does."

The chief marshal lets his words sit, weighing them.

Whicher thinks of the little he knows of Jessica McConnell—of Bella. Of the man, Travis.

With no kind of answer.

⁂

Van Horn, Tx

The view of the highway from the motel window extends up and down the road only a couple of blocks. Around the old sixties motor court, new-built stores, a gas station and fast-food restaurants have grown up—no matter, she tells herself; she can't keep a lookout—she can't keep watch all day and all night.

In the parking lot are only two other vehicles—a panel van and an ancient station wagon.

She makes a final check, lets the window blind settle against the glass.

Crossing the shabby room, she unlocks the door, slips the chain.

Striding outside she takes a set of keys from her jeans—approaches the twenty-year-old Nissan sedan on black, steel rims.

She unlocks the car, climbs in, starts the motor.

Staring out through the windshield, she scans her immediate surrounds.

Over from the motel is a tire and muffler center and a fried chicken restaurant, then a piece of dead ground given over to garbage containers and dumpsters—a wooden fence surrounding it on two sides. Beyond that, a spreading line of mesquite.

Pole lights are at the highway's edge—at the back there's nothing.

At night it will be dark.

She drives the car off the motor court lot, glances over at the booking office—its door closed, its windows barred and blacked.

She drives to the service area, noses the car past the row of dumpsters, past the line of mesquite. Turning in behind the fence and the trees the car is shielded from sight.

She kills the motor, waits a moment.

Nobody from the tire center comes out.

The lot in back of the chicken restaurant is deserted.

She pulls the keys from the ignition, steps out, locks the car.

Walking quickly, she keeps her eyes fixed dead ahead—until she's back outside the motel room.

Pulling a key from her jeans pocket, she unlocks the door.

She steps in.

Locks up again.

Hooks and slides the chain.

Her heart is racing.

She stands in the middle of the room before a sagging, queen-size bed.

Feels the rush of blood in her head. Takes a breath, tells herself to calm down.

Stepping into the bathroom, she eyes a window in the back wall. Its glass opaque. The shadow of a wire grille showing behind it.

She looks for any way to make it open. If she smashed the glass, could she get out?

She puts a hand to her mouth, gnaws at a nail.

Turning back to the room, she steps to the door, pushes against it, gauging its strength.

The lock is old. Feeble-looking. The door chain made of thin metal, a screw missing from its track.

She steps away, sits on the edge of the bed.

Faint sound carrying from traffic on the highway.

The air in the room is deadened, stale. She listens for any noise, any sign of other occupants. Hears only her heart beating. The hum of an overhead light.

An urge to run grips her.

An urge to flee, to get back into her car.

To drive, and keep on driving.

She puts her hands out to her sides, pushes her fingers into the coverlet.

The room swims.

Staring at a table by the window she focuses on a travel bag, a receipt—handwritten. One night. Room 4. Jessica McDonald.

She stands, suddenly.

Rushes to the bathroom.

Grips hold of the sink.

She retches.

Her body convulsing—expelling everything in her stomach.

Voiding everything inside.

⋏

Hudspeth County, Tx

The land to the rear of the property is empty, a wash line hanging slack above a hard dirt yard. Blinds and drapes are closed behind the windows, no seeing into any of the rooms.

Whicher passes along the side of the house.

Over at the neighbor's fence, the German Shepherd growls, pulling on its chain.

At the front, the marshal eyes the property.

No car.

No sign of life.

No word, no trace.

He scans the land beyond the house, bare caliche. A patch of wild violets breaking through the dry ground.

He thinks of Jessica McConnell, the day before, standing in her front room—smoothing her black hair from her face. Like some girl-band singer—with her pale eyes, paler skin. Lighting up an American Spirit. Mashing it out. In a one-floor, tumbledown with a tin roof, green-painted sides. Displaced in her surroundings, extrinsic, out of sync.

He takes out his phone, tries her number one more time.

No answer.

He can just make out the faint ring—from the phone inside the house.

Beneath the oak tree beyond the fence a man is looking at him.

Hispanic. In his sixties. With white hair, his face weathered, his body hard.

The man calls out to the dog.

Whicher takes off the Resistol. "US Marshals Service." He slips out his badge and ID. "Looking for Jessica McConnell?" Approaching the fence, he holds out the badge.

The dog snarls, its ridge is up.

"¡Cállate!" the man says. "She do something wrong?"

"I need to talk with her is all," the marshal says. "Have you seen her?"

"No, señor."

Whicher puts away the badge.

The dog circles, paws the dust beneath the tree.

"You know her?" Whicher says.

"She's new here." The man shakes his head. "She keeps herself to herself. I leave early, get home late. Running my construction business."

"You don't see her?" The marshal peers past the branches of the Mexican white oak, to the house beyond. "There anybody else around?"

"My wife's gone. The Lord took her, it's been three years. My kids are all grown up."

Whicher looks in the man's eyes.

"There's just me, now. Me and the dog."

The marshal takes out a business card. "If Mrs McConnell comes back, if you see her? There's concern for the daughter. She's missing."

"She ran off?"

"She's been living back in Fort Stockton."

The man looks at him.

"A residential center," Whicher says. "Right now I need to talk with Mrs McConnell. She's not answering my calls."

The man takes the business card.

"Sir, do you have a number for her?" the marshal says. "Apart from here at the house?"

"No, señor."

Whicher replaces the Resistol. "Let me know if she shows up?"

The man's eyes are hooded. "There was a truck here, the other night. I didn't recognize."

"A truck?"

"Light truck."

"You know what kind?"

"Toyota, maybe," the man says.

"What color?"

"Dark. Blue or something. Maybe gray."

"You see a plate?"

The man shakes his head. "See a Ram pickup out here a bunch. I didn't recognize this…this other one."

The marshal takes out his notepad, writes down the detail.

"I didn't think nothing of it," the man says. "But if something happened…"

"You see it again, you let me know?"

The man puts the card into a pocket, gives a bare nod. Turns to the dog beneath the tree. Speaks to it in Spanish, leads it away.

Whicher watches until they're gone from sight.

Silence hanging in the air, now that the dog has gone.

The only sound wind moving through the leaves in the big oak. Faint noise from the far-off road into town.

On his phone he opens up the picture of Bella McConnell.

He stares at it. Searching for something—some sign it might convey.

A flat image looks back at him.

A girl, twelve years old.

Blurring in his mind's eye, blurring with the face of another.

Far from there.

The image of his daughter.

Lori's face.

⚰

Dusk descending.

Coolness.

Air now turning.

Turning cold.

Fading light stretches shadows across the property—painting lines and shapes onto the barren yard.

The beaten-down, green-painted house sits abandoned.

Darkness deepens beneath the neighboring tree.

The Silverado is long gone, the marshal with it.

Amber eyes in the twilight scan the fence line—the German Shepherd prowling, its muzzle raised.

Sensing something.

Scenting the air.

Within the walls of the house, a clock in the kitchen ticks.

The refrigerator hums.

In a bedroom, Jessica McConnell's bedroom, drapes are closed.

The room is dim—light bruised.

In the front room, on the wall is a fine spray. Barely visible. Scarlet. Darkening.

On the floor of the bedroom is a body.

The body of a man.

Dried blood matted in his hair.

Legs splayed.

Eyes open.

Staring at the ceiling.

As if transfixed.

Bewitched.

On a point unknown.

Fixated.

On the view.

Of infinity.

Chapter Nine

Pecos, Tx

Sitting at the edge of the bed, he rests the folder marked *Child Protection Service* on his lap, the noise of feet thundering through the house pulling him out of the report.

His wife, Leanne, is speaking. The timbre of her voice through the wall pressed-sounding. His daughter's voice singsong. He gauges the exchange between them. Reads on in the report.

A paragraph by Rafaela Salinas, the Fort Stockton hostel supervisor notes; '*confrontational dynamics*' between Jessica McConnell and her daughter.

The door to the bedroom opens.

Leanne stands in the frame.

Her chestnut hair is undone, unruly, eyes quick in her handsome face. "Will you take her?"

He sets down the report.

"To school, you were going to take her this morning?"

"Sure." He looks at his wife. Graceful, still—despite the

rush of morning. "Pick out a tie for me?"

She spins around, eyes the armoire. Whips a dark blue necktie from the rack.

"They move the start time for Fifth Grade?"

"She needs to be there before eight…"

"Alright."

"Or I can do it?"

Whicher turns up the collar on a fresh white shirt. "I'll do it."

"You're heading that way anyway." Leanne eyes the folder. "What is that?"

Whicher threads the necktie, loops it into a knot. "The case."

"The missing girl?"

He takes the holstered, semi-automatic Glock. Two spare magazine holders. Clips them to his belt.

"There's still no word?" Leanne says.

Whicher catches the look in his wife's eye.

Reaching into the armoire, he takes out the Ruger in the tan leather shoulder holster. He slips the rig on over his shirt. "There's a problem with the mother, now. Nobody's seen her. She's not answering calls." He takes the jacket of his dark, gray suit from a hanger. Puts it on. "I'm headed over to Hudspeth County this morning, to see if she came back. Or find somebody else to talk to. The sheriff's office and Fort Stockton PD have nothing."

"There's no news this morning?"

He glances at his phone on the nightstand. "She's gone already. The question now is, where?"

"How long has she been missing?"

"Forty hours or so," Whicher says, "minimum."

Leanne looks at him. "I sure hope it's alright."

He nods.

"You need to leave," she says, "come on, you need to go."

He straightens his tie, sees his wife's reflection in the bedroom mirror—sees her uncertain face.

He turns around.

"You think you're really…best for this?" she says.

He cuts a look at her.

"It's not like you've done it before. Located a missing child."

The marshal holds her eye a moment. Picks the folder from the bed.

Leanne brushes by him, out of the room. "I'll go get Lori…"

Stepping into the hallway, he sees his daughter in the kitchen—in a shaft of sunlight. Dressed in jeans, sneakers, a yellow blouse with white dots. Her hair lit up. Chestnut hair like her mother's. A ribbon in it, a bright green thread.

She takes a glass of milk from the kitchen table, drains it.

Leanne grabs a red, canvas backpack from the countertop. Rifles inside it. "You have everything?"

Lori nods. Performs steps from a dance routine.

"The math worksheet?"

"Uh-oh." She dumps her milk glass onto the table—runs from the kitchen to her room. Spots her father. "Hey, dad…"

"Hey, yourself."

Lori speeds by him, beaming.

Leanne calls out, "You need the book Miss Pullen said to bring…"

"I don't know where it *is*…"

"It was under the plate I asked you to bring back in the kitchen."

A second later. "Found it…"

The marshal grins at his wife.

Leanne rolls her eyes.

Whicher grabs his Resistol.

Lori runs back in, the math sheet and book beneath her arm.

"You didn't bring the plate?" Leanne says. "Come on. Come on, you're going to be late."

The marshal takes out the keys to the Silverado.

Lori struggles with the pack on her back.

"You'll have to take it off again," Whicher says, "to get up in the truck."

She shrugs it off, slides it across the floor.

"I'm carrying it?"

"*Please*…"

He takes it. Swings it up on his shoulder.

Lori runs ahead, pushes open the front door, skips outside.

Whicher steps to his wife, kisses her. Lays a hand on the bare skin of her arm.

Leanne touches the side of his face.

Her eyes stay on his. "Go," she says, "go." And then,

beneath her breath tells him; "Find them."

⋏

Hudspeth County, Tx

The white, stuccoed church sits at the side of the highway—he sees the shine from its pitched, tin roof—approaching closer, sees a line of dark green cypress standing sentry along the dust-blown road.

He slows the Silverado.

At one side of the church is a picnic area—set back in the shade of live oak and ponderosa pine.

A man and a woman are seated at a bench among a group of tables.

Pulling in, Whicher parks the truck in a grit turnaround.

He steps down, fits his hat, buttons the jacket of his suit, covering the shoulder holster.

The seated man stands. White-haired, lean, dressed in work jeans and a plaid shirt. His face is open, welcoming. Eyes smiling behind steel-frame glasses.

The woman is thickset, with dark hair cut short.

Whicher raises his hat. "Morning."

"Good morning, brother," the man replies.

The woman nods. Her expression subdued.

Whicher takes out his badge and ID.

The white-haired man peers at it.

The woman's eyes slide away.

On top of the table is a pile of rags, two plastic buckets, a stack of newspapers, their edges curled in the breeze.

"Name's Whicher," the marshal says. "US Marshals Service, Western District. Out of Pecos. I don't mean to intrude. I was hoping I might talk with somebody from the church."

"I'm Winford Mullins," the man says, "I'm pastor here." He gestures at the woman. "And this is Miss Pearl Cooper."

The pastor steps forward, offers his hand.

Whicher takes it.

The man's grip is firm.

"How may we be of help?"

"I'm looking for a young woman," Whicher says. "I believe she may be a worshipper here. Jessica McConnell?"

The pastor looks at him steadily.

The marshal reads surprise in his face.

"Mrs McConnell is certainly a regular attendee," the pastor says. "Is something wrong? Has something happened?"

"Have you seen Mrs McConnell lately?" Whicher says.

"Not in a few days," Mullins replies. "I'd have to think about it..."

The marshal looks at the woman. "Ma'am?"

She sniffs. "No, sir."

"I need to speak with her in regard to her daughter," the marshal says.

Winford Mullins nods. "In Fort Stockton?"

Whicher looks at him.

"I know the daughter has been having...difficulties," the pastor says. "Jessica told me about it. That she's been living there, at a young person's center."

"The daughter's been missing a couple days," the marshal says.

"Oh." The pastor's eyes search his face.

"Mrs McConnell's not at her home, she's not returning calls. She may have gone someplace. I was hoping somebody from the church might be able to help. Y'all know much about her?"

"We know her a little," Mullins answers.

From the table, the woman speaks. "Did you try Jacob Harwood's place?"

"Pearl…" Winford Mullins clears his throat. "That's a little…out of turn."

The marshal eyes the woman. Her brows arched, her mouth pressed shut.

The pastor steps to the table, picks out rags from the pile. "We were cleaning the church windows," he says. "Pearl and I. With all the wind and the dust these last weeks."

The woman studies the back of her hands.

The pastor looks at her. "Why don't you make a start around the other side? There's the standpipe in back there, if you need more water."

She pushes up from the table, sullen. Takes a handful of rags. Picks a half-filled bucket from the table, wads a couple of newspapers beneath a thick arm.

She strides beneath the trees to the white-painted building.

"Jacob Harwood?" Whicher says.

"He's local," Pastor Mullins says, "he's a regular here. He and Mrs McConnell are friendly, I believe." The pastor picks up a bucket. "Do you mind if I continue? There's work to do, God's work, and the windows…"

Whicher reaches out a hand; "Let me carry that for you."

The pastor hands him the bucket, takes a pile of rags and papers.

Whicher follows to the side of the building. "How well do you know Jessica McConnell?"

"Not well, marshal. She hasn't lived here real long. When she moved in to our community we took the time to reach out. We deliver groceries and such to folk. Anyone who seems to be struggling. She seemed a little lost. She's separated from her husband. She didn't appear to know anyone."

Whicher nods. Sets the bucket down.

The woman, Pearl Cooper, disappears around the far side of the building.

"Her daughter found it difficult, I know that," the pastor says, his voice quiet. "Moving from back east. At her age. Jessica told me they have a…difficult relationship."

"She told you that?"

"I guess they fight. I told her what I tell all of my flock—I'm here if they need me, anytime. I'm not here to judge." Stooping to the bucket, the pastor wets the rag in the water. He wrings it out, wipes down a pane of glass.

"There something going on between Jessica McConnell and this Jacob Harwood?" Whicher says.

"Pearl can be uncharitable," the pastor answers. "She's a good person. But she's lived here all her life, the church is her church—she can be distrustful of strangers. Jessica McConnell's an attractive woman, she's different, she dresses a certain way. I guess she ruffles feathers."

"And Jacob Harwood?"

"He's a young man of good character, active in our ministry."

Whicher looks at Mullins.

"He's attentive to her," the pastor says. "People talk."

"You know him well?"

"Fairly well." Mullins wets the rag again. Cleans another part of the window. "I don't know that they're in any kind of a relationship," he says. "Then again, in good conscience, I don't know that they aren't."

"Know where I could find him?"

The pastor inclines his head.

"Jessica McConnell's private life is not my interest," the marshal says. "It's the daughter, Bella, I need to find. Nobody's seen her the last two days. She's a young girl, a child. It can be a hard world out there."

Pastor Mullins meets the marshal's eye. "God will be watching over her."

Whicher nods. "I hope you're right."

"And we'll keep her in our prayers."

"Do that," Whicher says.

The pastor stands a moment, studying on him.

"Sir, if you hear anything…"

Mullins touches his arm. "Have faith. The Lord will guide you."

"Yessir." The marshal takes out his notepad and a pen. "Meantime," he says. "Jacob Harwood? I'll be needing an address."

Pulling up in front of the house on Cammack Avenue Whicher lets the Silverado idle, eying the property, ranch style, three-to-four bed, the marshal guesses.

He scans up and down the street—houses set on plots fifty yards apart—most of them one-floor, rendered white or a dirty cream. Lean-to car ports, trucks in the driveways, older-model cars.

Between plots the ground is empty save for mesquite and yucca, and patches of burnt dry grass.

In front of the house is a dark red Ram pickup.

The marshal cuts the motor, steps out.

Walking up to the house, he places a hand at the front grille of the Ram—it's cold to the touch.

He knocks at the front door.

A strange sensation in him.

No sound comes back.

Stepping away, he looks along the front of the building. Moves to a window, tries to look inside.

The blind is down.

He tries the door again, calls out; "*US Marshals Service…*"

Still no answer.

He walks into the yard, looks around at the pickup.

Taking out his phone he finds the number for Jessica McConnell. He sends the call.

It rings over and over.

Switches to voicemail.

He clicks it off. Lets his gaze run out to the neighborhood houses.

He'll have to drive over. Check again. She won't be there.

He takes a breath, looks the property over, Jacob Harwood's house.

Something.

Gut tells him there's something. Three years leading the battalion scout platoon, Third Armored Cavalry. Twenty-two years a criminal investigator. He can feel it—a sixth sense.

He pictures Jessica McConnell. The strange allure in her.

Thinks of Harwood, a country boy, a congregant at a rural church.

Lining up on the tag of the Ram, he takes a picture, stores it.

Checks it.

Alongside the prior shot.

Of the girl on his phone.

⼈

People are everywhere, the walkways crowded, overhead lighting too bright, the store fronts glaring. A voice on a public-address system drones, the words of the announcer indistinct.

She tunes it out. Clutches a prepaid, flip phone, sweat running at her temple, dampening her hair.

Out of breath, she moves quickly. Passes food concessions, the smell of coffee and fries and donuts nauseating.

Walking the length of an aisle she searches out a place away from people.

Singles and couples are everywhere; families, groups.

She follows signs to the nearest exit. Stepping out, feels the coldness in the air. She gulps down breath, steadies herself. Sees an empty bench seat across from a taxicab stand.

She strides to it, sits down, dumps her bag on the floor.

Cars and buses pass in a steady stream. Taxis sit in the stand, their drivers talking, others looking at phones.

A uniformed cop appears at the side of the terminal building. A second cop behind him.

She grips the end of the bench.

Looks away. Looks at nothing.

Unfolds the flip phone. Forces herself to concentrate on its screen.

In her mind's eye she sees a room—a man's face. She feels a surge of fear. Her body jolts.

Focusing on the sounds of traffic, on the rumble of a bus, her vision swims, her eyes blur in and out.

Her hand trembles holding the phone.

People on the sidewalk are moving fast.

She stares over at the uniformed cops.

One of them talking into a radio.

Her fingers fumble on the keypad. She punches in a number.

Sends the call.

Clamps the phone to her ear.

Chapter Ten

Sonora, Ky

Travis McConnell scarfs down a third dollar-cheeseburger, a half-eaten carton of fries between his legs. He steers with one hand, stomach churning. Eyes sore from a lack of sleep.

Light rain falls from a gray sky on the town off the Kentucky Turnpike.

He drives the speed limit, searches the buildings along the sides of the road. Cuts a look at the man beside him. Looks away.

Reed Barbone crams the last of a beef patty and burger bun into his mouth.

"We need to get cleaned up," McConnell says.

Two days sleeping in cars, in the woods. Stubble on his face, ketchup stains on the ill-fitting tee.

Beyond the windshield, the edge of town gives out to white-fenced pasture and brick houses set between the trees.

"We don't look right. We look like we're sleeping rough," McConnell says, "like we don't belong in this car."

Barbone belches. "You want to walk?"

Beyond a black-painted barn at the side of the highway, a smaller road cuts down toward a group of stores and businesses.

"Your girlfriend got us these crappy clothes…"

McConnell ignores him. Studies the buildings—a convenience store, an auto repair. A pizza restaurant. Farm supply.

He comes off the gas, lets the SUV slow. Hits the blinker.

A handful of pickups and cars are spread around a grit lot.

"What're you doing?" Barbone says.

McConnell doesn't answer. He steers in, parks the Mazda by a power line at the edge of the road. Leaves the motor running, wipers and the blower switched on.

He lifts a soda from the cup holder, takes a pull. Grabs a handful of fries.

Barbone throws the wrapper from his burger over his shoulder. Shifts, turns in his seat.

McConnell feels the man's gaze—intense.

A semi rolls by from the interstate kicking up a wash of dirty spray.

"So, we got maybe three hundred bucks," McConnell says. "Most of a tank of gas."

"I'll tell you something."

McConnell looks at Barbone.

"I didn't break out of prison to live like this," the big man says. "Like an animal."

The wipers beat time on the windshield.

McConnell nods.

He picks out the billfold from the center well. Opens it, stares at the photo on the driver's license. "How long you think before somebody realizes this guy Dupris is gone? That his car ain't anywhere? That he ain't showing up for work?"

Barbone sucks in air through his nostrils.

"Back there," McConnell says, brooding, "that lake? Somebody might find him."

"So we make ground."

"We need to stay free." McConnell stares out through the rain on the windshield. "You want to make it to Detroit?"

On the pole holding up the power line is a blue panel-sign—an image on it, a hound running. A silver hound.

He points to it. "How about that?"

"A greyhound bus?" Barbone says. "Bullshit."

"Why not? Who looks on a bus?"

"You need ID."

"To ride it?" McConnell says. "You know that?"

"My ol' lady used to catch the greyhound bus, my third prison. No ID they don't let your ass on." Barbone shakes his head. Jabs a thumb toward the farm supply building. "Check it out…"

McConnell looks across—sees a horse and buggy.

"One of your boys. Amish."

"I'm not Amish," McConnell says. "I grew up around them, is all."

"Pennsylvania," Barbone says. "You plan on going back?"

McConnell takes another pull on the soda. They would have kept the first car, the Grand Marquis, they could have been long gone. Carlene must have given them up. Dumb hack. *Corrections Officer Jimerson.* The cop in Clarksville would've never happened. He taps the steering wheel. "This thing bothers me, you know? If they're looking for it."

"We need wheels."

"We need resources."

Barbone looks at the convenience store. "So we bust out a two-eleven…"

"Armed robbery?"

"Your specialty."

"With no guns?"

The big man scratches at his beard.

"We need better clothes," McConnell says. "We need to fit in." He points at the farm supply. "Maybe I'll take a look in there—see what they have."

"We need gas money."

"We got gas."

"You spend more than fifty bucks in there," Barbone says, "I'll kick your ass."

McConnell bridles.

Cuts the motor.

"Leave it running," Barbone says, "leave the heat on. It's cold out there."

McConnell thinks about it for a split second—thinks of stepping out, stepping into the store. The big man haring out of the lot, hitting the highway.

He opens the door.

Wordless.

Reaches to the ignition.

Slips out the keys.

⊥

Pecos County, Tx

The phone in the dash-holder lights up in the Silverado—Whicher reads the incoming number, Chief Deputy Marshal Fairbanks—he picks up.

"Ma'am?"

"Marshal, where are you?" she says. "Over in Hudspeth?"

"I left there an hour ago. I'm headed in to Fort Stockton, to the hostel," Whicher says. "I tried Jessica McConnell's place, nobody's home. I tried the address of a friend, a possible boyfriend, nobody was there either. Last night I talked with a neighbor—he said an unfamiliar Toyota truck was outside Jessica McConnell's house a couple nights back—a truck he's never seen before."

"He get a license plate?"

"No."

"You need to turn around," the chief marshal says. "USMS in Tennessee have just sent word."

"On Jessica McConnell?"

"They're set up monitoring bank transactions—credit cards, bank cards of immediate family members, for both escapees. They got a hit this morning."

"On her?"

"A gas station outside of Nashville."

Whicher stares at the road ahead.

"Her card. Used to buy gas."

"They're sure it's her?"

"They're double-checking, now," Fairbanks says.

"She drove to Nashville?" The marshal thinks of the distance. West Texas, to Tennessee.

"She might've flown," Fairbanks says.

"If she bought a ticket, would it show up?"

"Some transactions take longer than others."

Whicher thinks it over, eyes the empty interstate.

"Is there any word on Bella?" Fairbanks says.

"No, ma'am, not yet."

"Alright, I want you to turn around, head on back to Hudspeth, enter and search Jessica McConnell's house," the chief marshal says. "I'll arrange the warrant. I'll have the sheriff's office meet you there."

"A warrant?" Whicher says. "To look for what?"

"For Bella McConnell. Or any sign of her recent presence," Fairbanks says. "We need to know for sure she's not in there. People do some crazy things with kids, they'll hide them in basements, attics, under beds…"

"I don't believe she's there."

"If the mother's in Nashville, who knows where the daughter might be, now? We have to widen the search. But make certain we didn't miss something here," Fairbanks says. "I'll have people there. With a warrant, signed. Is there anything you want? Anything you need?"

"One thing," the marshal says.

"Go ahead, what is it?"

"Nobody goes inside till I'm there."

⁂

An ambulance and two sheriff's department vehicles are parked in front of the green-sided house—a female deputy in a black and white cruiser, a male deputy standing alongside an SUV.

Whicher pulls up in front of the property.

A woman in a zip suit stands in the yard—with an older man in a pale blue shirt and white hat.

Two paramedics look out from behind the windshield of the ambulance.

The man in the white hat steps off the yard, heads to Whicher's truck.

The marshal spots the brass badge on his shirt—he kills the motor, swings open the door.

"Odell Ingram," the man says. "I'm sheriff here."

"John Whicher, United States Marshals, Western Division."

The sheriff puts out a hand.

Whicher takes it.

"We have a warrant to enter the house," Sheriff Ingram says. "Marshals Office faxed it over, thirty minutes ago. It's signed. It's good to go. I have a crime scene investigator on site." He indicates the woman in the zip suit. "One of my deputies will get you into the house."

"You brought an ambulance?"

"I had your boss on the line," the sheriff says.

The marshal looks at him. Studies the man's lined face; quick eyes, the color of desert.

"I'm minded to say she's one thoroughgoing peace officer," the sheriff says.

Whicher inclines his head, steps out.

"We find this missing girl y'all are looking for, my office is ready to provide immediate medical assistance," Ingram says. "Or transportation to hospital in El Paso. For the record."

"Chief Marshal Fairbanks asked for that?"

"Insisted on it," the sheriff says.

Whicher scans the yard, eyes the neighbor's dog staring from beneath the tree.

Sheriff Ingram looks at him. "This girl's gone forty-eight hours?"

"Around that."

"Missing minors." Ingram sucks in air over his teeth. "They can take some finding. Some of 'em don't want to get found."

Whicher nods to the crime scene investigator. To the sheriff; "Y'all ready to go?"

Sheriff Ingram signals to the squat deputy by the SUV. "Vince. Let's open it on up."

The deputy reaches in back of the SUV—brings out a battery-operated drill and canvas tool bag. He steps to the front door, puts down the bag, places the drill against the lock.

Metallic grinding fills the air as the bit reams out the tumblers behind the plate.

The deputy reaches down into the bag for a wrecking bar. He fits the steel edge to the frame, rocks it in. Levers the front door open.

Sheriff Ingram addresses the female deputy. "Raylene? You want to help out with the search? Vince, you got the front, here, right?"

The deputy nods.

The sheriff addresses the crime scene investigator. "Grace?"

"I'm good to go."

Ingram turns to Whicher. "All yours then, marshal."

Whicher takes a pair of black, nitrile gloves from his jacket pocket, pulls them on.

He crosses the yard to the front door. Pauses by the deputy named Vince. "No sign of forced entry?"

"No, sir."

"You check all around the house?"

"All the way around, marshal, there's nothing."

Whicher feels the strange sensation returning, despite himself. He feels his heart rate tick up.

He steps across the threshold into the hallway. "*US Marshal entering...*"

The house is still, silent. The air deadened.

He enters the living room.

It's empty.

He backs out, steps down the hallway toward a kitchen at the rear of the house.

Behind him, the crime scene investigator moves inside— followed by the deputy named Raylene, and Sheriff Ingram.

The CSI pauses. Sniffs. Looks around. Sniffs again.

"Grace?" the sheriff says.

"You smell that?"

"Smell what?" Whicher says.

"Carpet cleaner," the woman answers.

The marshal breathes in air through his nose. Picks out a faint hint, a fragrance.

"Had to be a bloodhound in another life, Grace," the sheriff says.

"Not always a good thing," the woman replies.

Whicher meets her eye. "You smell carpet cleaner?"

The woman nods.

Continuing on into the kitchen he sees dirty dishes piled in the sink. Cupboard doors are left open. Glasses and cups and plates strewn around a countertop. The garbage can full.

The kitchen table is at an odd angle—not square with the wall. Chairs are pulled out at one side.

Whicher frowns.

Turning back to the hallway he sees the CSI, Grace, pointing at a closed door.

"Here," she says.

The marshal steps to her. Places a gloved hand onto the handle. Opens the door.

The room is a bedroom, drapes closed.

Flipping on the light, he sees a queen-size bed, unmade.

A wardrobe, a chest of drawers—all open. The scent of a cleaning product is in the air.

He steps in.

The crime scene investigator enters behind him.

She moves around the room, eyes the bed, the carpet.

At the far side of the room she kneels. "Here," she says. "Somebody cleaned this, right here."

Whicher moves around the foot of the bed, studies the spot. The color in the carpet is slightly lighter.

"Never a good sign," the woman says.

Sheriff Ingram calls into the room; "Y'all have something?"

Whicher walks back out. "Maybe," he says. "Maybe not."

Off the hall, by the kitchen, is a bathroom—the marshal steps in, scans the room.

A toilet and basin. Shower cubicle.

A bathroom cabinet; open. He looks inside.

Boxes of Tylenol and Motrin. Aspirin. Knocked over. A gap, a bare spot on the crowded shelf. Hair products. Lipsticks, makeup. No toothpaste.

He checks.

No toothbrush at the basin.

Passing again into the hallway, Sheriff Ingram is in the kitchen, his hat pushed back.

"Kind of a mess in here," the sheriff says.

"Kind of," Whicher answers. He steps along the hallway to another closed door—opposite the first bedroom.

"What're you thinking marshal?" Ingram says.

"I'm thinking she's not here."

Whicher opens the door. Steps inside.

A child's room, girl's room. Not unlike his own daughter's.

Clothes and soft toys, bright bangles. Sneakers, posters on the wall. A floral throw sits on top of the single bed.

Unease.

Unease is in him.

Thoughts of Lori. Of Bella.

Something more than that.

The room is neat, made up.

He turns back, steps into the hall.

The female deputy, Raylene, is exiting the front room. A pinched expression on her face.

He eyes her.

"You might want to see this."

"In there?"

She nods.

Whicher follows her into the living room.

The deputy crosses to a wall.

She squats.

Takes a pen from her shirt pocket, holds it between gloved fingers.

Pointing the pen at the base of the wall she looks up. "It's hard to see. It could be something."

Whicher stoops.

A faint speckle of marks is on the white wall—tiny droplets. A minute spray.

He feels his heart push in his chest.

The sheriff appears at the door. "You find something? You need Grace?"

Whicher stands, feels a black mood descending. He looks into the sheriff's face. "We need Grace."

Chapter Eleven

In a rest area off the interstate, Travis McConnell turns the Tennessee driver's license between his fingers. He studies the flat image, the face looking back at him. Considers the bare details of a man's life.

Kendrick Dupris.

Date of birth. Height, eye color.

Address.

He slides the license back into the billfold, sets it down.

Scanning the expanse of asphalt, he sees Reed Barbone emerging past a rank of Peterbilts and Macks and Freightliners. Fresh out of the rest rooms in a pair of new-bought jeans, a windcheater and boots from a roadside store.

McConnell glances at his own new clothes, canvas cargo pants and a fleece jacket from the farm supply.

Barbone strides the lot like a jailbird—chest pumped, big arms out at his sides.

From a hundred yards it sticks out.

McConnell pictures the prison, pictures Barbone within its walls. A world of brutal struggle. Hierarchy. Unceasing violence. Barbone thrived, a place like that.

He thinks of Carlene Jimerson, the female CO. The last weeks, working her slowly, piece by piece. Pushing, testing her limits. Leading. Never pushing too far. Sweet-talking, feeding her hopeful heart. Her dumb belief. In some fantasy bad-boy romance.

She'd been waiting her whole life for somebody like him. To save her.

Just as she could reach out; save him.

Feeding her, letting her believe.

That he'd been waiting his whole life, too, to meet a woman like her.

Never letting the slightest hint escape, not even for a moment.

Never letting himself laugh. Throw back his head and laugh in her face—at the fathomless depth of her stupidity.

Animal stupidity.

He watches Reed Barbone.

Another animal.

Too much had been riding on her—on her believing in him—that he was her destiny. What had she believed was going to happen?

Barbone nears the big Mazda, strutting now.

McConnell thinks of the last weeks, letting it flow, letting her see that he couldn't be without her, that he'd do anything. Risk it all. That he'd never known a thing like it. What he felt for her. If he could only get out, if he could find a way. They could be together. Love as destiny. Nothing able to stand in its path. No force. No law of man.

She'd showed him the cover of a book she was reading, one time. A guy on it, with a six-pack. Her bad-boy romance.

How could anybody believe it, he'd asked himself.

He'd had his answer.

Everything he'd wanted, she'd done for him, over time.

The money.

The car. Her dying uncle's car.

If only she would've held out. If only she'd had brains. They must've cracked her, the first day. The prison authorities and the cops. It couldn't have been hard. Among the COs there would have been suspicion.

He shakes his head.

Reed Barbone opens the door of the car. "What do you think?"

"Good," McConnell says. "Better. We got clothes, we got a change of vehicle."

Barbone nods.

"We need resources," McConnell says.

"We need to go north."

"I know where we can get some."

Barbone gets into the SUV—looks at him.

Travis McConnell picks up the billfold. Takes out the driver's license, reads the address.

"You want to go back to Tennessee?"

"I want to go someplace I know will be empty." McConnell holds out the keys from the ignition. He singles out a door key from the bunch. "A place we can get in."

"How you know it's going to be empty?" Barbone says. "How you know he don't live there with someone?"

"We can find out?" McConnell says. "If no one's there…"

Barbone's eyes show his lack of comprehension.

"I got you this far, man, I'm a thinker, right?" McConnell slows it down. "We get there, we make sure nobody's there."

"What if there is?"

Picking up the billfold he takes out the rest of the money. He puts it into Barbone's hand. "We put this in the tank, every dollar of it. Drive north. Far as we can get."

The big man glowers at him.

"But if we do that," McConnell says, "we got the exact same problem when we get there—we got nothing, we have to find something."

"We'll be long gone from where cops are looking for us."

"With nothing," McConnell says. "And no way to get anything. We go to family, they're watching. We go to friends, the same thing. You want to rob a store? Sure. With what? Bare hands?"

"You want to turn around?" Barbone says. "Head right back where we came from?"

"We buy time, get whatever we can get from this guy, Dupris. Get what we can from his place. Eat, sleep. Figure shit out."

"We could do that anywhere."

McConnell taps on the photograph of Kendrick Dupris. "We could do it the one place we know nobody will be coming."

⊥

Outside the rear of Jessica McConnell's house, Whicher finds the number for Chief Deputy Marshal Fairbanks up in Pecos—he keys it.

The squat deputy, Vince, stands guard at the front of the building. The ambulance is gone.

Sheriff Odell Ingram prowls the fence line speaking into a radio.

Inside the house, the CSI and the female deputy conduct a secondary search of the building, room by room.

The call picks up.

"Ma'am, this is Whicher—over in Hudspeth, at Jessica McConnell's place."

"What's going on?"

"The girl's not here. There's nobody in the house. We've checked every room, every space—there's no basement, no garage. Couple things—there's some sign of disruption in there. It looks like."

"What kind of disruption?"

The marshal eyes the back of the house. "Hard to say exactly. It looks like somebody left in a hurry. We can't be sure yet. But some kind of struggle may have taken place."

"What makes you say that?"

"The furniture in the kitchen looked like it'd been moved. Bathroom had the feel somebody maybe grabbed a couple things, headed out real quick."

"It doesn't sound like much," the chief marshal says.

"We found some blood inside the house, too."

"Blood?"

Whicher thinks of the gut feeling, the sense of unease

about the place. "Some deposits. A spatter pattern," he says. "CSI on site sees some stringing, she thinks it could be something."

Fairbanks is quiet a moment. "Is there anything else?"

"Yes, ma'am. In the bedroom, Jessica McConnell's bedroom—somebody cleaned something from the floor."

"What's the CSI make of that?"

"Interested," Whicher says. "It's recent. The carpet's not fully dry."

"Is there a chance the blood could be from Bella?"

The marshal stares past the house to the desert land beyond, dotted with ocotillo and prickly pear. "I sure as hell hope not."

The chief marshal exhales into the phone.

Whicher lets his gaze drift to the German Shepherd beneath the tree. On the ground, in the dirt is a dark spot, discoloration. Oil. A stain. He peers at it, tries to recall if it was there before. "Something bothers me about this place," he says, "about the house. I felt it last night. Again this morning. Now, with the blood...I'm thinking to go after this guy, Jacob Harwood, the possible boyfriend."

"I need you to go to Nashville," the chief marshal says.

"Say again?"

"I need you up in Tennessee. I need you to fly there tonight. USMS in Memphis are confirming Jessica McConnell's card was definitely used in that gas station. They have a record of an airplane ticket, now. Purchased by her, last night. For a flight this morning. Out of Midland, Texas, up to Nashville International."

Whicher thinks it over.

"You're booked on to a flight tonight."

The marshal rubs a hand across his jaw.

"USMS field office, Nashville, have a member of the Memphis task force up there now—they're asking that you meet with her. You know there's always the possibility an escapee will try to contact a spouse. If she went up to Nashville, better you're up there."

"How about Bella?"

"Maybe Bella's with her."

"We need to check out this guy, Harwood."

"The sheriff's office can pick him up," Fairbanks says. "They can bring him in. Talk to him. Your flight leaves at seven—out of Midland. You can fly armed, but let them know."

"How about if they can't find this Harwood guy?"

"If they can't, we start to worry about him. He becomes a person of interest."

Whicher lets his eye settle on the run-down rental property. "I'll tell the sheriff. But the guy's a person of interest now."

⋏

Joseph Avenue, East Nashville, Tn

All the way along the street twin spires stand stark across the Cumberland River—the AT&T building Gothic against a graying winter sky. A sight embedded, she tells herself. Through all seasons. Familiar feeling. Home.

Despite herself, despite the intervening years, nothing

has changed. Days fall away. None of them might ever have existed. It might be some new morning, nothing more; waking from some long, troubled dream.

The house.

Just as it always was.

Trees around it almost stripped bare—their leaves scattered over short-cut grass in the fenced-in yard.

She slows the compact rental car—signals, pulls in at the side of the road.

A two-story building. A cement-slab sidewalk. First floor of the house red brick, the second faced with weatherboard painted cream.

Louvered shutters on the windows. As if from some bygone age.

Security bars, but the neighborhood is coming good.

Better than good, rising, now. Rising fast.

In two years, restaurants and cantinas, beer gardens, French cuisine. Derelict units now coffee shops and bakeries. Art galleries. Hip cocktail bars.

Jessica McConnell shuts off the motor in the rented Hyundai. Studies the upstairs windows of the house. Recognizes the turquoise drapes.

Terracotta pots line the concrete steps leading to the front door. The plants in them dead or dying. She smiles. Thinks of buying the pots, a spring morning, years gone.

On the seat beside her is a pack of American Spirits. She looks at them a long moment. Tells herself she won't.

Staring out of the car at the house she focuses on its windows—sees no lights.

A kid on a cycle breezes by, raked back in the saddle, no hands. A Titans hat and a pair of headphones—freewheeling the descent of the hill.

Water over the dam, Jessica tells herself.

So much water.

Each day a little easier just to let it go.

No way back upstream—no way to push against the flow. Or drag the weight, deal with everything.

The time for explanations past.

Until a moment comes, a day, finally.

Until now, she tells herself.

She thinks of the owner of the house. How like herself. How unlike, in so many ways.

One content to dream and drift and build on sand. Addicted to the thrill of the new. To speed. Sensation. The love of life.

The other, connected, rooted. Grounded. Building day by day.

Amassing. By the force of application. Hard work. Willing life her way.

She clutches the wheel, steadies herself, breathes, looking out at the fixed point of the horizon. Downtown horizon. Towers of glass against the churning sky.

A sense of dread, now. The moorings cut.

Everything a spiral, spinning out of control.

A fixed point.

A known point.

In the ground.

Four walls, bricks and weatherboarding. And window bars.

She rips the keys from the ignition.

Pushes open the driver's door.

Grabs the bag from the back seat, stares at the house, its windows.

Fights down nausea.

Body tense, electric.

Stepping out.

⋏

Pecos, Tx

From the bedroom closet, Whicher takes a box of .357 Magnum rounds for the Ruger. He lays the large-frame revolver and the tan leather shoulder holster at the foot of the bed.

In a drawer of the nightstand is a fifty-round box of .40 S&W. He takes it out, tosses it onto the coverlet, places the magazine holders for the Glock alongside it.

Leanne sits on an edge of the bed.

The marshal lifts a canvas holdall from the floor. "There still two shirts in there?"

"You packed it," Leanne says, "it's your go-bag." She sips on a cup of coffee. "They should be in there."

Placing the holdall on the coverlet, he checks beneath a USMS rain jacket—sees the folded shirts inside. He feels down to the bottom of the bag for a pair of jeans. "It's all there," he says, "thanks."

"The flight's at seven?"

He nods. "I should head out soon." The marshal takes a

dark red tie from the closet, rolls it, puts it on the top of the bag. "There's a layover. At Dallas, Fort Worth. Then a couple hours up to Nashville."

"You know where you're staying?"

"Downtown. By the convention center."

Leanne picks a clear, plastic document wallet off of the bed. She studies the top page—the photograph of Jessica McConnell. "I'm not sure I like you chasing around the country after her…"

He grins.

Leanne looks at him.

"She's married."

"It's kind of strange, though," she says. "A missing child case."

"The kid's father broke out of prison. The mother disappears," Whicher says. "She shows up a thousand miles away. It's not a regular missing minor case—there's a USMS task force assigned to find the father."

"But your brief is to find the girl?"

"I find people, don't I?" The marshal packs the ammunition and the magazines for the Glock into the holdall. "The daughter could be with the mother. The task force is trying to track her, in case she meets with the father, tries to help."

Leanne stands. "You think she's a normal woman? A normal mother?"

Whicher places the Ruger on the rain jacket.

"You think she took her daughter from the hostel?" His wife puts her head on one side. "Why disappear?"

"I met her one time, is all. I can't say."

"Unless she took her daughter?"

The marshal swings the bag off the bed, doesn't answer.

"That's what I mean," Leanne says. "I'm not sure you're right for this."

"You said that already."

She glances at him. "I don't mean…" She leaves the thought unspoken.

"I'll fly up, liaise with the task force," Whicher says. "We'll see where it goes from there."

Leanne stands at the bedroom door. "You have a couple of minutes for Lori?"

Whicher softens. "Sure."

He follows his wife into the hall.

In the kitchen, Lori is at the table. She looks up from scribbling on a notepad with a colored pen. Sees the bag in his hand. "Where are you going?"

"To the airport."

"Oh?"

"Up to Midland. Like we did last fall?"

"Am I coming?" She looks at her mother.

"No, it's daddy's work," Leanne says. "Feel like reading some of your new book to your father? Give him a story to think about while he's away?"

Lori smiles, jumps from the table, runs to get the book from her room.

Whicher watches his daughter.

Thinks of Bella McConnell.

Lori, two years on.

He thinks of Jessica McConnell—of the green-painted house.

Leanne studies his face. "What's wrong?"

The marshal rubs at the back of his neck. "Nothing."

"You'll find her."

The image of the house is in his mind. And the uneasy feeling.

"I know you," his wife says. "You'll find both of them."

He thinks of the dog on its chain and the silence.

And the blood on the wall.

Chapter Twelve

Rutherford County, Tennessee

The motel room is at the end of a long row—traffic on I-24 hammering past fifty yards away. Beyond a service road, the stream of headlamps and tail lights merge with the drone of gray-white noise.

Trucks and pickups and panel vans are in the lot outside—the Toyota sedan the only car.

At the doorway to the room, he stands watchful. Eyes the reception office. The other doors along the row.

She pushes past him in her purple, hooded top. "I left something in the car…"

"I can get it for you…"

She steps out quickly—reaches the Toyota shielding the view of the motel door.

She yanks at the handle on the passenger side. It won't open.

He takes the keys from his pocket, presses on the fob—unlocks it.

She opens up, reaches inside, rummages on the floor.

Stepping away, she works a bright, fabric hairband over one hand, a plastic grip held in the other. Pushing back her hood, she slides the grip into her long, dark hair.

"Would you do that inside?"

She walks back in. Her blue eyes flat.

He closes the door behind him. Locks it.

She sits on the bed.

Her silence oppressive. A statement.

"What?" he says.

"This place sucks. I want to go get dinner."

"We can't do that. You know that."

"Nobody knows us here."

He shakes his head. "We'll get take out."

She stands, takes a pace around. "Why can't we stay someplace else?" In front of an aging full-length mirror she regards herself. "We're right on the interstate. It's horrible. It's old, it's too loud."

"We'll be there tomorrow," he tells her. "Everything will be different. Like I told you. We just need to do this, get it done."

"We've been on the road all day. Why do we have to be stuck here?"

He looks at her.

"What are you afraid of?"

"Do you want to go back?" he says.

Her face reacts, as if slapped.

"You want to go back to Fort Stockton?"

"I never want to go back there again."

He nods. Stares across the room into harsh light from the open door to the bathroom. "What you want, what's available, what you can get—it's all complicated, you know? It's not that simple."

She glances at him, face uncomprehending.

"Life gets complicated. You got yourself in trouble," he says. "Question is, can you get yourself out?"

She walks around to the side of the bed, sits. Lays back, swings up her legs.

"You want to take off your shoes?" he says.

She looks at him.

"Your shoes. You've got your feet up on the bed." He lets his eye meet hers a moment.

She breaks off. Stares at the ceiling.

He walks to the window, eases back the blind. Sweeps the lot in front of the motel. Watches lights on the interstate flashing by. "We'll get something to eat. You like pizza?"

"I don't care."

"We'll pick something up. Bring it here."

She lays back on the bed. Eyes vacant. "One night…"

He lets the blind fall back against the cold glass.

⁂

Clarksville, Tennessee

The house is on a wooded lane—a mix of new-built condominiums, gated dwellings, discrete older properties. Three times they've driven by it. Three times. Rolling slow. In full dark.

No light is on inside the building.

No vehicles nearby.

On the deserted sidewalk, Travis McConnell pulls the zipper on the fleece jacket all the way up. Breath clouding around him in the light from a streetlamp. Keys bulging in the cargo pocket of his pants—the likely door keys already singled out; removed from the ring.

Reed Barbone stomps along beside him.

The SUV is two streets over—in a strip mall lot.

Approaching the home of Kendrick Dupris, McConnell slows, touches the arm of Barbone's jacket.

The big man checks stride.

McConnell takes in the building.

The house is brick and shingle, two story. From the nineteen-fifties. A separate garage.

Woodland surrounds it—next building over is a condo—not too close.

The nearest house is new-built, a stuccoed property behind iron gates. A line of cypress and pine to screen it. Across the lane in the condo, bright lights shine from the windows.

McConnell nods. "I say we try this. No sign anyone's home."

"Says you."

McConnell chins toward the house. "Look for yourself."

"How about if someone's in there?"

"Sitting in the pitch dark?"

"How about if there's a dog?"

"See if we can get around back, take a look."

"You know the deal?" Barbone says. "Anybody's in there, we turn around, walk on back to that big-ass SUV. And blow. We can be in Michigan by morning."

McConnell moves up the sidewalk. A post-and-rail fence is all that separates it from the grounds of the house—pine and oak in a half-acre of grass. "We're here, right? We made it. So, let's try it…"

Barbone looks toward the back of the house. He pulls a hand from his windcheater. Rubs at his beard. "Son of a bitch. How about if we can't get in?"

"We leave. Run back two streets," McConnell says. "Pick up the car. Do it your way. Hit the road."

Barbone grunts.

McConnell steps from the sidewalk, ducks between the rails of the fence.

He walks quickly over damp grass, eyes a long, kitchen window—pinpricks of red showing in the dark.

At the back door, he takes a key from his pocket, tries it. It won't fit.

He takes out another. Slides it all the way in.

He turns the key, pushes open the door.

Breathes the stale scent of the air inside.

No dog. No animal.

No smell of food or any garbage. No perfume.

Heat is on in the kitchen.

Barbone hustles by him.

McConnell steps inside, pushes the door closed. "You hear anything?"

Barbone stands mute.

"Leave off the lights." McConnell leads the way from the kitchen to a living room—just enough light from a street lamp to make out couches, recliners, a coffee table in the center of the room.

In the hallway is a big staircase—doors, some of them open. One of them a bathroom, another some kind of office—with file cabinets on one wall.

"Upstairs," McConnell says. "Then we come back down, see what's around."

Barbone grabs a hold of the banister, pulls himself up.

McConnell feels his heart beat in his chest.

Nobody is in there.

But somebody could be coming back.

At the top of the stairs he sees Barbone disappear inside a room.

McConnell picks another door, throws it open. The room is filled with exercise equipment—a cross-trainer, exercise bike. Dumbbells on the floor.

Stepping out, he pushes open doors to a third and fourth room—beds inside, bags, cardboard boxes.

He circles back.

Barbone is still inside the first room.

He enters, sees the big man sitting on the edge of the bed. From the nightstand he whips a dark, heavy shape.

Barbone turns, holds it up. Grinning. Tosses it onto the bed.

A black, squared-off semi-automatic pistol.

He reaches back into a drawer. Pulls out another.

McConnell sees the glint from the big man's teeth in the light from the lane.

"Party time," Barbone says.

"What else? We need resources."

"That's what I'm talking about. Why I broke you out of the hole…"

McConnell looks at him.

Barbone's eyes shine in the dim light.

"We need more," McConnell says, "if we're going to stay free."

"No shit."

"So, come on, let's keep at it, let's see what's in here."

"Mister two-eleven."

"Come again?"

"Armed robbery." Barbone shakes the pistol in his hand. "Robbery with violence. What I'm talking about. And now, brother. Now we got the guns…"

Chapter Thirteen

Nashville, Tn

The blue sky of a crisp November morning arcs above the sprawl of high-rise towers and auditoriums. In the meeting room of the USMS office, high in the Federal Building on Ninth, Whicher stands at a window, looking out over rooftops, the downtown street busy far below.

He takes out his phone. Keys to send a call to Texas—the Sheriff's Office in Hudspeth County.

Staring out of the window, he gazes along the wide avenue of Broadway—to where it meets with the river—the twin-spired AT&T building looming tall.

Sheriff Odell Ingram picks up the call.

"Morning," Whicher says.

Ingram's voice is low-key, gruff. "I do something for you?"

"Jacob Harwood."

"It's not yet eight in the morning, marshal."

"Right. I'm an hour ahead. I flew up to Tennessee last night.

To meet with a task force marshal looking for Bella's father."

The line is quiet but for the sound of the sheriff moving about his office, pulling out a chair. "We can't find Harwood," he says, finally.

"He's not home?"

"Not at the house. I had deputies talk with the neighbors, nobody's seen him in a couple days."

"How about friends? People he knows? Y'all try at the church?"

"I spoke with Pastor Mullins. I know Win personally," the sheriff says. "They haven't seen hide nor hair of him."

"How about your crime scene investigator?" Whicher says. "She turn up anything at Jessica McConnell's place?"

"We're still on that…"

"How about the blood? Y'all get a sample?"

"Yessir."

"How soon can you get it tested?"

"We'll send the sample to the lab in El Paso this morning."

The marshal hears the creak of a chairback as Ingram sits. "Tell 'em it's urgent."

"Tell 'em yourself," Ingram says.

A dark-haired woman in a black skirt and jacket enters the room. Beneath one arm she holds a leather attaché case.

"Call me if you find Harwood?" Whicher finishes up the call.

The woman walks forward, she's in her mid-thirties, sharp-looking. Toned.

"Evelyn Cruz," she says. "USMS, Western District of Tennessee."

"John Whicher. Pleased to meet you."

She puts out a hand. Cruz's grip is firm. "You flew in last night? Where are you staying?"

"The Sheraton," Whicher says. "Up the hill."

"I just came in from Memphis, yesterday," Cruz says. She walks to a long, polished table at the side of the room. Puts down the attaché case, unzips it. "What do you know about the case?"

"Yours, or mine?"

Cruz takes out a slim, laptop computer. "The two escapees."

"Not much." Whicher crosses the room to the table. "I'm trying to find a missing minor."

"The daughter. Bella McConnell. And now, the mother," Cruz says. From the attaché case she takes out printed papers and a thumb drive. "I have footage for you to look at—it's from a gas station in south Nashville." She pulls back two chairs from the table. "Please," she says.

Whicher sits.

Evelyn Cruz looks at him. "Can you believe prisoners worked out how to jimmy the locks at a prison? They jammed them up with paper, they got to where they were popping them open at night just for fun. Reed Barbone. Serving life for murder in the first degree. McConnell on a sixty-stretch for Class A felony, aggravated robbery."

"Nobody knew?"

"People knew," Marshal Cruz says. "But nothing happened. You know about the CO?"

Whicher nods. "They had help."

"She left a car for them—parked close by. Along with some cash. McConnell told her he'd come get her, once things quietened down. The car was spotted by law enforcement in Clarksville. That's an hour northwest of here, fifty miles."

"Long way from the prison," Whicher says, "from Memphis."

"Two hundred miles. I know," Cruz says. "Highly unusual. Which is why we have a big problem. They breach a searchable radius it can escalate anywhere."

"What happened when the car was spotted?"

Marshal Cruz fires up the laptop, enters a password. "A unit followed them. Then lost them. They ditched the car in a supermarket lot. Disappeared."

"Y'all had nothing since?"

"They've vanished into thin air," Cruz says. "As of now we have no leads. The corrections officer has no idea where they were going. Or if she does know, she's not saying. The only thing we have is the wife of Travis McConnell—turning up right here in Nashville."

"Plus the daughter missing," Whicher says.

Evelyn Cruz taps a key on the laptop, bringing up a bright-lit screen.

Inserting the thumb drive, she launches a folder, clicks on a moving image file. "Our IT guy picked up this gas station purchase down in south Nashville. I spoke with the manager, had them check their CCTV. We think they might have captured footage of her." Cruz clicks on the file, expands the image to fill the screen.

An overhead shot shows a gray-blue compact car, the color washed out, contrast in the picture unnaturally high.

A woman exits the car from the driver's side. In a ball cap, a loose jacket, jeans.

Her hair is long, dark. She's wearing sunglasses. She walks from the car toward a mini-mart in back.

The camera cuts away. Switches to an interior shot.

"IT stitched this together from three overheads," Evelyn Cruz says. "She's headed inside to pay for gas before she can pump it."

Whicher peers at the screen, studying the woman in the ball cap and dark glasses.

She walks down a store aisle, toward the cashier desk.

He tries to make out the face through the low-res, grainy image.

The woman reaches the cashier till.

"Not picking anything up…" Whicher says.

"How's that?"

"For herself. For anybody else. Anybody with her. I have my daughter with me, she'll usually ask for something."

Evelyn Cruz inclines her head.

The image on screen jumps to an overhead from behind the counter.

The marshal studies the face of the woman offering a bank card—the shape of her mouth, the line of her cheekbones. The fine nose. A stray hank of black hair hanging from the cap.

"Is it her?" Marshal Cruz says.

"I think."

"You're not sure? The time stamp on the footage

matches with the transaction time of purchase."

Whicher watches the grainy image jump again—to a shot of the woman walking back out of the store.

And then to an overhead view as she walks toward her car. She goes around it, takes the filler cap from the gas. No interaction with anybody inside the vehicle.

She takes the nozzle from the pump housing. Starts to fill the car.

"We get the tags?"

Cruz shakes her head. "A separate camera captures vehicles exiting to the road. A delivery truck was parked in front of it."

"We know make and model?"

The film recording ends abruptly.

"That's all there is," Cruz says. "The cameras rotate on a cycle. There's no shot of her pulling in."

"The car's what—Japanese? Compact?"

"Something like that," Cruz says.

"Dark in color."

"Not enough for any kind of BOLO." Marshal Cruz clicks on the image file. "You want to see it again?"

Whicher shakes his head. "I get a copy of it?"

"Not a problem."

The marshal leans back in his chair. "Jessica McConnell flew into Nashville yesterday morning?"

"According to our IT guy—it's on record."

"She rented a car?"

"Not from the airport," Cruz says. "We checked with all the concessions."

"So, what else?"

"If she took a bus or a cab from the airport, Nashville-metro area has any number of private rental companies."

"You working that?"

"We've got people on it. But there's scores listed. With smaller companies, bank transactions can take days."

"But she's up here somewhere," the marshal says. "In Tennessee."

Cruz closes the laptop. "So it seems."

"Maybe she was. Maybe she's not now."

"We're ready to move if we get a solid lead," Cruz says. "She's not breaking any law being up here. But given the daughter's disappearance, and her husband's, it's pretty strange. If she shows up, I'm sure you'd want to be here, to talk with her."

Whicher shifts his gaze to the view of the high towers across town.

"Anything you can tell me might be useful," Cruz says. "If there's no further sign of her, you're not obliged to stay."

"How about if she's a lure, a decoy?"

Evelyn Cruz looks at him.

"Get us here," Whicher says.

"Why get us here?"

"Get us busy. While her husband gets away."

⋏

In the master bedroom of Kendrick Dupris' house in Clarksville, Travis McConnell puts a finger to the receiver of the landline—silently replacing the handset onto the cradle.

He sits on the edge of the bed, mind turning, tightness in his stomach.

Three times he's tried to call—two times overnight, in darkness, Barbone sleeping.

He stands, moves noiselessly from the bedroom to the ensuite bathroom. Steps to the toilet, flushes it. Runs water in the faucet.

Looking at himself in the bathroom mirror, the fleece jacket and the cargo pants seem alien—unfamiliar after prison blues and whites. The handsome face looking back is haggard at its edges, bags under his dark eyes, stubble at his chin.

His skin is slack from lack of sleep. From stress.

He runs a hand through his head of dark brown hair. Takes a breath. Walks out of the room, jogs back down the stairs.

Strewn across the kitchen table are graham crackers and saltines, an empty milk carton. A box of .44 Magnum rounds.

A Highways Department map is weighted open with a Browning Hi-Power semi-auto and a Sig P226.

Standing where he can see from the window, Reed Barbone holds a brushed-steel Desert Eagle—a giant pistol, even in his outsize hand.

"What's going on out there?" McConnell says.

"Nothing."

Walking to where he can see, McConnell checks the condo on the opposite side of the lane.

"We should be long gone," Barbone says. "Should've left

before daylight. Look at us now. Anybody could spot us walking out of here."

A car makes its way up the tree-lined lane. McConnell tracks it, a dark green Mercedes. "Every hour that passes is better."

Barbone grunts; "Better for what?"

The car drives by the house, on up the hill.

"Better for us," McConnell answers, "better for getting away. Anybody in law enforcement it's the opposite—longer we're out, the more chance we stay out."

Barbone turns from the window, swings the big pistol back and forth in his hand.

McConnell notices the red dot above the grip on the side of the gun. "You want to put the safety on that?"

"What?"

McConnell points to the lever.

Barbone swings up the gun. "Pussy."

Locking eyes with him for just a moment, McConnell steps away to the kitchen table.

He takes a graham cracker from the pack, puts it into his mouth.

"The deal was we blow," Barbone says. "Get back in the car, tank the sucker. And go. Ain't nothing for us here." He steps away from the window, grabs a handful of saltines from the table.

"Head north," McConnell says, "for Michigan. Right?"

Barbone looks at him.

Travis McConnell steps from the kitchen—walks through the hallway on into a ransacked office. From the top of a file cabinet he takes a plastic box filled with 9mm ammunition and two spare magazines for the Sig. Unredeemed goods from Dupris' pawn business, McConnell supposes. There'd been little else—eighteen hundred dollars in cash from an unlocked safe in the bedroom. Three semi-automatic pistols, the Desert Eagle, the Browning, the Sig. Ammunition. At least he'd kept himself in ammunition. In the kitchen were dried goods, Campbell's soup, creamed corn. Jars of pickles. Ketchup. Nothing else to eat.

Barbone appears in the door frame.

McConnell sticks the magazines for the Sig into a pocket, rattles the box of ammunition at him. "We did right to come here." He walks out of the office, back to the kitchen. "But you were right about one thing."

Barbone follows.

McConnell dumps the plastic box onto the table. He checks the time display on the cooker. Almost ten o'clock in the morning. He thinks again of the phone in the bedroom. He can't risk it again, before leaving. Can't risk it with Barbone.

The big man moves to stand in McConnell's line of vision. "Right about what?" A look on his face. Dumb. Flattered in equal part.

The man had something, though, McConnell reminds himself. He was dangerous. In the jungle. He had a value—something that could make things work.

Picking up the Browning Hi-Power, McConnell drops the magazine from the handle. He eyes the 9mm rounds in the magazine. Racks the slide, checks the chamber is empty. "Aggravated robbery."

Barbone eyes him.

"What we're going to need," McConnell says, "to keep us rolling. Keep us in green." He sits at the kitchen table. Takes out the magazines for the Sig.

"How about the shop?" Barbone gives a sick grin. "The guy's pawn shop?"

"Uh-uh."

"Why not? Dupris ain't going to be there. Right?"

"Somewhere else."

Barbone swings the Desert Eagle in his big hand. "How about if a crap ton of money's in there?"

McConnell shakes his head. "People around the place will be wondering what happened. How come the guy's not coming in? We show up, then what? Besides, the place will be alarmed. You think a bloodsucker like Dupris would leave money lying around the office overnight?"

"He might have a safe?"

"Yeah. An alarm. A safe."

"You got a better idea?"

McConnell nods. Weighs the Browning pistol in his hand, raises it.

Looks along its iron sight.

Chapter Fourteen

Nashville, Tn

In the office in the Federal Building, Whicher sips a cup of coffee staring from the window down on Broadway. An ornate stone building topped with Gothic spires dominates the opposite side of the road. In his mind's eye he sees the pastor at the Hudspeth County church, Winford Mullins.

He thinks of the woman with him.

Remembers her disapproving tone at the mention of Jessica McConnell.

Behind him, the door to the meeting room opens.

Marshal Evelyn Cruz enters—holding a single printed page. "The Memphis office are collating reports of vehicle thefts overnight," she says. "Break-ins, any new or unexplained incident from law enforcement."

"Looking where?"

"Statewide."

"Too much ground to cover," Whicher says.

"It is," Cruz answers. "Anyhow, we have to look. So far,

there's nothing that stands out. You want to see any of this?"

Cruz crosses to the desk, places the print-out beside the marshal's notes.

"How about your IT guy?" Whicher says. "There been any more bank transactions?"

Evelyn Cruz shakes her head.

"Nothing on rental cars?"

"It's a waiting game," Cruz says. "She could pop up anywhere. I'm in room 509, down the hall if you need something."

"Got it. 509."

Cruz backs out of the room, gives a rueful smile, pulls the door behind her.

Whicher picks up the USMS compilation of incident reports—a bullet-point list from the big cities; Memphis, Nashville, Chattanooga—down through Tullahoma, Knoxville, Franklin, Jackson. A long list.

He reads a few entries. Vehicle thefts. Breaking and entering.

He picks up his notepad, an idea sifting to the front of his mind.

Flipping back through the pages he reads a name—*Karyn Dennison*.

The cousin.

Travis McConnell's cousin.

The reason Jessica moved out to Texas.

He keys the number written in his notes.

Puts the phone to his ear.

A woman's voice answers.

"Ma'am. Ms Dennison?"

"Yes."

"Good morning. This is Deputy Marshal Whicher, we spoke the day before yesterday—regarding Bella McConnell. Regarding her mother, Jessica."

"Oh."

"I need to ask you a couple follow-up questions, ma'am. About Jessica. She's from Tennessee?"

"Yes."

"You said she moved out to Texas after her husband was sent away to prison."

"Yes. I don't understand," the woman says, "has there been some news?"

"No, ma'am, not at this time. But I need to ask if you know if Jessica is close to any family member in particular?"

"Her mom died. Five, six years ago."

Whicher writes in his notes.

"Her dad left the family when she was young. I don't think she sees him."

"How about in the Nashville area?"

"There's her sister."

"She has a sister?"

"Ursula. She lives in Nashville."

"You know where?"

"No," Dennison says. "I have no idea. I don't know her. But Jessica's talked about her."

"What's the sister's full name?" the marshal says, "do you know?"

"Carney. I think. Ursula Carney."

Whicher writes the name in the notepad. "Are she and Jessica close?"

"Yes and no. A little of both," Dennison says, "you know how sisters are."

"You tell me anything about her?"

"She's older, I know that. Older than Jessica. I think she works at some bar."

"You have some way I could contact her?"

"No. I'm sorry, I don't."

"If you hear from either Jessica or Bella, call me?" Whicher says.

"I will. I've said I will. So, you haven't found either of them?"

"No, ma'am." Whicher stands, tosses the pen onto the notepad. "Not yet. But we will."

⁂

Five minutes, two internet searches later, an address for Ursula Carney is written on to a fresh page in his notes.

McFerrin Park.

Across the river, past the Titans stadium. Off of I-24.

The marshal buttons the jacket of his suit. Fits his hat. Steps from the room, walks the corridor to 509.

He knocks, enters.

Evelyn Cruz is seated at a computer terminal, wearing black-rimmed eyeglasses.

"She has a sister here," Whicher says. "Jessica. Here in town. In east Nashville."

"Really?"

"Maybe it's nothing. But I want to go see her."

Cruz says, "Do you want me to come?"

The marshal shakes his head. "I'll go talk with her. If I can find her—I need a car."

"Take one from the law enforcement pool," Cruz says. "Are you sure you don't want me to come?"

"Better you're here if something comes in."

She takes off her glasses, looks at him.

"I have an address. There may be no one there," Whicher says. "If I need backup, I'll call."

⋏

Five miles out of Clarksville, past the diamond interchange, Travis McConnell steers the black SUV off the interstate toward a long, low, glass-front commercial unit.

He drives up onto the lot, finds an empty bay close to the Exit-11 Sporting Goods Store.

He stops. Kills the motor.

Barbone stares out through the windshield.

"This is good," McConnell says.

Third stop of the morning.

First two stops the locales were well placed, but too busy, too much going on.

McConnell grabs the road map from the back seat, spreads it over the steering wheel. "We're off of I-24 and…" he traces a finger, "Martin Luther King Parkway. A highway interchange. Good to run. North, south, east or west."

"Yeah? Well, so what?"

"We hit a store, we have to get the hell out."

Barbone looks at him.

"Somebody's bound to see us. Say they see us heading for I-24 south? We get off the next exit, turn around run north. We get off the next one, track east, west, anywhere."

"That's your plan?"

"Eighteen-years-old I got started with this," McConnell says. "It took 'em twenty years to catch me."

The big man shakes his head. Stares at the storefront. "Look at it, man. You even like this?"

"People spend a ton of money on some of that outdoor gear," McConnell says. "That's premium-price shit. Golf clubs, cycles, hunting gear, fishing. Guns."

"Guns, uh?"

McConnell says, "We're already locked and loaded."

Barbone looks around the parking lot, agitated.

McConnell takes the keys from the ignition. He reaches in back for a gym bag taken from a bedroom in Dupris' house. Takes out a ball cap, a wool hat. Puts on the cap, tosses the hat to Barbone.

Lifting up the fleece jacket, he pushes the Sig P226 into the waistband of his cargo pants. Covers the butt of the gun with the jacket. Pushes open the driver's door. "Come on. Let's get out. Let's go take a look."

Barbone reaches for the Desert Eagle in the glove box.

"Leave it," McConnell says. "Take the Hi-Power. The Browning. It's smaller. Easier to hide."

Barbone takes the Browning from the floor beneath the passenger seat, stuffs it into the waistband of his pants. He covers it with the windcheater. Pulls on the woolen hat.

McConnell steps from the SUV, scans the other units around the lot—a dry cleaner, a shoe store, pet store—two gas stations up the road. A half a mile off, budget motels. An Arby's.

In the lot are a dozen or more cars and trucks.

"We go in," he says, "don't look at folk. Look at shirts or boots. Pick something. Don't talk to me. Leave first. After five. Walk across to the pet store, wait for me."

Barbone grins. Scratches at his beard.

"Don't walk in with me." McConnell sets off. Walks thirty yards to a double-wide door.

Entry.

Plus a separate exit.

He slows, tips the bill of the ball cap down.

Entering the store he sees a cashier station—a large, open floorspace—long aisles, display areas, promo stands.

In back are cabinets, counter areas. Firearms and fishing rods and mountain bikes.

He looks without looking. Feeling his way around.

Four staff, that he can see. Two cashier desks, one in the center of the store, the other by the exit.

No line at either of them. A half-dozen customers inside.

Cameras will be mounted in the ceiling, filming, he doesn't look for them. Nothing he can do. The ball cap will cover his face some.

At the far side of the store is a doorway—beyond it, a bright-lit office space.

Through the open door he sees a man in a white shirt and dark suit.

McConnell stops at an accessory aisle for camping gear, scans a rack of flashlights.

Good enough.

All in.

Good enough to bankroll a couple weeks.

Not enough for a big score. But enough.

From the corner of his eye he sees Barbone leaving.

A middle-aged man in a plaid shirt approaches. Eyeglasses. Bald. "Sir? Can I help you with something?"

McConnell smiles, easy. "Thanks. I'm just looking. I'm all good."

Moving toward a display of camo rain gear, he pauses to check on a couple of the jackets—sliding them out on their hangers, studying the price tags.

Then he turns, heads for the exit.

A bored-looking blond woman at the cashier station eyes him. "You have a nice day, honey."

He doesn't respond.

Outside, he cuts along a concrete sidewalk.

Barbone is by the pet store, hands shoved in his pockets, watching traffic on the parkway. He says, "So what do you think?"

"We light it up."

"You want to do this?"

McConnell nods.

"So, you like the roads and shit," Barbone says. "But right here, this place? You really think?"

"We hit something on the run up to Michigan we pull them after us," McConnell says. "Law enforcement. We're showing 'em where we went."

Barbone eyes him.

"Do it here, we get 'em looking in the wrong place." McConnell searches the service lanes running alongside the store units. "We'll put the car where nobody sees it. Around back someplace." He fishes the keys from his cargo pants. "I'll get the car, I'll move it. Then you stay with it, I'll go on in…"

"I'm going in with you," Barbone says.

"You ever do something like this?"

"There's a bunch of people in there."

"You won't know what you're doing."

"So, tell me, I'm listening…"

McConnell doesn't answer.

He turns around, heads back for the car.

Chapter Fifteen

Pulling over at the curbside in a dark blue Ford Crown Victoria, Whicher eyes a mailbox on the side of the road. He checks the street number.

Satisfied, he drives another twenty yards. Stops the car.

The house is two story, red brick with cream weatherboarding.

Shutters at its windows. Security bars.

Across the river, the AT&T tower rises—its spires twin needles of black.

He takes the Resistol from the passenger seat, steps from the car, locks it. Crosses the street to a rusted steel gate.

Opening it, he makes his way up a set of concrete steps lined with earthenware pots.

A name plate by the doorbell reads, *Carney*.

Whicher takes out the Marshals Service badge and ID.

He presses on the bell.

Thirty seconds pass.

A striking, dark-haired woman opens the door. Luminous eyes. High cheekbones.

She's dressed in jeans, a black lace blouse, her face made-up, jewelry and beads strung at her throat.

Almost a twin to Jessica McConnell. A little older.

In his mind's eye Whicher sees the footage from the gas station, the figure in the grainy image.

The woman studies the photo ID in the marshal's hand.

"Ursula Carney?"

She looks at him.

"John Whicher. I'm with the Marshals Service. Out of West Texas."

Thoughts pass behind her eyes as she stares at him.

"Like to ask you a couple questions. About your sister, ma'am. About Jessica McConnell."

The woman puts a hand to her chest. Blanches. "Is she alright? Is everything alright?"

"Ma'am. Do you think I could come in?"

She blinks, moves aside in the doorway—waves him forward.

Whicher steps inside.

The woman closes the front door, leads him into a living room—soft couches and throw rugs, antique lamps.

By the window is a rosewood table, hard-backed chairs.

"Has something happened?" Ursula says. Her eyes search the marshal's face.

"Ma'am, did you know that Jessica's husband broke out of prison three days back?"

"Travis?" she says.

"Yes, ma'am."

Her eyes widen. The same pale shade of blue-gray as her

sister's. She pulls out a chair. Sits down, her back to the window. "He broke out of prison?"

"Him and a second inmate. The Marshals Service is looking for them now."

She steadies her gaze across the room.

"Have you spoken with your sister lately?" Whicher says.

"No."

"When would be the last time?"

She sits forward. "A month? Three weeks? I don't know…"

Whicher takes out the notepad from his jacket, takes out a pen.

"Is she in trouble?" Ursula says. "I can't believe he broke out…"

"Last time you spoke to Jessica, did she talk to you about her daughter?"

"A little. You mean—that she's been in trouble? About her going into care? Look, Bella's a little off the rails…"

"She has a Juvenile Court case pending."

"She shouldn't be in a home."

"Did your sister give you the impression she might try to do something about that?"

The woman looks at him.

"Bella McConnell's been missing three days."

"What do you mean, missing?"

"Absent from the care home she's been living at. Nobody's seen her," Whicher says. "Nobody's seen your sister, either."

Ursula Carney swallows. "That's why you're here?"

"We have reason to believe Jessica flew into Nashville yesterday. We have information she was in the south of the city."

"Here in town?"

The marshal looks at Ursula Carney a long time. Animated. Flustered.

A phone rings in the house.

She stands quickly. "I need to get that."

She darts from the room into the hallway.

He hears her answer the phone.

"I need you to open up for me," she says, "can you? Something came up, I'll be there as soon as I can." A pause. "I don't know, I'll try. I'll get there as fast as I can. I have to go. Okay? Thanks. No, it's okay, I'll be there soon."

A moment passes. She walks back into the living room. "I was just leaving for work," she says. "I have a bar. I run a bar."

"Downtown?"

"Here, in East Nashville."

"Can you give me a couple more minutes?"

She folds her arms across her chest. Walks back to the empty chair at the table. Sits.

Whicher sits down. "Can you tell me a little about your sister?"

Ursula lets out a long breath. She slumps a fraction in her seat. "Since Travis, and all. Since his conviction?" She shakes her head. "I mean it broke her. Jessica. She couldn't deal with it. She couldn't deal with it for Bella. She just left. She just got herself out, she had to, she couldn't handle it. She ran."

"To Texas," Whicher says.

"She couldn't stand the thought of spending the rest of her life making prison visits. Taking Bella. To a place like that. She said it would've been easier if he were dead."

"She told you that?"

"I can understand it."

"Were they together long?"

"They got married for Bella," Ursula says. "They were together a couple years before that. Fifteen years I guess."

"You tell me anything about his background?"

"He was always kind of the bad boy, sort of glamorous, I guess she liked that. I guess she didn't know how bad. And she was young, she was twenty when she met him. He came to Nashville crewing for a band, some rock band. He liked it here, he stayed."

"Doing what?"

"All kinds of stuff back then. He worked bars, managed a couple restaurants. He worked a lot with another guy, running road crews for tours. Kind of a business partner. But then he got to flipping houses, he was doing that with Jess."

"You remember the partner's name?"

"Ackerman, or something. Erv Ackerman."

Whicher notes it down.

"Travis always had some hustle or another, always had a gig on the side."

"Like robbery?"

"Nobody knew," Ursula says. "Until they caught him."

"Did she know?"

Ursula takes a moment before she answers. "Jessica could kid herself. She was always good at that. I don't know if she knew or not, to tell you the truth. She said not. She's my little sister, she kind of drifted her way through her whole life, right up until him getting arrested. Doing whatever, always some new dream. Travis was kind of the same. Except," she says, "it turned out he'd do some of that with a gun in his hand."

Whicher looks at her.

"I didn't know about any of it," Ursula says. She gives a dry laugh. "I was always too busy working. Buying this house. Paying for the bar. Just working at it. Everyday. Plus the weekends. I'm not much like her. She's not much like me."

"When did she decide to leave here?" Whicher says.

"Soon after he was arrested. They charged him. She told him she wouldn't bring Bella to see him. They started to fight. It got nasty. Pretty quick. That all came as a surprise. I think it hit her real hard. Her whole world kind of came in on her. There was no money, the house was owned by the bank. She wanted to get as far as she could from everywhere."

"To West Texas?" Whicher says.

"She didn't know a soul. She knew a cousin of Travis, is all."

"Karyn Dennison?"

"Karyn. Right. She helped her find her feet, find a place to rent. But Bella was miserable."

"Miserable enough to run away?"

Ursula Carney puts both hands to her face, smoothes the

skin beneath her eyes. "I don't know. Really. I don't know, I couldn't say."

"You have any idea where she might go?"

"I'd have to think…"

Whicher takes a business card from his suit. "If Jessica contacts you, call me. If I don't find her, if I don't find Bella, she could be facing a charge of felony kidnap."

"Of her own daughter?"

"Yes, ma'am." Whicher holds the woman's eye.

Ursula breaks off, stares at the floor.

The marshal looks at her. "She still love him, you think?"

"After what he put her through? She's afraid," Ursula says. "Afraid she never really knew him. I'd say she fears him, hates him even."

"Hate's a strong word."

"The threats came soon after the fighting started."

The marshal lets the words hang.

Ursula Carney only looking at him. Looking away.

⊥

The gym bag is slung from his shoulder, ball cap jammed down on his head.

Beneath the fleece jacket, the butt of the Sig sticks from the waistband of his pants—hammer down, the gun hot, fifteen rounds plus one in the chamber.

The gym bag is empty. Zipper open.

He moves fast without looking. Trusting Barbone to come in behind—the last words to him simple—post up on the handgun counter, get a wide sweep of the store.

Boss the room.

Boss the people.

McConnell feels his heart race moving toward the far-side office.

Barbone behind him.

With the Hi-Power and the Desert Eagle. Wool hat pulled down.

Nobody stopping them.

Nobody saying a word.

The door to the office is open.

Inside, the man in the dark suit stares at a computer.

A woman in a turtleneck types at a desk.

She looks up as he enters. "May I help you?"

She's heavy, middle-aged, her face fleshy.

The suited man looks around the side of his computer. Thinning gray hair, startled eyes.

Whipping out the Sig, McConnell levels the gun at him.

He looks from the man to the woman. Back again.

Stricken silence hangs in the air.

A white, square metal door is in the wall at the back of the room.

His voice even, locking eyes with the man, Travis speaks: "So, we know what this is. Everybody stay calm." He slips the gym bag from his shoulder, tosses it onto the woman's desk. "All the money, right now. Everything from the safe."

The woman stares—disbelieving.

He points the Sig at her. "You fill that bag. I walk out of here. Nobody gets killed."

A flash of anger is in her eyes. She sits rigid.

"Ms Turner…" the man says from his desk.

McConnell barks, "*Open the safe.*"

"It's only money," the man says, "it's insured…"

McConnell looks right through her, raises the gun in line with her chest.

"Ms Turner, please…"

The woman stands, backs away. Eyes shining.

She steps to the safe, taps on a keypad in the wall.

"Get the bag," McConnell says.

The woman takes the gym bag from her desk.

Turning to the safe she opens the door, starts to empty it.

McConnell sees thick bundles of bills.

He steps to where he can see the woman and the man and the open doorway.

The woman stops, holds out the bag in her hand.

McConnell grabs it from her.

She stares at him, eyes wide.

"You step outside with me," he tells her.

The manager starts to stand up, slowly.

"Sit your ass back down," McConnell breathes.

The man hesitates, eyes hollow. Lowers himself.

McConnell sees the closed-circuit monitor suspended from the ceiling—four pictures split across the screen. "The guy in the hat? He's with me." He stabs the Sig at the woman's stomach. "We walk out of here. We stop at the cashier registers, you open them, put the money in the bag."

"I hope they catch you," the woman spits, "and lock you up. Or kill you…"

McConnell lashes out, hits her between the eyes with the butt of the gun.

She staggers, folds forward, clutches at her face with both hands.

The man rises from the desk.

McConnell points the Sig at him. "You walk out with us. Keep everybody calm. Don't piss me off."

The man stops. His mouth working.

McConnell grabs the woman by her arm, pulls her hand from her face.

A thin line of blood runs from her nose.

She straightens, stares out through the open doorway.

He pushes her forward. "Come on, move."

Stepping from the office, he sees Reed Barbone in a center aisle.

The bald store assistant in the plaid shirt turns.

Barbone draws the Hi-Power and the Desert Eagle.

McConnell hustles to the center cashier desk, pushing the woman, pushing the manager.

Barbone shouts out; "*Everybody stay where you are.*"

Customers in the aisles look up startled—confusion in their eyes.

The manager speaks to a pale-skinned youth on the cashier desk. "Robert—please open up the register and take out all of the money."

"What?" The young man looks at him.

"Please—just do it."

"Move," McConnell says. He shoves the woman forward. "Get it. Put it in the bag."

The young man fumbles open the register. Lifts out a wad of bills.

The woman takes them, puts them into the bag.

Barbone makes a sudden move. "*Hey*," he shouts. "*You…*"

A bearded man is at a counter in back of the store.

"Don't move." Barbone draws a bead on him with the Desert Eagle.

The man stops.

McConnell waves the Sig at the young man on the cashier desk. "Keep going…"

"That's it," he says. He takes the last rolls and wads of bills, hands them over to the woman.

McConnell pushes her forward to the cashier desk at the exit.

The blond woman standing rooted.

Barbone prowls the center of the store, eyes darting to left and right.

The manager raises his voice, "Everybody stay calm," his voice hoarse, "please—just stay calm."

McConnell points the Sig at the blond woman. "Let's go, let's go…"

She takes out bundles of bills, gives them to the woman with the bag.

Two customers near the cycle section stand frozen, another is at the gun counter, more by the camping gear—all staring.

"That's it," the blond woman says.

Something moves in the corner of McConnell's eye.

The bearded man at the gun counter disappears—ducking down from sight.

Barbone bounces on his toes, points both the pistols. "*Hey. Hey, hey…*"

The bald store assistant takes a step back.

McConnell whips the Sig onto him.

At the gun counter, the bearded man jumps up, a compact semi-auto between his hands.

He fires.

Barbone fires.

Shock and noise fill the room.

The gun counter shooter drops from sight.

Barbone fires the Desert Eagle—display cabinets shatter at the back of the room.

McConnell backs to the exit door. "*Let's go, let's go…*"

Reed Barbone starts to back away, the Hi-Power held out.

McConnell shoulders open the door.

Outside, a man and woman stare from a pickup truck.

A van enters the lot.

Barbone reaches the exit.

McConnell shouts out; "*Everybody stay inside—you come out, you'll be shot…*"

Stepping into cold air he grips the gym bag, sprints the concrete sidewalk to the edge of the store.

The Mazda is fifty yards from the turn.

Spinning around he sees Barbone a pace behind him—craning his neck to see the exit door.

The gun counter shooter and the bald store assistant step out.

McConnell raises the Sig. Fires three times.

Both men drop to the ground.

Barbone fires fast, over and over.

McConnell lunges for the side of the building.

The sound of shots rings out. The SUV is in back of a shoe store, keys in its ignition, doors unlocked.

Barbone dives around the corner of the building, trying to clear the line of fire.

His face twists, suddenly—he stumbles forward, whips a hand to the back of his thigh.

McConnell stares as the big man wheels, staggers.

Ears ringing.

Heart hammering in his chest.

Chapter Sixteen

Nashville, Tn

Driving the streets a nervousness is in him, a nervousness he tries not to let her see.

He cruises slow in the Toyota. Passes the same landmarks as minutes before—McFerrin Park, its trees stripped of leaves—tennis courts, a Salvation Army center, run-down apartment blocks.

In the passenger seat beside him, the girl picks at the sleeve of her hooded top, pulling at a purple thread, twisting it between her fingers.

She looks at him. "Why don't you just call her?"

The man doesn't answer.

He signals, turns onto the avenue a second time.

Drives slow. Eyes open. Trying to take it all in.

Automobiles are parked both sides of the wide street—cars and vans and pickups. On the skyline across the river, downtown Nashville rises in a cluster of high towers.

The car is still there.

Still parked at the curbside.

A dark blue sedan.

The man still in it.

Fifty yards from the house.

Was he waiting for someone? Why would he be waiting?

A score of different reasons, he tells himself.

He turns to the girl; "Put up your hood."

She looks at him. Irritated. "Why?"

"Put it up." He reaches across to her.

She pulls away. Drags up the hood. Sits low in her seat.

He pushes down on the gas.

Stares at the back of the blue sedan—a Ford.

And the man inside it—dressed in a dark suit, a Western hat.

"Just look straight ahead," he says.

No response from the girl.

Approaching the car he tries to take in everything in front of him—a suburban street, nothing out of the ordinary, deserted sidewalks.

He sees the house, now—its windows—unlit on both floors.

Pulling level with the dark blue sedan he sees the man in the suit and hat, upright behind the wheel. Maybe talking into a phone.

He drives the Toyota to the intersection with the next block.

The girl says, "What're you doing?"

He slows, checks his rear-view mirror. Signals, turns.

"I've been here, like, a hundred times," she says, "I know this area, it's all fine."

He pulls over, parks the car at the side of the street. Watches in his rear-view for anything turning. "I need you to wait here a minute."

She throws back her head. Yanks on the cords of her hooded top.

He shuts off the motor. "Just wait here. Let me make sure."

"I don't know who you even think would *be* there?"

He looks at her. Waits until she looks at him. "I'll be a couple minutes. You can wait that long."

Her eyes cut away.

Taking the keys from the ignition, he pushes open the door.

He steps out, looks around the street. Brick and timber ranch homes, empty yards.

Pushing the door closed, he shoves the keys into his pocket, walks back to the intersection with the avenue. Crosses to the opposite side.

The dark sedan is still there—two hundred yards up. Daylight reflecting from its curving windshield. The man in the hat just visible behind the wheel.

He starts to walk in the direction of the house. Studying it, looking for any signs of life.

If he could see her, if he could just talk with her.

He puts his head down, leans into the slope of the grade.

A white, metro-area police car appears at the brow of the hill.

It drives toward him, down the middle of the street.

Mind racing, he searches for a route out—an escape

route through the lots and yards.

Throat tight, a prickle of sweat blooms on his skin.

The police car continues toward him.

Two officers inside, a man and a woman.

It pulls level.

Rolls past.

The sound of its tires, its motor, unnaturally loud.

He fights an urge to turn around.

He slows his pace, stares ahead at the two-story house.

Tells himself to calm down—that the dislocated feeling is only road fever—paranoia after two days—the girl setting him on edge.

Focusing on the gate in the fence, he starts to move toward it.

The dark sedan is still there.

But is the man inside looking at him now?

Has he started to watch?

⋏

An early crowd is at the bar in Five Points—college kids, tourists, East End incomers—loose and loud.

Ursula Carney clears a table at the front window of the nineteen-forties bar room—a gaudy mix of dive and hip, serving Frito pies and cocktails, burritos and wines and craft beers.

Short-staffed, again. Two girls taking orders at the bar, Deano in back working the kitchen.

She stacks three emptied plates in the crook of her arm, pins them against a barkeep apron, grabs beers, mugs and a coffee cup, carries it all to a basket at the end of the counter.

A low-level buzz drowns out the ball game on a wall-mount TV.

In her head she pictures the man in the suit and Western hat staring at her in her living room.

She thinks of Jessica, her little sister. Feels a twist in the pit of her stomach.

No answer from the house, from the place in Texas. Voicemail only when she calls her cell.

She thinks of Bella.

Of Travis.

Of the reason she lied.

She stacks glasses into a dishwasher at the back wall behind the counter. Thinking of the TV report—the news, right there at the bar, up on screen. Three days back. Travis's face. Another man, another prisoner. A Tennessee-wide hunt.

She'd said nothing, told no one. She'd been afraid.

The man turning up at the house—the marshal—had been a shock. She hadn't known what to say—to try not to make things worse.

Bella, though.

Bella disappearing.

A wave sweeps through her; nausea, a sickening feeling.

She scans the tables, customers, all the way to the far side of the room. Looking for any task, distraction.

Deano shouts out from behind her; "*Boss?*"

She spins around.

Standing at the kitchen door, Deano wipes his hands on

a dish rag. "Boss, you got someone?"

"What?"

He thumbs behind over his shoulder. "Somebody just showed up. Out back. In the lot. There's a car."

"Who?" she says.

"I don't know. Want me to go on and check?"

Ursula swallows. "No, no, I'll do it. I'll do it, it's okay."

"We got the garbage truck coming by," Deano says, "they'll need to get all the way up."

"Alright," she says. "It's alright, I'll go."

She unties the apron, tosses it by a coffee machine.

Stepping into a small office at the side of the kitchen, she crosses to the window, pulls back a slatted blind.

The nose of a car is just visible outside between twin dumpsters.

She unlocks the back door, steps out.

Crosses a cluttered rectangle of broken asphalt—steps around the dumpsters, stares at the car.

Nobody is inside it.

She moves from the lot into a narrow service road running along the backs of the neighboring businesses—a car wash, a paint store.

A figure is standing at the intersection where the service road meets the street.

Ursula feels a lurch inside. "Oh, my God? What are you doing?"

The figure turns.

"What are you doing here? Do you know they're looking for you?"

She nods. "I was going to walk around—I was going to walk around to the front…"

Jessica.

White-faced.

A wisp in the sunlight.

Drained.

Stark.

Slight as a ghost.

⸸

The black Mazda barrels down the state highway—the sound of its tires pink noise against the thoughts inside his head.

McConnell drives the speed limit. Eyes everywhere. Fingers wet with sweat against the wheel.

Thoughts running, cycling—images popping, flashing.

He casts a sideways glance. Sees the blood not yet dry on the seats.

Briley Parkway is behind him—trees and farms and fields now turning into urban sprawl. Pushing along the Clarksville Pike, fast as he can, adrenaline in every sinew, the Sig on the floor.

Barbone forty miles back—in a patch of woodland next to standing corn.

With the Browning and a wool hat full of bullets and McConnell's fleece jacket.

And the gym bag of money.

Collateral.

A reason to go back.

He thinks of the big man; his eyes feral, face gray with pain.

Blood seeping from his leg. A chunk of thigh missing. A through-and-through, entry and exit wounds. T-shirt tied around to stop the bleeding.

They could have taken the woman.

Taken her with them, taken her hostage; he should have done it, nobody would have run outside.

They could have kicked her out—two minutes, all they would have needed—nobody would have fired a shot.

Cresting a ridge in Bordeaux north of the river, he sees the outline of Nashville, half a dozen more miles.

He checks his speed, dabs the brake, checks the rearview.

Thinks of stopping, thinks of turning around.

Running back up to the field of corn and the patch of woods.

He could be dead in the next hour.

Dead by the time he can get back.

Or still alive—the animal survivor.

McConnell stares through the windshield—*don't cross the river*, he tells himself.

Take Buena Vista Pike.

Work a way around.

Chapter Seventeen

Headed over the Woodland Street bridge, Whicher eyes the raked seats of the Titans stadium above the lots and warehouses on the Nashville riverside.

No word on Jessica McConnell.

Nothing from the stakeout of her sister Ursula's place.

He drives the Ford Crown Vic across the Cumberland River. Phone calls to the sheriff's office in Hudspeth have yielded nothing on Jacob Harwood. The blood sample from Jessica's house is at the lab, awaiting testing and results.

Whicher steers along the four-lane onto Union. Thinks of heading for his hotel.

He keys a call to the USMS office in Pecos, Chief Deputy Marshal Fairbanks.

The call rings twice.

His boss picks up.

"I'm thinking to head back," Whicher says. "Maybe tonight. Unless you want me up here?"

"Tell me what you have so far?" Fairbanks says.

The marshal slows for a stop light, scans Union—the

hotel is just a few blocks over. "We've had no further sightings of Jessica McConnell," he says. "The task force marshal out of Memphis showed me footage from a gas station where she used her bank card."

"Was it her?"

"It looked like her." Whicher thinks again of the sister; Ursula Carney.

"Do they have anything else?"

"Not yet," the marshal says. "I found a sister, here, Jessica's sister, I talked with her. She reckoned there's some bad blood."

"Oh?"

"With the husband making threats," Whicher says, "fights between them."

Fairbanks is quiet a moment. "You think it might be worth staying?"

"If Jessica shows up, local law enforcement can notify us. Or the task force can. I don't think Bella's with her." Whicher pictures the footage from the gas station—the woman in the store, buying nothing—walking back to her vehicle, no interaction with anyone inside.

"Why not?"

"Gut," he tells his boss.

"Just gut?"

"I need to start over," Whicher says, "go on back to Fort Stockton, to the hostel—find out where Bella might've gone…"

An incoming call flashes up on the phone's screen.

Evelyn Cruz.

"Ma'am, I have another call—from the task force."

"Alright," Fairbanks says. "Let me know what you want to do?"

The marshal clicks out the call, switches over. "Yeah, Whicher. What's going on?"

"Where are you?" Cruz says.

"Headed downtown."

"We think they might've just pulled an armed robbery."

"Say again?"

"McConnell. And Barbone. Outside of Clarksville, I'm headed up there now."

Whicher brakes. "Where?"

"Off of I-24," Cruz says. "Two people hit a sporting goods store, robbed the place—witness descriptions sounded like it could be them. This was two hours ago, but if they're still here I want them nailed in here, before they get out."

"Where's it at, you have an address?"

"About forty miles from you. It's right at exit-eleven."

Whicher signals, shifts lanes in the Crown Vic.

"They were still in Clarksville," Cruz says, "you believe that? Nobody's seen them in two days, I thought they were gone—but they're still here."

The marshal stares grim out of the windshield.

"Just forty miles from the last-known-sighting of Jessica McConnell—the mother of your missing child?"

"That's what bothers me," Whicher says.

"Do you want to come up here?"

The marshal presses down on the gas. "I'm already on my way."

The lot in front of the sporting goods store is filled with black and white cruisers—Whicher slows at the entrance, rolls the window, shows the Marshals Service badge and ID to the patrolman standing guard.

Evelyn Cruz is with a handful of people by a silver Ford Taurus.

Whicher drives in, finds an empty bay, parks. Steps from the car.

Cruz breaks off from a dark-suited man with thinning, gray hair—she calls over; "I think this was them…sheriff's office and the Clarksville PD have a BOLO out. I showed the store staff their pictures…"

"How come we didn't hear sooner?"

"NCIC logged it," Cruz says. "USMS Memphis heard an hour ago, they called me."

Whicher scans the people in the lot.

At a squad car, a police captain talks into a radio. Crime scene technicians work a section of sidewalk at the front of the store.

Among the group at the Ford Taurus is a middle-aged woman in a turtleneck—bruising across her face; two black eyes.

The gray-haired man in the suit steps closer.

"This gentleman is the manager," Cruz says.

Whicher eyes him. "Y'all have cameras in the store?"

"We do," the man says. "I'm afraid they're not that good. The footage is stored off site, we'll be able to retrieve it. But really, it all happened so fast—we think they came into the store about forty minutes before coming back in to rob us."

"They come in together?"

"Not according to my cashier," the man says. He points to a blond woman smoking on a cigarette. "She said they weren't together. She said one of them was wearing a baseball hat…"

Marshal Cruz cuts in; "McConnell, we think."

"The other man was wearing a wool hat."

Cruz nods. "Pretty sure that was Barbone."

The manager frowns. "He didn't look much like the picture you showed me."

"Clean-shaven in the picture of record," Cruz says, "the beard's recent."

"Anybody with them?" Whicher says. "How about a woman? A dark-haired woman?"

"I wasn't aware of anyone like that," the manager says. "I was back in the office, with Ms Turner." He angles his head toward the woman with the facial bruising. "The man in the baseball hat came in. He pulled a gun. Demanded all of our money. He told Connie, Ms Turner, to open up the safe. Then he hit her. With his fist, with the butt of his gun."

Whicher looks to Marshal Cruz. "Where you think he could've gotten that?"

The woman in the turtleneck steps over. "It was him," she says. "That bastard. In the photograph."

"Travis McConnell?" Whicher says.

She nods, her face bitter. "I got a good enough look."

"He was carrying a bag," the manager says. "Connie put

the money into it. Then he told us another man was in the store with a gun. He made us go out, empty the cash registers. There were customers, I just tried to keep everybody calm. We gave them the money. Then Gary drew a gun on them, he and the man in the wool hat started firing."

"Gary?"

The manager indicates a short, bearded man at the trunk of the silver Ford. "Mister Seaton. He operates the firearms counter."

Whicher waves him over. "Sir? You took a shot at these guys?"

The man steps across the lot. "The big guy in the wool cap was firing a Desert Eagle."

"You're sure on that?" Cruz says

Whicher looks at the man. "Nothing else like it."

Seaton nods. "I was at my counter. I had my Glock 26 with a fifteen mag. I took a shot at him when I thought I could. He fired back. Then they ran like hell out of it."

"Mister Seaton gave chase," the manager says. "Along with Mister Dooley, my chief salesman." He points at a bald man in a plaid shirt and glasses.

"The big guy had a Browning, also," Seaton says. "Hi-Power, semi-auto. The other guy was carrying a Sig."

Whicher looks to Evelyn Cruz. "Three weapons? Maybe it wasn't them?"

The woman in the turtleneck speaks; "That bastard in the photograph is the man who hit me."

Whicher looks at the store manager. "How much they get?"

"Between ten and twelve thousand. They got lucky, we were carrying over from yesterday, it wouldn't normally be so much."

Evelyn Cruz addresses the bearded man, Seaton. "You think you may have hit one of them while they were escaping?"

"Pretty sure I nicked the big guy in the leg."

"Mister Dooley thought he was hit, too," the manager says.

The man in the plaid shirt nods, adjusts his eyeglasses.

Whicher looks toward the front of the store, takes in the yellow, numbered square markers on the sidewalk. "Y'all know which way they went?"

"No," the manager answers. "I called everybody back inside."

"They went around in back," Seaton says, "we weren't about to go on after 'em."

"Any idea what kind of vehicle they might've been in?"

Seaton shakes his head.

Whicher eyes the lot, eyes the parkway, the service roads running in and out. The interchange with the interstate—any number of exit routes.

Evelyn Cruz steps from the group, gestures at Whicher. He follows.

"What happened this morning?" she says. "You were looking for Jessica McConnell's sister?"

"I found her, talked with her—Jessica wasn't there."

"You get anything of use?"

Whicher doesn't reply.

At the squad car, the uniformed captain, a black man in his fifties stares across at them.

Cruz calls over. "Marshal Whicher's with me…"

"We've got units at all the major roads," the captain says, "all the interchanges."

"What kind of vehicle you think they're in?" Whicher says.

The captain looks at him. "Witnesses in the lot said a black SUV. The sheriff's office are trying to help us lock down a fifty-mile radius. We've got air support, helicopters from districts one, three and eight. We need to talk about where to put them. I've got a map you might want to see."

The phone in Whicher's pocket starts to ring.

He takes it out, looks at it—doesn't recognize the number.

Cruz steps toward the captain's car.

Whicher holds out a hand, presses to answer the call, crosses the lot to the Crown Vic.

He opens up the door. "Hello?"

The line is live.

But nobody answers.

"Yeah, this is Whicher," he says, "go ahead?"

Clamping the phone against his ear, he swings in behind the wheel of the pool car.

"Hello?"

A woman speaks. "I think…I need to see you."

He straightens. Stares through the windshield.

Feels a prickle at his skin.

"It's me," she says. "I need to see you. It's Jessica McConnell."

Chapter Eighteen

Twilight turning to full dark. The lightweight jacket barely warm enough in the cold evening air. Walking along Eleventh, past a timber-clad roadhouse, he glances in at a window—sees drinkers, flashes of colored neon.

Revelers.

At an ungodly hour.

The smell of pizza drifts along the street from a down-home restaurant.

Ahead is a stop light—a five-way intersection.

Five Points.

Getting close now, he tells himself. He checks for parked cars, for cops.

The girl is back in the car, still in the car. Locked in.

He crosses the road toward a flat-roofed building, its walls spray-painted garish colors—a mural of stars and rainbows by its door.

A scrolled message is painted on one wall; *lose yourself— to find yourself.*

He bunches his shoulders, picks up the pace.

Passes a two-pump gas station. No cars filling up.

Nobody is out on the street.

The cold and the wind, he guesses. The between-times hour.

Lose yourself to find yourself.

Turning the words over. Was that it?

Was that what he'd done?

Whatever it was, he'd known one thing; he'd known it was wrong.

His conscious mind had known.

Obsession.

It had turned into obsession.

Little by little.

In the depths inside himself.

Some fundamental thing in him needed her. Longed for her. Ached for her. Infected him with anguish and guile.

Pursuit.

It had been pursuit—like an animal.

Was that what he had become?

Standing at the intersection he sweeps the cold sidewalks. Light pooling beneath the streetlamps, music spilling from rowdy bars.

He can see it. Finally.

Past a karaoke joint, past a tapas place. A low-roofed brick building. He checks the board out front, reads the sign above the door.

Nothing is parked along the street for fifty yards.

He walks on. Tries to take it all in.

Absorb everything.

See without being seen.

⋏

Ten minutes later, slowing the Toyota at the corner of a block. Still nothing is out on the street, the lots and side alleys deserted.

The girl speaks from the passenger seat. "That's it, there it is…"

He steers past a car wash, past the front of the bar, past a paint shop—spots the service road. Feels his heart beat faster.

He turns in on the narrow, unlit track.

Forty yards in he sees the back lot of the bar.

To the girl; "Is that it, is it there?"

"I think." She looks, sits forward, nods.

A pole light throws a dim wash on the edge of the rear lot. Tucked into the space between two dumpsters is another vehicle.

Part hidden.

Black.

A Mazda SUV.

Its headlamps off.

Chapter Nineteen

Second Avenue, downtown. Whicher takes the stairs to a pedestrian bridge over the Cumberland River.

Up lighters pick out steel trusses, grids of pale gray etched against the evening light.

In the sky to the north, navigation lights circle on a helicopter.

A solitary female stands at a scenic overlook midway across the bridge, leaning out over the rail.

Slender. Her long, dark hair moving in the breeze from the water.

Nobody with her.

The marshal closes down the last yards.

Jessica McConnell turns, her face caught in the lights of the bridge.

She gives a half-smile.

Her eyes are luminous above the wide mouth. "Marshal."

She stands at the rail, uncertain.

Whicher studies on her, feels the same strange sense; distance and allure.

"My sister told me you're looking for me?"

The marshal looks into her face, into the strange light in her eyes. Trying to pin down the feeling, the misaligned feeling.

"She said you came to her house? Have you found my daughter?"

"No, ma'am."

She turns to the river. Leans into the iron railing. "I thought, maybe….maybe you might have…"

She exhales a long breath.

"You want to tell me what you're doing in Nashville?"

Rocking lightly, she stares at the water down below.

Lights reflect in the river's surface, from the bank-side eateries and bars.

"Have you spoken to Bella?"

"No."

"Have you had any form of contact?"

"No," she says.

"Why are you here?"

No response.

"You got on a flight," Whicher says, "out of Midland, Texas?"

"My family is here." She looks at him. "I'm not allowed to care for my daughter. She can't live in my house."

"That's why you left?"

"The people taking care of her lost her. What am I supposed to do? My family is here. Not there."

Whicher looks into the side of her face. The smooth skin is stretched taut, he sees the tiny muscle working at her jaw.

"Hudspeth County Sheriff searched your house yesterday."

She turns, slowly. "They searched my house?"

"We're trying to find your daughter."

"I told you," Jessica says, "she's not with me. I don't have her. I don't know where she is."

"There's been no sign of Bella. Next thing you know, there's no sign of you."

She turns back to looking at the river. Eyes hooded. Her mouth pressed shut.

"A forensic investigator found traces of blood in your house," the marshal says. "A spray pattern. On one of the walls."

In the light from the bridge her face blanches.

"They sent a sample to analyze it."

Her body stiffens. She doesn't move.

"There were signs of disruption in there, also," Whicher says.

She shakes her head.

He glances up at the sky, tracks the navigation lights on the helo. "Marshals Service found a record of you up here in Nashville—buying gas. The south side of the city. Did you know the Marshals Service were already watching you?"

"Why would I?"

"Your husband robbed a sporting goods store at gunpoint today." Whicher eyes her. "About fifty miles from here. Less than an hour away."

Jessica McConnell shivers in the cooling air. "Can we go someplace?"

She turns to meet his stare.

Again the look, the strange feeling.

She dips her head a fraction, gives her half-smile. "Anywhere," she says.

"You want to go somewhere?"

"Can I buy you a drink?"

⊥

She sits with her back to the river at a double-height window, the bar on the riverside muted, barely half full.

Whicher watches her sipping on a long-neck.

She sets the bottle onto the table. "Why did you come here?"

He doesn't answer.

"Did you really think I'd be with my daughter?"

"The Marshals Service out of Memphis have a task force assigned to recapture your husband," he says. "The task force thought it significant. You moving, heading across the country like that."

"Why significant?"

"Your daughter goes missing. You leave the family home."

She shakes her head. "I panicked. I lost my head. I couldn't stand to be there anymore." She breaks off looking at him. Gazes out across the room. "I promised myself I wouldn't let it get to me." She draws herself up, sits straight suddenly. "But it freaked me out, I just needed to get out, get away from there. I thought, "what if he tried to come here?""

The marshal doesn't respond.

She sits back a fraction. "I know it's crazy. But he hated

that I went out there, that I took Bella, that I wouldn't take her to see him. I thought, somehow, he could try to get to me. I was alone, in that place, I was afraid. I panicked. I wanted to be someplace else. Right now, things don't make a lot of sense. But Bella has a lot of friends, I think that's where she'll be—with one of them—I think she's just trying to punish me, to make my life as miserable as it can be. Make me pay for taking her away from here, for ruining her life. For everything…"

She stops, checks herself.

Looks at Whicher.

"How about the house?" he says. "The disruption we found?"

"What disruption?"

"The kitchen."

Her eyes glaze a moment. She frowns, looks away. Looks back. "That? I was angry. I just got into this whole thing. Pissed. Mad at everything. I kicked over the chairs, I kicked the table, it doesn't mean anything—it's not a crime to trash your kitchen."

"How about the blood?" the marshal says.

Her mouth parts slightly. "I don't remember any blood." Opaqueness is in her eyes, now. "Maybe it's old. The house is rented."

"Crime scene investigator said something was cleaned from the carpet. The bedroom carpet. It was still wet."

Jessica McConnell takes a sip on her drink. Her voice is quiet. "I spilled coffee. I don't understand. Are you accusing me of something?"

The phone in Whicher's pocket starts to ring.

He takes it out, looks at it. Reads the number on the screen.

⊥

Outside on a deck overlooking the river, the marshal clamps the phone against his ear.

Sheriff Odell Ingram from Hudspeth County is on the line. "You still up in Nashville?"

"Still here."

"You find Jessica McConnell yet?"

Whicher turns to face the window of the bar. "I found her. I'm with her now."

"Right now?" the sheriff says.

"I'm looking at her."

"Well, listen, there's something I thought you ought to hear. We had a call from El Paso, the lab," the sheriff says, "on the blood. It's definitely human. It's recent—but the sample size is small. They're going to run more tests, PCR-DNA analysis. It's going to take some time. Plus, we don't have reference samples."

"We don't have a victim, either," Whicher says.

"There's no word on the daughter?"

"No word as yet."

"Alright. Well, Grace tells me the pattern analysis suggests the blood on the wall could have come from an injury. A court wouldn't take it, as it stands. But the likes of you and me, that means something. So I wanted you to know that."

Whicher thinks about it, doesn't reply.

"But there's something else," the sheriff says. "I've been talking with folk around here, I talked with Pastor Mullins. From the church. And a woman from the congregation, Pearl Cooper, she says she met you?"

"Yeah, I met her."

"Well, the thing of it is; there's no sign of Jessica McConnell's boyfriend, or whatever he is—Jacob Harwood. Nobody's seen him in days. He's not home, he's not out working. I'm starting to think maybe that blood on the wall here could've come from him."

"Say again?"

"The feller's gone. Nobody's seen him. He never misses church, never goes much to anyplace. It's out of character."

Whicher stares at Jessica McConnell through the window.

"According to Pearl Cooper, this guy Harwood's kind of strange around girls," the sheriff says. "Around Bella, you know, young girls? Whenever she sees the two of them together she don't like it."

"Well, what's that mean?"

"Well, how about if Harwood had some interest there with the daughter? Something more than he should have. And Jessica got to hearing about it?"

Whicher stares at the door to the bar, mood darkening.

"Maybe I'm reaching," the sheriff says. "But maybe that's why Bella upped and disappeared? She started getting in trouble. We know that. Maybe that was part of it? If something was going on, I could see the mother reacting…"

Whicher thinks of the disrupted kitchen, the blood. The newly cleaned carpet in the bedroom.

He pictures Pearl Cooper at the church. Thinks of her cold air, her disapproval.

He thinks of Jessica, the strange disconnection. Like held-in anger.

"We don't have evidence," Sheriff Ingram says. "But I been around long enough to know something's going on. I don't know what to advise you, marshal. But we have human blood, a potential injury pattern—I wanted you to know."

▲

Back inside the bar her eyes are on him.

Whicher sits. Puts away the phone.

"Is something wrong?" She searches his face, leans forward. "I don't know where my daughter is. I came here yesterday, I bought a ticket, I wanted to see my sister…"

"That it?" Whicher says.

"Last night I slept at a motel. I needed to get straightened out. I saw Ursula today. I spent some time with her, I went to the bar she owns. You can call her up, ask her."

"I'll be sure to do that."

Jessica's eyes widen. Color is at her throat. "We talked things over," she says. "I just needed someone…"

"You can't call on the phone?"

"I don't have to make excuses to you." She takes a fast sip on her drink. "I came out. I was always going to go back to Texas. I haven't done anything wrong. I haven't committed a crime, I'm not breaking any law."

Whicher lets his thoughts run, says nothing.

"There's not a damn thing you can do about it, anyway," she says. "Why does every man I ever meet seem to want to control everything? Including me?"

The marshal keeps his eyes on hers, doesn't answer.

She lets out a sharp breath. Sits forward. "If there's nothing else, I think I'm done here. I think I'll go." She stands, quickly. "I have nothing to do with my husband's escape from prison. Or with my daughter running off. It might seem like it to you, from the outside…"

"Sit down," he tells her.

"You don't know a thing about my life. You don't know me. What do you want?" She stares at him, face flushed, now, eyes shining. "I'm walking out of here."

He shakes his head. "Mrs McConnell. Please sit down."

⁂

Wind is blowing through the tops of the standing corn—rustling, reaching in to the empty black woodland space.

For the last hour, the sound of the corn has been the only thing he can hear—but now there's something.

A faint hum of something.

Something moving along the road, the rural lane close by.

Reed Barbone lies still, only listening. Night and the cold and the loss of blood numbing. Everything a fog.

He pulls the collar of McConnell's fleece jacket up over his bearded chin. Breathes into it, trying to preserve the warmth.

Hours, now. Long hours; watching. Afternoon light fading—the onset of dark through the trees. Sometimes half-out, dreaming, woken by pain gripping his leg.

The gym bag is in the dirt at his side, the Browning in his hand, fully loaded.

He lays his head back, listens.

Above the wind in the corn, hears it again—the moan of a motor.

He thinks of dragging himself to the edge of the woods—two times he's tried already, limping, staggering to stand where he can see a section of the distant road. To search for any sign of a house or farmstead, any light. And find nothing.

But the sound is louder, now. The sound of a motor more defined.

He sits up, listens.

Stares into the dense dark of the woods.

Maybe it will pass by.

He grabs the gym bag, pulls it closer.

McConnell would be back. Sooner or later.

Nashville was a risk—but there were people he knew there.

They'd have to lie low, find somewhere, find help. No choice, now. With the wound to the leg.

The wind moves again in the corn. Barbone pulls himself up against the trunk of a tree.

He stuffs the Browning into the waistband of his pants. Lifts the gym bag, strains to see through the dark to the near-edge of the wood. Twenty yards—to where a dirt track runs along the side of the corn between the field and the trees.

Dragging his leg, he winces from the pain—breath coming short.

At the edge of the wood, he stops. Crouches.

Listens again.

Hears it.

His heart beats faster.

Along the dim line of the trackway he sees no sign of light.

But a motor is humming low.

Coming closer.

Barbone takes out the Browning, grips it. A round already chambered, the hammer cocked. He pushes off the thumb safety.

The T-shirt tied around his leg is cold. Heavy with his own blood. He fights an urge to sit down.

Something is coming.

He hears the motor, makes out a dim shape.

A big, black shape rolling slow toward him.

Light from the moon is on its windshield. Headlamps out.

It slows.

Stops thirty yards distant. The motor dies.

Wind blows in the corn.

Barbone holds on to the trunk of a tree.

The door of the vehicle opens.

An interior dome light flicks on.

Travis McConnell steps out.

He stares into the dark along the edge of the wood.

"Reed," he calls out. "It's me, man. I made it…"

He waits for an answer.

Barbone raises the pistol.

"Are you out there? Where are you?" McConnell says.

Barbone points the Browning at a second figure sitting inside the vehicle. He shouts back, voice ragged; "What's going on? Who the hell is that?"

Chapter Twenty

In the Federal Building on Ninth Street downtown, Whicher checks his watch in a bright-lit corridor.

The double-door at its end swings open.

Marshal Evelyn Cruz emerges through it—hair tied back, the black skirt and jacket exchanged for navy chinos and a rollneck top. In her hand is the leather attaché case, her sidearm and badge clipped to her belt.

Whicher thumbs over his shoulder at a door behind him. "She's in there."

"I got here as fast as I could. Did you make a start yet?"

"I thought to wait on you."

Cruz stops in the corridor. "We have no idea where they went. We have nothing. We had helicopters in the air, ground units everywhere…"

"I don't know if this all is going to help," Whicher says. "She's not under arrest. This is just a conversation. She's a person of interest, both my investigation and yours."

"She has to know something," Cruz says, "she came here. She consents?"

Whicher nods. "To give her version of events. I came down after she called from Clarksville. She went quiet on me, I thought she was backing out. She called again, I persuaded her."

He gestures for Cruz to follow, opens up the door behind him, enters a small interview room.

Jessica McConnell is seated at a plastic-topped table. A cup of coffee in front of her in a cardboard holder.

Whicher takes off the Resistol, sits.

Jessica regards him from the other side of the table. Sullen. Glancing up at a camera fixed high on the wall.

Marshal Cruz pulls out a chair. Sits alongside Whicher. From her leather attaché case, she takes out a digital audio recorder.

"She's not under arrest," Whicher says.

Cruz switches on the recorder. "My name is Deputy Marshal Evelyn Cruz. With me is Deputy Marshal John Whicher from USMS Texas, Western Division." She turns to Jessica. "Please state your full name for the record."

"Jessica Ava McConnell."

"Mrs McConnell, your husband escaped from a prison facility outside of Memphis, Tennessee three days ago…"

"Estranged husband," Jessica says.

"Estranged," Cruz repeats.

Whicher looks at Cruz, then at Jessica in turn.

"Are you legally separated in the state of Tennessee?" Cruz says.

"No."

"Your husband has been convicted of a felony and

sentenced to serve time in a penitentiary."

"Excuse me?"

"Those are legally adequate grounds to file for divorce."

Jessica McConnell sits in her chair, her face a mask.

"But you're still his wife," Cruz says. She sniffs. Leans forward an inch. "You don't have to be. But you are."

Whicher clears his throat. "Marshal Cruz is from the task force assigned to locate and recapture your husband. Along with a man that escaped with him."

"Which has nothing whatever to do with me," Jessica says.

Cruz looks at her. "I spent this afternoon up in Clarksville. Where we believe your husband committed an aggravated robbery today."

Jessica stares blank at the top of the table.

Whicher speaks; "Tell us about your movements since you left your home in Texas?"

"I already told you," Jessica says. "I caught a flight out of Midland yesterday morning…"

"Why?" Marshal Cruz says.

Jessica looks at Whicher. "I told you all of this. I was alone in the house, I was freaking out. I was afraid, with Travis breaking out. I was frightened for my daughter. I have nobody back there, everyone I know is here."

"You left the family home with your daughter missing," Cruz says, "because you were afraid?"

"I wanted to see my sister. I planned on going back again."

"You left your home, you took a flight from Midland. Alone?"

"Yes, alone."

"You arrived here when?"

"About noon."

"Then what?"

"I took a bus from the airport. I rented a car."

"Why not rent at the airport?" Cruz says.

"There's places all over town, cheaper places. I just rode the bus is all, I found a rental place…"

"Not trying to cover your tracks?" Cruz says. "Make it harder to find you?"

Jessica McConnell looks at Evelyn Cruz slowly. "Why would I want to do that?"

"Maybe if you thought people could be watching you?"

McConnell bugs her eyes.

Cruz says, "People like me. Monitoring family members of an escaped felon."

Whicher cuts in; "You took a bus—then what?"

"I got a motel room."

"Where?" Cruz says.

"Luna Heights," Jessica answers. "A couple of miles from the airport. I saw a rental place from the bus, I got off. I rented the car—there were motels around there, cheap rooms."

"Why not go to your sister?"

"My sister runs a bar—she works nights. She sleeps late."

"Why not go to friends, or go to people you know?"

"I don't know," Jessica says, "alright? I was messed up. I wasn't thinking straight. I didn't know what I wanted."

Cruz looks at her. "Did you meet with anyone?"

"No."

"Then what?" Whicher says.

"I took a nap at the motel. I drove to East Nashville. To see my sister."

Whicher thinks of the interview with Ursula Carney. Around midday. Ursula hadn't seen her—or else she'd been a practiced liar. "So, did you see her, yesterday?"

Jessica shakes her head.

"Why not?"

"I don't know."

Cruz repeats her words. "You don't know."

Jessica drops her head between her shoulders. "I backed out of it. I wanted to see her, but I didn't want to, at the same time. I didn't know what to do, I didn't know what she'd say to me. I didn't know if I could handle it, if she started in on me…"

"So you didn't see her?" Whicher says. "You see anybody?"

"No."

"What *did* you do?" Cruz says.

Jessica's eyes glaze. She puts her hands over her belly. "I drove around a while. I went downtown. I sat by the river. Tried to straighten out, you know? Get my head right, get my thoughts together…"

Marshal Cruz shoots an eyebrow. "What else?"

"I went around the neighborhood," Jessica says, "my old neighborhood. Thinking about everything. My life here, Bella growing up, the friends she had, the school she went to. All of it."

"And?"

"I got something to eat. Then I drove back to the motel. I went to bed."

"You didn't see your sister?" Cruz says. "The person you came all this way for?"

"It got late. I was upset. I figured she'd be at work, I didn't want to see her that way, you know? In a bar. With everything going on. I wouldn't be able to talk to her. I saw her today."

Cruz nods. "Tell us about today?"

"I got up. I left the motel I guess around eleven."

"Alone all this time?" Cruz says.

"Yes, alone."

"Then what?"

"I drove into town. I went over to the bar, to Ursula's place. This afternoon. I knew it would be quiet, but she'd be there. We talked. She told me you were looking for me. That you were here, that you came out…"

"What else?" Cruz says.

"Ursula said I had to call you." She looks at Whicher. "She had your card, your number. I was going to fly back. Tonight. I was going to buy a ticket. But Ursula said to see you first."

Whicher studies the young woman's face. "A sheriff's department team entered your house yesterday, searched it. I asked you about a blood stain on the wall?"

"I told you, I don't know anything about it."

"Tell me about Jacob Harwood?"

A flash of something passes behind her eyes.

"What about him?" A slight constriction is in her voice.

"He a friend of yours?"

"Yes," Jessica says.

"Hudspeth County sheriff says nobody's seen him in three days."

Color leaches from Jessica's face. She doesn't answer.

Evelyn Cruz is looking at him, now.

Whicher thinks of the man, Harwood. So far, only a name without a face.

He thinks of the sheriff's words; talk of Harwood's awkwardness around girls. "Are you and Jacob Harwood in a relationship?"

"What business is that of yours?"

"Members of your local church seem to think y'all are close."

Jessica's eyes harden. "So what? He and I are friends. What does that have to do with this, with anything?"

"The Hudspeth County sheriff says the man's disappearance is out of character," Whicher says. "And we found a blood spatter pattern in your house you've given no explanation for. Plus evidence of some kind of disturbance when we searched the place."

Evelyn Cruz leans in to the table.

Jessica shakes her head, mouth open.

"Did you and Harwood have a fight?" Whicher says.

"No." Jessica swallows, sits forward.

The marshal looks at her. "You don't have anything to say about his disappearance? Your daughter's? Either one of them?"

"I told you, Bella's just a runaway, she'll come back…"

Evelyn Cruz cuts a glance at Whicher. Catches his eye, holds it a long moment. "You and your daughter lived here," she says to Jessica, "in East Nashville? Along with your husband, prior to your husband's conviction. Correct? This was your home. Why was your husband here, less than an hour away? Today. Shouldn't he be trying to get as far from the state of Tennessee as possible?"

The young woman stays silent.

"Mrs McConnell, did you come here to Nashville to meet with your husband?" Cruz says. "Did you come here to meet with him, to give him aid?"

"No."

"Your husband stayed in Clarksville, just fifty miles away. Was that to give you time to get here? To support his escape?"

Jessica lets out a tight breath.

"How do you explain his presence—the fact he's been on the run for days? He could've gone anywhere. And yet he chose to remain here?"

Spreading her hands wide, Jessica looks at Cruz and then at Whicher. "I have no idea."

The marshal feels the pent-up energy in Cruz. In the force in her words, in her body language. Sensing her poised to strike.

He changes tack; "I'm going to ask you again, how do you account for what we found when we searched your house in Hudspeth County?"

Confusion is in the young woman's face now. "Nothing happened." Her voice is hollow.

"Marshal…" Evelyn Cruz says.

Whicher holds up a hand. "I believe you have information about the disappearance of your daughter…"

Jessica McConnell shakes her head.

"I'm placing you under arrest."

Marshal Cruz sits back, stares.

"You have the right to remain silent. Anything you say can and will be used against you in a court of law. You have the right to speak to an attorney, and have an attorney present during questioning."

Cruz reaches out, stops the audio recorder. "What?" she says. "On what charge?"

Jessica eyes him.

"Obstruction of my inquiry—obstructing a federal officer in a felony investigation. I'm taking her back to Texas," the marshal says. "I'm taking her tonight."

⁂

The moon hangs low above the field of overwintering corn. At the edge of the woods Travis McConnell shrugs off the cold night air. He rifles a bag of items from a gas station outside of Nashville—energy drinks, candy, burritos.

Reed Barbone sits in the dirt, clutching at his wounded leg.

"You want something?" McConnell says. "Something to eat? Drink?"

"Finish this," Barbone says.

Distraction, McConnell tells himself. Make the man believe things can work out.

He takes out a new-bought first-aid kit and flashlight. Snaps on the flashlight, unrolls a bandage, wraps it around the gauze pad already taped to Barbone's leg.

Fixing it in place, he ignores the blood already starting to seep back out of the wound.

Barbone shakes his head, stares at the dark outline of the SUV between the cornfield and the woods. "I don't know what the hell you think you're doing…"

"I told you," McConnell says. "I found a way into town. All the way back—to my old neighborhood…"

"You go back in your old neighborhood?" Barbone says.

"What choice did I have?" McConnell looks at him. "Who else is going to help? You got people in Detroit, I got people here."

"You're lucky you made it back."

"I was hanging around this bar, my wife's sister owns it. Looking for someone I could trust. Reed, she showed up."

"And you bring her?"

"She latched right onto me. Wanting to know what was going on. She's my daughter, it's not like she was going to let it go…" McConnell ties off the last of the bandages. "You know what?"

Barbone grunts.

"I stopped to get this? A gas station outside of Nashville?" He nods at the bag. "I filled the tank so we can drive all night. I was going to leave her there. You know, leave her? I went inside with her, to pay, to buy shit. Nobody bats an eyelid. Some dude and his daughter. First time since we busted out I don't look like some kind of fugitive."

"The hell are you talking about?"

"This can work for us."

"What?"

"Her being here."

"Are you out of your mind?" Barbone's eyes are wild in the beam of the flashlight.

"She's seen me, she's seen the car. You think law enforcement ain't about to force that out of her? If they get a hold of her. This can work."

"Bullshit…"

"We drive all night, by morning we'll be gone." McConnell closes up the first-aid kit, tosses it into the bag with the drinks and the food.

"Put her out someplace," Barbone says.

Inside the Mazda, motionless in the dark, McConnell sees the outline of his daughter, the hood of her top, her head pressed against the window. "We drive all night. We get to Detroit, we can get you fixed up. Eight hours, we can be there. We can get your leg taken care of…"

Barbone shifts on the ground, holds his weight on his arms. "How about if cops are there looking?"

McConnell squats low.

Barbone lets out a guttural grunt—pushes to his feet.

McConnell puts the man's arm over his shoulder. "If cops are there, we take you somewhere else. I can take you out to Pennsylvania."

"My leg's on fire…" Barbone lets out a breath through gritted teeth. "It's burning up, you got to fix me up, man."

"Two holes in it," McConnell says. "Two ways to bleed.

We get you drugs, we'll get food—she can buy the food, we won't have to go in any store."

Barbone pants, struggles across toward the car. "You're crazy, man. You're one crazy-ass son of a bitch…"

"I get you out of prison, or what? Did I get you out of Clarksville when you stopped a bullet?"

The big man doesn't answer.

"I'll get us where we need to go," McConnell says.

"Think you got this?" Barbone's voice is low, ragged. "You think you got it all?"

"I guess we'll find out."

"You ever take it all the way?" Barbone says. "Huh? You ever kill, though—to get what you want?" He juts his chin at the Mazda. "The guy that owned that, uh? You know?"

"I know."

"He ain't the first…"

McConnell leans the big man on the side of the SUV.

"I know I can do it," Barbone says. "Push comes to shove. Next time, I might be out of it. Way my leg is."

McConnell looks at him.

Barbone stares in the dim light. "You want her there, man? Next time. Next time—it's going to be on you."

Chapter Twenty-One

Pecos, Tx

He hears her enter the room, not yet fully awake, no longer asleep. Mild pain in the back of his head. Face squashed into a pillow.

He opens an eye, focuses on the outline of his wife looking down at him.

"Didn't mean to wake you," Leanne says.

He reaches out a hand from under the coverlet.

She takes it.

He smiles at her, squeezes her hand.

"I made coffee, you want some?"

"Thanks." His voice is dry in his throat. He lifts his head an inch from the pillow. "Where's Lori?"

"In school. She wanted to come see you this morning, before she left, I told her not to wake you."

"She okay?"

"She's just fine." Leanne steps away from the bed, out of the room into the hallway.

Whicher turns, pushes himself upright. Thinks of the overnight flight; Nashville to Midland. An hour at DFW. Arriving four o'clock in the morning.

And then the drive down to Pecos with Jessica McConnell. Silent. Handcuffed in the truck.

Not the usual kind of passenger for him. Still uneasy at retrieving her that way.

Leanne re-enters the room. "I didn't hear you come in last night?" She sits on the edge of the bed, puts down a cup of coffee on the nightstand.

"I stopped by the Reeves jail facility," Whicher says, "booked in Jessica McConnell. I got in around six." He rubs a hand over his eyes. "I have to speak to my boss, let her know what's going on."

"So, you arrested her?"

Whicher picks up the cup of coffee, takes a sip. "I think she knows something about her daughter's disappearance. No one's seen her in four days. She says she thinks she ran away, is all."

Leanne looks at him.

"Memphis task force think she might have gone to Nashville to help her husband. The county sheriff in Hudspeth thinks she might be responsible for a man going missing. A boyfriend."

"Somebody else is missing?"

"Three people," Whicher says. "The daughter, the husband. This other guy. The church she attends, there's a rumor there's something between them."

"Why would he go missing?"

"We don't know. The boyfriend might've been—involved with the daughter." Whicher sees the change in his wife's face. "We don't have evidence yet."

Leanne eases off the bed, walks to the window. She angles the slats on the blind, lets the sunlight stream in.

Whicher takes another pull on the cup of coffee.

"Anybody ever tried a thing like that with Lori…" Leanne says.

"I know."

She steps to the built-in wardrobe. "Want me to find you something?"

"No, I'll take a shower."

"You want to eat? You want eggs?"

He smiles at her. Sees the look in her face. "I ask you something?"

She nods.

"If somebody ever did something like that. To Lori. You think you'd have it in you to do something about it?"

Leanne flushes. "Like what?"

"Something serious. Violent."

She swallows. "You mean; hurt them—do something to them?"

Whicher only watches her.

"Maybe," Leanne says. Her gaze downturned. "If I got the chance…"

"If you had the chance?"

His wife says nothing further.

Her face is dark as she turns from the room.

⋏

From the parking lot at the side of the courthouse building, Whicher crosses the broad stretch of Cedar Street to the county sheriff's office on the opposite side of the road.

Inside the building, a group of uniformed deputies stand at one side of a wide lobby—on the opposite side civilian staff are gathered by a water fountain and drinks machine.

Whicher spots the tall, Hispanic woman dressed in a dark suit—Silvia Gonzales—attorney with the public defender's office.

Gonzales sees him. She picks up her briefcase, makes her way over.

Whicher tips his hat. "Ms Gonzalez. Good morning."

"Marshal." The defense attorney looks at him, eyes unsmiling. "I've spoken with Mrs McConnell already. About her arrest. Made without a warrant in the state of Tennessee?"

"Yes, ma'am."

"You arrested her last night?" Gonzalez says. "On a charge of obstruction?"

"Yes, I did."

"Did she assert her right to counsel?"

"No, ma'am."

"She does now. You have twenty-four hours to get her into a probable cause hearing." The defense attorney looks at her watch. "And the clock is running. You think you'll make it? It's almost noon."

"I guess it depends," Whicher says.

Gonzalez looks at him. "On what?"

"On the interview," the marshal says. "On whether she talks."

"If she chooses not to?"

"I'm trying to find the woman's daughter, Ms Gonzalez."

"You have evidence? To present to the court for obstruction?"

Whicher eyes the defense attorney, doesn't answer.

"Mrs McConnell says she traveled to Tennessee to see family," Gonzalez says. "In distress. Over her missing child."

"She tell you her husband broke out of a prison up there?"

"Estranged husband."

"They're still married."

"And?"

"I don't believe her story. I suspect her of trying to prevent me from finding her daughter. I requested counsel from your office. I'm hoping she'll reconsider what she has to say."

"Then I'll see you in the interview room," Gonzalez says. "But I think you're mistaken, marshal. Unless you can back up what you're saying, I think she'll walk."

Whicher nods. "I have a phone call I have to make. I'll be right with you."

Gonzalez takes out a security pass on a lanyard. She turns on her heel, walks away across the lobby.

The marshal steps to a window looking out onto a bright street. He takes out his phone, keys a number. Puts the phone to his ear.

It picks up—Sheriff Odell Ingram in Hudspeth County.

"I have Jessica McConnell in an interview room over in Pecos," Whicher says. "I'm about to go talk to her."

"You brought her on back?"

"Arrested her. Last night. For obstruction."

"You did, huh?"

"I'm calling about Jacob Harwood."

"There's still no sign of him," the sheriff says. "I had a unit go by the house last night, another one went over this morning. Nobody's there."

Whicher runs his tongue around the inside of his cheek. "Y'all are sure on that?"

"Yessir."

"How about the lab in El Paso—you get anything on the blood spatter?"

"Not at this time."

"I'm going to ask for a sample from her," Whicher says. "A blood sample. To see if we could match it or not. If she won't agree, you think you could get a judge to issue a warrant?"

"My office?"

"It's your county," Whicher says. "Plus, we widen this thing out it gets her attorney off my back."

"Alright," the sheriff says, "I guess. If that's what you want."

"Let me know if there's word on Harwood?"

"When I hear, you'll hear," the sheriff says.

Whicher finishes the call.

⚰

Inside the interview room, video cameras point at each side of a small table.

Whicher sits straight in his seat.

Jessica McConnell leans in, handcuffs around her wrists.

Whicher regards her. The formal start to the interview over. An audio recorder between himself and Silvia Gonzalez.

"Yesterday you told me you traveled to Nashville," he says, "to see family. That correct?"

Jessica answers. "Yes, it is."

"You saw your sister Ursula. She told you I was looking for you."

The young woman nods.

"Your sister was the only person you saw. I asked you to account for the time you spent up there—around thirty-six hours?"

"I told you," Jessica says.

"You claim you saw no one. You told me you visited your former neighborhood, you were upset."

"I told you I was messed up. And scared. With everything going on."

"You stand by the fact you saw no one?"

"Because it's true."

"And then I asked you about evidence we found—of a disturbance in your home."

The defense attorney sits forward. "What evidence? What disturbance?"

"It's nothing," Jessica says.

"A forensic investigator from the Hudspeth County Sheriff's Office found a blood spatter pattern on your living room wall," Whicher says. He glances at Silvia Gonzales, then back at Jessica. "You say you don't know anything about it?"

"I don't." She looks at him. An edge in her voice despite the outward calm.

"What disturbance?" Gonzalez says. Rising alarm in her face.

"I told you," Jessica says to Whicher, "that was me. The kitchen getting messed up. I was mad, I wanted to…bust things up. I kicked some chairs around, I kicked the table over. Then I straightened things out, no big deal."

"Well," the marshal says, "that may be so." He leans in, puts his elbows on the edge of the table. "If it's no big deal, I'd like you to provide a blood sample, Mrs McConnell."

Silvia Gonzalez raises a finger. "Marshal. Do you have a warrant for that?"

"No, ma'am."

The defense attorney turns to Jessica. "You don't have to consent to give a sample if you don't want to. I recommend that you don't consent."

Whicher looks at Jessica. "If it's your blood on the wall, it could help clear things up."

"Clear what up?" Gonzales says.

"There's nothing to clear up," Jessica says, "I told you the house is rented, it could be anybody's, it could have been there years."

"Do you intend to apply for a warrant to take a blood sample?" Gonzalez says.

"No, ma'am. The sheriff's office in Hudspeth will request the warrant."

"On what grounds?"

"On the grounds that a man thought to be in a relationship with Mrs McConnell has been missing. For four days."

Jessica shakes her head.

"My client does not consent," Gonzales says.

The marshal nods. "Understood."

"You'll have to get your warrant," Gonzalez says. "Is that the purpose of your questioning here, marshal?"

"No, ma'am."

She looks at him. "You have further questions?"

"Just one."

The defense attorney eyes him.

Jessica McConnell draws her hands in to her chest.

Whicher sits back. "What do you know about the disappearance of your daughter?"

"Nothing," she says.

"Nothing at all?"

No response.

"My client is not obstructing you," Gonzalez says, "if she doesn't know anything."

The marshal keeps his eye on Jessica McConnell. "Did Jacob Harwood have some kind of an involvement with your daughter?"

The woman's eyes flare.

Whicher feels the attorney looking at him, now.

"I don't know what you're talking about," Jessica says.

Whicher lets her words sit unanswered.

He buttons the jacket of his suit.

"Is that it?" the defense attorney says.

"No further questions."

Gonzalez turns the audio recorder off.

Whicher stands. Looks at Jessica. "I sure hope for your sake that's the truth."

⁂

The sun is high over the mountain. The wind cold. Biting cold.

He sees the darkness in the sky to the north, watches it for just a moment. Feels the sense of foreboding, approaching, troubling him. The constant feeling, for days.

He says a silent prayer, the latest in an unending litany.

Tries to shrug the weight of sapping fatigue.

Picking a wooden-handled shovel from the dirt he bends low. Returns to digging. The brush is thick all around him—mesquite and shinnery oak and creosote bush and ocotillo.

The land is his land, owned by his father before him, grandfather before that.

A single dirt road onto the property—dry ranch land—a couple of aging barns, timbers missing from their sides.

The nearest ranch is six miles east, the little town of Sierra Blanca way over on the other side of the mountain.

Still the sense of being watched haunts him. As if eyes were upon him, at every moment of the day.

He sends the blade of the shovel singing into the dirt. Scoops out another load, lifts it onto the growing pile of earth at one side.

The sight of God, he tells himself.

The eyes of God, watching.

In all corners of the earth, in the hearts and minds of every man.

Seeing.

Knowing.

He digs on. Wipes a line of sweat from his brow.

The hole in the ground is six feet long, a little under two feet deep.

He pauses. Carries the shovel to a Ram pickup by one of the decaying barns. Reaches in back for a water bottle in the box of tools by the winch in the bed.

Taking out the water bottle, he unscrews the top. Drinks a little. The water is cold, sluicing down inside him. He feels a burning sensation, like ice. He grimaces. Snatches the bottle away.

No comfort.

Not even in simple refreshment.

The cold water sits in his gut, like some poison, he tells himself.

Elixir to poison.

He tosses the bottle back in the bed of the truck.

Turning around, he eyes the hole in the dirt.

By its side a green tarpaulin, dark green, the color of leaves. Or of river water. Or the cover on his first Bible— way back, given to him as a boy.

Beneath the tarp, rolled in a tangle of arms and legs, a man lies enshrouded.

Shutting down the thoughts inside, he strides to the hole, grips the shovel harder. Bends his back.

To shut out the overwhelming feelings.

Dig down.

Bury them.

Along with the tarpaulin. Now fluttering in the wind. The dark green images. A baptizing river. A Bible cover.

And the body of the man wrapped inside.

Chapter Twenty-Two

Pecos, Tx

Inside the USMS office at the courthouse building, Whicher sits at his desk staring into a computer screen.

A search on Jacob Harwood shows scant information—Harwood listed as owner-operator of a drywall company—with a business website little more than a holding page. A phone number that won't answer; generic voicemail. Social media pages for the church have references to him, no moving image, no stills.

The marshal picks up the phone, keys the number for the sheriff's office in Hudspeth County.

Sheriff Ingram answers on the third ring. "So, Jessica McConnell?"

"Refuses to give a sample," Whicher says.

"You want me to go ahead, make the warrant request on behalf of the county?"

"Had a thought to run by you—on this guy Harwood…"

"Oh?" the sheriff says.

"There's still no sign?"

"Not a thing."

"Could you open up a missing person's file?"

The sheriff is silent a moment.

"A judge might be more inclined on the warrant if y'all have a missing man in the county," Whicher says. He glances at the screen, waits for Sheriff Ingram to answer. "If her boyfriend's officially missing. A blood sample from Jessica McConnell could rule her out. Aside from that, rule out it being her daughter's blood, potentially."

"Nobody reported the guy missing," Ingram says. "I can't open the file myself."

"How about somebody that knows him? Pastor Mullins from the church?"

"You want me to get Win Mullins to report him gone?"

"There's no way to check if it's Harwood's blood—unless we can find him. If someone were to report him missing we can look."

From the far side of the office, the squat figure of Deputy Marshal Booker Tillman approaches.

"I'll put in for a warrant for a sample of Jessica McConnell's blood," the sheriff says. "Let me think about Harwood."

Marshal Tillman gestures at the open door to Chief Marshal Fairbanks's room.

"Sheriff, I appreciate it. I'll let the on-call doctor know." The marshal clicks off the call. Turns to Tillman. "They didn't blow you up?"

"How's that?"

"The courthouse? You had some nut threatening to light it up."

Tillman grins. Tips back his black Stetson. "Guess it never came to that." He looks at Whicher. "You find your missing minor?"

The marshal shakes his head. "I found the mother. Up in Nashville."

"She run off to be a singer?" Tillman thumbs back over his shoulder. "Boss wants to talk to you."

Whicher nods. Shuts off the screen, stands.

He crosses the office, knocks at the chief marshal's door.

Fairbanks is seated at her desk dressed in a navy two-piece, metallic gray hair neatly groomed.

She waves him in.

The marshal pulls out a chair.

"Reeves jail sent over custody forms," she says, "on Jessica McConnell? You arrested her?"

"For obstruction, yes I did."

Fairbanks reads the note on her desk. "You're going to put her in front of a judge?"

"Working on it."

She places a pair of eyeglasses on the top of her head. "On what evidence?"

"Hudspeth county have evidence," Whicher says. "From the search of Jessica McConnell's house—the blood spatter pattern she can't account for."

"You have that analysis already?"

"No, ma'am."

"You know whose blood it is?"

Whicher shakes his head.

"Then how's this going to work? For the judge."

"I've asked Jessica McConnell for a sample of her blood."

"What's she say?"

"She's refusing."

Fairbanks sits back. "So you need a warrant for that? Twenty-four hours on a misdemeanor charge. You need something fast." She looks at her watch. "This afternoon, marshal…"

"I know that, ma'am."

"You think you can get this through?"

"Marshal Cruz was close to arresting her last night," Whicher says, "for the task force. She thinks she was in Nashville to help her husband. I needed her back here."

"That's why I have a message from them? To call?"

Whicher sits forward in his seat. "I think something else happened, here. Something else to start this whole thing off."

Fairbanks looks at him. "You want to fill me in, marshal?"

Whicher blows out his cheeks. "A man Jessica McConnell knows has disappeared—a man she's close to. Nobody's seen him in four days. Name of Jacob Harwood, the guy's some kind of a friend or maybe a boyfriend. He attends the same church over in Hudspeth County."

"And?"

"There's speculation the guy might've taken undue interest in the daughter."

"In Bella?" Surprise is in the chief marshal's face.

"If he did," Whicher says, "it might explain the daughter going off the rails…"

"You mean the burglary charge?"

"If Jessica got wind of something, it might've led to some kind of confrontation. Between her and Harwood. The search of the house showed signs of a disturbance. It could've been a fight," Whicher says. "Maybe it could've been more than that."

Fairbanks looks at him a long moment.

"She said she went to Nashville, to family, in a blind panic."

"Why a panic?"

"She says she's scared of him. Her husband, McConnell. Afraid, now that he broke out."

The chief marshal makes a face. "You think she's credible? How about if the judge throws this out?"

"I've been thinking on that. I'll rearrest her."

"On what charge?"

"Felony kidnap of her daughter."

"With what evidence?"

"A felony charge, I get forty-eight hours, ma'am. Another forty-eight before she goes in front of a court."

Fairbanks picks a pen off the desk, turns it in her hand. "You're going to *develop* it? Develop the evidence?"

Whicher looks at his boss.

"Meaning you don't have it?"

"I keep her from running."

"That going to be enough?"

The marshal puts his head on one side. "It's going to have to be enough."

⭐

The lot in front of the elementary school is filled with cars and trucks, every space taken.

Whicher parks on a dirt verge a street over—kids streaming from a long, glass and pale-brick building.

He shuts off the motor in the truck, pushes open the driver door.

A flurry of light snow is in the air as he steps out.

Cold wind from the north lifts his necktie from his shirt front. The flag at the school's main entrance snaps. He pushes down the Resistol onto his head.

Groups of parents wait, standing, talking.

Clipping across the road, he heads into the lot.

Lori is with three girls; animated, laughing. Waving their hands around. Bouncing.

The marshal feels a lift in his heart.

He nods at other parents, maneuvers along a line of automobiles to where he can catch his daughter's eye. A day and two nights since he's seen her. So much going on already beyond him, Lori growing up, living her life.

She spots him.

He waves, smiles.

Surprise is on her face.

The other girls turn to look—serious, now, at the sight of him. A big man in a suit and hat.

Lori grabs her school bag, trots over.

"Where's mom?"

"I'm picking you up today, sweetheart. Want me to get your bag?"

"Uh-uh. I can do it."

Whicher fights the urge to reach out and take her hand. He waits for cars to pass in the street. Crosses the road with her. Tiny flecks of snow blowing, Lori dressed in a light, cotton top.

"Aren't you cold?"

"*No*," she says.

She rolls her eyes.

He opens up the truck.

Lori throws in her bag.

Whicher walks around to the driver door, climbs in. He starts the motor. Waits as his daughter fastens her seatbelt. Signals, pulls out into the street.

Lori turns, waves at kids on the sidewalk.

He feels a familiar sense of gratitude, the uncomplicated bond for his child.

He turns to her. "So, you okay?"

She sits forward, smiling. At some new thought. Reaches out a hand. "Sure," she says. She stabs at a button on the dash. "Can we put the radio on?"

Pulling onto a four-lane highway, sun breaks through the gunmetal cloud. Bruised cloud, filled with the threat of snow, of weather to come.

He thinks of Jessica.

Thinks of Bella.

At the house, at the kitchen table, Whicher finishes up a plate of chicken-fried steak and white gravy. He watches snow falling from the November afternoon sky. Settling in a thin white layer out in the yard.

Leanne sits at the breakfast bar with Lori; Lori writing into a notebook.

The marshal pushes the plate aside, fatigued, three scant hours of sleep since returning from Tennessee.

"I get you anything else?" Leanne says.

"Thanks. I'm all good."

"Are you headed back in?"

"Have to make a preliminary hearing," Whicher says, "before the court day is through."

Lori slides from her stool, skips across the kitchen to put the notebook onto the table.

Whicher studies the page, sees the score for math, reads the teacher's comments. He smiles at her. "Excellent."

His daughter bounces from foot to foot.

"You get your brains from your mother."

She takes back the book.

He squeezes her arm.

"You want to finish that up in your room?" Leanne says.

Whicher stands, walks to the kitchen window.

Leanne pours coffee from the pot. "You alright?"

Lori runs out of the kitchen.

The marshal takes a cup of coffee from his wife. "Waiting on a blood sample."

"Blood?"

"From Jessica McConnell," he says. "Something

might've happened—at the house where she's living."

"It's not…" Leanne lowers her voice, "not the daughter?"

The marshal stares at snow gathering on outdoor furniture in the yard. "Bella was in a hostel in Fort Stockton, last time anybody saw her."

"It couldn't be her?"

"It could," Whicher says. "If that's where she went."

Leanne clears away the empty plate from the table, puts it onto the countertop. "How long was she missing before anybody knew?"

"Not long," Whicher says. "At the hostel, they reported it when she didn't come back. It was probably less than an hour." The marshal watches his wife. Watches her move around the kitchen. "You think a woman would divorce her husband—if he was sent to prison for a long time?"

She meets his eye.

"Jessica McConnell's still married." The marshal thinks of Evelyn Cruz, of the interview in Nashville. "Criminal conviction is grounds for divorce. The state of Tennessee."

"Her husband is the father of her child."

Whicher turns back to watching snow falling silent beyond the kitchen window.

"What do you think she's done," Leanne says, "this woman?"

The marshal doesn't answer.

Only studies the wide, bleak sky.

Outside the Public Defender's office in the courthouse building, Silvia Gonzalez watches him walk in. She stands, weight on one leg.

Whicher tips the brim of his hat.

"I saw your truck come in the parking lot." Gonzalez pushes back the sleeve of her suit. Checks her watch. "It's getting late. You still intend putting my client before a hearing for probable cause?"

"I'm waiting on the sheriff's office in Hudspeth…"

"Based on what you've got," Gonzalez cuts in, "the court will dismiss for sure. And my client will sue for wrongful arrest if this is thrown out."

The marshal looks at her.

"Furthermore, I think it's in the best interests of your investigation if you release her."

"Ma'am. I'll let the judge make that determination."

Gonzalez gives him a cool look.

"My interest is the well-being of the daughter. I have a blood sample warrant pending on Jessica McConnell. I expect to serve it."

"I think you're making a mistake."

The marshal touches a finger to the brim of his hat again. Steps away.

Gonzalez re-enters her office.

Whicher takes a set of stairs to the second floor.

Opening a door with a security pass, he clips along polished tile to the USMS office.

He enters a code, steps inside.

Chief Marshal Fairbanks's door is open, she sees him,

waves him over. "I just spent the last half-hour talking with the county attorney…"

Whicher steps into her office.

"You want to close the door?" Fairbanks says. "They're not happy—with charging Jessica McConnell. They think it's premature. You're going to have to turn her loose."

"Ma'am?"

"If the judge dismisses the charge of obstruction, it could prejudice the case. Silvia Gonzalez is threatening to sue on behalf of McConnell, citing lack of evidence."

"How about if the judge upholds it?"

"I don't think they will," Fairbanks says. "Based on what you have."

"Ma'am, the blood sample could change things, we could get that today."

"So get it," Fairbanks says. "And rearrest her."

Whicher leans his weight against his boss's door. "How about if Evelyn Cruz issues an arrest warrant for her?"

"If she has evidence, let her," the chief marshal says. "Listen, I'm not saying you're wrong about this, I'm saying we can't hold her. Not yet. Last thing we want is to have it look like we mishandled the case, exerted undue pressure."

"I want Jessica McConnell under pressure," Whicher says, "I'm trying to find her daughter, I want her talking. I had reasonable grounds to bring her back."

"Your evidence is thin, marshal. I want you to go over to the Reeves jail—and sign her out."

"And if she takes off again?"

"Then we'll find her again. Go see her, turn her loose.

You get your warrant, we'll demand the blood sample, we'll bring her in again. I want you looking for her daughter, marshal. I'm not interested in Jessica McConnell. Whatever she did, whatever she didn't do. That's what you're here for. Find the child."

Chapter Twenty-Three

The view from the window of the bus on the interstate highway is a blur of shape and movement in the freezing rain.

Jessica McConnell breathes the overheated air, nausea in her stomach heightened by the motion of the bus.

She sits alone at a window seat. Staring out at the road. Eyes unfocused. Thinking of the marshal, the jail. Lack of sleep. The distance to Nashville. The words of the attorney, Silvia Gonzalez. The emptiness of words. Urging her to stand up, to not give in.

To oppression. To men coercing her, against her will.

Barely breathing, now. Sitting on a bus, arms around herself. Trying to hold back the sick feeling. A brittle hollowness, inside.

She thinks of the blood in the house, her house.

The image of the marshal. Resolve behind his eyes.

Talk of a warrant from the sheriff's office—a warrant for her blood.

Shuddering in the seat, she glances up the aisle between the rows. A few other passengers are spread out along the bus. None of them noticing.

Her.

The turmoil inside.

Though weight pins her, deadens her thoughts, her limbs.

She stares at ice rain on the window.

Takes the prepaid phone from her bag.

Stares at it. Says a silent prayer.

She enters in a number from memory. Studies the network bars.

For long seconds only dead space stretches between bursts of a ring tone.

She presses the phone against the side of her face.

And then his voice is in her ear.

"Jessica?"

The sound of him far away, distant.

"Where are you?"

"On a bus." She swallows. "I have to go get my car. I was arrested. Last night," she says. "By a marshal. Brought back here."

Only silence answers her.

"Here?" he says, finally.

"To Texas. Now they've let me go. I have to get my car. From the airport. I left it, when I flew out."

"Why were you arrested?"

"They thought I was lying. Lying to them, obstructing them. They're trying to find Bella…"

"Who is?"

"This marshal."

The line goes quiet.

And then his voice is back again. "I've been waiting hours for you to call."

"I couldn't call." Jessica stares at the blur of land outside the window.

"I didn't know where you were," his voice rising, "I didn't know what was going on…"

"Just listen," she says, "please." She sinks in her seat. "Where are you? Where are you now?"

"I'm back. I drove all night."

"You're back here now?"

"I slept in the car on the road. It took me all night, I just got in."

"Did you leave Bella?"

"She's with your sister, with Ursula."

Jessica closes her eyes a moment. Opens them. "Alright. I need to meet you."

His voice is wary. "Where?"

A prickle of cold sweat is on her brow, now, despite the heat. She says, "You know where."

⅄

Light snow is on the scrub-covered hills, a world of tans and dirty whites against a primer-gray sky.

Jessica McConnell drives the aging Nissan deep onto the Harwood property.

She can see him.

She can see him by the side of the big barn—its plank sides patched in places, shingles missing from the roof.

She sees the Ram pickup parked to one side.

He stands long-limbed, a raw-boned cowboy.

Pulling in front of the barn, she sits, looking out. At wind blowing in the mesquite beneath the wintry sky.

She cuts the motor, pushes open the door. Pulls herself out against the wheel.

He starts toward her. Looking half-dead. In a Carhartt work jacket, jeans and boots.

"Jacob," she says.

He stops. Stands to watch her.

She brushes her ink-dark hair behind her ear.

"I came straight here," he says. "After I got back. I dumped the car. Got my truck."

She studies his face—the skin lined, fatigued. His blue eyes sunken. Dark-blond hair matted, a mess.

He manages a tired-looking smile. Takes another step toward her. Handsome, despite the weariness in his face.

She moves, uncertain.

He puts his arms around her, pulls her in, holds her.

She breathes against his chest.

Moment after moment. In the cold wind. Paralyzed. Numb.

"I moved it," he tells her.

She doesn't respond.

"It's gone. It's gone, now."

She takes a half-step back, looks toward the big barn, searches his face.

"I put it in the ground."

She nods, no words.

He takes her arm. Starts to lead her into the high-grown brush. "I got it out of there, out of the barn, dragged it out."

Jessica sees a small clearing—newly dug earth covering a spot on the ground.

"Jacob…"

"It can't stay like that," he says, "showing like that. I'll come back. Tomorrow. With a chainsaw."

She looks at him, wildness in her eyes.

He shakes his head. "I'll clear some of the land, cut down a bunch of mesquite, greasewood, palo verde. I'll make a pile. I'll burn it. I'll burn it all. Burn the tarp with it…"

Jessica stares at the spot on the ground.

"Burn what's inside," he says.

She puts her arms about herself. Watches snow settling, whitening the pile of raw earth.

"No one can ever know…about this."

Harwood looks at her.

She nods, quickly.

"No one can ever know."

"If you make a big fire…will people be…suspicious?" Her voice is tiny in her throat.

"Folk clear their land all the time. Else it gets choked, you can't get on it. Wintertime I can burn it. Besides, nobody ever comes. This is private acreage." He sweeps an arm in the direction of the hills.

Jessica gazes at the twin barns, pictures afternoons spent away from prying eyes.

Long afternoons in the September heat. The two of them, alone. Alone upon the surface of the world. Only blue sky above them. A blanket beneath. Warmth in the wind, an icebox of cold beer. No rules. No expectations. No demands.

Free from all of it. From responsibility. From getting by, trying to make ends meet. From wagging tongues at the church, the gossip of a small town.

From resentful daughters.

She turns back to stare at the spot in the clearing. "Will it snow tonight?"

"It's cold enough," Harwood says.

"Will it cover it? Will you have to…dig it up?"

He lets his eyes meet hers a moment. "I'll do what I have to do."

She puts her hands over her face.

Harwood touches her on the shoulder.

She flinches, despite herself. "Tell me about Bella?"

"I took her, like you told me. Took her right there."

She lets her arms fall limp to her sides. "Why did he have to bring me back? The marshal. If they're watching, now, how can I go there?"

A bitter edge is in the wind.

Harwood only stands and stares.

At the sky darkening above the hills.

Chapter Twenty-Four

Little Molasses River, Gladwin County, Michigan

The first light of dawn is at the window of the cabin, cold and dim and dank and hard. Travis McConnell pulls the sleeping bag about himself. He listens to the wind outside in the mass of oak and pine.

Two hours by road north of Detroit.

A deer camp. A forest clearing. Miles from anywhere. From people. From cops.

He peers into a corner of the cabin at the sleeping figure of his daughter on a canvas cot. Thinks of Reed Barbone in the second cabin. Jacked on animal-grade antibiotics. Fentanyl for the pain.

Half the time in a sweat of fever, half the time out of it. Raving.

One phone call into Detroit.

One call. All it took.

To know that law enforcement were set up—looking out for Barbone. Around his neighborhood, around his old home. No way of going in there, nowhere safe in the city.

But a deer camp, two cabins, out in the sticks.

Good enough.

A friend of Barbone's owned it. Drove up to Flint, gave them keys. Drugs. A few days to hole up.

On the cot in the corner, Bella turns on her side, hutches the sleeping bag and the blanket higher.

She lifts her head an inch from a pillow. Looks at him. Eyes half open. "Dad? Are you awake?"

"Uh-huh."

She draws up her knees.

"You alright?" he says.

"Mmm."

"Can't you sleep?"

"I don't know." Bella turns again, lays on her back. "How long are we going to be here?"

He sees her face now, in the light seeping into the cabin window. Sees her gazing up at the roof—at the rough wood joists and planks overhead.

"I mean, how long will we stay?"

"Not long," he answers. "Not too long."

She stares up at the ceiling. "Why'd we have to come all the way up here?"

McConnell thinks of the eight-hour trip from Tennessee up to Michigan. Counting on Detroit to be something. "Reed just needs to rest up," he says. "Then we'll move again."

"It's cold," Bella says.

"It's not so cold."

"It's colder than Texas."

In his mind's eye McConnell pictures Jessica, he feels a familiar pull in the pit of his gut.

He watches his daughter. Frames and reframes a question in his mind—careful to think of the right words to say before he speaks them. "Your mom...was going to be there? That night?"

"I told you."

"In Nashville? The night I got there?"

Bella turns, looks across the cabin toward him. "*Yes.*"

McConnell thinks it over again, saying nothing—thinking only of the tone in his daughter's voice; matter of fact, neutral. "And she had this friend bring you on up? She was going to be there? Meet you there? At Ursula's?"

"That's what she told me."

McConnell thinks it over for the hundredth time.

Why hadn't she been there?

Bella sets her head back on the pillow. "She told me we were going away. Because of all the...trouble."

He looks at her. "With the court?"

"That. And everything else going on. The crowd I got mixed up in," she says. "And the juvenile court. I had nothing to do with that burglary, I told mom, I told everybody. I told the woman from child protection. But no one ever listens. I've told them over and over. I was just *there*, I didn't *do* anything, I didn't even go in that house."

Her head turns a fraction.

"I believe you," he says.

He sees the smile; her smile directed at him, through the gloom of dawn.

"I told the others to leave it. They were just…fooling around. Mom thinks they're going to put me in a center, some youth detention center, you know? Lock me away. They already put me in that lame hostel."

McConnell sits up higher on the makeshift bed.

Bella looks at him. "I need to go outside."

"Uh?"

"I need to…you know…"

"You want to go out? You want to go to the outhouse?"

She nods. "Will you come?"

"What for?"

"I mean, it's dark outside. It's horrible. I don't like it."

McConnell pushes the sleeping bag off of him, still fully dressed from the night before. He grabs an old wool coat from a bunch of jackets on the wall. "You don't need to be afraid."

Bella maneuvers from under the tangle of blanket and sleeping bag.

"You got me," McConnell says, "you've got your father now. I'll take care of you. Nobody's going to do a thing."

Bella pulls up the hood on her purple top, covering the mess of long, dark hair.

She stands. Shivers slightly.

"Put on one of those coats." McConnell points at the row hanging from hooks on the wall.

"They're disgusting."

"Yeah. They'll keep you warm." He stands, pulls on his boots, fastens the plaid wool coat about himself.

Bella slips on her sneakers, takes down a battered camo

parka, puts it around her, makes a face.

McConnell steps to the door, unlocks it. He squints out into growing twilight. Scans the forest, the clearing. Hears the sound of water running in a nearby stream.

He pushes the door wide. Walks out to a rough timber porch.

Twenty yards off is the outhouse—built from planks and a rusted tin roof.

McConnell steps down, starts to walk toward it.

Bella follows.

Ten yards short, he stops. Lets his daughter go on ahead.

"So yell," he says. "If you need me."

She walks on in front of him, reaches the outhouse, yanks open the door. "Gross," she says.

McConnell steps back to the cabin. Sits on the edge of the porch.

He eyes the line of the forest, leaves already down from half the trees. Their branches a crazed skein in the dawn's early light. He thinks of his Jessica. Silent. Still no word. No sign.

No sign of her in Nashville.

No word from Texas.

But she was bound to come; Bella was everything. The best thing to ever happen in her life.

The good life, he tells himself; their life together. Nashville—he'd made it a good life. But then he'd pushed too hard.

Taken one too many risks.

The time that followed was all dark time. Prison. Slow death. Days spent inside a cage. He stuffs his hands into the pockets of the coat, feels the hard edges of the Sig. Nothing would ever take him back again.

The door on the outhouse opens.

Bella steps out.

She shudders in the parka.

"You alright?"

"It smells disgusting in there."

"So, don't breathe in."

She walks over, holds the coat closed at her front. "I have to *breathe*."

McConnell grins. "Quit sassin'."

Bella sits on the edge of the porch. Her mouth open. "What's that?" she says.

McConnell follows the line of her gaze to where a stream skirts the edge of the woodland—grass and reed growing from its banks.

Two men are standing beneath the trees.

Two men.

Rifles slung at their backs.

They're dressed in woodland gear, boots and hats, overtrousers, camo pattern coats.

McConnell feels his pulse quicken.

He pushes up from the porch.

The men are staring right at the cabin—right at them. Staring, silent, from out of the woods.

"What's going on?" he calls over.

They both look at him.

Look at Bella.

But neither man answers.

⊥

Hudspeth County, Tx

A thin covering of snow is on Cammack Avenue—Deputy Raylene Lapointe sees the Ram pickup on the driveway of the three-bed ranch.

A light in the house catches her eye as she studies the property—a light in a window at the front.

She takes her foot off the gas, slows the cruiser.

The truck has moved, the Ram—it's moved slightly.

Twice a day she's seen it going in to work, coming back.

It's parked a few feet closer to the road.

She stops the cruiser at the foot of the driveway, stares at the house. At the light showing in the kitchen window.

No light was on before.

She checks her watch.

Just gone seven-thirty in the morning.

She takes out a notepad from her shirt pocket. Writes down the time.

Switching off the motor, she steps from the car, pulls on a sheriff's department ball cap.

Walking over the snow in the driveway, she sees faint footprints.

Footprints leading all the way to the door.

She looks in the kitchen window, sees nothing. Checks the other windows along the front. Nothing in there either.

She knocks hard.

Listens for any sound.

Somebody is moving around inside the house.

She hears the muffled sound of footfall.

Takes a half-pace back from the door as it opens.

Jacob Harwood stands looking out. Dressed in jeans, boots, a sweat top, his dark blond hair a mess.

She searches his face. "Jacob," she says. She sees tension.

Harwood peers over her shoulder at the county sheriff's cruiser at the foot of his drive. He dips his head. "I do something for you?"

"Matter of fact," the deputy says, "I didn't really expect to see you here."

"How's that?"

"I've been coming by. The last three days. Every morning. Every night. Trying to find you. Looking for you."

Harwood stares at her, blank-faced.

"No one's seen you in church," the deputy says.

"You were looking for me?"

"Nobody's seen you around, nobody's seen you anyplace."

He shrugs. Runs a hand through his hair.

She looks past him into the hallway. "Jacob. Can I come in?"

"I don't get it. What's going on?"

"Is anyone here with you?" the deputy says.

"Excuse me?"

"Are you alone in the house?"

He looks at her. "Am I alone?" He nods, slowly. "Sure."

"Nobody else is in there?"

"I told you, no."

"Can you show me?"

He frowns. "Why would you want me to show you?"

"I need to come inside."

Harwood stands a moment. Then moves back, away from the door.

She follows him into a kitchen.

He crosses the room, leans against the sink, against the drain board.

"I need to make sure," the deputy says.

"Make sure of what?"

"That nobody else is in here. That there's nobody else."

He shakes his head. "What's going on, Raylene?"

"Where have you been?" she says. "The last few days?"

His face is clouded. "I've been out of town, away."

She looks at him. "Doing what?"

"I went over to a buddy of mine…"

"Oh?" Deputy Lapointe puts her head on one side. "Male, female? Maybe I'd know 'em?"

"No." He shakes his head. "What's going on? How come you're asking me that?"

"Where'd you go?"

"What?"

"Where d'you go to see this 'buddy'?"

"What're you even doing here?" Harwood says.

"Sheriff's office have been trying to speak with you for three days straight," the deputy says. "You haven't been here, you haven't been around. In church. Or anyplace else…"

"I can't go someplace?"

"Sure you can."

"So?"

"So, where were you?"

He folds his arms over his chest. "Out of town."

"Have you seen Jessica McConnell, lately?" Deputy Lapointe looks at him.

"Jessica? No."

"You haven't seen her?"

"Should I?"

"Well," the deputy says. "Thing of it is, nobody's seen her either."

Harwood unfolds his arms. "That all has something to do with me?"

Deputy Lapointe eyes the empty dish rack, the bare countertops in the kitchen, sees no sign of anything in use. "The two of you seem pretty friendly."

He makes a face.

"I'm not saying you shouldn't be. But I mean, most folk in church," she says, "they think you're, you know. An item."

"What is this?" he says. "What's going on?"

"I need you to show me that nobody else is in your house, Jacob."

He pushes off the drainer. "Where do you want to start?"

She looks him up and down. "No matter. Wherever. Just show me."

Harwood reddens, stalks from the kitchen.

He stands outside the door to a living room. Walks inside.

Deputy Lapointe follows.

Nobody is in the room.

"You seriously want to look in the bedrooms?" he says. "The bathroom?"

"I'm sparing you having your house searched by a team with a warrant."

His eyes are wide as he looks at her.

Lapointe regards him steadily.

Harwood leads her down the hall to a closed door. Opens it. "I don't use this," he says. "It's a spare."

The deputy looks inside, sees a large armoire. "Open that, please."

"Seriously?"

"Yes, Jacob."

"What do you think I've got in there?"

"Just open it," the deputy says.

"Why does the sheriff's office want to talk to me, Raylene?"

"Because the Marshals Service want to talk to you, Jacob."

"The Marshals?"

"Because they're looking for a missing minor. Jessica's daughter. The girl's been gone six days."

⋏

Lying on her side, bone awake on the bed in her house, Jessica McConnell stares at the discolored mark on the carpet—visible, still, despite all the cleaning—its outline clear in the early morning light.

Drained. Her body drained from lack of sleep.

Trying to banish an image that keeps on coming—the hills, the barns, Jacob's property, the ranch land north of town.

She thinks of a fire.

To burn everything. Burn to nothing what was buried.

Rising suddenly from the bed, she steps to the window. Stares out at light snow still covering the ground. Grateful. Grateful for that, at least. A mask; a white mask for the raw earth, for the new-dug grave.

She shakes herself.

She should eat something, get something. Then go to Jacob, help him. Help him set the fire. Feed it. Keep it going. Till everything was burned away.

She sits at the edge of the bed. Picks a cardigan sweater from the floor.

The telephone starts to ring.

She moves into the hallway, stares at it, snatches it up.

"Jess?"

The sound of her sister's voice on the line is jolting—a shock to her brain.

"You're in Texas? You went home?"

"Ursula? Yes…"

"You weren't going to *call* me?"

She stands mute, the heat in her sister's voice working into her. "So much has happened…"

"You couldn't call? Why didn't you come see me before you left?"

"I couldn't."

"Why the hell *not?*"

"I just couldn't…"

"You just take your daughter and go?"

"What do you mean?" Jessica says.

"You didn't think to tell me?"

"She's not with you?" Jessica stares down the hall, a hand at her midriff, breath stopped.

Ursula's voice is high, tight. "Are you telling me she's not with *you?*"

Jessica forces herself to be calm. "What happened?"

"What do you mean what happened? Your guy showed up with her, at the bar. Jacob?"

"Jacob, right."

"He said you were coming. To get her."

"I know…" Jessica says.

"So he left. He left Bella, he said you'd be there. We were busy, running the damn bar, I was running the bar for Christ's sake—then later she was gone."

"Okay, okay…"

"What do you mean 'okay'?" Ursula's voice is on the verge of breaking. "If she's not with you, where is she? I haven't seen her since then…"

"She runs off," Jessica cuts in. "She's always running off…"

"What?"

"She's been doing it for months, it's her thing, it's what she does."

Moments hang in silence as the line goes quiet.

"She ran off?" Ursula finally says.

"She's home, she's home in Nashville," Jessica says, "she's where she grew up, she knows the neighborhood, she knows everybody—she'll be with some friend, some friend from before…"

Ursula stops her. "You're not worried?"

"Of course I'm worried…She's been doing this over and over," Jessica says, "it's been going on for months." She leans her back against the wall, steadies herself. "It's all part of all the trouble, it's what she does. I've had to learn to deal with it."

Jessica listens to the sound of her sister's breath.

"Well, I don't know what to say."

She massages her brow, kneads the skin between her fingers. "Look, I was coming," Jessica says. "And then I was arrested."

"Jess. What the hell?"

"I went to see that marshal, like you told me. I went to meet with him. I just went to talk. And then he made me go downtown, we went to this office. And then he interviewed me with this other marshal. This whole thing. And then he just arrested me, he just came right out. And he flew me back down here. And he put me in jail, I was in the jail till yesterday afternoon…"

"God, Jess. What for?"

"Obstruction. That's what he said. I got a lawyer, she told him to let me go."

"I've been calling and calling…"

"I was in jail."

"My God, Jessica. What are you doing, what's going on?"

"I'll come back up, I'll find her." Jessica chews a thumbnail, thinks of Jacob, of the fire, of the fire she has to make. "Tomorrow..."

"Tomorrow?"

"I'll call everybody, I'll call around, see if anybody in the neighborhood knows who she's with."

"What if she's not with anyone?"

"She will be," Jessica says, "she will. Look, I know it's a shock—to think like this. But, honestly..." her voice is flat, "it's what I do, I've gotten used to it."

"Really?"

"Truly. I've had a lot of nights on my own. Days without her. Days and days. And a lot of nights. I've learned to live with it."

"I don't know how you can..."

"I had no choice."

Ursula softens, "What can I do? What can I do here?"

"Just be there," Jessica says. "Until I can get there. If she needs you, she can find you, she knows she has a safe place."

"You really think she's alright, Jess? You really think she's okay?"

Jessica sinks to her haunches. A sick feeling at her stomach, dryness in her mouth. "I told you," she says. "I've learned to believe it. I don't have any other choice."

CHAPTER TWENTY-FIVE

Pecos, Tx

Approaching the intersection with West Third on South Eddy, Whicher pulls up at a stop light in front of a vintage clothes boutique. The wipers on the Silverado beat time on the windshield. A light fall of snow is in the air.

Heat is cranked in the cab of the truck, blowing hard. He runs a hand across his freshly shaved jaw.

Through the steel bars on the clothes store window, racks of old-time dresses from the fifties and sixties hang immobile, misfits out of time and place. Gowns from long-forgotten proms and balls. Slashes of color suspended in the pale morning air.

He pictures Jessica McConnell. Her strange look—luminous eyes.

Out of step with a far West Texas town. Out of sync.

The stop light changes.

He shifts the truck into drive, pulls away.

Thinks of two calls—the first to Georgia Eastman from

the Juvenile Protection Service. The second to the hostel in Fort Stockton—to Rafaela Salinas, the supervisor there.

Eastman had been a callback. Straight to voicemail, then she'd called; anxious. Too used to breaking bad news to disbelieving parents.

Rafaela Salinas had nothing for him.

Jessica was back, he told them. But there was no word on Bella. No word yet.

The marshal drives the cross-town highway. Low sun in his eyes, the road covered in a dirty brown slush of snow.

Thinking on Bella. A young girl. Barely two years older than his own.

A daughter rested, fed, dressed in clean clothes. On her way to school like any morning.

He thinks of Jessica on the Nashville bridge. Lights of downtown behind her. And in the jail cell. The white-painted interview room. Out of reach. Somehow unknowable, still.

Half a mile up the road he spots the sign for the Mexican diner.

He checks the time—just gone eight-thirty in the morning.

The phone in the dash-holder lights up.

Whicher reads the name on screen.

Deputy Marshal Evelyn Cruz.

He clicks to speaker.

"Marshal. I tried your office," she says, "you weren't there."

"I'm headed out to breakfast. With my boss. You still up in Nashville, where you at?"

"Michigan. I've got news. On my escapees."

"Hold on," the marshal says, "I'm pulling over."

He checks the highway, turns in on the lot of a truck and auto parts store.

"What's happening with Jessica McConnell?" Cruz says. "Is she talking?"

"Not talking."

"She's pleading the fifth?"

"She'll answer questions," Whicher says. "She won't tell me what's going on. You have news on your escapees?"

Cruz ignores the question. "Will you let her go?"

"Already done."

"You let her walk?"

"She has a defense attorney threatening to sue for harassment. I might arrest her again."

"What for?"

"Felony kidnap."

"You think she has her daughter?"

"I think she might know where she is," Whicher says.

"You take her away," Cruz says, "and now she's out again?"

"So far she is. I've asked the county sheriff to apply for a warrant—for a blood sample."

Cruz lets a beat pass.

Whicher peers through the windshield at flakes of snow settling on the Chevy hood. "There's blood on the wall in her house…"

"If you wanted to pressure her," Cruz says, "you should have left her with me, in Nashville."

"You about to tell me what's going on?"

"Two things," Cruz says. "First, we've been trying to figure out how they're moving. We think we have a lead on a vehicle these guys could be in. The task force looked into the incident in Clarksville—where they were first spotted—driving a Grand Marquis. We know about that, we know the prison guard supplied the vehicle. But they abandoned it in the lot of a Kroger store."

"Right."

"Now we think we know how they're moving. A guy that owns a next-door business has gone missing—he's been missing this whole time. Nobody reported him gone. The guy lives alone. His business is next door to the supermarket. His name is Dupris, Kendrick Dupris. He owns a pawnbroker business and credit agency right over in the next lot. We think they might have taken him against his will. His car's gone, they might have taken it. It's a Mazda. A black SUV."

"Nobody's seen this guy? Nobody's seen the car?"

"No. And witnesses at the robbery of the sporting goods store mentioned a black SUV," Cruz says.

"You have the guy's home address?" Whicher says. "Have law enforcement been inside?"

"Yesterday. Metro-area police went in, they said it looked like somebody ransacked the place."

"So, there's a possible vehicle."

"We've put out an attempt-to-locate."

Whicher thinks about it. "ATL should get you something. You said two things?"

"The other thing," Cruz says, "is the reason I'm up here—up in Michigan."

⋏

Inside the Mexican diner, business is brisk—the talk muted among the morning crowd. Whicher sits with Chief Deputy Marshal Fairbanks at a table by the window—eating migas and breakfast tacos filled with chorizo and eggs.

"Evelyn Cruz thinks they left Tennessee," Whicher says. "She thinks they've been gone twenty-four hours. Maybe more."

"There's been no further sign of them in Tennessee?"

Whicher shakes his head. "They had a report—from Detroit, Michigan. One of the escapees is from Detroit. The task force suspect Jessica McConnell of being in Nashville to help her husband. If they're gone, they could be looking for help in the other guy's neighborhood."

Across the street from the restaurant, Hispanic day laborers gather at the front of a construction yard. Whicher watches the men, an uneasy feeling nagging at him, a thought sitting in the back of his mind.

The chief deputy marshal looks at him. "Are you going to eat?"

Whicher takes a bite on a burrito. "I'm eating."

"Tell me about the report?" Fairbanks says.

"A Detroit area cop saw a Mazda SUV," he says, "three people in it. The driver was male, wearing a ball cap, he didn't get a plate. The vehicle was waiting at a stop light. The cop noticed it, drove by, didn't think much about it. A couple of blocks down he thought about it some more—he turned around, went back up the road. But the car was gone."

Chief Marshal Fairbanks nods, takes a sip on a cup of coffee.

"The cop said he searched but couldn't find it again. He reported it just in case. Detroit was one of the places the task force targeted, he'd seen a BOLO—law enforcement knew to look out. The guy in the ball cap tweaked his interest. But it's a common enough vehicle," Whicher says. "The thing that threw him was seeing a young girl in the car—in the front passenger seat. He thought it couldn't be them."

"What're you saying?" Fairbanks leans forward. "You think that was her?"

"Evelyn Cruz does."

"She thinks that could be Bella McConnell?" The chief marshal stares at him. "How about you?"

"I got a bad feeling."

"Have there been no other sightings of her?"

"No, ma'am."

Fairbanks exhales a long, drawn-out breath.

"Maybe we'll get lucky," Whicher says. "Maybe someone else will spot them."

"You think this guy could have his daughter with him?"

"I want to know if he could've talked to her," Whicher says, "before he broke out."

Fairbanks looks at him, a question in her face.

"He conned a female CO at the prison into helping him. Maybe he conned the CO into getting him access to a phone.

I need to speak to the hostel, in Fort Stockton," Whicher says. "I need to go on back to Hudspeth."

Across the table, thoughts work behind the chief marshal's eyes.

Whicher regards his boss a moment.

Finally she speaks. "Could Jessica McConnell have taken her to him?"

Chapter Twenty-Six

Across from the house the German Shepherd shifts from its place beneath the oak. On the hard dirt yard is the twenty-year-old Nissan. The marshal cuts the motor on the Silverado. Steps out.

The dog growls as he walks by.

Whicher checks the neighbor's yard—no sign of any vehicle.

At the front door he knocks. Bunches his shoulders at the cold wind blowing from the north. A ranch coat is on the rear seat of the truck. He thinks of going back to get it.

The door opens.

Jessica McConnell stands in the frame.

She's dressed in jeans and a hooded top. Her face pale, guarded. "Marshal," she says. "You let me out of jail, now you're back again?"

The marshal's eyes cut to the hallway. "If I could come on inside?"

Jessica McConnell steps back.

Whicher follows her down the hallway to the kitchen.

She stands at the window, folds her arms over her chest.

"Has your daughter made contact with you?" the marshal says.

"I guess that means you haven't found her?"

Whicher takes in the view from the kitchen window—bleak scrub, clumps of prickly pear, low hills covered with snow. "We think Bella could be with her father, now. With your husband. With Travis."

Her lips part.

No words come out.

"A police officer in Detroit thinks he spotted a vehicle we believe your husband may be using."

"I don't understand…"

"The officer said a girl was in the vehicle. Riding in the vehicle."

"They spotted Travis? Somebody saw him in a car?"

"The vehicle disappeared. The officer couldn't find it again."

Jessica says nothing. A vein pulses at her throat.

"It's possible it's just a mistake."

"De*troit?*" she says.

"The escapee with your husband has connections to the Detroit area. It's possible they'd go there. To get help."

"With my daughter?"

Whicher watches Jessica McConnell a long moment. "We think your husband was in the Nashville area, ma'am. You know that. We're pretty certain he pulled a robbery fifty miles from there."

No response.

"You were in Nashville."

The young woman's face colors, "We've been over all this…"

"Was Bella out in Nashville, too?"

Turning from his gaze, Jessica touches the back of her hand to her face. She stares at the floor. "You're telling me my daughter is in Detroit?"

"I asked you was she in Nashville?"

She shakes her head, eyes blank. "How could she possibly be in Detroit?"

⚔

Outside in the yard, Whicher keys the number for the Hudspeth County law enforcement center. Reception puts him through to Sheriff Ingram.

"It's Whicher," the marshal says, "I'm over at Jessica McConnell's place. Did you get that warrant? For the sample of her blood?"

"No can do," the sheriff answers. "The judge won't agree it. But there's something I need to let you know here—our missing boy is back."

"Say again?"

"Jacob Harwood. He's back. One of my deputies was by this morning, she's been driving by every day."

"He's here, now? At the house? What did he say?"

"It's what he *didn't* say."

"Excuse me?"

"He's given no account of his whereabouts the last three days. The deputy did a walk-through of the house. Nobody was there, there's no sign of your girl. But his demeanor was troubling, according to my deputy. She knows him pretty well, they attend the same church. He can't or won't account for his absence—so, I telephoned the on-call judge. I have a warrant issued to search his property."

"You're going in?"

"We're heading out to execute it, marshal. It's your case—but my office has the right to know what's going on here—I won't have my deputies' questions go unanswered. This thing's happening, this morning. If you want to be there, you best get over."

⚔

Whicher pulls up in front of the three-bed ranch on Cammack Avenue.

Two cruisers and an SUV from the sheriff's department are out on the street in front of the house.

On the drive is the Ram pickup.

Blocking it in, a silver cargo van—a GMC Savana, its sliding rear-door open.

At the side of the pickup, a man in a blue zip suit swabs the handle of the passenger door.

Posted at the edge of the property a uniformed deputy watches.

The marshal cuts the motor on the truck.

He elbows open the door, swings down from the Silverado. Takes out the USMS badge-holder. Holds it out.

The deputy checks it—a lean Hispanic in his forties.

"Like to talk to the sheriff. Is Jacob Harwood here?" Whicher says.

"He's with Sheriff Ingram, inside, sir. I think."

The marshal watches the evidence recovery technician place a sample from the door in a zip lock bag.

"I'll go see if the sheriff can come out," the deputy says.

Whicher nods. Watches the deputy walk back up the driveway to the front door.

Faces are at the windows of some of the neighboring houses, people watching—a few already out in their yards.

Sheriff Odell Ingram appears in the doorway. Dressed in a winter coat, a Western hat. He raises a hand.

The Hispanic deputy walks back down the driveway.

Whicher takes a pace up the yard. "You got a warrant for the house and the truck?" He inclines his head toward the pickup.

"The property," Sheriff Ingram says, "plus any vehicle on the property."

"Looking for what?"

"Any sign of Bella McConnell."

"Judge thinks you have probable cause?" Whicher says.

"In the case of a missing child, yes."

"But not for the blood sample from Jessica McConnell?"

The sheriff's eyes narrow. "Different judge this morning."

"So, you find anything?"

Ingram shakes his head. "So far, no."

"How about Harwood?"

"Says he was out of town the last few days." The sheriff scowls. Stuffs his hands into the pockets of his coat. "The deputy that spoke to him this morning said she thought he was flat-out lying."

Whicher eyes the house. Scans the yard, the Ram pickup. "USMS have reported a possible sighting—of Bella."

"Say again?"

"In Michigan—the Detroit area."

"You serious?"

"I just heard this morning," Whicher says. "A patrol car reported a vehicle she may have been in."

"How the hell they figure on that?"

"They think she could be with her father. They think they spotted the vehicle he could be using."

The sheriff pulls on the brim of his hat. Confusion showing in his face.

"The task force think it's credible. The guy that busted out with Bella's father is from Detroit. Law enforcement were looking for them."

"How about you," the sheriff says, "what do you think?"

Over at the Ram pickup, the evidence technician takes a sample from the passenger seatbelt.

"I want to know where this guy Harwood's been the last few days," Whicher says. "Why he's lying—if he is."

"You and me both," the sheriff says. "He's had a little time to work on his story, it still sounds like a crock. He contracts for drywall. Says he was between jobs. Says he took off, out of town, just to kick back, get away, get a change of scene."

The evidence tech climbs down from the cab of the Ram, steps around the side of the pickup to the open door on the van. He puts two zip lock bags into a plastic tray. Turns back to the pickup, lets down the tailgate. Leans low to the bed.

Whicher looks at the sheriff. "Harwood take off in that?"

"Nope. That thing's been here the whole time, my deputy drove by every day, she saw it, it never moved. But it's included in the warrant, we may as well search it."

"He has another vehicle?"

"A sedan he keeps at a warehouse he rents—he keeps a car there, plus a bunch of materials, tools, work gear."

"You going to look in there, too?"

"I need a separate warrant for that."

"You need to find something here," Whicher says.

The evidence tech climbs in the back of the pickup. He squats low, places his gloved hands on the truck bed. Searches inch by inch.

"I speak with Harwood?" Whicher says.

The sheriff nods. He looks across to the nearby deputy. "Miguel? You bring out Mister Harwood for me? He's with Raylene in there."

"Yes, sir."

The deputy clips up the yard to the front of the house.

The sheriff looks to Whicher. "If Jessica McConnell's daughter is up in Michigan with her father, what's this guy have to do with it?"

A tall figure emerges from the house—rangy, in his thirties, Whicher guesses. Lean. Good-looking. With collar-length blond hair. He walks down the yard with the Hispanic deputy. Dressed in jeans and boots, a sweat top.

The sheriff addresses him. "Mister Harwood. This here is Deputy US Marshal Whicher, he's a federal officer, he's looking into the disappearance of a minor. Bella McConnell, Jessica's girl."

Harwood gives the sheriff a nod.

"You're a hard man to find Mister Harwood," Whicher says.

The man looks at him. "Didn't know anybody was looking for me."

"Four days back I came by here. Hoping to see you."

"I would have been in El Paso."

"That right?"

Harwood nods. His eyes guarded.

"Sheriff says you contract for drywall?"

"That's right."

"Your own tab?"

"I have a team of guys."

"You're not working right now?"

Harwood rubs the forearm of his top. "I told the sheriff. I'm between jobs, I have some time till the next one gets rolling."

"That's why you weren't around?" Whicher says.

"I got done on a job in El Paso," Harwood says. "The hangers had the panels up, I have a float crew, tapers and mudders, they come in, they get it finished up. There's no need for me to be there."

"So you got done, you decided to take off?"

"Right."

"Why was that?"

Harwood looks at him. "Well, why not? Why shouldn't I?"

"Why now?"

"I told you. I had the time free."

"So, where'd you go?"

"I stayed a night in El Paso."

"Where?"

"A motel. I went out to a Mexican restaurant. Had a few beers. Hit the sack."

"Alone?"

"I went out with a couple of the guys, I ended up alone."

"Then what?"

"I took off into New Mexico for a couple days."

"What did you do?"

"Nothing much. I was just kicking back."

"Were you with someone?"

"No," Harwood says. "I wanted some time away, some time alone."

The marshal eyes him. "Mister Harwood, are you involved with a woman named Jessica McConnell?"

Harwood sniffs, looks away, then back again. "Yeah," he says. "As a matter of fact, that was part of the reason I wanted to go, to get away."

"Oh?"

Harwood looks to the sheriff and back to Whicher. "We kind of needed a break. I kind of needed a break. You know? From her."

"You broke up?" Whicher says.

Harwood blows out his cheeks. "We didn't break up. We just needed to not be around each other for a while."

"Why would that be?" Whicher says.

"I guess we have our disagreements—same as most people do."

"Did you know Jessica's daughter is missing?"

Harwood nods.

Whicher says, "Was your disagreement over Bella?"

The young man shakes his head. "No." He looks at Whicher. "Why would it be? Her daughter's her daughter…"

"Has Bella McConnell ever been inside your house?"

Harwood's expression hardens. "No."

"How about in that truck?" Whicher angles his head in the direction of the Ram pickup.

"No." Harwood glares at the man in the zip suit searching the pickup bed. "And I don't appreciate the line of questioning."

The marshal eyes him. "Why's that?"

"What do you mean by a thing like that? What do you mean? Has she been *in* there?"

"Straight question, Mister Harwood. I'm just looking for a straight answer."

"She hasn't been to this house," the young man says. "But if she had been, so what?"

"I'm trying to find a missing minor," Whicher says. "A girl that could be at risk. She's been gone six days."

Jacob Harwood's jaw tightens. "You can go ahead and search all you want to, and search the truck, too. I'm not hiding anything, I haven't done anything."

In the bed of the pickup, the evidence tech works his way toward the cab of the Ram.

Sheriff Ingram clears his throat. "Were you with anyone that could vouch for your whereabouts? The time you were away?"

Harwood looks at him. "I don't know, I guess."

"We have to look at things from all angles, Jacob," the sheriff says. "Folk around here know you and Mrs McConnell are close. If her daughter goes missing, we have to ask, we're obliged to know, we got to cover all the bases."

"You search all you want, sheriff," Harwood says.

The man in the zip suit sits up, swings his legs out over the side of the pickup. He slides to the ground. Looks across at the sheriff.

Whicher reads something in the man's face.

"Mister Harwood," the sheriff says. "Excuse us."

Whicher follows Sheriff Ingram across the yard to the side of the truck.

The evidence tech looks up into the sky. "If it keeps on snowing I need to get a canopy over this."

"The truck's been parked on the drive the last few days," the sheriff says. "And Mister Harwood doesn't seem concerned about it."

The evidence tech leans over the truck side. He points a gloved finger at an inboard winch mounted in the bed behind the cab. He keeps his voice low. "Blood on that. It looks like. On the casing of the winch and the floor around it."

Whicher leans over, studies the spot where the man's pointing. Sees nothing.

"Not much there," the man in the zip suit says. "But there's something."

"It's a work truck," the sheriff says. "Could be a nick or a cut."

"Get it covered up," Whicher says to the evidence tech.

"It might not be much of anything," the man replies.

Whicher looks at the sheriff. "Blood spatter in Jessica McConnell's house—blood here."

The sheriff eyes him.

"I want to know where it came from," Whicher says. "I want to know whose it is."

Chapter Twenty-Seven

Pulling up in front of the small high school on the main drag through town, Whicher finds an empty parking bay, pulls in, cranks down the heat in the cab. The search at Harwood's property is ongoing, nothing more there he can do.

At the door to the school a tall, thin woman with long, brown hair emerges. A single phone call eliciting a meeting.

She stares across at the truck.

The marshal steps out, fits his hat.

"Laura Emerson," the woman says, "I'm assistant principal here."

"John Whicher, US Marshals Service."

"I'm not sure we can be of much help." The woman gestures to the door of the school. "But if you'd like to come this way…"

Whicher follows the woman inside to the assistant principal's room off of main reception; in the air the same cleaning product and disinfectant smell as his daughter's school back in Pecos.

From the office window is a view out over a wing of the small high school.

Laura Emerson sits, clears papers from her desk. "Please," she says, "take a seat."

Whicher pulls out a chair.

The woman folds her hands lightly on the desk. "Bella McConnell has been away from us—out of school six weeks. She's currently taught by specialists at the hostel back in Fort Stockton—which means I can't really help any with recent developments."

"I'm interested in how she was before," Whicher says, "before she left."

"Well," Emerson says, "she relocated here—from Tennessee. There was some difficulty settling in—settling into a new life. For some children it can be problematic. For girls, all the more so—with all their friends, their little cliques. I'd say things were okay, by and large, up until about six months back. There were signs something wasn't right."

The marshal takes out a notepad and pen.

"It was nothing major, at first," Emerson says, "but her work started to drop off, she wasn't completing assignments. Her scores were suffering. As time went on, she became unresponsive. Disruptive, too."

"In what way?"

"In class. In her general attitude. Toward staff, to other students. She always seemed to be in trouble."

"Anybody have an idea why?"

Emerson shrugs. "We did our best to find out, of course. But we couldn't get to the bottom of it, she wouldn't talk to anyone here. We had her mother in…" The assistant principal looks at a letter on her desk. She holds it up. "Three months back. We agreed an action plan to get things back on track. But it didn't really work."

"She got in trouble—with law enforcement? With the court?"

"That was outside of school," Emerson says, "we were unaware of any activity she might've gotten into, we can't do anything about things like that."

"But do you know anything about it?"

"As far as I know, she was hanging out with boys she shouldn't have been hanging out with. Older boys. Problem boys. And some girls, too, the wrong kind of girls."

Whicher turns the pen between his fingers. "How about Bella's mother? Was she any help?"

The assistant principal sits back a little from her desk. "Mrs McConnell was protective of her daughter, of course. And broadly supportive. But I found her a strange woman. Helpful one minute, combative the next. Just an odd mix. She was, sort of, defiant, somehow. I don't really know. I mean, she hasn't lived here long, I can't say that I know her. I don't know anybody that does. I know she attends church here in town, I've heard she's there often. I believe she's 'born-again.'"

The marshal eyes the woman behind the desk.

"But then, the way she looks," Emerson says, "her demeanor, the way she dresses—she's very striking looking. Quite overtly…compelling. In some way. Wouldn't you say?"

Whicher says nothing, lets the woman talk.

"It's all a bit of a confusing mix," Emerson says, "I didn't really know what to make of her, to be completely honest. We never really managed to get to grips with either one of them—neither Bella nor her mother. We couldn't single out something that was causing Bella to behave the way she started to behave. We tried as best we could to be supportive. Then when the police got involved it was…taken out of our hands."

"Juvenile Protection Service stepped in?"

"They did, yes."

"Do you know a man name of Jacob Harwood, Ms Emerson?"

The woman looks up, nods. "Yes."

"You tell me anything about him?"

"He's local, most people know him." The assistant principal flushes slightly, pushes back a strand of hair. "There was some gossip over him and Mrs McConnell, I know that."

"They were in a relationship?"

"According to the local grapevine."

"What do you know about him?"

"He'd be quite a catch," Emerson says. "He's single, good-looking, he runs his own business. He's pretty quiet, I guess sort of shy. He's not a drinker or a womanizer. He's a devout Christian. Regular attendee in church."

"But he got together with Mrs McConnell?"

"The thought is, he was easy prey for her. Someone like her. With her looks and her…I don't know what you call it. Whatever she has. But people think she hooked him, reeled him right in."

The marshal thinks it over. "You think she was aware what people thought?"

"I couldn't say."

"You think the daughter was?"

⊥

Five minutes later, Whicher takes in the girl sitting nervous in a chair in the assistant principal's office. Aimee Douglas, dressed in a skirt, a red and white baseball jacket, hi-top sneakers. Her blond hair cut short at one side of her scalp, the rest of it pulled up in a loose knot on the top of her head.

"Marshal Whicher is here to ask about Bella," Ms Emerson says. "She's been missing for six days—there's a lot of concern for her well-being."

"Is she in trouble?" Aimee says.

In her face is uncertainty. Something else; sweet-natured, a contrast to the would-be urban look.

"She's not in trouble," Whicher answers. "We just need to know she's okay."

"Don't be worried," Emerson says. "You can tell us whatever you know, there's no need to be afraid."

Whicher softens his voice. "You're friends? You and Bella?"

Aimee nods. Sits forward in her chair.

"Have you heard from her?"

She answers quickly; "No."

"Have you heard anything?"

The girl shakes her head.

Emerson cuts in; "If you have, Aimee, it's important that you tell us."

The girl lets out a breath.

"She never calls?" Whicher says. "You never try to call her? Speak with her?"

"She doesn't have a phone," Aimee says. "Not since she went to that hostel."

The marshal nods. "So when's the last time you spoke?"

"I don't know," the girl says. "Not since she left."

"I need to ask you something about her," Whicher says.

The girl glances at him sideways. Nods.

"Did Bella ever hear from her father?"

The girl stares dead ahead, blank looking.

"Did her father call her? Did she ever call him, talk to him?"

Aimee shakes her head.

"You're sure?" Whicher says. "Sure on that?"

"She never says anything about her dad. At least, not to me. She told me she wished he was still around a couple times. She just says he went away. She never tells you anything about him. Has something happened?"

The marshal doesn't answer. "Did Bella ever mention anyone connected to her mother?"

The girl's eyes are hooded.

"Any friends. Men she might know?"

"Boyfriends?" Laura Emerson puts in.

The girl colors. She rocks slightly in her seat. "Sort of. There's this one guy. That her mom knows. That she…I don't know. I mean, Bella doesn't like him."

Emerson looks at her. "Did she say why?"

"She just doesn't like him. She says he's always coming

around. Her mom's always going out to see him. Or they're in church, doing whatever. Like, she wishes her dad was there, that's all, she wishes he was around…"

"Do you know his name?" Whicher says.

The girl stops herself.

"Is it Jacob Harwood?"

She nods. "She calls him 'Hard-on.' I mean she's always going to church, her mom—but it all just seems like bull…"

"Aimee," the assistant principal says.

Whicher half-raises a hand. "It's alright. Let her talk."

"He's like, all over her mom," Aimee says. "It creeps her out, she just wishes he'd go away."

The marshal catches the tone in the girl's voice. "The guy bother her? You think? Does he bother Bella?"

Aimee folds her arms in front of herself. Stares at the floor.

"Did she talk to you about him?" Whicher says.

"No. I don't know."

Whicher keeps his voice even. "Was any of this part of things getting messed up for Bella? Her hanging out with people, getting in trouble in school?"

"I don't know. I just know she didn't like him," Aimee says. "She didn't like that her mom was always with him."

"It sounds like the classic cry for attention," the assistant principal says.

The young girl's face is sour when she answers. "She wanted her dad back. Mainly. She just wanted her old life back."

⋏

Outside in the lot Whicher sits in the Silverado, motor running, winter sky reflected in the windows of the school.

He thinks of Bella McConnell. Aimee Douglas.

Two girls, like his daughter; but different. Without the laughter. Smiling eyes replaced with wary looks, tension. Crossed wires.

He thinks of Travis McConnell. Serving sixty years for armed robbery.

Jacob Harwood at his house on Cammack Avenue.

And Bella. A child, nothing more.

Marshals Service handled child abuse cases—but never him.

The worst kinds of cases.

Enough to strip a man's belief. In a benevolent creator. Justice in the world.

He sits looking at the fall of snow.

Weight of the large-frame Ruger in the shoulder holster rising and falling at the side of his chest.

Chapter Twenty-Eight

Mosquito Alley truck trail,
Gladwin County, Michigan.

The forest to either side of the dirt trail is dense, primeval, the look of a never-tamed land.

Deputy Marshal Evelyn Cruz stares from the sheriff's department SUV into a mix of evergreen and deciduous woodland—trees densely packed, breaks of wild grass and brush.

A fair-skinned deputy steers along the rough track. Tad Haskie. Pale eyed, knuckles protruding from his hands at the wheel.

Evelyn Cruz sits back in the passenger seat. Thoughts turning over inside her head.

She thinks of driving two hours upstate from Detroit.

Leaving her downtown hotel. Taking a car from the federal pool.

And driving up to Gladwin County.

Thinking about a report.

A weak lead—according to her boss. Most likely nothing.

She lets the trunks of trees blur to an indistinct jumble—branches, browning leaves, green pine and fir. Trying to feel it, feel if they could be out there—out there somewhere.

In hunting country, lumber country. Sparsely populated. Scant three thousand in the county seat.

The task force was spread out, now—from Memphis, out to Clarksville and Nashville—on up to Detroit.

A northern Michigan county had recorded the report—a member of the public—disquieted over a man and a young girl sighted at a woodland hunting camp.

Camps were all over the forested northern counties.

Nothing much more out there, according to marshals in the Detroit office. Trees and lakes and game—few people.

The report had come in to a county sheriff's deputy. Hunters, unused to seeing 'young girls' with rough-looking men in deer camps in the woods.

A phone call from Cruz to the local sheriff's office had turned up more information. The deputy had been on break at a roadside bait store—a hunter stopped him. The deputy had taken note of the man's concern.

Any number of innocent explanations might be possible. But the deputy had checked NCIS for updates on the mobile terminal in his car. He'd looked for anything pertaining to the county or the state. Seen federal notices from USMS. One filed in the Missing Persons section. Two filed under Wanted Persons.

He'd added the report from the hunter to the addendum sections of both files.

Evelyn Cruz had seen updates to the NCIS records. She'd called the county sheriff's office. By then the reporting deputy had been off-shift.

And so she'd come.

Two hours up I-75 and Highway 61. In a navy blue Crown Vic. To meet with the sheriff—an austere northerner, name of Burbank.

And Deputy Tad Haskie. Her current guide.

She pushes down the thought of fruitless searching.

Of hundreds of square miles in all directions.

Two steps behind. The task force always two steps behind.

Like the Clarksville police entering the house of the man, Dupris. Dupris still missing, guns he owned now thought to have been taken from the house.

Deputy Haskie raises a hand from the steering wheel, points out a small, white shack just visible off the trail, set back in the woods. "That's the kind of thing…"

Cruz focuses on it. "That's a hunting camp?"

"They're mostly pretty rough," Haskie says. "Majority of 'em are owned by folk from the cities. Up from Flint, Detroit. Grand Rapids, wherever."

"They get used a lot?" Cruz says.

"Whenever the owners have a mind," the deputy answers. "They're mostly empty. But people come up. Guys with deer rifles. A yearning for the great outdoors. They'll stay a weekend. Then hightail it back to hot water and pizza. Comfortable beds."

"It's pretty remote," Cruz says.

"Remote as you need to get." Haskie points out of the windshield. "Right now, before the snow's started it's okay. Come winter, you want to come down one of these trails you'll need an ATV or a snowmobile."

Evelyn Cruz nods. She thinks of the sighting of the vehicle in Detroit. Clutching at straws, according to some on the task force. She'd taken it further. Now this—a wild-goose chase in the woods.

Or maybe a chance at a breakthrough. Or another dead end, a credibility stain.

"Right around the next bend is the Molasses River," Deputy Haskie says. "According to the report, that's where they were seen. We don't have an exact location."

"Why not?"

"Officer filing the report said the hunter he spoke with reckoned they were somewhere over here—by the Molasses. They said the camp was by the side of running water. But there's a bunch of streams, separate branches to the river. They said they passed a small lake, right before they came on the cabin. Sheriff reckoned this might be the spot."

Haskie pulls off the dirt trail onto a patch of grass and fern. He shuts down the motor. "I guess from here we take it in on foot." He looks at Evelyn Cruz from behind the wheel. "There a plan if we spot them?"

"Withdraw," Cruz says. "Call for backup. Why can't you get a hold of the reporting deputy?"

"Glen Creel?" Haskie says. "If he was buying bait he's probably up on Lake Lancer, now. He'll be fishing, maybe working on his boat. Sheriff left a message to call."

"We could go find him?"

"Could be on Lake Houghton. Could be somewhere else."

"How come he doesn't answer his phone?"

"The networks are no good," Haskie says. "I guess he'll pick up his voicemail soon enough."

Marshal Cruz unfastens her seat belt. "We think they're driving a black, Mazda SUV," she says. "But they could've changed vehicles."

Haskie nods.

"If we spot a black Mazda SUV, we back off."

"Understood."

"They're armed and dangerous. We believe they might've killed somebody in Tennessee already."

Haskie gestures in the direction of the woods. "We can search on foot, marshal—but you'd need a helicopter to really get above it, get a look at what's going on."

"They'd hear it a mile off," Cruz says. "They'd know we're looking for them."

"Least we'd find them."

"If they have a minor in tow we have to be careful."

Deputy Haskie nods.

Evelyn Cruz opens up the door, steps out. Dressed in olive pants, nubuck boots, a dark blue Marshals Service jacket. She takes the Glock 22 from the nylon holster clipped to her belt.

Deputy Haskie climbs out from behind the wheel.

Cruz drops the box magazine, checks it over, pushes the magazine back, chambers a round.

"Thought we were just looking?" Haskie says.

"We are." Cruz puts the semi-automatic pistol back into the holster—leaving the retaining strap undone. "But then again…"

Haskie starts toward the edge of the forest. "You any good with that thing?"

"I'm from Tennessee," she answers.

He looks back over his shoulder.

"I shoot straighter than you do," Cruz says.

"I'm the worst shot in the department."

Cruz grins. "Go ahead. Let's see what we've got." She takes a breath.

Steps forward into the woods.

Hudspeth County, Tx

At the drive-through window of the fast-food restaurant, Whicher pays for coffee, steers the truck into an empty parking bay. He turns to his notepad. Thinks of the juvenile hostel in Fort Stockton. Two hours away.

Too far.

He reaches for the phone. Keys a call.

The hostel supervisor comes on the line, Rafaela Salinas.

"Ma'am," he says, "This is Deputy Marshal Whicher. Calling from over in Hudspeth County. About Bella McConnell?"

The woman's voice is guarded. "Is there news?"

"No, ma'am. We're doing everything we can to find her," the marshal says. "I was just over at her school, I was wondering if you might help me out with something?"

"I can try," Salinas says.

"Could anybody from outside of the hostel contact the young people staying there?"

"No." The supervisor's voice is firm. "Phones are not allowed. If they need to call somebody, they go through my office. But only under strict control."

"Sure on that?"

"Absolutely. Why do you ask?"

"I want to know if Bella's father could have called her. While she was living with you."

"I don't understand," Salinas says. "Her father was in prison. How would he get access to a phone?"

Whicher stares across the snow in the half-empty lot.

"If the prison placed a call on his behalf," Salinas says, "we'd know about it. If he'd called here, I'd know."

The marshal eyes the notebook on the empty passenger seat. "Her father got into some kind of a relationship—with a female corrections officer at the prison. It's possible he could've persuaded her to bring a cell phone to him. It's not unknown."

"He didn't call here, marshal." The supervisor's voice is certain. Brittle. "Bella's father didn't call."

⋏

Gladwin County, Michigan

In the dense-packed woodland, visibility is down to fifty yards. The sound of the wind is in the tree tops, bright sky splintering the canopy overhead.

Evelyn Cruz follows the path picked out by Deputy Tad Haskie, stepping over dead-fall of branches, maneuvering through the underbrush, handing off between the trunks of trees.

The sense of stillness deepens every yard farther. The air fetid with decaying leaves, with sap oozing from the stands of pine.

Cruz keeps pace behind the deputy. Conscious of the gun at her side. A sense building, a sense of being watched.

Haskie keeps a measured pace—his movements careful, aware.

Thirty yards on, the feel of the wind is stronger, colder. The woodland opening out.

Sunlight glints from the surface of a body of water.

The deputy moves faster through the thinning trees.

In her mind's eye, Cruz sees the faces of McConnell, of Barbone—believed injured.

If they were here they'd be on edge.

Through a tangle of birch and maple and jack pine, wind ripples the surface of a small lake. Young saplings and rough breaks are along its edges. Haskie comes to a stop at the limit of the trees.

He stands by a sugar maple, afternoon sun lighting it up in amber.

Cruz closes the space between them. "Is that it?" she says, beneath her breath.

The deputy nods.

"So, what now?"

"We track around the edge of the water, there should be a stream we can follow," Haskie says. "After that we'll come to the camp."

Cruz gives a silent thumbs up.

The deputy moves off along the edge of the woods.

The ground is soft at the rim of the body of water. Twenty yards farther, the channel of a stream is in view.

Haskie bends low.

Cruz mirrors the movement.

The wind is strong over the water, blowing among bare branches, in the tops of pines.

No other sound is present. Just a feeling of isolation.

Cruz fights an urge to break out her gun.

Overhead a buzzard circles. A high keening splits the air.

Haskie tips back the bill of an olive ball cap.

Beyond the water is a clearing—fifty yards ahead, surrounded with birch and oak and a few tall fir. Two cabins stand side by side—tin-roofed, built from rough planks.

Around the cabins are frames for dressing game—an outhouse, stacks of cordwood. No vehicle in sight.

A vehicle could be back among the trees, Cruz tells herself.

Tracking Haskie along the stream's edge, she fights a mental image; McConnell in the near cabin—gun in hand.

Entering the clearing now, Haskie keeps close in to the edge of the woods.

Cruz looks for disturbed ground, for vehicle tracks, for bootprints. The ground too rough, too overgrown to see its surface.

Deputy Haskie waits. "No sign of anybody," he says,

beneath his breath. "It feels kind of weird, though, like there's something…"

"We get up close, we check the cabins," Cruz says. "One thing—break out your weapon."

"You're sure, marshal?"

"This close, definitely."

The deputy slips out a square-sided semi-automatic pistol.

Cruz takes the Glock from the holster at her belt.

Separating a few yards from him, she walks toward the door of the nearest cabin.

Heart pumping.

Breath constricted in her chest.

Chapter Twenty-Nine

The steel is heavy—the links ice-cold as Jacob Harwood wraps a length of chain around the base of a screwbean mesquite.

He squats, places a hook through a link in the chain, securing it.

Turns back to the Ram pickup, gets in the cab behind the wheel.

He puts the truck into low, eases forward—taking up slack in the chain.

Feeling it tighten, he pushes down on the gas.

The truck wheels dig down through snow into hard dirt.

With a crack, the tree breaks at the base, the Ram lurches.

Harwood gets off the gas, moves the shifter—drags the tree toward a new-built fire.

Piled around it is a mess of lumber, brushwood, cans of gasoline mix.

He eyes the flames. Drags the mesquite to the fire side, cuts the motor, steps out.

A shovel, a rake and two chainsaws are by the side of the burn pile. Picking up a chainsaw, he puts a boot through the handle, rips on the starter, sparking it into life.

Gunning the engine, he cuts through a branch of the mesquite, cuts another, a third.

He hits the kill switch, sets down the chainsaw. Swings the branches onto the burning fire.

Heat and flame engulf them.

He stands back. Feels smoke sting his eyes.

A cold wind lifts the sweat from the top of his scalp.

Beyond the barns a vehicle appears—an old sedan, hub caps missing from its wheels.

He eyes it.

Jessica McConnell.

Inside him, a mix of grim resolve—resentment, longing. Conflicting emotion. Feelings he can't unwind.

He breaks off to stare into the fire—a mix of dread in him, dread and wildness.

Flames consume the mesquite. He hears the hiss of boiling sap. A high pitch squeal of steam escaping from cuts in the wood. Like a scream. A muted, strangled scream.

He shudders. Braces something inside.

Jessica pulls the car up alongside the barn.

She steps out. Dressed in old jeans. Boots. A wool jacket. Raven hair blowing. Her face a mask.

He lets his eyes glaze as she approaches, staring into the fire.

"Jacob? Are you alright?"

"All day they've been at the house," he says, "since this morning." He turns, looks at her. "With a warrant."

She swallows.

"They don't believe me, they don't buy where I was."

"What did you tell them?"

"I told them I took a break," Harwood says. "From the job. From you. From everything."

"From me?"

"I had to tell them something. They've been watching the house, the sheriff's office have been by the last four days. I know these people—they know me—it's different for you…" Harwood drags a clump of brushwood off of the pile. He heaves it through the air into the flames.

"Where did you tell them you went?"

He looks at her. "I told them I got done on a job in El Paso. I told them I went and hung out with a couple of the guys. And then I went on up into New Mexico. Just cooling out, tooling around."

"Did they ask you about it?" She stares at him. "Did they want you to prove it?"

He shakes his head. "Not yet."

"We'll think of something…"

"Will we?" Harwood steps to the chainsaw, pulls on the starter cord, fires it up.

He cuts more branches from the mesquite, pulls them clear.

Jessica shouts above the noise. "What's *that* mean?"

Harwood snaps off the kill switch. "I barely know what I'm doing anymore. Since I met you. You know that? I hardly know my own mind…"

"Don't say that." Her face softens. "We can be together, Jacob. After all of this."

Harwood stares into the fire, the skin of his face reddened, slack. "I have to face my maker. One day. So will you. After all this."

"Look," Jessica says, "just hold on. Just…" She breaks off.

"What?" he says. "Keep quiet? Just say nothing, hope this all goes away? The sheriff? That marshal? Our sins before God? We have to answer for it, one day, don't you know that?"

She nods. "I know. I know."

Harwood grabs another bundle of cut brush, hurls it up onto the fire. "For the wages of sin is death…"

"Jacob, listen—I came here to help."

He stops. Stares at her.

"I'm sorry. I'm sorry the sheriff was at your house."

"You came here to help?" Harwood says. "Did anybody see you? Did anyone follow you?"

She looks at him a long moment. "There was no one."

Harwood eyes her. "You came here to help?"

She folds her hands together. "Don't look at me that way. Jacob, you're scaring me."

He grabs the shovel, rips it from the ground. "I'm scaring you?"

Jessica steps back. Half-turns toward the car at the barn.

"Get the rake," Harwood says. He stomps across the snow, ten yards, starts to dig. Working fast, his eyes transfixed. "Rake this soil away," he grunts.

She takes the rake, reaches out with it, starts to pull at the loosened earth.

Exposing the seam of a dark green tarp, Harwood drops to his knees, flings the shovel aside.

He claws at the dirt with his bare hands. Clears the snow and earth, grabs an end of the woven green fabric. "Get a hold of the other end…"

"Jacob…" she says.

"We have to do this."

"I don't know if I can…"

Harwood scans the hills, the snow-flecked scrub and brush. He looks at her, eyes shining.

She bends low, grabs the tarp.

Dragging it to the fire, she stumbles. "Oh God, Jacob…"

He takes a can of gasoline, unscrews its cap. "Don't take the Lord's name in vain."

He douses the tarp, moving up and down it.

Jessica gives him a hollow look.

Harwood grabs the tarp, drags it on to the edge of the fire. "I can't get this done on my own," he says. "We have to swing this…"

She stoops, sets her legs to take the weight.

"On three," Harwood says.

He counts down.

Jessica's eyes are locked in front of her.

"One—two—*three*…"

The tarp sails the few feet toward the bed of the fire.

A ball of flame explodes—Harwood grabs her arm, pulls her away.

Flame and black smoke roil, the tarp vaporizing.

Exposing the body of the man concealed inside it—

clothes burning, shreds curling.

Jessica recoils, scrambling. "Oh God…Jacob, what do we do?"

He grabs wood from the pile.

Pours gasoline on it.

His voice choked in his throat on a single word.

"Pray…"

Chapter-Thirty

Hudspeth County, Tx

Out in front of the law enforcement center, Whicher spots the black and silver pickup—Sheriff Odell Ingram's truck.

He pulls the Silverado into the empty bay beside it, cuts the motor, heads inside.

A thick-set sergeant in reception eyes him.

"US Marshals Service," Whicher says. "Like to talk to the sheriff."

From an open door at the side of the reception space, a voice calls out; "*In here…*"

Whicher recognizes Ingram's voice.

The sergeant nods.

Whicher steps to the sheriff's door, enters a bright, cluttered office—cork boards on the walls, file cabinets, a printer, a radio receiver. Swivel chairs surround an oak-veneered desk. Sheriff Ingram sits behind a computer monitor, face lit up by the screen.

"I take a minute of your time?" the marshal says.

Ingram waves him in. "I got arrestees to process, I want folk out of my cells."

"How's that?"

"I don't have the room. Deputies seized a package of illegal drugs at a checkpoint this morning," Ingram says. "Forty pounds of marijuana—on two guys. I need them in the county jail. Plus we had a wreck on the interstate, a Trans Am and a farm truck. I got the Trans Am driver and two passengers under arrest—all intoxicated."

"Busy man," Whicher says.

Ingram dips his head. "You best believe it."

Whicher closes the office door. "I was over at the school, yonder," he says, "Bella's school?"

The sheriff looks at him.

"I came back by Harwood's property—everybody was gone."

"We're all done." Ingram gestures at an empty chair.

Whicher sits.

"We searched everything we could—according to the terms of the warrant. There was nothing outstanding, nothing obvious—none of the girl's clothes, nothing like that. Nothing to indicate her presence in the house. Voluntary or otherwise. There may be trace evidence, my guys took swabs, samples, if there's DNA from her in there, we ought to find it."

Whicher leans forward in the seat. "How about the guy's Ram pickup—your tech said there was blood on the winch?"

"There's some hair samples, too," the sheriff says, "around the hinges on the tail gate. Some in the bed of the truck. We'll get everything looked at—get it up to El Paso."

"USMS can help with that."

"Noted," the sheriff says.

"Was there anything else?" Whicher asks him.

"The guy had a laptop computer, I'd like to take a look at—but we're not allowed. The terms of the warrant were pretty precise."

"So we wait?" Whicher says.

"We got no other choice, partner. We put in the work, we see what comes out."

⊥

Outside in the parking lot, Whicher takes out his keys. He steps across to his truck, eyes the white-capped ridge of Sierra Blanca to the northwest of town, the loaded sky above it.

The phone in his pocket starts to ring, he takes it out, answers.

"Marshal, this is Georgia Eastman—from West Texas Juvenile Protection Service."

"Ma'am."

"Rafaela Salinas just called me."

"She did?"

"From Fort Stockton—she said she spoke with you?"

Whicher stands by his truck.

"She says there's been no development—as such—on Bella's case, is that right?"

"Not exactly," the marshal says. "We have persons of interest we're talking to."

"She said there's been no word on her."

"Nobody in law enforcement has had contact with Bella. That's not to say there have been no developments."

Eastman is silent on the line. "The department has…concerns," she says, finally. "My supervisor has concerns. You know that the longer these cases go, in general, the worse the outcome…"

"I know that, ma'am."

"Ms Salinas says that nobody from the hostel has heard from her, nobody in Fort Stockton's seen her…"

"She's gone from there," Whicher says. "We think Bella's further afield than that."

"Oh?" Eastman says. "Oh." An uncertain note in her voice. "Well, that's part of the reason I was calling."

"Ma'am?"

"Look, the department think that now would be the time…there's a view it would be a good idea to publicize Bella's disappearance. At this point. If she's gone from the area—couldn't it help? If she's gone far, we need eyes looking for her. Her welfare is paramount in this. If law enforcement were to make some kind of an announcement…"

Whicher thinks of news crews, cameras. Updates from that point on, constant questions.

"Marshal?" Eastman says.

"I'd have to talk to my boss," Whicher says. "That kind of thing needs consideration."

"Where do you think Bella might've gone?"

"At this point," the marshal says, "I can't discuss that."

"In a child's disappearance," Eastman says, "we need to

be sure every base is covered. Especially a child placed in care of the state. If somebody were to look at what we're doing to safeguard Bella, we don't want any potential avenue closed off. If you understand me? Our actions need to be beyond reproach."

⁂

Back inside the law enforcement center, Whicher clips across reception into the sheriff's office. "Can you get a warrant for blood samples from Jacob Harwood and Jessica McConnell?"

Sheriff Ingram looks at him.

"Based on the blood in Harwood's pickup," Whicher says. "And the blood spatter in Jessica's house?"

"Can't you?"

"I got Jessica McConnell's attorney to think of."

"I could try," the sheriff says.

"How about this other vehicle Harwood owns?"

"How about it?"

"You get a warrant to search that, too?"

Ingram shakes his head. "We didn't find enough to justify it with the first search. A judge won't buy it right now."

"I say we need it."

The sheriff grunts. "If you can get a warrant, marshal, you can go ahead and be my guest."

⁂

Little Molasses River,
Gladwin County, Michigan

Travis McConnell stands at the window of the deer camp cabin—staring outside at the big man staggering across the clearing toward the outhouse. Stopping, bending double. Swaying, gripping hold of his knees.

He hears his daughter behind him. "What's the matter?" she says.

He doesn't answer.

A worried note is in Bella's voice. "What's going on?"

McConnell looks back into the room—at Bella, on the bed, wrapped in the camo parka, half-asleep, half-awake.

"Nothing," he says. "It's just Reed. Out there."

She stares across at him, blank eyed.

"I need to go talk to him."

She nods, lays her head back on the pillow.

McConnell opens up the cabin, steps out onto the rough wood porch.

The pine is tall against the late afternoon sky. He surveys the line of beech and maple and fir at the edge of the clearing.

Barbone reaches the outhouse, straightens—puts out an arm to take his weight.

He cranes his neck, catches sight of McConnell. Stares across the camp ground at him.

Travis drops from the porch.

He strides across the rough grass and weed. "What's going on?"

Barbone's face is flushed, his eyes glassy. "Uh?"

"What're you doing?"

"What do you think?"

McConnell lowers his voice. "I mean, staggering about like this?"

Barbone clutches at the bandage wrapped above a strip of cloth. "My damn leg's on fire. I need to take a crap…"

"How about if somebody sees you? It don't look right."

"Screw you."

McConnell scans the debris scattered about the camp. "Maybe there's a bucket, somewhere…"

Barbone only stares.

"If somebody sees you, they'll see you're injured. They get to thinking about it, they'll ask themselves how come a guy injured didn't go to any hospital. What's he doing in a deer camp, the middle of nowhere?"

"Somebody like who?" The big man looks around the clearing.

"I told you," McConnell says. "Hunters were by here this morning. Early. There were hunters."

"Bullshit."

"I saw them, man."

"Nothing happened."

McConnell stares across the clearing. "So far, nothing happened. Maybe they'll be back."

"Uh?" Barbone says. "You saying you want to split?"

"We need to let your leg heal." McConnell eyes the big man—sweat on his skin, color in his face. His hair is matted, breath coming hard.

"It hurts, man," Barbone says, "it ain't good. Maybe it's the damn drugs. They're meant for animals—horses, or something. I got my guy coming tomorrow, remember…"

McConnell nods.

"Don't forget," Barbone says.

"I know, I know. Into Standish," McConnell says, "meeting him at three."

Sweat blooms across Barbone's forehead. "That little pissant town…He'll have food. Better drugs…"

"I'll be there." McConnell thinks it over.

Thinks of the time to fix a bullet wound. Barbone getting worse instead of better.

The big man shifts, grunts; "Maybe we could get moving, after that…"

"We need to lay low."

"We could find something."

McConnell stares along the line of the stream at the edge of the camp, into the forest beyond it, listening for any sound.

Barbone pushes off the side of the outhouse, a fevered look in his eye. "Your damn fault I end up shot…"

McConnell thinks of Barbone at the sporting goods store—firing at the gun-counter clerk—turning it into a fight.

Instead of getting out.

Nobody ever shot at him—in any robbery—he'd never let it come to that. Not even close.

His own fault.

Barbone's own fault.

Let him say what he liked.

The big man pulls the Browning pistol from the waistband of his pants. "Anybody comes looking—any goddamn hunter or anyone else…"

"What?" McConnell says.

"We take 'em down. Shoot 'em."

"That's the plan?"

"Bury 'em in the woods." Barbone eyes him. "You cooking up something else?"

McConnell doesn't reply.

"Uh?" Barbone says. "Like, maybe taking off…"

"Yo, Reed." McConnell meets the man's stare. "Nobody said that."

"How about that little princess you got back there?" Barbone juts his chin at the cabin. "You don't think that's some weird shit? People see some little girl in these woods?"

Travis feels a beat of temper.

He shuts down the impulse of anger—careful not to let the big man see.

Barbone paranoid, adept at sniffing out hostility. Quick to set himself against perceived threats. Many times he's seen it in prison—Barbone working a pent-up energy, only for it to break in a blur of violence.

Barbone lets the Hi-Power pistol hang from his side.

"We just need to be careful is all," McConnell says. "Careful about being seen."

"That go for her, too?"

"We get that leg of yours fixed, we'll get out of here. I'll meet your guy tomorrow. Like you say."

Barbone raises the gun again, looks at it, a new thought working on his face. "You get the car hid?"

"I moved it," McConnell says. "It's back there in the woods."

Barbone's eyes narrow. Gun in hand he starts to edge toward the outhouse door. "Just the three of us…" he says beneath his breath.

McConnell looks at him. "What?"

"Nobody around to bother us…"

His eyes are hooded. Malevolence threaded in his face.

He shuffles, opens the door. Hand gripping the Browning, fingers flexing.

Muttering, verbalizing.

The thoughts floating through his fevered head.

CHAPTER THIRTY-ONE

Reeves County, Tx

In the USMS office back in Pecos, Whicher finds the note from Chief Marshal Fairbanks on his desk.

He takes off his jacket, shrugs off the Ruger in the shoulder holster. A two-hour ride east on I-10—time enough to think on Jessica McConnell. On Harwood. On two missing federal felons. And a vanished girl.

He carries the Ruger to a wall-mount gun safe, hangs the rig inside.

The chief marshal's note in hand, he steps to Fairbanks's door, raps a knuckle against it.

Hears her voice, "Come on in…"

Fairbanks is seated behind her desk, writing onto a yellow legal pad. "I just spoke with the Office of Public Affairs," she says.

"Ma'am."

"The head of the Juvenile Protection Service wants to publicize Bella's case."

"Ma'am, I know that. Georgia Eastman called me."

Fairbanks looks at him.

The marshal eases the door closed. Sits.

"Any request originating from a child protection agency we have to listen to," Fairbanks says. "Make sure it's handled according to guidelines. It's been six days. The child's still missing. She's still at risk." The chief marshal clicks onto a file on her computer. "OPA recommendation is begin with a press release at a minimum—you can write the press release yourself. Also, we need to file with the National Center for Missing and Exploited Children."

"I have no problem with that."

"But you do with the press release?"

"National Center for Missing Children is a specialist agency," Whicher says. "They'll be good for the case."

"But not the media?"

The marshal doesn't reply.

"We're going to have to go public," Fairbanks says. "From experience, I think we'll get interest, fast. Radio within the hour, local TV within half a day."

"There'll be interest," Whicher says.

"So, maybe it can help us out. Multiply potential sources of information."

"Somebody will need to spend time fielding that."

"I'm not asking you to man the phone." The chief marshal studies him from across the desk.

"If Bella's with her father, we don't need some raw deputy or a rookie cop pulling a gun," Whicher says. "We don't need people calling in with false leads…"

"I'm talking about policy," Fairbanks says, "procedure we have to follow."

"I'm talking about a girl's life."

Chief Marshal Fairbanks taps a pen against the yellow notepad.

"Most of the reports will be false," Whicher says, "it could pull us halfway over the damn country."

"You're a good investigator," Fairbanks says. "But I need to put out the press release."

Whicher eyes her, says nothing.

"Did you find Jessica McConnell?"

"Yes, ma'am."

"What's she have to say about the idea of her daughter up in Michigan?"

"Not a whole lot. But she was rattled, I'll say that. Her boyfriend, Harwood, is back in town."

"In Sierra Blanca?"

"Sheriff had a warrant issued to search the man's house," Whicher says. "The guy's been missing for days."

"You have him in this?"

"He says he was out in New Mexico. Says he was between contracting jobs. He told me he needed to get away from Jessica."

"He said that?"

"I don't know what the hell's going on, but there's something. A forensic tech found blood in the back of a pickup he owns. We got blood spatter in Jessica McConnell's house," Whicher says. "And now blood in the back of Jacob Harwood's truck. I've asked the sheriff to put in requests for samples from both of them."

Fairbanks turns a page on the yellow legal pad, writes a note on it. "If he can't get that, we will…"

"Ma'am, you wanted to see me?" Whicher holds out the note.

The chief marshal nods. "Evelyn Cruz's boss called. Cruz is still up in Michigan. She thinks that lead might've developed."

The marshal sits forward in his chair.

"Somebody in one of the lower peninsula counties reported a sighting—of a man with a young girl in a hunting cabin, out in the woods. A deputy there saw notices outstanding, the Marshals Service alert was live for Michigan, so he filed the report. Marshal Cruz went up there," Fairbanks says. "She went out to search for the camp."

Whicher looks at his boss.

"They were looking in the wrong place—but now they think they know where to look she wants to go search again."

"You know when?"

Fairbanks clicks her pen, eyebrows arched. "I mean, she wants to go do it now, marshal. If you want to talk to her about it, you best make it fast…"

⅄

Standing at the window by his desk, Whicher finds the number for Evelyn Cruz.

He keys it, waits as it rings. Stares out over the car lot, at snow on the roof of the Silverado.

The call picks up.

"My boss tells me you have a report of a man seen with a young girl?"

"Marshal, yes," Cruz says, "you heard right. I think it could be something."

"At a camp up there in the woods?"

"A deer camp, in one of the northern counties here, Gladwin—it's pretty remote."

"Last sighting of McConnell was urban Detroit," Whicher says. "Plus we don't know it was them."

"Gladwin's three hours north of there," Cruz says, "granted. But these hunting camps are mostly owned by people from the cities—from Detroit, Grand Rapids. We got a hold of the deputy that took the original report—he knows the country—we're going to look again, we're just getting set up."

"You need to back that up," Whicher says.

"Excuse me?"

"This all needs figuring out—before anybody goes in."

"I'm working with the sheriff here," Cruz says.

"They'll take it in hot."

"They'll what?" Cruz hesitates at the end of the line.

"If they think they've got escaped felons, armed felons," Whicher says, "they'll go with overwhelming force. If Bella McConnell's there—if she *is* there—she could be a victim in this."

"I can't risk losing them."

"If they're there—why would they move?" Whicher stares at his reflection in the office window, a bad feeling blowing the length of his spine.

"I think it's them," Cruz says. "If you'd been here today, at the camp we found, you'd think the same. It's the perfect place to hide out—if Barbone was injured at that robbery they need to be somewhere, they can't keep moving."

"I'll get the first flight up."

"What?"

"I'll come up."

"I want to do this now," Cruz says, "before nightfall."

"You do what you want with your escapees," Whicher says. "But not with Bella McConnell. If she's there, I want her out."

▲

Two blocks up from the rodeo arena across town, Whicher tops off the gas in his truck in the Sunoco station. He hits the Stripes store to pick up a beef fajita taco. Cold wind scything off of the highway. Thinking on the conversation with Chief Marshal Fairbanks.

The Memphis task force had unlimited powers—apprehending their quarry mandatory.

Fairbanks had put through a call to the Memphis field office—made clear the position—the chief there had given a hard-limit, twenty-four hours.

Whicher could fly up in the morning. If the escapees were there, an intervention would have to be agreed.

The marshal thinks of the photograph of the young girl on his phone. Tries to picture her at the center of it all.

Back out of the store, he climbs up into the truck, dumps the taco on the empty passenger seat.

His phone rings.

Whicher fires up the motor. Sees the name on the screen—Hudspeth County Sheriff.

He hits drive, parks in an empty bay by the side of the store. Answers.

"Marshal. I got news," the sheriff says.

"Oh?" Whicher hears the testiness in his own voice.

"Everything alright?"

"Yeah. I got more intel regarding Bella and her father, now—not good news."

"Really?"

The marshal grabs the food from the seat. "USMS think they could be up in rural Michigan. If she's with him, that's not a good place to be. I'm flying out there, tomorrow, early."

Ingram grunts. "You think she could be?"

Whicher takes a bite out of the beef fajita taco. "Too early to say."

"If she is, then what?"

"We have to keep her safe, somehow."

"Right. Well, I was calling to let you know my office put in for warrants for blood samples from Jessica McConnell and Jacob Harwood. The warrants have been granted," Ingram says. "They're back in my office, I'm looking at 'em now."

The marshal eats, nods. "Good. That's good."

"I sent out a couple deputies, looking to find them," Ingram says, "to bring 'em on in. I even had the police doctor come by."

"But?" Whicher says.

"But damn if anybody can find 'em."

"Y'all can't find them?"

"No, sir," the sheriff says. "And I'm starting to wonder if maybe they've cut and run."

Chapter Thirty-Two

Laid out on the coverlet on top of the bed is an open canvas travel bag. Whicher places a box of .40 calibre Smith & Wesson for the Glock into a zip-up pocket inside.

Along with ammunition for the Glock he puts a box of .357 Magnum rounds for the Ruger on top of a USMS Kevlar ballistic vest.

Leanne stands with her back to the walk-in wardrobe. "You want a pair of jeans? Or cargo pants?"

"Jeans will be warmer."

She reaches in to a shelf, takes out a pair, tosses them to him. "How cold is it up there?"

"Warmer up in Michigan than it is in Texas right now," Whicher says. "According to the task force marshal."

Leanne glances out of the bedroom window—at flakes of snow blowing through the air. "How long you think you'll be gone?"

"One night, two at the most." Whicher opens up a drawer takes out a sweater, puts it into the canvas bag. On top of the sweater, he places the Glock semi-automatic in its clip holster, a brace of extra magazines alongside it.

"Are you going to need all of that?" Leanne says.

The marshal brushes by his wife, takes out a wool ranch coat from a hanger. "I don't plan on needing any of it."

"But you think this girl could be there?"

"We've had no word," Whicher says, "since she disappeared from the hostel in Fort Stockton. Six days gone."

Leanne leans against the wall of the bedroom, folds her arms across her chest.

"We don't know where the mother is. Last credible sighting of the father was at a robbery in Clarksville, Tennessee, three days back. Yesterday, law enforcement in Detroit logged a possible sighting that could be the girl with her father. The second escapee is from Detroit—it's possible they'd look for help there."

"Why not let the task force and the local sheriff's office handle it?" Leanne says.

"I could do that." The marshal looks at his wife.

From the kitchen is the sound of Lori's voice.

"I'm back here," Leanne says.

Lori calls out. "*We're supposed to go pick up Amelia…*"

"One of her friends," Leanne says to Whicher, "you've met her. I told Lori she could come over. I thought maybe we'd pick something up. You want to eat?"

"Sure."

Leanne looks at her watch.

"Go," Whicher says, "I got this."

Leanne nods. "Do they know about the missing girl up there?"

Whicher takes a pair of winter socks from the back of a drawer. Stuffs them into the bag, padding the magazines for the Glock. "She's listed with the National Center for Missing and Exploited Children. They have access to the data. Plus personnel. They can give on-site assistance to law enforcement."

"They sound like the right people for the job…"

"We're talking about violent men," Whicher says, "they've staged an armed robbery already, they may have killed a man."

Leanne regards him, coolly.

"Michigan law enforcement know that. The task force aren't obliged to bring back felons alive."

"But they'd take care if there's a child involved."

"People get hurt around those guys," Whicher says.

"How could she even be with them?"

Whicher hunts out a pair of buckskin gloves, throws them into the bag.

"Does the task force want you there?"

"Bella's my responsibility."

"She's everybody's responsibility," Leanne says.

Lori calls out from the kitchen, "*Mom*—we need to go…"

"I took this," Whicher says. He fastens the zipper on the canvas bag. "It's my job to bring her back."

Chapter Thirty-Three

Little Molasses River, Gladwin County, Mi

Sunlight splinters through the woodland, the low sun of early morning. Travis McConnell stands dead still—holding onto the trunk of a jack pine—senses on high alert.

He breathes shallow, his mouth open.

Wind shifts in the branches overhead.

He feels for the pistol in the pocket of his heavy coat.

A jay flits between trees, dipping, diving.

Sound comes again—faint, indistinct. The sound of voices.

Wind is swirling.

Wind in the breaks of ground, in the rough patches of sapling—the long grass and shrub and weed.

Disorienting.

But his senses tell him where the voices are.

He tracks between trunks of beech and pine, half-crouched, profile low to the ground. Breathing silent. Toward a sloping ridge of underbrush and fern.

Moving uphill, snatches of sound come.

Men talking. Somewhere close.

Somewhere between himself and the camp.

The camp—safe ground—a place to hide, a place where nobody would come. The nearest town little more than houses, a sawmill, a handful of stores.

Safe.

But to be found was danger.

A man's raised voice reaches him.

McConnell drops in the underbrush. Stays entirely still.

Taking out the Sig he grips the semi-auto in his hand. Feels his pulse quicken. Rises, crouches low, moves fast to the top of the ridge.

He flattens to the ground. Crawls forward. Peers down over the crest into a dipping vale.

Among the trees, two Jeep Wranglers and a Tacoma pickup are parked a hundred yards off. The trucks on outsize tires, raised suspension. A group of men gathered about them—six men—with rifles. Dressed in woodland camo. Hi-top boots.

McConnell stares down. Eyes the party of hunters. Standing talking. Drinking coffee. Setting up to move out. The deer camp barely half a mile along the river. They'd know it. The men the previous day had known it—two men that had stared at them, silent, from across the stream.

If they stopped, then what? If these men stopped?

If they saw Barbone. The state he was in—the wounded leg, the fever in him.

Or Bella.

The way she looked, a young girl.

Another thought hits—the SUV.

Hidden in a patch of brushwood and oak and maple at the head of an overgrown trail. On out-of-state plates—Tennessee plates. Tennessee—six hundred miles south.

How would they not notice?

A group of hunters.

If they saw the camp.

If they saw the car.

With a last look McConnell eases back from the top of the ridge. Raises up, pushes off to run.

Into the tangle of broken country.

Heart racing, toward the dense, dark woods.

⚚

Hudspeth County, Tx

Lying on top of the bed in her empty house, Jessica McConnell listens to the silence—staring up at brown stains of water on the popcorn ceiling.

The air in the house is still. Dry. A faint smell of carpet cleaner rising from the floor.

Her stomach turns over. Empty. But the hunger barely touches her, she barely feels it.

A day and a night.

Day and a night, now.

A string of hours. A parcel of hollowed time.

Nothing from her daughter. No word, no sign.

She thinks back, across the weeks and months.

At first it had been sleepovers—weekend stays with her friend. Aimee—her friend from junior high; staying over, never thinking to call. Those first times painful. Hurtful to be shut out, left aside. Alone.

The first times, she'd mourned, almost grieved her daughter's absence.

Soon it became more frequent, weeknights gone from home. Hanging out not with Aimee, but with boys, Jessica suspected. Aimee was sweet—but not a good liar. Slow torture accompanied the waking hours, then, waiting for her daughter's return. Unwilling to ask Aimee's mother. Unwilling to ask for help. Trying to hide the full dysfunction of their relationship—the mess of it.

But then the trouble had come.

The trouble with cops, with the juvenile service. With the court.

And then the day—the day the axe fell—Bella ordered into care.

Jessica driving her there, her own daughter, her baby, her flesh and blood—trying to pretend it was just a little thing, some little thing, a break, that it would do them both some kind of good. That it could give them time and space to think and breathe and see things differently. And not let her daughter see that she was falling apart inside. Mortified. Consumed with sadness. With shame, with self-loathing. With crushing misery. Biting back tears when she thought of her little carefree girl. Gripping tight, steering her ancient car, as if the bones of her whitened fingers might break against the wheel.

Learn.

She'd told herself.

Learn.

Adapt.

Survive.

Put one foot in front of the other. Keep on. She'd learned that, too.

Learned to live shut out—shut off—locked out from her daughter.

From the self-obsessed adolescent who'd replaced her.

Learned to not give in to panic, terror—all manner of bleak things.

She would be alright.

Bella would be alright, wherever she was.

She would be okay, she would get by, squeak by—keep just enough of her wits about her to make it through.

A mantra.

A silent prayer—ever ready. On her lips, in the back of her mind.

Even as morning broke, alone, with nothing. Loneliness, an emptiness so hard to bear.

Aloneness.

A void.

Into which *he* had stepped.

Jacob.

With his Faith. Belief.

His smile. His understanding.

He'd helped her see. Believe. And so much more. Revealed meaning. A depth of understanding. Illumination.

She'd found her church.

She sits up on the bed, swings her legs out, puts her feet onto the floor.

Pushes back her ink-black hair, stands. Looks out of the window—at the mid-morning sun on the hill in the distance, yesterday's snow melting to ocher-red.

The smell of carpet cleaner lingers.

In her mind she sees herself, on hands and knees. Scrubbing at the dark stain of blood held deep within its fibers. Scrubbing till her skin was raw.

She lets her gaze roam the vista beyond the bedroom window. Images flashing behind her eyes—the tiny splatter of blood on the living room wall—a thing she'd never noticed. Shuddering, she holds her arms about herself. Holds back a nameless dread.

Until the thought breaks in on her consciousness—standing in the fall of snow on Jacob's land.

Piles of cut brush, of pulled-up mesquite. A can of gasoline. Black smoke.

The crackle of the tarp bursting into fire.

The horror of the body concealed within it.

Consumed, roiling before her.

Consigned to flame.

Gladwin County, Mi

In an annex room of the Gladwin law enforcement center, Whicher studies the county sheriff—a lean, tough-looking fifty-year-old name of Burbank. Along with the sheriff are four deputies, plus Evelyn Cruz from the USMS task force.

Sheriff Burbank takes a note from a plastic jacket, he checks it, gestures to a deputy named Creel.

Creel is short, his sandy hair erratic-looking. His skin weathered. Eyes watchful. The look of an outdoorsman, Whicher decides.

The marshal sits at the corner of a scuffed desk, canvas travel bag and his gear at his feet. A dark blue ranch coat on the back of a chair, hat between a finger and thumb.

Evelyn Cruz has her hair tied back, she's dressed in a USMS jacket and chinos, her ballistic vest on a nearby seat. Alongside her is another deputy—Tad Haskie. Two others—a bear-like officer name of Grogan, and a dark-complexioned man named O'Donnell complete the group.

Whicher rubs on the back of his neck—feels the dislocated sensation of long-range travel. The flight up from Midland to Detroit—and then a two-and-a-half hour ride up I-75 with Marshal Cruz.

The sheriff finishes his discussion with Deputy Creel. Burbank clears his throat. "Alright, everybody—if I could have your attention. There's just a couple things for me to cover, and then Glen will take you through the details and any questions." The sheriff looks at Cruz and Whicher in turn. "Marshals? Anything you want to add, we can do that, too."

Whicher nods, leans back an inch, fits the Resistol onto one knee.

Evelyn Cruz stands, arms folded across her chest.

Sheriff Burbank checks the note in his hand. "Our objective this afternoon is preliminary reconnaissance," he says. "To establish the likely presence of any of our current persons-of-interest. USMS Tennessee looking for two escaped felons out of Memphis. And USMS West Texas looking for a missing minor—the daughter of one of these two men."

Deputy Glen Creel looks across the room at Whicher. His eyes flint, hard to read.

"The operation is limited to establishing their presence," the sheriff says, "without alerting them of our interest. We're simply looking to confirm if they're out here. If they are, we pull back, scale resources—only then engage."

Whicher glances at Marshal Cruz. Back in Memphis, she told him, the effort was now on follow-up of reliable incidents. Detroit-area law enforcement setting up on known locales for Barbone. USMS trying to trace the disappearance of the man from Clarksville.

Sheriff Burbank gestures for Deputy Creel to step forward.

Creel looks around the room. "Alright," he says. "Well, good afternoon. So, I'll make this brief." He hooks his thumbs into his duty belt. "I took the original report—from what the witnesses said, a number of possible locations present themselves. Sheriff and I have it narrowed down to two spots. In my opinion, the most likely is a camp I know, out by the section twenty-three Township Road and the Fire Lane Trail. There's a deer camp there, out by the Little Molasses River. Flooding area three."

Deputies Grogan and O'Donnell exchange glances.

Tad Haskie listens, hands at his hips.

"If they're not there," Creel says, "they could just as well be at a spot around three miles to the north—the other side of sixty-one. There's a hunting camp around the east Fire Lane Trail. It's on the Little Molasses, same as the first camp—there's a small lake, right enough, a couple of streams, there's wetland up there…"

Sheriff Burbank cuts in; "We have a map print-out for everybody, both locations are marked. We also have recent photographs of our persons-of-interest, from the Marshals Service. You'll each be issued with them. Glen, you're looking to take this in at flooding area three?"

"Right," Creel nods, "we start from there, take a look, see what's going on."

"The idea is, post up," Burbank says, "and observe without approaching too close."

"If there's no sign of folk there," Creel says, "we move up north across Highway 61 into the woods around east Fire Lane Trail."

"We're talking about a substantial area of woodland," the sheriff says. "Wild country, hunting country. With few trails. What trails there are, are only dirt tracks. If they're out there, we'll need more than just the six of you to securely contain them—we'll need air support, state police, National Guard maybe. We can get support, if we need it. But we need to show good cause."

Evelyn Cruz holds a hand up to speak. "The camps I've seen are isolated, little-used. It's credible they'd hide out somewhere like that."

"It's dense woodland," Deputy Creel says, "but we have enough people. Six guns is more than enough to control that acreage…"

Deputy Haskie looks at him. "We're not hunting whitetail, Glen."

"We go mob-handed," Whicher says, "this all could get ugly…"

The sheriff raises his hand. "Alright—look, we have to find them, then we'll worry about bringing them in. There'll be time to make whatever points anybody wants to make—but Glen you want to close this out? Run us through the plan of ingress?"

Deputy Creel nods. He turns to a whiteboard in a corner of the annex room. Uncaps a marker pen, draws a horizontal line in the center of the board. "You all have maps," he says, "you'll be able to see this close-up." He points to the board. "But this line here, we'll say is Highway 61."

Grogan, the bear-like deputy speaks; "That's out near the county line?"

"Correct," Creel answers. On the whiteboard, beneath the horizontal line, he draws two verticals—and then another horizontal—forming a box. In its center he draws a rough oval. "Right there is flooding area three," he says. He points to the bottom line. "That's the Grim Road. And then to the left and right you have the center Fire Lane Trail and the County Line Road. The camp is right around the flooding area, surrounded with trees. There's a clearing, that's the camp. We keep 'em in the box here, we don't need to get real close. We should be able to observe from the woods."

"How about if we can't see anybody?" Evelyn Cruz says.

"There'll be signs, ground sign," Creel answers. "I track deer, I can track disturbance by a bunch of jailbirds. We'll post up around the box, work in toward the flood area. Then hold short. I'll go in closer."

"How about the second locale?" the other deputy, O'Donnell, says.

"We'll draw the play, run that if they're not at this one," Creel says. "I'll take the board. Right now, we need to focus on this."

Whicher holds up a hand.

The sheriff nods.

"Everybody needs to maintain distance," the marshal says, "not allow visual contact."

"Understood," Creel says. "I'll be the one that gets in close. You have experience, this kind of thing?"

"Battalion scout platoon," Whicher says. "With Third Armored Cavalry."

"I guess I meant with tracking, hunting?" Creel says.

"My job to find the enemy, bring him out," the marshal answers. "Right now, we only want to find them. The men we're looking for are violent and dangerous. Since they broke out of prison, it's believed they've killed at least one man and robbed a store at gunpoint. I don't think they'd hesitate to kill again."

"They don't get a free pass," Cruz says.

Deputy Grogan grunts. "Somebody pulls a gun, I'm defending myself—for damn sure."

"That goes for me, too." O'Donnell's face is cold.

"Nobody fires," Whicher says, "nobody offers up a target." His eyes are hard as he looks around the room. "Nobody sparks this off here. Nobody lights the flame."

Chapter Thirty-Four

Hudspeth County, Tx

Behind the wheel of the sheriff's department cruiser, Deputy Raylene Lapointe studies the green-sided house, the aging Nissan parked out front. A dog watches from behind the fence on the neighboring property. She fits her hat, pushes open the door.

The dog, a German Shepherd starts to growl.

She looks at it; "What's your problem?"

The dog growls louder, white teeth bared.

Deputy Lapointe reaches the front door of the house. She stops, looks into the window.

Nobody there.

She knocks hard. "*Sheriff's office*," she calls out.

No answer comes back.

Lapointe knocks again, harder.

She moves around the side of the house away from the dog, to the kitchen in back.

Stepping to the window, she sees Jessica McConnell,

seated at a table—staring back toward the hall.

Lapointe taps on the window.

The young woman whips around in her seat—color drained from her face.

"Ma'am," Lapointe says, her face close to the glass. "Could you open up the door?"

Jessica only sits motionless.

"I need to speak with you." Lapointe gestures to the kitchen door. "Mrs McConnell? Could you open up, please?"

Standing quickly, Jessica moves to the back door—dressed in black jeans, a skintight top hugging the curves of her figure.

She unlocks the door, opens it. "Is it Bella?" she says. Her eyes are wide, shining. "My God, have you found her?" She puts a palm to her chest.

"No, ma'am," the deputy says, "it's not that."

The young woman folds in on herself. Lets out a breath.

"Why weren't you answering the door?" the deputy says.

"What?" Jessica looks shaken.

Lapointe stares at her.

"I don't know…" she says.

"Sheriff's department tried to find you yesterday, Mrs McConnell."

The young woman doesn't reply.

"You leave town?"

She shakes her head. "I was around."

"Where?"

"Is that any of your business?"

"Ma'am?" Lapointe says. "We need to talk to you."

"Why can't you find my daughter?"

"You need to come with me, please, Mrs McConnell."

"What for?"

"I have to take you to the sheriff's office. To see the doctor."

"What're you talking about?"

"Court's issued a warrant. You'll need to come with me. We have a warrant to take a sample of your blood."

*

Gladwin County, Mi

In the dim light of the deer camp cabin, Travis McConnell zips the fastener on the hunter's jacket. He takes out the SUV keys from his pocket, holds them in the palm of his hand.

Sitting on the bed, Bella watches him—face sullen, black hair loose about her shoulders.

Her clothes are strewn across the end of the bed and on the plank floor. Rolled up socks, a pair of jeans pulled inside out, a T-shirt, a top.

McConnell looks at her few possessions. "I'll be gone an hour at most," he says. "Fifteen miles into Standish. I'll meet with Reed's people at the Family Dollar. Get whatever I get from them. Then that's it. I'll come right back."

"I want to come."

"You can't."

"I'm not staying here."

"I'll bring fried chicken."

Bella bugs her eyes.

"Donuts? You want chicken?"

His daughter doesn't answer. She jumps off of the bed, stalks to the window. Looks outside. "Where is he?"

"In his cabin," McConnell answers.

"Doing what?"

"Sweetheart, he's sick. You know? He's not doing much of anything."

"So why do I need to be here?"

McConnell stares at his daughter's back at the window.

He slips his free hand into his jacket, feels for the Sig. Takes his hand back out, chews at a hangnail. Thinks of the hunting party—six men—in the early light. Half the day spent wondering if they could come the way of the camp. Bella cooped up, him trying not to show his fraying nerves. Watching Barbone's cabin, watchful of the big man coming out. "I have to leave," he says. "I can't be late."

Bella turns from the window.

He crosses the cabin to the door. Opens up.

His daughter pushes past him, onto the rough porch outside.

She jumps down—into the clearing.

McConnell steps out, pulls the door.

He eyes Barbone's cabin. No movement from it.

Bella starts to sprint for the woods.

He jumps down, runs. Fast as he can—after her, into the trees. Clearing deadfall of beech and tangled underbrush. Reaches Bella. Grabs her arm, pulls her around, fights his shortness of breath.

Anger is in the set of her jaw, heat in her face.

He holds a finger to his mouth—willing her to calm down, to stay quiet, to not make any sound.

She glares at him.

He checks back over his shoulder. Beneath his breath he tells her; "Walk with me."

Scanning the forest in front of him, he fixes on a spot.

He moves fast, pulls his daughter through the tall pine, leafless birch, grass and fern and bright-leaved maple. "You can't come," he breathes. "You can't come with me."

"Why not?"

"He'll think we're running out…"

She stumbles at his side, looks at him.

"I don't want him even thinking that…"

"I don't care what he thinks."

"Maybe you don't. I do."

"He won't even know I'm gone," Bella says.

Travis pulls her on faster. "Reed's friends don't know you're here…"

"What?"

"With us," he says. "They don't know you're with us—so you can't be there. They can't see you."

"What's it matter?"

McConnell scans ahead, sensing shapes of trees, keeping a tall, blue-green fir ahead of him—the marker for the route. "If they see you, they'll want to know what's going on. They won't like it."

"You said they were helping you…"

"Helping Reed, they're Reed's friends, not mine. Look,

we have to play ball, do this."

"I don't want to be here," Bella says. "I don't want to be with him."

Travis stops suddenly.

He looks at his daughter.

She stares into his face.

"You don't have to worry," he says. "He's sick, he won't bother you."

"He's gross, he creeps me out."

McConnell pictures the big man—base, an animal—the thought of him alone with his daughter like a knife to his gut. "Go back."

Bella stares at him.

His words in his own ears the words of a stranger. "I can't take you. I'll be gone an hour—I'll be back with food, with medicine. With drugs for Reed. To fix his leg. We'll be here just a little while longer. Then we'll be gone…"

Bella's eyes drill him. She stands mute in the forest.

McConnell pictures a deer, surrounded on all sides.

He reaches into his jacket.

Takes out the Sig semi-automatic pistol.

His daughter's eyes widen.

He holds the gun out. "Take it."

She makes a choking sound.

"Take it."

"I don't know how to shoot…"

"You won't have to."

She swallows. Reaches out.

"It's loaded," he says. "Hold it in both hands, brace your

arm if you have to shoot. Squeeze the trigger, grip tight, it's going to kick back…"

She only nods.

"But you won't have to," McConnell says.

"What if I do?"

"You stay here. Right here. All you have to do." He takes her shoulders. Feels the tightness in his throat. "Stay here. I'll be back in less than an hour…"

Chapter Thirty-Five

Gladwin County, Mi

Whicher tightens the straps on the ballistic vest, adjusts the Glock in the holster at his leg. *Grim Township Road*—a dirt trail flanked with overgrown woods. He breathes a lungful of cold, clear air—the scent of pine and decomposing leaves on it. In the wind, the raucous call of a bird.

He takes the keys from the Silverado, closes up the truck. A static burst sounds on the portable two-way radio fastened to his woolen ranch coat. Whicher recognizes the voice of the search team leader, Deputy Glen Creel.

"All elements—radio check…"

Stationed on the bottom edge of the search zone, the marshal listens to Creel work his way through the team posted up around the deer camp, the forest, the flood area. Evelyn Cruz on the right-hand edge, the County Line Road. Deputy Tad Haskie on the west flank, the Center Fire Lane Trail. Creel and the bear-like Deputy Grogan set to work toward the camp on left and right diagonals. The final deputy, O'Donnell, holding post on the highway, up at the top.

"Three?" Creel says, "come on back?"

Whicher answers; "Three—receiving."

Adjusting the volume down, he moves off the dirt trail through a line of high-grown rushes, the ground wet beneath his boots.

A mix of underbrush and sapling woods stand before him—he picks out a path toward raised ground, a ridge covered with beech and maple and birch a hundred yards ahead.

⚹

Among the light and shadow of the trees Deputy Tad Haskie keeps a steady pace, mindful of the words of Glen Creel—slow and easy.

He thinks of birds breaking from the trees; signs and tells. Creel the King-of-the-woods, Haskie the city guy out of Saginaw.

The Ford Ranger is parked at the end of a deep-rutted dirt spur three hundred yards behind him. He stands a moment, wondering is he too fast—ahead of everybody else?

Wind is all he hears.

Wind in the needles of the tall pine. The rustle of withered leaves.

He takes out Sheriff Burbank's print-out, traces a finger along a line of the map. A couple of hundred yards should put him on the edge of the woods—with a view of the flood land, the area surrounding the camp.

Despite the cold in the wind he feels sweat prick his skin.

He moves forward, searching left and right among the trees.

Unsnaps the strap over his Sig.

⮚

Travis McConnell follows a line at the edge of the forest, gripping the wheel of the big Mazda—he sees a glimpse of road through tall grass and brush and a stand of brown cattails.

He slows, brings the SUV to a stop.

Nothing is moving on the highway.

Nothing he can see.

He checks the clock on the dash—thinks of the town of Standish a dozen miles distant. Tension in the set of his shoulders, in his grip on the wheel. He lets go, shakes his hands, tries to loosen himself out.

Barbone's people would be waiting—better not to let them see the wire drawn tight inside him.

He slips his foot off the brake, eases back onto the gas. Drives the few remaining yards to the highway's edge, the big car bouncing over rough ground, dry brush screeching against its underfloor.

At the road's edge, he checks again.

No car, no vehicle.

Nosing out onto asphalt, he turns, heads east.

Along the two-lane road is a stretch of open ground and then the dark green forest, pine and fir closing tight to the roadway.

A vehicle is parked there.

Five, six hundred yards ahead—between the trees.

A man standing.

Not moving.

McConnell stares through the windshield at the man's back.

He's dressed in olive drab—a coat, a hat.

A uniform.

Across the top of the vehicle is a strip of something. Light bar mounted over the roof.

McConnell stands on the brake, his chest tightens.

Adrenaline surges inside.

He cranks the steering around, hits the throttle. Fights a rising panic.

Locks eyes on the rear-view mirror.

▲

Whicher studies the ground in front of him, brush and wetland, the sky reflecting from the standing water.

Nobody can leave to the south—not without being seen.

From the tree-lined ridge, the view of the camp is only partial. But nobody can pick him out—if anybody is there.

He moves in shadow to the edge of a line of withered fern.

Sees a man tracking between stands of trees, clumps of brush and reed. Grogan. Deputy Grogan—moving in toward the camp.

The other deputy, Creel, would be moving through the woods to set up close.

Close enough to make the call, observe, decide if anyone was in there.

Whicher scans the ground beyond Deputy Grogan. Forest along the right-hand flank, edging the flooding area. Evelyn Cruz at the County Line Road beyond that—no way out if anybody broke east.

Wind shifts in the trees overhead.

A feeling of unease is in him.

In his mind's eye he sees his own daughter, in place of Bella McConnell. Armed officers closing in. Violent men around her. A hair trigger's breadth from danger.

A broad-winged hawk sweeps from the top of a jack pine.

Sunlight breaks on the figure of Grogan as a cloud moves across the sky.

Lighting up the big man in the tan and gray-green landscape. A black vest covering his torso. White letters on its back.

Grogan stalks on—picked out—lit up.

Whicher stares across the dead ground.

Willing him to feel it.

Sense it.

Recognize his mistake.

Chapter Thirty-Six

Racing through the woods toward the camp clearing, Travis McConnell fixes on the far cabin, Barbone's cabin—he scans the ground that he can see—heart beating like a triphammer.

Nothing.

Nothing among the grass and weed and piles of cordwood.

No one.

No faces in the woodland.

Nobody along the edge of the stream.

He breaks cover. Runs for the back of Barbone's cabin. Pushes open the door.

Barbone is at the window—staring outside, his hands at his knees.

The big man turns around, color in his face, sweat on his brow, his beard and hair matted to his face. "Somebody's out there…" He turns back to the window. "Out *there*."

Travis takes a step closer.

Barbone sways on his feet. "You're supposed to be gone.

You're supposed to be in Standish…"

"There's a cop on the road."

Barbone's voice is dry, a rasp in his throat. "Say what?" He turns. His eyes glazed. Uncomprehending.

Through the grime on the cabin window, McConnell sees the figure approaching.

Barbone gapes. Malevolent. Lurches back to stare from the window.

McConnell steps to a rough wood table, whips up the Browning Hi-Power pistol.

He flips it, grips its barrel. Braces. Smashes the butt into the back of Barbone's head.

The big man drops—felled—he hits the plank floor, face first.

McConnell reaches to the gym bag beneath the bed—rips it clear.

Scrambling out of the cabin he sees nobody in the camp, nobody in the woods.

Sprinting to the second cabin, he grabs the door handle—it won't open, it's locked.

Sweat blooms across his face, his voice sticks in his throat. "Bella…"

No answer.

"Bella, it's me—open up…"

He hears a bolt slide back in its runner.

His daughter's face is at the door.

"You need to come with me—right now. Grab your bag."

Her eyes lock onto the gun in his hand. "Dad…"

"Just do it."

"Wait, why?"

"We've got to go—*now*—*right now*…"

⭟

The sound of the shot exploding lifts the birds from the tops of the trees.

Whicher stares across the sweep of open terrain before him.

Grogan is on the ground.

Flat.

A void of silence returning on the wind as Whicher eyes him.

He pulls the Glock from its holster. Stops his breath to listen.

No sound.

Nothing.

Another shot rings out. Two more.

The marshal grabs the radio.

Different rounds crack out.

Grogan firing now—lying prone, arms out. His pistol recoiling, climbing in his hands.

Whicher holds down the call switch; "Cease fire—*hold your fire*…"

Shots boom out—a third weapon firing.

"This is call-sign three—Whicher. All elements cease firing—find cover. Withdraw, now…."

Creel's voice comes on the radio; "This is six—I have gunfire coming from the camp—I see call-sign five under fire."

The marshal sees Grogan push up from a prone position. More shots ring out.

Whicher hits the switch. "Five—get on the ground—stay down, find cover."

He sees the man flop forward, roll to one side. Then start to crawl toward a patch of tall brush.

Eveyln Cruz comes on the radio; "This is two—moving in."

Another voice, O'Donnell, at the highway; "You need help? Should I come in there?"

"Everybody stay back…" Whicher gets to his haunches.

Cruz speaks as he lets go the switch; "We need to keep them contained."

The marshal runs at a crouch to the left flank of the flooding area—to the cover of trees.

More shots boom out.

Whicher tears through the woods. "*Hold fire. Five—get in cover.*"

Tad Haskie's voice crackles, "This is four—moving in—I'm almost at the camp."

Racing through the trees, Whicher pictures timber-skinned cabins, rounds whipping through them, no protection inside.

Ragged fire is ripping through the air.

Whicher keys the switch. "Cease fire—and hold position—we need everybody alive."

⋏

Travis McConnell's hands are greased with sweat, his jaw clamped, body wired.

He steers along the bed of a dry creek beneath a line of overhanging trees.

Seconds pass.

Seconds turning to minutes.

Bella in the passenger seat, silent. Scarcely breathing.

He listens through the rolled window of the SUV.

Above the sound of the motor is gunfire—distant now, slowing, fading.

A quarter-mile till the roadway, it can't be more—a quarter-mile.

Only trees and the dry creek before them.

But would more be coming?

How many?

How much more time?

⋏

At the clearing's edge Whicher spots Deputy Glen Creel—advancing onto the back of the cabins. A second deputy—Haskie—is behind a pile of firewood thirty yards away.

Shots explode from the furthest cabin—incoming rounds smack low against its sides.

Haskie leans around the woodpile, gun arm out—he fires twice in the direction of a shattered window on the cabin front.

Whicher breaks from the tree line, runs to the woodpile, throws himself in behind it. "Quit firing…"

Haskie stares at him.

"There could be a minor in there," Whicher says.

The deputy's eyes are wide. "Grogan's out there getting shot up."

More rounds crack out from the cabin's interior.

Deputy Creel edges closer.

Whicher checks the second cabin—no sign of any movement.

Evelyn Cruz is crouched low on the far flank—the letters on her USMS vest picked out against the color of the woods.

He keys the radio switch; "Cruz, get in cover…"

More shots splinter the side of the cabin.

Rounds explode from inside it.

Whicher turns to Haskie; "Get to the road—call for backup. Ambulances, a medevac helo…"

"I'm staying right here."

"Get a siege negotiator…" Whicher locks eyes with him. "You know who to call, get whatever you can get…"

The deputy takes a breath. Then runs from the pile of cordwood to the cover of the trees.

A burst of shots boom out—Evelyn Cruz flattens to the ground.

Whicher leads with the Glock, closing the angle on the cabin, running in line with its corner.

Deputy Creel breaks out into a run.

Flattening to the cabin side, Whicher takes the Glock between both hands.

Inching wide he stares down its iron sights.

A bearded man is just back from the edge of the smashed-up window—his eyes wild—a Desert Eagle in his hand.

The marshal's finger curls around the trigger.

The man's eyes move to him—but his gun is pointed out—onto Grogan.

He can drop him.

Whicher knows.

The man knows. He stands completely still.

A crash erupts at the back of the cabin.

The man spins around.

Shots explode.

Blood flies against the back wall.

The man drops out of sight.

⋏

Through the shattered window Whicher sees the shooter slumped at the foot of the wall.

Deputy Creel stands in the doorway, gun out before him.

The marshal runs around the cabin to the door, pushes past Creel, takes the gun from the fallen man's hand.

A mess of clothes and bedding and spent shell cases is on the floor, the air fetid—nobody else inside.

Whicher eyes the deputy—sees the shock in his face. "Stay here."

Creel barely nods.

Whicher pushes out of the door.

Glock out front, he moves to the second cabin, jumps onto its porch. "*US Marshal. Open up.*"

He drops low, to one side, puts a hand to the door—it opens.

He scans the interior, leads with the Glock.

Nobody is in there.

⋏

Nowhere.

The girl is nowhere.

The man in the first cabin is Reed Barbone.

If McConnell was here, Whicher tells himself, he's gone now.

Deputy Grogan wanders the perimeter of the camp—uniform smeared with dirt, eyes hunted.

Radio chatter drifts from Cruz in the shooter's cabin—back and forth with Haskie and O'Donnell at the road.

Whicher re-enters the second of the cabins—a bed and camp bed are set up—unmade. Cans of food and soda bottles litter the place. He squats, gets to his hands and knees, scans the plank floor, peers beneath the bed and the camp bed. A flash of color catches his eye.

Reaching beneath the camp bed he pulls out a balled-up top—a purple sweat top. Wrapped up in it is a single sock—a pale pink sports sock.

The same as one of Lori's, a little bigger.

He stands.

Holds it in his hand.

Stares out through the open door into stark afternoon light.

Chapter Thirty-Seven

Hudspeth County, Tx

The sheriff's department is practically deserted—a dispatcher in the comms room, a female secretary working civilian support.

Sheriff Ingram reads the file on a low-level marijuana bust the county likely won't proceed to prosecute.

The phone on his desk rings, Ingram puts down the file, picks up.

"Sheriff, this is Carlos Sanchez—calling from the lab in El Paso."

The sheriff cradles the phone against his neck. "Yeah, go ahead."

"It's about the material we're processing in regard to the search of the Harwood property—Jacob Harwood's house and truck."

"You have something?" the sheriff says.

"Yes and no," Sanchez replies. "I wanted to give you an update, your office said it was urgent."

"It's a missing minor," Ingram says, "a girl we need to

find. We need whatever we can get."

"Well, so far, the samples we've processed from Harwood's house are all associated with him, there's nothing out of the ordinary," Sanchez says. "The blood sample from the Ram truck is looking problematic at this point. The sample we tested was contaminated with gasoline and some kind of oil, maybe chainsaw oil, dirty water, too."

"It's no good?"

"We'll run another test, see if we can extract a cleaner sample. We won't know till tomorrow—but there's another sample, a hair sample—from the bed of the truck."

The sheriff pictures Harwood's Ram pickup, the forensic investigator crawling over it.

"The hair doesn't seem to be from Harwood," Sanchez says. "Harwood's blond, the hair we have is dark. We have a root on it, though, we can run STR analysis, we'll be able to extract DNA."

Sheriff Ingram scowls. "That pickup's a work truck, I'd guess a hair could be from just about anyone, a co-worker maybe?"

"Maybe," Sanchez says. "But it looks like it was pulled out forcibly—a hair breaking or shedding naturally, wouldn't look the way this does."

"Can you tell if it's from a man? Or a woman?"

"It's short, it's from the head area, I'd say male at this point."

The sheriff pictures Bella McConnell, long haired, like her mother. A co-worker then, a drywaller maybe? Somebody at a construction supply? He clears his throat.

"We're sending blood samples from Harwood, and the child's mother—we just took them today. How soon can you process them?"

"We'll process the samples as soon as we receive them," Sanchez says.

The sheriff nods. "So, I wait to hear from you? On the blood sample from the pickup?"

"We'll have it tomorrow."

"And you'll test the hair root for DNA?"

"I can't promise, sheriff. But it could be something."

⊥

Gladwin County, Mi

Whicher reaches into a pocket of his ranch coat—pulls out a pair of nitrile gloves, puts them on.

Marshal Evelyn Cruz watches.

The cabin is empty, now, Deputy Creel outside with the big deputy, Grogan. A faint sound of sirens in the air—more units arriving on the highway, out beyond the trees.

Whicher approaches the body slumped at the foot of the cabin wall.

In the chest and upper abdomen are three entry wounds. Center mass. Well placed. Creel's accuracy high under duress.

In the wall to one side is a bullet hole—a miss, a single round.

The marshal squats, regards the bandaged wound on the leg of the man, Barbone.

Blood is visible on the bandage, the wound not yet

healed—likely from the robbery at the sporting goods store.

The man's face is wild-looking; the matted hair, the beard. On the floor is spent brass and broken glass, splintered wood from incoming fire.

Whicher stands, turns to Marshal Cruz.

She looks at him, her face immobile, set hard.

"This a good result for you?" he says.

She bridles. "We have one less escaped felon to relocate. To house, to feed."

Whicher eyes her. Moves across to the window. Glances out into skeleton-branched trees. The caw of a single crow sounds above the sirens in the distance.

"You have something to say?" Cruz's voice is flat.

"She was here," Whicher answers.

"Bella?"

The marshal turns back from the window, gestures with his head. "Girl's clothes. In that other cabin back there."

Cruz stares at him, coldness in her eyes.

Whicher breaks off looking at her—studies the blood on the plank wall above the body of Reed Barbone—blood splattered, smeared downward in short, broad streaks.

He takes a step toward it.

Something in the marks catches his eye.

The blood is spread from exit wounds to the torso, dragged downward with the man's fall.

But above it is another patch of blood.

Smaller. Small but separate, distinct.

The marshal steps to it, leans in, studies the stain.

Striated marks are visible within it, linear marks—made by hair.

He steps away from the wall, kneels at the body on the floor.

Placing his gloved hands on Barbone's shoulders, he grips him.

"What are you doing?" Cruz says.

Whicher pulls the man forward, away from the wall.

Carefully, he leans his head over on his chest—rolls him slightly to one side.

Cruz steps closer. "Marshal?"

At the back of Barbone's head is blood.

In his dark hair, glistening.

Soaked in through the collar of his jacket.

Whicher puts a gloved finger into the man's hair, parting it slightly. Feels the lump and the blood and the broken skin at the back of the scalp.

He holds his hand up for Evelyn Cruz to see.

"What?" she says. "What the hell is that?"

"Somebody hit him. Back of the head," Whicher says. "Before we got here. Somebody put him down."

Chapter Thirty-Eight

Reeves County, Tx

A shaft of sunlight cuts the still air of the kitchen in the house in Pecos. Whicher sits alone drinking coffee, ranch coat on the back of a chair.

The Ruger revolver and the Glock are laid out on the table with the extra magazines, the boxes of ammunition, the ballistic vest.

Outside, the snow is gone from the ground, now. The air still cold and sharp when he'd stepped from the plane. One night at a hotel in Detroit. Return flight to Midland. A world away from the Michigan woods.

At the front of the house is the sound of a motor.

He drains the cup of coffee, moves through the hall to the front door. Opens up.

Leanne is outside, parking a dark gray Chevy Impala by the Silverado in the drive.

She sees him. Her smile behind the wheel is warm.

He steps to her as she climbs out, puts his arms around her.

Her kiss is full, sweet.

"I went to lunch," she says. "That new Mexican place. With Katelyn. Katelyn? From yoga class?" She cocks her head.

"Sure."

"You have no idea, do you?" She makes a face. "Did you eat yet?"

"I got a sandwich. And breakfast at the hotel." The marshal eases his arms from his wife. Leads her back into the house, into the kitchen.

She glances at the guns on the table, the ammunition, the Kevlar vest. "Like an armory in here."

"I'll get it squared away."

"I'm sorry about..." her face slackens, "about what happened...that you didn't..."

Whicher meets his wife's eye.

"But she was there?"

He nods. "Looks like it. We found clothing we can test."

She takes his hand, squeezes on it. "What now?"

"I have to go in, talk with Chief Marshal Fairbanks. There's a whole mess we'll have to clean up. A fatality. Failure to apprehend a felony prisoner. Bad medicine. Not to mention Bella."

Leanne takes off her coat, throws it onto a chair, brushes back her auburn hair.

"How's Lori? She miss me last night?"

"She knows you come back, now."

Whicher takes the guns from the kitchen table, dumps them back among the clothes in the go-bag on the floor.

"She's ten years old," Leanne says. "She's in a world of her own. You want to pick her up from school?"

"I have to go in."

Leanne brightens; "Don't worry. She's okay."

Whicher carries the bag into the bedroom. Grateful for his daughter's school day, its mundanity. Far from ragged woods, from gunfire.

He hears the ringer sound on the phone in his coat.

"John…"

He clips back into the kitchen. Takes out the phone, checks the screen, answers.

"Marshal. This is Sheriff Ingram—calling from Hudspeth County."

"I do something for you?"

"No. But I got something for you. I just got done talking with the crime lab over in El Paso. Where are you?"

Whicher steps to the window. "I'm home in Pecos."

The sheriff's voice is wary. "You didn't find Bella McConnell?"

"We didn't find her," the marshal says. "But we think she could've been there."

"Up in Michigan?"

"We found a camp, a hideout our escapees were using. We found kids' clothing. A purple top."

"You think she was there?"

"I do now," Whicher says. "We nailed one of the escapees."

"You caught him?" Ingram says.

"Killed him."

The sheriff is quiet a moment on the line. "What happens now?"

"We keep looking."

"Well," the sheriff says. "I got something you'll maybe want to hear. I talked to the lab in El Paso yesterday, to a guy name of Sanchez—processing samples from the search of Jacob Harwood's home."

"Y'all have something?"

"They been running tests on the sample of blood—from Harwood's truck? Yesterday, the lab said the sample was corrupted, contaminated. But now it looks like they managed to get a cleaner sample. And it looks like it could be a match for the blood spatter at Jessica McConnell's house."

Whicher glances at his wife's reflection in the window.

"The blood from her living room wall," the sheriff says.

"Could it be from either one of them? From Harwood? From Jessica?"

"No, sir."

"You sure on that?"

"We found 'em yesterday, brought 'em in, took samples from them both. El Paso already ran the first tests. The blood in the pickup and the house is neither one of 'em."

The marshal thinks it over, mind starting to hunt. "They tell you where they were at? How come nobody could find them?"

"No, sir. But I'm submitting requests for warrants," Sheriff Ingram says, "to impound Harwood's truck, to search it again. And search that other vehicle he owns—the car, a Toyota sedan. He keeps it over at a work yard here, I want to search inside there too."

"Where's the work yard at?"

"The highway north out of town, just beyond the city limit."

The marshal finds a square of yellow paper on the countertop, notes it down.

"You're the investigator, I thought you'd want to know."

"You thought right," Whicher says.

"There's something else, too," the sheriff says. "My evidence guy found a hair sample, the same area he found the blood—around the winch in back of that Ram? The feller at the lab, Sanchez, says one of the hairs has the root attached. They'll try to profile the DNA."

Whicher turns from the window. "When are y'all putting in for the warrants?"

"I have a deputy on it now."

"I have to head into the office," the marshal says. "It'll take me a couple hours to drive over. I'd like to be there for the search."

"We get the warrants, we're going right out and get it moving," the sheriff says.

"I'll be there," the marshal tells him. "I'll be there just as fast as I can."

※

In the USMS suite on Cedar Street Whicher steps into Chief Marshal Fairbanks's office, pushes the door closed.

The chief marshal looks at him from behind her desk, face pinched. "Take a seat."

Whicher pulls out a chair.

"Yesterday?" Fairbanks says. "What happened?"

"We located a site. With local law enforcement. Approached it."

"And?"

"Somebody started firing."

"You know who?"

The marshal shakes his head. "Somebody in the camp, the deer camp. By the time I made it in it was a goddamn shooting gallery."

"Then what?"

"I tried to get everybody to stop. I got close. One of the deputies broke through the back of the main cabin, opened up on the shooter. That was it."

"They shot and killed this man, Barbone?"

"Yes, ma'am. They did."

"I've had the senior marshal from the Memphis task force, plus the county sheriff's office from Michigan on the line. There's a lot of friction," Fairbanks says.

"I told 'em right out not to go in hard."

"Because of the girl."

"Because of Bella…"

"The task force think she might've been there?"

Whicher leans forward, works his palm with his thumb. "There was clothing that might've belonged to Bella. If it didn't, I don't know what the hell it was doing there. Marshal Cruz took it in evidence, for their investigation."

"Do you think Bella could have been present when you arrived?"

"We didn't find any vehicle," Whicher says. "Maybe she got out, with her father. Maybe she wasn't there."

"The county sheriff's office said they found wheel tracks. In the woodland. Across several fields."

"Maybe that was the missing SUV," Whicher says.

Chief Marshal Fairbanks clicks her pen in irritation. "We just made the case public—now this."

Whicher eyes his boss.

"If it gets out a minor was in there..." Fairbanks lets her sentence trail off.

"Hudspeth County sheriff called me," Whicher says. "They're putting in for warrants to search vehicles and a work yard belonging to Jacob Harwood—the friend or maybe boyfriend of Bella's mother. They found blood in his truck matching a blood spatter sample found in Jessica McConnell's home."

Fairbanks looks at him, her brow creased.

"If the warrants are issued," Whicher says, "I want to be there."

"You have any idea whose blood it could be?"

Whicher shakes his head. Lets his eyes meet the chief marshal's.

"Have you spoken with Jessica?"

"Not yet. But we think the deer camp might've belonged to one of Barbone's associates. Evelyn Cruz is looking to trace the owner."

"And?"

"If Barbone's dead, who's going to help McConnell now?" Whicher says.

Fairbanks gazes down at her desk a moment. "You think Jessica?" The chief marshal nods. "Alright, good. You're going after her?"

"Yes, ma'am," Whicher says. "And there was something else."

"What's that?"

"Somebody hit the man, Barbone, in the back of the head. Before we got there. There was an injury to the back of his skull, a recent injury—still bleeding."

"You think McConnell hit him?"

"Maybe he thought he was slowing him down."

The chief marshal thinks about it. "Could he have seen you coming? You know, I can see this from the point of view of the Michigan sheriff's office; the action they took. Those men were convicted criminals, violent offenders, they were guilty. A public inquiry would likely reflect that."

"Not the kid," Whicher says.

Fairbanks looks at him.

The marshal stands. Opens up the door to the office. "They may be guilty," he says. "Not the kid."

⸸

Seated at his desk in the main office, the marshal checks his notepad, dials a landline number.

A woman answers.

"Mrs McConnell? Jessica? This is Deputy Marshal John Whicher."

"Have you found her?" Jessica's voice is shaky.

"No, ma'am."

"It's been two days—I didn't know what to think…"

"Sheriff's department said they couldn't find you."

"I didn't know they were looking for me."

"Where were you?"

"I've been around."

"You can call here," Whicher says. "You can call the juvenile protection service, Georgia Eastman."

"I didn't know what to do, what to think…"

"I told you last time we spoke there were reports your husband might be in the Detroit area."

"You said you thought Bella might be with him."

"A child was thought to be a passenger in a vehicle we've been looking for. I traveled up to Michigan, yesterday, ma'am."

"You think she's up there?"

"Ma'am, does your daughter own a purple top—a purple, hooded sweat top?"

Jessica McConnell is silent on the line.

"Ma'am, does she?"

"I think."

"You think?" Whicher says. "You don't know?"

Her voice falters. "She swaps clothes with friends. One of them had a top like that, I think, from school. But she's been living away at the hostel…"

"What friend?"

"A girl, Aimee."

The marshal checks his notes—finds his interview with the girl from the high school. "Aimee Douglas?"

"Have you talked to her?"

The marshal ignores the question. "Ma'am, has your daughter made contact with you?"

"Why would you say that? I would have called."

"Mrs McConnell, if you hear from your daughter—or your husband, I want to be the first person you call…"

"Why would my husband try to contact me?"

"Call me. If Bella calls you, I want to know. You pick up the phone. Night or day."

⁂

Hudspeth County, Tx

From the two-lane highway, Whicher studies the rugged mountain to the north of town—*Sierra Blanca;* white mountain, the land surrounding it harsh, empty, broken only with desert scrub, scoured by wind.

Sheriff's department vehicles are ahead at a small warehouse set back from the road.

Slowing the truck as he approaches he spots a blue panel van—a man in a zip suit kneeling at a white Toyota sedan.

The sedan's four doors are open, the man in the zip suit leaning into a footwell.

Deputies wearing gloves move in and out of the warehouse.

Sheriff Ingram is at the perimeter of the property—standing with Jacob Harwood at the edge of the yard.

Whicher pulls the Silverado over at the side of the highway.

The sheriff spots him.

Harwood stands rigid, arms folded across a dirty-looking canvas work jacket.

Cutting the motor on the truck, the marshal climbs out.

Sheriff Ingram walks toward the gates at the front of the yard.

Harwood watches; face pale. Hair blowing in the wind.

Whicher stops at the gate. "What's he doing here?"

"Demanded to be present. No law says he can't be."

"Y'all get your warrants?"

"We got them," Ingram says. "We impounded his truck, he's got no other ride—he rode over with me."

"What's he saying?"

"So far, squat."

Three deputies search inside the warehouse building, examining piles of boxes, lumber, stacks of drywall panel.

"Anybody find anything?"

The sheriff inclines his head toward the evidence technician at the Toyota. "There's some hairs in the car. Long, dark. Could be Jessica. Could be Bella. There's prints. And fibers around the passenger side. Partials on the door handles, the window."

"I want to talk to him."

"He wasn't talking on the ride over."

Whicher crosses the yard to Harwood.

The young man stares.

"Sheriff says your whereabouts are unaccounted for the last couple days."

"What's going on here?" Harwood says. "How come everybody's in my business?"

"A young girl is missing," Whicher says. "And the sheriff's office found blood in your pickup. And in Jessica McConnell's house. It's not your blood. It's not hers. We find blood in a missing persons case we get interested."

Harwood eyes him, swallows.

The marshal goes on; "We find blood in a spatter pattern, it likely comes from an injury. Not a scratch, or a cut. We match that with a blood sample found elsewhere—we need an explanation."

"I feel like I need a lawyer."

"You're not under arrest."

The young man shakes his head. "What are you accusing me of?"

"How come you feel like you need a lawyer?"

"My house gets searched, the sheriff impounds my truck? My warehouse gets turned over? I don't know what all's going on. How do I know somebody's not about to plant something?"

"Nobody's planting anything, Mister Harwood."

"I feel like I'm being set up."

"Did you wash the truck?" Whicher says.

"I'm entitled to wash it."

"Did you?"

Harwood doesn't answer.

"You've been out of town. You've been asked where," Whicher says. "Sheriff's office says you don't seem real clear."

"I told the sheriff, El Paso, New Mexico…"

"Sheriff wasn't satisfied with your explanation," Whicher says.

At the gate to the work yard, Sheriff Ingram watches. Shoulders bunched against the cold.

"Your being out of town coincided with Bella McConnell's disappearance." The marshal studies the young man, thinks again of Sheriff Ingram's theory—of Harwood; his behavior around the girl. "You know what my job is?"

Harwood looks at him.

"I'm a criminal investigator." Whicher scans the yard, the deputies in the warehouse, his gaze settling on the evidence technician at the car. "The pastor at your church says you're a good man, a God-fearing man Mister Harwood. That right? Pastor Mullins says so. He had no time for talk about you; the rumors, you and Jessica."

"What rumors?"

"Her a married woman an' all."

Thoughts work behind the young man's eyes.

"You believe in a just God?"

Harwood's mouth is clamped shut, he juts his chin.

"I believe you do," Whicher says.

"You believe what you want to believe."

"If you won't talk to me, that's your right. Same as it's the county's right to search your property. Your vehicles. Your home. But you'll stand before a court and make your account. One way or another." The marshal takes a cold look at Harwood. "Here," he tells him. "Or in a Higher court than that."

Chapter Thirty-Nine

Whicher sits in front of the green-painted house behind the wheel of the Silverado, eying the marked-up Nissan in the yard.

He kills the motor in the truck, climbs out.

The dog in the neighbor's yard barks, its amber eyes shine.

The marshal steps to the front door, knocks hard.

The door opens on its chain.

Jessica McConnell peers out.

"Mrs McConnell. Like to talk to you."

She stares, silent. Dressed in black jeans, a white sweat top, her dark hair piled on top of her head. A few dark strands are loose against her neck, stark against the pale skin. Whicher thinks of the hair found in Harwood's Toyota sedan.

"I come in?"

She slides back the chain, pulls the door wide.

Whicher follows her into the living room.

She looks into his face, eyes luminous. "What's going on?

Is there news—about my daughter?"

"No, ma'am."

Her voice is dry in her throat. "You still think she's somewhere—up in Michigan?"

"I believe she was." The marshal studies the spot on the front wall—barely perceptible. "I need to talk to you about the blood that was found here, Mrs McConnell."

Jessica stares at him. "I already told you this place is rented. It hasn't been redecorated in years. It could be anybody's."

He shakes his head.

"I don't know anything about it."

"It's not yours. We know that."

She sinks down onto the arm of the couch.

"Sheriff's office took blood from you yesterday," the marshal says. "They tested it already. They know it's not yours."

She rocks forward, lightly.

Whicher eyes her, takes in the studied composure. "Your daughter's been gone how long? Eight days, now?"

She nods.

"You don't seem that concerned?"

"I have to not fall apart, wouldn't you say, marshal?" She touches a hand to her face. "If I gave in to the things I'm feeling, everything inside me…" She stops herself. "I might walk out—right now. And throw myself under some train."

"She's been gone eight days…"

A flash of anger is in her, now; "Longer than that, marshal. She's been gone a lot longer than that. She's been gone since they took her to that damn hostel. Since they took her to Fort Stockton. To *'ensure her proper welfare.'* She's been gone weeks. Months. Slipping away from me even before then."

"If she's with her father, now…" Whicher waits until she looks at him. "She's not safe. A man was shot dead yesterday afternoon, the man that escaped with your husband. The folk charged with bringing him back have no compunction about that."

"Shouldn't you be talking to them?" she says.

"Her best hope, Bella's best hope, is I get to her first."

Jessica steadies herself, says nothing.

"So anything you can tell me," Whicher says, "anything that gets me to her ahead of anybody else, you need to tell me."

"What could I possibly know?"

"If either of them were to contact you." The marshal looks at her. "Your daughter. Your husband. Either one."

She shakes her head, allows her gaze to rise toward the ceiling. "I don't know where she is. I told you…"

"One of them may try to call. You're her mother. You're his wife."

She lets out a constricted breath. Face drained.

"There's something else you could maybe answer for me?"

Her eyes flick onto his.

"The blood we found in this room—matches with a sample of blood we found in Jacob Harwood's truck."

Jessica's eyes go flat.

"Sheriff Ingram's searching it again. He's searching Harwood's warehouse—out on the highway. Searching that other vehicle he owns, the four-door Toyota. I just came from there."

Still she only stares.

"How could that be?" the marshal says. "That there's blood in here? This house. And the same blood, in your friend Jacob's truck?"

She stands, suddenly. "I don't know—I have *no idea* what you're talking about." She sways on her feet.

"I'm just looking for an answer to a question. A question that's going to vex me," Whicher says. "And vex the sheriff. Till the answer's out there, one way or another."

She puts her hand in front of her mouth, "Please… excuse me for a moment…"

She disappears out of the door, into the hallway.

The marshal hears her enter another room, pull the door.

He stands in silence, in the stillness within the house.

Hears a sound—a retching sound. Muffled, from behind a closed door.

A minute passes. He hears the flush of a toilet. Faint noise of water running in a basin.

A door opens.

Jessica appears in the hallway.

He looks at her.

She stares back, ashen-faced.

"Ma'am?" he says. "Is everything alright?"

Jessica nods, wordlessly. "I'm afraid I'm going to need you to leave. I don't feel too well. Unless there was something else?"

Whicher lets his eyes rest on hers a moment. "Think about what I've said here. You have my number. Anytime, day or night, you can call."

⋏

The sun is sinking in the winter sky above the trees at the edge of the truck stop—cars flashing by on Interstate Eighty, the traffic steady, noise of the road a low drone.

Bella McConnell sits up front in the passenger seat of the SUV; finishing up a burger and fries, her father beside her, already done eating, now sipping on a can of soda behind the wheel.

The parking lot is half-filled. Cars and pickups and RVs, rows of trucks line-astern. Bella watches strings of people moving around—in and out of food concessions, a convenience store.

"I wish we could just keep on driving…"

Travis rests the can of soda on the top of the wheel, says nothing.

"Like this." She thinks of the camp in the woods—the man Reed. Stifling a shudder at the thought of him. His eyes. Face. Hands. The big, brute body. The whole feeling around him. Threat and heat; something barely under control.

The best thing that happened since Nashville, since seeing her Aunt Ursula, was being with her father—no doubt. But getting out of that horrible place, the camp, those woods. Running out on Reed was the best thing.

"I like this," she says. "Just you and me." She looks across at her father. His handsome profile. "I've missed you."

He pats her leg. "I missed you, too."

"I could just keep doing this forever," she says, "you know? Just keep on, going wherever we want to, doing whatever we want…"

Tension is in her father's face, despite his smile.

"We could just keep going." She finishes the burger, screws up the wrapper, eats the last of the fries, flattens out the carton.

Runaways.

The pair of them.

Rebels against the system. Out from underneath it all.

In the trunk of the car is the gym bag.

Filled with money—more money than she's ever seen.

Enough to go and keep on going. To never have to go back.

To never see the hostel in Fort Stockton again, never see the juvenile court. Never talk to any more 'protection' officers. Never see the crappy house in Texas, never lie on the bed in her crappy room.

For her father, enough to never be put back—to never be put back in some cage.

"We'll drive a couple of more hours," he says. "Then find someplace. Get a motel."

"I meant after," Bella says. "After tonight. Tomorrow. The day after that. We could just keep right on, keep going." She smiles at him.

He smiles back.

But he doesn't feel it.

She can see it—something in him, coiled, hyped-up. Like

he's all the time on edge.

"Don't you want to see some of my old stamping grounds, a few of my old places?" he says.

"You mean, Nashville?"

"Before that." He flicks the opener on the top of the can of soda. Stares out the front of the car.

She looks at him, blank-faced.

"I grew up in Pennsylvania, you know that. When I was a kid. When I first got started in Nashville I was with a guy from there, a buddy of mine, Erv Ackerman. A guy from my hometown. It's not far from here."

She shrugs.

"Tomorrow we could be there."

Something about the way he speaks—something about the way his words come out. All the time it's there.

"You done eating?" he asks her.

"Yeah."

He reaches into the pocket of his jacket. "I need you to do something for me." He brings out a bunch of twenty dollar bills, holds them out in his hand. Points at the convenience store across the lot. "I want you to go on into that store back there. There's a travel section. With a bunch of phones, prepaid phones. I want you to go get one. Can you do that?"

"Why don't you?" she says. "I don't know what you want?"

"Just pick one," her father says. "A cheap one."

She feels it in him now—the way he is. The same unease. "Will they sell one to me?"

"Why not?"

"I'm just a kid."

"There's no contract, you don't need a credit card."

"What if they ask me about it?"

"Just give them the money," he says. "Look, the less I show my face, the better. If I don't have to, if you can do it, you know? So nobody sees anything, says anything. Nobody reports anything. We just get what we need, we roll on by. Out of here. Like you said."

She takes the money, pushes it into the pocket of her jeans.

Pops the door, steps out. Feels the cold air on her skin.

"It's okay," he says.

She nods.

"Just walk on over, pick out a phone, pay for it. Come on back."

He smiles at her, the same brittle smile, the skin stretched at the edges of his mouth.

And a coldness in his eye.

On the floor beneath his seat she sees it—stepping back to swing the door shut. The pistol, the barrel of the pistol. Always there, or in a pocket, or in his jacket, or down in the small of his back. Concealed, but there. Like the edge in his smile. The tension in his arms, the way his hands grip the wheel.

The sound in his voice.

The sense.

The wire running through him.

The knife edge.

A fire waiting to catch hold.

Chapter Forty

Pecos, Tx

The kitchen is dark—a strip lamp above the countertop the only light. Whicher sits at the table. The morning sky above the yard an ink-black.

The house is still. The world silenced.

He sips on a cup of coffee. Leans into the table. Tiredness in him. But restless. Always restless. Mind turning. Tracking, hunting ahead.

In the pre-dawn sky beyond the glass sliders he lets his mind range.

A sound is in the hallway—footsteps.

He turns.

A light is on.

Leanne stands in the doorway, a bathrobe about her.

She pads into the kitchen. "You alright? Can't you sleep?"

"I was trying to be quiet."

She puts a warm hand on the back of his neck.

"You want coffee?" he says, voice low, "I made coffee."

"You won't wake her," Leanne says.

The marshal thinks of his daughter—sleeping safe in her room.

His wife takes a china mug from a cupboard, fills it from the pot.

"Busy day ahead," he says. "It gets into your head."

"I know."

The marshal turns his cup on the table. "Sheriff over in Hudspeth has his sights on a guy that could be something."

"That why you're awake?"

"They searched a work place and vehicles yesterday. I think the guy's going to lawyer up. Wouldn't mind talking to him before he does."

"Who's the guy?"

"Involved with the mother."

Leanne settles against the countertop, takes a sip on her mug. "Are you getting anywhere with her? Didn't she already have a lawyer, the woman who told you to back off?"

"Silvia Gonzalez," Whicher says, "the public defender. She was under arrest, then. She's not now."

Leanne looks out into the yard, into the still dark sky.

"There's something going on with all of this," the marshal says. "It's a missing person case. A missing minor. It feels like something else, more than that." Whicher rubs a hand over the growth of stubble at his jaw.

"You have any idea?"

"I don't understand the mother." The marshal sits back at the kitchen table. "She's not the way I'd expect her to be."

"Not every woman's the same kind of mother."

"She says she's gotten used to her daughter being gone—because she had to. With the kid in care. She's learned to live with it."

"You don't believe her?"

"Doesn't feel that way."

"You think she knows what happened to her?" Leanne looks at him. "You said you thought the girl was up there—in Michigan. You think the mother knew?"

Whicher regards his wife. "You know, I think you might be right, what you said before? Maybe I'm not the man for this. This job."

She puts down her mug on the countertop. "Don't think that."

"Maybe you were right."

"It's not what you do, that's all…" She steps to the table, leans in. "You'll find her."

Turning to the refrigerator, she opens it.

"You want breakfast?" she says. "Want me to fix something?"

The marshal nods. Lets his eyes blur on the hint of dawn in the sky at the east.

"You'll find her. You *will* find her."

"I hope I find her alive."

⊥

Hudspeth County, Tx

At reception in the county law enforcement center Whicher recognizes the lone deputy from the search of Jessica McConnell's house.

Raylene Lapointe's face is guarded.

"Here to see Sheriff Ingram," Whicher says. "He around?"

"He's around. I can see if he's free?" The deputy picks up a desk phone, keys a number. "Sheriff? I have the marshal—out of Reeves County. Asking to speak with you?" She listens to the reply in the earpiece. Puts down the receiver. "He says he'll be right out."

Whicher cuts a look at her. "Something going on? Something I ought to know about?"

A door opens at the side of reception—Sheriff Ingram stands in the entrance to a corridor. "Marshal. I was going to call you."

"Oh?" Whicher gives the man a look.

"We had news," Ingram says. "From the lab in El Paso."

The marshal crosses the floor.

The sheriff takes a pace back into the corridor, gestures for Whicher to follow.

"What's going on?" Whicher says.

The sheriff closes the door to reception. "The lab called about fibers in Jacob Harwood's car? Purple. Cotton. Distinctive," Ingram says. "You told me you found a purple top. Up in Michigan?"

The marshal nods. "A sweat top."

"Maybe we can match it."

"I'll speak with the task force marshal holding it in evidence," Whicher says, "they can test it."

"Do that," the sheriff says.

Whicher looks along the bright-lit corridor, doors to

three rooms leading off it, all the doors shut. "I want to talk with Harwood."

Ingram looks at him.

"I came out to find him. I thought to speak with you first. If there's evidence Bella McConnell was in his car, we can pressure the guy, get him talking. Before he lawyers up."

"Too late for that," the sheriff says.

"How's that?"

"He's here."

"You have him here?"

"Pastor Mullins called me this morning, Winford Mullins?" the sheriff says. "He said Harwood went over to see him last night. He said the man was troubled. He told him about us searching his house, his work yard, impounding his truck, searching his car. The pastor told me he was concerned for Harwood. Asked if I'd go over, this morning with him. Speak with him."

"And?"

"I went over. But Harwood flat out refused. He said he wanted a lawyer. I told him he needed to talk to us, one way or another. Pastor Mullins told him the same. But he went on back in his house, called a lawyer, he wouldn't come out till the guy arrived."

Whicher blows out his cheeks.

"The lawyer showed up—advised him to come on over here, make a statement—Harwood rode with him, in the man's car. Listen," Ingram says, "I haven't had a straight answer out of Jacob Harwood since this all got started—if the boy's ready to talk, I'm ready to hear it—he has the right to counsel, too, if he's a suspect in an investigation. You know that."

"What's the lawyer say?"

"That his client is co-operating."

"This a custodial interview?"

The sheriff shakes his head. "The man's not under arrest."

"Let me talk to him," Whicher says. "You know Harwood, personally. You don't want a defense team citing conflict of interest."

"I know half the people in the county," Ingram says, "I can still investigate 'em."

"Let me question him," Whicher says.

"You want in on this?" Ingram says. "You making it federal?"

"We got blood already, we got hair," Whicher says, "we got a spatter pattern in Jessica McConnell's house. This all could get ugly."

The sheriff nods. Unfolds his arms.

"Five minutes," Whicher says. "I have to make one call."

⁂

Evelyn Cruz answers the phone on the second ring.

"Marshal? I got news."

"On your missing girl?" Cruz says. "Or my escaped felon?"

"On the girl," Whicher says. "You have that hooded sweat top you took in evidence? It looks like fibers from it could be in a vehicle belonging to the mother's boyfriend."

Cruz is silent on the line.

"If Bella McConnell was in his car, he may have played a role in her disappearance. The sheriff's office here found blood and hair in a pickup truck this guy owns."

"What's that mean? What're you saying?"

"The blood looks to be a match for an unidentified sample found in Jessica McConnell's home. This guy, the mother's boyfriend, Jacob Harwood. I'm starting to wonder if he might've taken Bella to your man Travis. I don't know how Bella got up to McConnell—up in Tennessee—if that's where she met him. I do know Jessica didn't take her there, she flew up alone. But there's evidence Bella was in this guy's car."

"What about this blood, this hair?" Cruz says. "It's not Bella? Bella's alive, no?"

"I believe she's alive."

"You want the top? You want me to get it to you?"

"Test it there," Whicher says. "Send down the results, send a sample, too. I'll get the address for the lab, you can send it direct. Where are you now?"

"Memphis," Cruz says. "With the rest of the task force."

"You went on back? Y'all have any idea where McConnell is at now?"

"None," Cruz answers.

"Have there been any sightings?"

"I wish I could tell you different. We're ready to deploy. But we're back to square one, unless we get something."

"You think they're using the same vehicle?"

"That's our best guess. But nobody's seen the vehicle,

nobody's seen its owner—the pawn shop guy, Kendrick Dupris. I've been making a lot of calls, I spoke with a Nashville detective from McConnell's case—a guy that helped put him away. He told me there were suspicions McConnell had money they never recovered, held back someplace. If he does it's only going to make it harder to find him."

"How about the injury to Reed Barbone?" Whicher says. "To the back of his head?"

"Coroner's Office are dealing with the body. Full autopsy, they'll be reporting back."

"Somebody hit the guy. Hard. You and I both think that."

"And the best guess is Travis McConnell," Cruz says. "The question is; why?"

"Nothing but questions," Whicher says. "Listen, I'm about to go talk with this guy, the boyfriend."

"If you get answers," Cruz says, "be sure and let me know?"

⋏

The interview room is cramped, airless—a harsh glare from the strip light overhead.

Jacob Harwood sits with a balding man in his fifties, Harwood in a rollneck top and denim jacket, the older man beside him dressed in a dark brown suit.

Whicher sits with Sheriff Ingram on the opposite side of a table from the two men—notepad open, pen in hand.

The man in the suit eyes Whicher, wary. A light sheen on his fleshy face.

Ingram starts a digital recorder on the desk. He states the date and time out loud. "Here present," he says, "are Mister Jacob Harwood—with Mister Dean Pemberton, attorney at law. Myself, Sheriff Odell Ingram." He looks at Whicher.

"And Deputy US Marshal John Whicher, Western Division, Texas," Whicher says.

The lawyer, Pemberton, sits forward an inch at the desk.

"Mister Harwood is not under arrest," the sheriff says. "And is free to leave at any time."

Pemberton nods.

Whicher looks at Harwood. "I'm a criminal investigator. I'm tasked with locating a missing child on behalf of the United States Marshals Service."

The young man's face is a mask.

Pemberton sits poised, hands folded.

"The child in question is the daughter of a woman I believe you to be in a relationship with. Is that correct?"

"I've been spending time with Jessica," Harwood says, "that's all. I don't have anything to do with her daughter."

"Bella McConnell went missing nine days ago," Whicher continues, "from a juvenile hostel in Fort Stockton. At around the same time you yourself were out of town. Several days in a row…"

"I already told the sheriff about that," Harwood says. "I was between jobs, up in El Paso. I took off a couple days, kicked back…"

"Nevertheless," Whicher says, "the answers you've given have failed to satisfy the sheriff, they've failed to satisfy me. Added to that, you've produced no evidence corroborating your story. Nor witnesses who can attest to the same."

"Because I wasn't expecting to need to," Harwood says. "You know? I mean, you think you could produce evidence of where you been, if I were to ask you?"

"There'd be card payments in stores," Whicher says, "at gas stations."

"I just finished a job, I had a bunch of cash," Harwood says. "I'm allowed to spend it, aren't I?"

The marshal nods. "During a search of properties and vehicles owned by you, a blood sample was obtained from a pickup, a Ram pickup. A matching sample was also found in the home of Mrs Jessica McConnell, Bella's mother. What do you have to say about that?"

Harwood looks at his lawyer. Looks back at Whicher. "I don't know anything about it."

"That's not a satisfactory answer, Mister Harwood."

Dean Pemberton speaks; "My client has answered your question, marshal. Whether you're satisfied with it or not is another matter."

The marshal looks at him. Flips the pen back and forth between a finger and thumb. "You might point out to your client that if an investigator is not satisfied with an answer, they'll likely pursue it further."

"I'll also point out to him what he's obliged to say and not say."

Whicher looks at Harwood. "Do you have any information regarding Bella McConnell that might help us?"

The young man shakes his head. "I have no idea where she is."

"When's the last time you saw her?"

Harwood looks off across the room. "I'd have to think about it. A couple weeks, I'd guess."

"What was she wearing?" Whicher looks directly into Harwood's eyes.

"I don't know…"

"You don't know?"

"I don't take an interest."

The marshal glances at Sheriff Ingram.

From across the desk, Pemberton regards him with gimlet eyes.

"You like her?"

The attorney cuts in; "That's a leading question."

Whicher addresses Harwood. "I'm trying to find out how well you know her. Whether you spent any time with her."

Harwood's face is flushed. "I see Jessica, is all. I'm not interested in her daughter."

"Could you account for where you were those days?" Whicher says. "Now that you know we're interested?"

The young man shifts in his chair. "I don't have receipts for gas or motels…"

"There any way for you to show us where you were, who you were with?"

Pemberton answers; "My client has already explained that, he's already accounted for it."

"Yesterday I was present at the search of a work yard you run your business out of," Whicher says. "A vehicle there was also searched, a vehicle you own. Is that correct?"

Harwood nods.

"What do you use it for?"

"What kind of a question is that?" Harwood says. "It's a car. What do you think? I use it for getting around."

"But you have a pickup, also? A Ram pickup."

"A work truck, right."

"Which one did you use to take off in? To kick back?"

Harwood doesn't answer.

"Your Ram pickup was on the yard out in front of your house while you were gone," Whicher says. "The sheriff's office had deputies go by there."

Sheriff Ingram nods, "They saw it there."

"If you were on a job, how come you weren't in your work truck?"

"I use the car, too," Harwood says. "I use the truck when I'm hauling supplies. But I use the car, too."

The marshal lets a beat pass. "During a forensic search of your car, the Toyota sedan, fibers were found from a cotton sweat top." He looks again into Harwood's eyes. Senses rising alarm.

Pemberton lays his hands flat on the table top, fingers spread.

"We believe Bella McConnell was wearing that top," Whicher says. "When she disappeared."

Harwood's voice falters slightly. "I don't know anything about that…"

Pemberton raises up his hand. "Gentlemen, I'd like to stop this interview, temporarily. I'd like to speak with my client a moment—alone."

Sheriff Ingram speaks; says the time out loud; then, "The interview is suspended."

⋏

In the corridor Whicher pulls out his phone, checks for messages.

Sheriff Ingram chews on a nail, his face tight. "You think he's about ready to talk? Boy's got something on his mind…"

A message is on his voicemail—Whicher shakes his head. "I don't think he knows what he wants to say."

The sheriff looks at him.

The marshal presses the key for voicemail, clamps the phone to his ear.

"Please call me," Jessica's voice is halting, strained-sounding, "as soon as you get this. I've been thinking, all I've been doing all night is thinking—since you left. I think I might know something. I think I might know where they are…"

Her voice stops.

The message clicks to end.

Along the corridor, the door to the interview room opens.

Dean Pemberton steps out, expression strained, his eyes flat. "Mister Harwood does not wish to continue. We won't be resuming the interview."

The sheriff steps forward. "He said he wanted to talk."

The lawyer looks from Sheriff Ingram to Whicher. "I assume he's free to leave? He's not under arrest, there's no charge against him. Correct?"

Whicher nods.

"Then I'll leave you to develop your evidence, marshal," the attorney says. "I don't believe you have very much."

"We can put a missing minor in his car," the marshal says, "y'all might think about that."

"I'll be sure to talk it over with him."

Whicher looks to Sheriff Ingram. "You consider him a flight risk?"

Ingram shrugs, the corners of his mouth downturned. "Everything he owns is right here."

The marshal takes a business card from his suit jacket, presses it into the hands of the attorney. "If the guy's memory improves, call me."

"My client is co-operating here."

"Advise him not to run," Whicher says. "It only makes the dogs come on harder."

Chapter Forty-One

The last sign of civilization is fifteen miles behind them, a Pennsylvania college town—limestone and ivy and old-time brick stores. Travis McConnell waits at the head of a grit road, a private track down through pasture and light trees toward dense woods.

A sign posted by a cattle guard reads—*Ackerman*.

He settles his hands at the wheel of the SUV. Hits the gas, feels the tires bump on the steel bars of the guard.

In the passenger seat, Bella looks at him.

"It's right down here," McConnell says.

"What is it?"

"A homestead, a farm."

"I didn't know it would all be so…out in the country. Can we go see your house?"

"Later we can see it. It's not much to look at. It's back a ways." McConnell thumbs over his shoulder. "That last little town?"

Bella nods.

"My dad died, your grandma moved out. Moved to

Florida, before she passed. I'd already left."

"I'd still like to see it."

McConnell steers along the grit road between denuded trees. "It's just an old house, you know? Nothing special. Anyhow, I couldn't wait to leave, get the hell out."

His daughter smiles—a knowing smile, a co-conspirator.

Emerging through the woodland into winter pasture, Travis McConnell slows, peers through the windshield at the property ahead—a timber house built on a base of river stone, a red-painted barn with a white gabled roof. Twenty-plus years since he's seen it. Memories float back—of summer nights and dirt bikes. Smoking grass. Shooting rifles out of deer hides, getting drunk in the barn.

Parked at the house is a flame-blue Ford Raptor. Alongside it, a black, Chevy Camaro with tinted glass.

McConnell drives in slow, thinks of the last time he would have seen the current occupant—Finn Ackerman. A Titans game, was it? In Nashville. Six years gone?

The tickets would have been a favor pulled in. Just to show him the way he lived now in music town, show him the way he was living.

"Are we staying here?" Bella says.

"Maybe," McConnell answers. "Maybe just tonight. We can get off the road one time. We're good here."

His daughter looks uncertain.

"I can show you around, show you some of my old places."

"Could we see your old school?"

"Not my favorite place."

Bella grins, "Me neither."

McConnell steers past the big Ford Raptor. Parks behind it—out of sight from the entranceway.

"So, who is this again?" Bella says, her nose wrinkled.

"Folk I knew when I lived here, good friends, a family. I used to be up here all the time, hanging out. With Erv, mainly, my buddy. Ervin Ackerman. I knew Finn, too, the guy's older brother. He's living out here, now. But I knew the family well, this all was kind of a second home, growing up." Travis shuts down the motor, looks around the property—not much has changed. An old John Deere parked at the far side of the barn—little sign of any gear, of agricultural supplies. More a country home, now, than any kind of farm.

A man and a woman appear in the doorway to the house. The man heavy, muscled—his arms inked with tattoos. On his head is a ball cap, he's wearing a black tee, jeans, engineering boots. Sporting a long, dark, forked beard.

The woman with him is skinny, blond, chewing gum in jeans and a sweat top. Her face brittle-looking, chest inflated—Travis thinks of Nashville nights, pole dancers, neon, dry ice, cold beer.

Stepping out of the SUV, he ushers out his daughter to stand at his side.

Finn Ackerman stomps a couple of paces forward. Gives a flat grin. "Hey."

Travis puts a hand on his daughter's shoulder.

"How's it going?"

"Good, man," McConnell answers. "Yeah. Good. Good

to see you." He looks to the woman.

"This is Krista," Finn says.

The woman gives a bland smile. "Hey."

Ackerman looks at her. "This is my old buddy, Travis…"

McConnell chips in; "And this is Bella, my daughter."

Finn nods.

Krista repeats the smile. She flashes her teeth. Chews on the gum. "Hey, honey."

"Long time, man," Travis says.

"Long time." Ackerman stands looking out from under the ball cap, big arms at his sides.

Travis looks around the place. "I tell you what, it takes me back, man, years—seeing all this again. Like, twenty years. Since the last time I was here."

"Twenty, huh?" Ackerman says.

Krista puts her head on one side. "Y'all want to come on in?" She turns back to the house.

Finn shrugs, follows after her.

McConnell looks at his daughter—staring ahead, blank-faced.

He nudges her forward—lets his hand fall from her shoulder.

At the house, a mudroom filled with coats and boots and sneakers opens onto a big kitchen—with long windows on three sides. A view of the barn, of the pasture sloping down toward a creek—of the woods, a large pond at the edge of the tree line.

The kitchen is cluttered, warm. On the table a motorcycle brake caliper on a metal tray.

A double-doorway connects with the living space—rugs on a wood floor, old corduroy and leather couches. Native American art is on the walls, dreamcatchers and antler racks. A TV on in one corner.

Krista looks to Bella. "You want to get a soda, honey? You want something?"

Bella glances at her father. "Okay," she says, "sure."

"Come on in here. We got Doctor Pepper. Fritos. There's Oreos by the TV if you're hungry."

McConnell watches his daughter step through to the living room with Krista.

The woman pulls the doors behind her.

Travis thinks of the phone call—a single phone call to the man now standing at the kitchen sink—staring out of the window at the driveway descending through the trees.

"Anybody see you come?" Ackerman says.

"No, man."

"You sure about that?"

"Yeah, I'm sure." Travis sees the semi-automatic in the tactical holster in back of the man's waist.

Ackerman turns around, grim-faced. "So, what's going on?"

"You heard from him?" McConnell says.

The man shakes his head.

"You heard anything?"

"Like what?"

"I don't know, man." McConnell looks toward the living room door. Lowers his voice "How about, uh, Krista?"

"I told her you're just an old friend," Ackerman says. "I

mean, I don't want nobody knowing you even came here."

"They won't. They won't."

"What do you aim to do?"

"Get a hold of him, man, I just want to find him. Did you try calling?"

Finn makes a face. "What do you think?"

"There's nothing?"

"I want to know what happened with him, man," Ackerman says. "It's starting to freak me out."

McConnell levels his eyes on the man. "I know," he says. "I know. That's why I'm here."

⸸

Hudspeth County, Tx

Jessica McConnell sits at a picnic bench in the public park in back of the county courthouse—leather biker jacket loose about her shoulders, wind blowing hair across her alabaster face.

Kids clamber in a play area, beneath a cobalt sky.

On the opposite side of the bench Whicher studies the blue-gray mountains on the distant horizon. "Sheriff's office had your boyfriend in for questioning this morning," he says. "Pastor Mullins is worried about him. Says he came to see him last night."

The marshal notices the lack of protest—at his description of Harwood as a boyfriend.

Jessica's eyes are luminous, alive.

"The pastor called Sheriff Ingram this morning.

Harwood called a lawyer. Then he came in."

"What did he say?"

Whicher sees alarm, a lick of fear in her eyes. A new look. A look he's never seen before. "I can't tell you that, ma'am. It's privileged information. One thing I can tell you—he's pretty close to getting himself arrested. Samples we have from vehicles he owns need explaining—sheriff's not satisfied with what he's getting. Neither am I. He was out of town days on end. I don't buy what he says about it."

"What crime is he supposed to have committed?"

The marshal looks at her a long moment. Trying to read her, read her face, read the tension in the set of her body. "You mean what evidence is there of an actual crime?"

"He's a good man," Jessica says, "you ought to just leave him alone. You're supposed to be looking for my daughter."

"Mrs McConnell…"

"Don't call me by my married name. Call me Jessica. Call me who I am."

"You wanted to see me?" Whicher says.

She unclasps her hands.

"You said you might have information?"

She takes a breath. Nods. "I think so. I think maybe I do. Have there been any more sightings? Of Bella? Of Travis?"

The marshal shakes his head.

"You know why?" she says.

"Do you?"

"Because you're looking in the wrong place. You're looking for him in Michigan. He won't be there now. You were looking for him in Detroit because of the man he escaped with."

"Reed Barbone," Whicher nods.

"You looked for him in Nashville, like you looked for me—because it was our home." She stops, swallows. Braces her shoulders. "He's not from there, Travis—he lived there a long time. But he's not *from* there. He grew up in Pennsylvania."

Whicher eyes her.

"I'm not sure I even want to tell you…"

"Where in Pennsylvania?"

"After what happened," she says, "the last time. Bella might have been killed."

"If you know where your husband might be…" The marshal stares. "If you know where Bella might be, you need to tell me."

Jessica only leans into the picnic bench. Sick-looking.

Thoughts racing behind her eyes.

Chapter Forty-Two

A block up from the public park, Whicher sits in the lot at the law enforcement center—phone on speaker in the Silverado. It rings three times, picks up.

Chief Marshal Fairbanks answers.

"Jessica McConnell just told me she thinks she knows where her husband might be," Whicher says. "And her daughter."

"Come again?"

"She says she thinks they'll be in Pennsylvania."

"Really?" Fairbanks says. "Did she tell you why?"

"McConnell's from there. According to her. She says he grew up there, he only moved out to Nashville later on."

"Where in Pennsylvania?"

"She said he's from a place called Ridgway—close to there. It's up to the northeast of Pittsburgh. That'd be a half-a-day's drive out of Michigan, I checked."

Fairbanks is quiet on the line.

"We know they went up around Detroit looking for assistance," Whicher says. "They were close to Nashville before that, maybe looking for help. It'd fit with that."

"Did she tell you anything else?"

"No, ma'am. She says she's afraid. Of potential danger to her daughter—after what happened before."

"Well, was there anything more specific?" Fairbanks says. "An area? A part of town, an address?"

"She wouldn't tell me any more."

"We'd need to look at family," Fairbanks says, "former friends."

"The task force in Memphis need to know," Whicher says. "I can call Marshal Cruz, she's back in Memphis. I don't know how much they know of McConnell's past."

"I'll call them," Fairbanks says, "I'll talk to her boss."

The marshal stares through the windshield at a car pulling into the lot—a beat-up Nissan—Jessica McConnell's car. "Alright, ma'am," he says. "I'll let the sheriff's office here know."

Jessica drives in.

Staring at him from behind the wheel.

She steers in, swings her car directly in front of the Silverado, blocking it. She brakes to a stop.

"Ma'am," Whicher says, "I have to go, I'll call you…"

"Let me know what's going on," the chief marshal says. "Ridgway, Pennsylvania—I'll call the task force, I'll let them know."

Jessica McConnell is out of her car, stepping to the door of his truck.

Whicher pushes it open. "What the hell are you doing?"

"Take me," she says, her eyes wild-looking. "Take me there, to Pennsylvania."

Whicher steps from the truck.

"I can help you," she says, "I can help you find them."

"If you know where they are, you need to tell me."

"You already tried that—look what happened." She stands before him, arms out at her sides.

"Mrs McConnell. Jessica," Whicher says. "You're not making any sense."

"I've been up there, with him," she says. "With Travis. He took me up there. Before Bella was born. And after. Bella used to stay behind, we'd leave her with Ursula. He showed me places, he showed me all around—places he used to go—I don't know their names, but I could remember. I can remember where we went."

"What makes you think he'd be at any of them?"

"But he *could* be. They could be."

The marshal looks at her. "He have relatives back there? Family living around there?"

"His parents both passed, his mom was out in Florida…"

"Brothers? Sisters?"

She shakes her head.

"Then what?" Whicher says.

"*People*, you know? Friends," she says, "friends he had growing up."

"Local law enforcement can handle it."

"Nobody's handled anything," Jessica says.

"The Marshals Service will send people. They have a task force charged with bringing Travis in."

"All I want is my daughter…" Jessica's voice trails off.

Whicher swings the truck door shut. An uneasy feeling inside, despite himself.

She looks at him. "I'm not going anywhere."

"You do what you want to do."

"I'm not moving my car."

"Ma'am. I understand how you feel…"

"Oh?" Jessica says. "Really?" Heat is in her eyes, now. "You understand? You have a child. Where is she now?"

"I have to go in and talk with the sheriff."

She only stands and stares.

"Find someplace else to park. Better yet, go on home."

Her eyes drill him.

She only stands, transfixed, a statue.

Black hair blowing in the wind.

⋏

Inside the law enforcement center, the door to Sheriff Ingram's office is open.

Whicher knocks, walks in.

The sheriff is at the far side of the room, his back to the window. "Judge agrees we have sufficient probable cause—to arrest Jacob Harwood."

"You want to charge him?"

"In connection with the disappearance and possible abduction of Bella McConnell," Ingram says. "I talked it over with the county attorney. We'll charge him with abducting a minor, for now."

"Can you get him arraigned?"

"I'll get him before a court today," the sheriff says. "If

not today, then tomorrow. We lean on him hard enough, we might get a straight answer. If he's innocent of all this, we'll drop the charges."

Whicher eyes the sheriff. "Jessica McConnell just told me she thinks her husband might have her daughter up in Pennsylvania."

Ingram tips back his hat. Walks from the window, sits at a corner of his desk, mouth open. "You have any idea what's going on here? We've got fibers in Harwood's car that could be from the daughter's clothing. And blood in his truck—the kind of thing we'd find if somebody transported a victim."

"And the mother has a blood spatter pattern in the front room of her house," Whicher says.

The sheriff nods. "I'm sending over a deputy to pick up Harwood right now."

"My priority is the girl," Whicher says.

Ingram looks at him. "I can't help you if the kid's in Pennsylvania."

The marshal dips his head. "I need to head back to USMS in Pecos. Work background on McConnell. But you get Harwood talking, you find out anything…"

"I got your number."

"Anything at all, let me know."

⚞

Barreling down I-10 east, pushing eighty in the truck. Whicher's phone lights up on the dash.

He presses to answer, shifts lanes passing a brace of RVs.

Marshal Evelyn Cruz is on the line. "Your boss says Travis McConnell could be in Pennsylvania?"

"Y'all heading up?"

"No, we're not. We don't have enough to go on. All we have is a town—Ridgway."

"That's what his wife told me."

"There's no report, no sighting. We'll put out a BOLO," Cruz says. "Local law enforcement can look for the Mazda—that's if McConnell's even using the damn car…"

The marshal eases back on the gas.

"I mean, it could be something," Cruz says. "My boss won't greenlight moving on it. You think she's being straight with you?"

"Hard to say."

"We'll dig, check background, find out what there is on record."

"I'm headed back to my office," Whicher says, "I'll do the same. The Hudspeth sheriff is arresting Jessica McConnell's boyfriend. I think he's good for something. I don't know what."

"The girl might've been in his car, though." The tone of Cruz's voice changes; "Why would the mother not be straight with you? If she wants her daughter back."

Whicher fixes on the farthest point ahead through the windshield—barren hills, gray-blue peaks above the scrub.

"You think the daughter wants to be found?" Evelyn Cruz says. "You think she knows the risk she's running, being with her father?"

The truck tires whine on the washboard-flat road.
Whicher turns it over and over.
Still with no kind of answer.

Chapter Forty-Three

Elk County, Pa

The sound of twin motors cuts through the air. Travis McConnell searches the tree line, sees the dirt trail into the woods. Two ATVs emerging from it, Krista up front, his daughter, Bella, riding along behind.

He eyes the private road snaking down through the trees at the top of the property.

Finn Ackerman steps from the house, cigarette in his mouth, motorcycle brake parts in his hands.

He crosses the yard toward the big barn, hem of his T-shirt caught on the semi-automatic holstered in back of his jeans.

McConnell follows him over.

Ackerman slides back the door on the barn.

Inside is a Big Twin Harley—dirt bikes, old farm trailers. An aging half-ton truck.

"I called everybody I know to call." Ackerman takes the cigarette from his mouth. "I've called Erv fifty times, man."

McConnell looks at him. "I told you everything I know."

"You spoke to him from prison? Through this hack girlfriend?"

"Carlene, right. Officer Jimerson," McConnell says. "She called Erv, told him I was getting out."

Ackerman puts a brake caliper and pads on the seat of the Harley. "He agreed to help?"

"Like I told you."

Face sour, Ackerman takes a drag on the cigarette. "Then you got yourself caught up, you and this guy you broke out with?"

"I couldn't make contact with Erv, man, I couldn't do a thing about it. I was running, there was no time. The guy with me, Barbone, he didn't know…"

"You never told him?"

McConnell shakes his head. "Didn't want him knowing. Not his business. Erv was meeting with me. That's all."

Ackerman blows out his smoke. "And you asked him to find you a boat?"

"Right."

"On Lake Erie?"

"He knows I'm good for the money. You know I got money, Finn."

Ackerman's eyes are dark.

"I got money put away. Money I robbed, money I hid. He knows that, he knows I can pay him. Hell, I spent half my life stealing, I always put some of it aside. And me and him are tight, you know that. He lived with me out in Nashville, I staked him for half the things we ever did."

"This boat? It waiting for you right now?"

McConnell nods. "He left a key for it, I know where to find it, all of that. It's two hours from here, it's good to go, man."

"Why come here, then?"

"I thought he'd call, that he might've talked to you."

Ackerman steps out through the open door.

McConnell follows the man around the side of the barn.

"So, you asked him to go down in Texas? And bring back your wife?" Ackerman says. "You were paying for all of this?"

"He knows I can, he knows I've got it. I'm going to Canada. To disappear. He's not afraid of any of that. I asked him if he wanted to make the money, he was in. From day one. No second thought."

"For how much?"

"A hundred."

"A hundred grand?"

"For the boat," Travis says. "For the rest."

"For driving down to Texas? Finding your wife?"

"For being Erv, man. You know? Getting it done. No bull."

"And what about your woman?"

"Jessica? She'll be here. She'll come."

"Sure on that?"

McConnell looks at him, nods.

Finn Ackerman takes a long drag on the cigarette. Blows the smoke out of the side of his mouth. He puts a thumb and finger to his long, forked beard. Eyes small, bead-like.

"Everybody that helps you seems like they get burned. Like they disappear, Travis."

"What do you mean?"

"The hack that helped you break out. She's burned, right? What's happening to her now?"

Down the grass slope at the tree-rimmed pond, Krista stops her ATV. Bella pulls up behind her.

Ackerman eyes him. Moves away from the side of the barn, starts to walk down toward the pond.

McConnell follows. "That was only ever a crock, man—the thing between me and her. A corrections officer? Come on. I just played her, worked her, you know, to get the hell out…"

"This partner you broke out with?" Ackerman stomps on down the hill. "He's shot, right?"

"Right. By a bunch of cops," McConnell answers. "What do you mean, man?"

Ackerman smokes the cigarette down. "Erv helps you out. And where is he?"

McConnell keeps in step. Eyes his daughter climbing from the ATV, now.

"It's like—they do what you want—you get what you need from 'em—and then bam. You know? They're gone."

"I don't know what happened to your brother, man." McConnell keeps his voice steady, looks dead ahead. "But don't be talking like that."

Ackerman takes the cigarette from his mouth, sails it out into the cold, damp grass. "Yeah, but you save a hundred grand. If my kid brother don't show up."

McConnell stops.

Ackerman turns to look at him.

"You better be kidding me."

Finn Ackerman holds his stare a beat too long.

McConnell shakes his head, breaks off looking at him. "If I did something to your brother, I'd come here?"

Ackerman turns back down the slope.

McConnell walks slow to the edge of the water—pewter sky reflected in it, sky and the spindle shapes of leafless trees. He thinks of the wood in Kentucky. Barbone dragging the man, Dupris, from his vehicle, through the trees. Grim-faced. Disposing of the man's body. In the black waters of a woodland pond.

At the waterside, Bella crouches, peering in, weaving side to side. The woman, Krista, bent forward, her arm outstretched to point.

Ackerman grunts. "I'm worried about my brother, man."

McConnell nods, "That's what I'm saying."

Krista brushes a strand of platinum blond hair from her face. "In the weeds, there."

"I can't see," Bella says.

"Its head. You can just see its head."

McConnell looks at his daughter. "What's going on?"

"There's snapping turtles," she says. "I'm trying to see. There's one there…"

"It looks like a piece of wood, honey," Krista says, "just its head there."

"Oh," Bella says. She smiles. "I see it. It's funny. It's kind of cute."

Ackerman steps to the water's edge. Pulls his ball cap low on his head. "Don't be fooled."

Bella looks at him. She shades her eyes. "What do you mean?"

"They're top of the food chain," Ackerman says. "They move around real slow, all of that. Like, no problem, nothing's going on. But they got a set of jaws on 'em like a vice. Snap like you won't believe."

"Really?"

Ackerman nods. "Take your finger right off."

Bella moves a fraction back from the water's edge.

"He's just kidding, honey," Krista says.

Ackerman grins. Looks at Travis.

The smile at his mouth doesn't reach his eyes.

⏺

Pecos, Tx

Riding east up I-20 into Pecos, Whicher eyes the double-stack freight train running along at the side of the road. Graffiti on the well cars, containers out of China and Mexico and the Gulf. Bright, painted steel against the washed-out tan of oncoming winter. He passes the local RV park—white trailers arrayed beneath the giant sky.

He checks the time, thinks of stopping by at the school, picking up Lori.

No word from the sheriff—no word on Harwood, any arraignment would take time.

At the office, he could search out background on Travis

McConnell—on any associated places.

He could take his daughter home first, pick up something—ice cream or tacos or maybe fried chicken.

He thinks again of the fibers in Harwood's car—thinks of holding the purple sweat top in his hands. Asks himself why Bella would have been in Harwood's car. Tries to remember the last time he told his own daughter not to get in any stranger's vehicle.

He can't bring it to mind.

He must have told her, Leanne must have, between them they must have done it a score of times.

At the upcoming sign he takes Exit 37 east for Pecos.

Crossing the interstate overpass, the phone on the dash stand lights up.

The number on the screen is the USMS office across town.

Chief Marshal Fairbanks comes on the line. "What happened in Hudspeth County this morning?"

"Ma'am?"

"I have Jessica McConnell outside my office—she just drove up from there. She's threatening to go to the nearest TV station and tell them she knows where her missing child is—and the Marshals Service won't help her."

"She drove up here?"

"Are you in Pecos?"

"Yes, ma'am."

"Then you best get over here—make it fast."

Upstairs in the courthouse Whicher steps into Chief Marshal Fairbanks's office.

Jessica McConnell faces Fairbanks's desk. Arms wrapped about herself in her leather biker jacket.

"You want to take a seat?" the chief marshal says.

The marshal inclines his head, a lick of temper in him. "I'm just fine," he says. "I'll stand."

"I asked you here to speak with Mrs McConnell."

"I have work to do," Whicher says. "On background. On Travis McConnell. Relating to Ridgway, Pennsylvania."

"I spoke with the senior task force marshal in Memphis," Fairbanks says, "they're on that."

Jessica turns to Whicher. "Why aren't you?"

"I was picking up my daughter."

"Oh? You were picking up *your* daughter?"

Fairbanks cuts in; "Mrs McConnell says she remembers places her husband took her."

"I could find them again," Jessica says.

"She knows where to look, she doesn't remember names, she can't tell local law enforcement."

"Can't or won't?" Whicher says.

"I want to be there for my child." Jessica looks at him. "I want to find her. Is that so hard to understand?"

Fairbanks speaks; "Mrs McConnell, if you were to talk to the press it likely wouldn't help—it's more likely to act as a warning to your husband or daughter. If they were to hear of it, it could alert them that law enforcement were on their way."

"If you won't help me, I'll go there myself," Jessica says,

a hot-looking flush at her face. "But I'll talk to everyone I can find. I'll tell them you're refusing to help."

"Nobody's refusing anything," Whicher says. "No sightings have been made of your husband or your daughter in more than twenty-four hours."

"So?"

"So, maybe they're nowhere near Pennsylvania."

"It's half-a-day's ride from their last known location," the chief marshal puts in. "We're pretty sure they're mobile."

"Why wouldn't he look for help there?" Jessica says.

"Because he'd know we might be watching," Whicher says.

Jessica's voice rises; "But nobody *is*."

"Jacob Harwood was just arrested," Whicher says, "in connection with your daughter's disappearance."

Jessica eyes him, angry.

"Mrs McConnell," Chief Marshal Fairbanks says. "If you wouldn't mind, I need a moment with the marshal here. Alone?"

The young woman stands, blades of color at her throat.

She steps to Whicher at the door.

The marshal moves aside, feels the energy in her.

She wrenches open the door, stalks out.

The marshal shuts it.

Fairbanks looks at him over steel-framed glasses. "There's a flight out of Midland. Six-thirty tonight."

"Say again?"

"You can be in Pittsburgh tonight. We can arrange a hotel, a car."

"We have no idea where to look."

"But she does," Fairbanks says.

"Ma'am, we have a suspect under arrest in Hudspeth County."

"You can fly up there, take rooms for tonight—this town, Ridgway, it's a two-hour ride from Pittsburgh. You can be there by morning, you can start to look."

"The sheriff's office get Harwood talking there could be more information…"

"The task force aren't going out," Fairbanks says. "They're staying in Memphis. Local law enforcement will only be looking for McConnell as a federal escapee. I won't have Jessica McConnell bring the Marshals Service into disrepute—she's threatening to take this public, drag the Juvenile Protection Service into it."

"How she's going to do that?"

"She says they wanted to take this all public earlier…"

"And I told you why not."

Fairbanks takes off her eyeglasses. "I'm not here to canvass opinion. I want you up there. With her. I want this right on the political end. No reproaches later. There'll be a car waiting at Pittsburgh International arrivals. Rooms will be booked. You take Jessica McConnell up there with you. Six-thirty. You be on that flight."

⚞

Pittsburg, Pa

Rain glistens on the cobbled stones of the downtown market square, a cold rain haloed around the street lamps. On the hotel balcony, Whicher grips the wet rail, eyes the few remaining revelers tipping out of bars and restaurants far below.

He scans the high-rise buildings beyond the square. Lights of the metro-area winking out of the city night beyond the river.

A bitter note is in the wind, the tang of snow.

He thinks of Ridgway, the little he's learned of it; a county seat, just a few thousand strong. A record of Travis McConnell at the school there—according to the voicemail from Evelyn Cruz. Nothing else significant from the task force.

Somewhere McConnell is out there.

Somewhere out in the black, wet night.

Maybe in Pennsylvania—maybe back in Michigan.

Michigan, where they almost found him, holed up, the middle of nowhere, in some wood.

Ridgway law enforcement were alerted to the stolen Mazda. State troopers would be watching the main roads.

On the adjacent balcony the glass doors slide open.

Jessica McConnell steps out from the room adjoining his. A pack of cigarettes in one hand, a phone in the other. She moves forward, unaware of his presence—takes a cigarette from a pack of American Spirits—lights up, inhales a shallow breath.

She raises her head, notices him.

The marshal nods.

"I didn't see you there. It's raining," she says, "what're you doing? Taking in the view?"

"Maybe."

She steps forward to the rail, stares out over the lights of downtown.

A rumble of traffic is in the air, the horn sounds on a nearby car.

She brushes a strand of hair from her eye. "It makes me kind of homesick."

"For Nashville?"

She nods, takes a light hit on the cigarette, barely drawing it in. Blows out the smoke in a wreath of fogged breath. "Are you angry?" She looks at him. "That I dragged you up here?"

Whicher doesn't reply.

"I don't believe you'd abandon my daughter," she says.

The marshal eyes her.

"I believe in you." She stubs out the cigarette, scarcely smoked. "I have to," she says. "I have to take it all on trust. That my daughter is alive, well. That I'll see her again, hold her."

Whicher lets his gaze rest on the silhouette of a high-rise office building, its windows dotted with yellowed lights.

"You don't believe me?"

The marshal ignores the question. Cuts a glance toward her, to the phone in her hand. "Calling somebody?"

"My sister," Jessica says.

"It's pretty late."

"She runs a bar. She's always up."

The marshal breaks off to stare out over the city square again. "You really think we're going to find Travis somewhere out here? Find your daughter?"

"I can't bring myself to think the opposite," Jessica says. "That someone else will find them. Or her. Or that something else will happen. Something worse."

"So you cling to that?" Whicher says.

"It's wet out here. It's cold," Jessica says.

The marshal watches as she steps away from the balcony's edge—turns back to her hotel room. She pauses for just a moment. Looks at him. Pulls the glass sliders behind her, pulls the drapes closed, blacking out the spill of light.

Whicher wonders, not for the first time since arriving on the flight, since checking in.

Will she still be there?

Will Jessica McConnell be there in the morning?

Chapter Forty-Four

Peterbilts and Macks and Freightliners fill the lot of the truck stop—an early morning sun rising over the top of green, wooded hills.

Travis McConnell swings the half-ton Sierra pickup off of the two-lane highway.

He pulls in, parks on a bare patch of oil-stained grit.

Only light traffic moves on the highway in the winter pall.

On the passenger seat beside him is a burner phone.

He takes it from its place, holds it a moment—eyes the big rigs, stationary, silent. Searches his thoughts again, asks himself for the hundredth time. Sees no choice, no other option.

He grips the phone, keys a number from his memory, despite the risk.

Pushes back in the seat as the call connects, starts to ring.

A woman's voice answers—her voice thick, blurred from sleep. "Hello?"

"Karyn," he says.

The woman only breathes into the phone. "Who is this?"

"Karyn, it's me," McConnell says.

"Oh my God…" Karyn Dennison's voice catches in her throat, constricted with surprise.

"Don't talk," he says, "just listen."

"What're you doing? Why're you calling?"

"Just listen for me—will you do that?" The grunt of a man's voice is in the background, McConnell hears it somewhere off of the phone. He checks his watch—an hour earlier in Texas, she must still be in bed. "Listen," he says, "I have to make this real quick. I need you to do something. You don't need to speak, just hear me out, okay?" Only a faint hum tells him the call is still live. "I need you to talk to Jessica. Tell her there's no time, there's no more time."

No response.

"Can you do that?" McConnell says. "I can't call her. I just need you to let her know. She has to get moving."

"No," Karyn breathes.

"No?" He fights to keep his voice low, even. "Why not?"

"I can't."

"Why can't you?"

"She's gone," Karyn says.

His mind races, trying to process the words.

"She's gone already. I went over. Last night." Karyn's voice is flat. "Her car was gone. The neighbor said she was gone; I asked him."

McConnell feels his heart pump in his chest.

On the road.

Jessica was on the road. Moving.

"How long?"

"I don't know. I have no idea."

McConnell swallows, grips the wheel with his hand. "What about…the guy?"

Karyn hesitates.

McConnell's voice is dark, "You know?"

"Gone, too."

"You know that?"

"I went over. To see if she was there," Karyn says, "with him, at his house. She wasn't. Nobody was there."

McConnell breathes into the burner a few more moments. "Alright," he says. "That's it. That's it, I'm sorry I had to call."

⁂

The Waffle House is busy, filled with the scent of pancakes and fried bacon—Whicher eyes the man opposite in the booth—a Captain Defoe of the Ridgway Police Department; square-jawed, in his fifties, his dark hair graying at the temples.

The captain scans the diners in the restaurant—construction guys, office workers, store assistants—he nods to a couple at the back of the room.

Jessica McConnell leans into the booth, tightly coiled. The leather biker jacket zipped to her throat.

"So far you've had no sightings?" Whicher says.

"We have a live BOLO," the captain answers, "we've had sightings of Mazda SUVs—two that we've stopped, that didn't amount to anything."

"No reports from the state troopers?"

Captain Defoe shakes his head. "I can let you have a patrolman, a unit, to help you look?"

Whicher takes a forkful of bacon from his plate. "Thanks," he says. "But we ought to be okay."

"You come up armed?"

The marshal thinks of the go-bag in the airport rental car outside—the ballistic vest, the extra ammunition. He nods. "I'm all good."

"Well, if you need anything?" the captain says.

Jessica cuts in; "We'll be okay."

The captain eyes the marshal.

"We're kind of feeling our way," Whicher says. "This all may not amount to anything."

"I can tell you this much," Defoe says, "we have nothing current on record for McConnell. Going back five years, the active files stay open. We've checked the archive—but there's nothing on him in any recent time-frame. He left the area twenty-something years back, there's no family around that we know. The parents are both deceased. If there's anybody else, we don't know about it." He looks to Jessica.

She turns her face to stare out of the restaurant window.

Defoe addresses Whicher; "Before you head back to Pittsburgh, let me know how it went?"

"I'll be sure to do that."

The captain drains his coffee cup, stands, fits his hat. "If he's still with the vehicle, I say we'll find him. If he's here. If not, if he's switched into something else he could be anywhere. We got half a million acres of the Allegheny

National Forest right on our doorstep. Good luck finding anybody in that."

⋏

Travis McConnell leaves the half-ton pickup in front of the red-sided barn.

He crosses the yard, enters the house, hangs his jacket on a hook inside the mudroom.

In the kitchen, Bella pads to the sink, feet bare, her hair in disarray. She runs water from the faucet, rinses her hands.

"What's going on?" McConnell says.

"Oh, hey. I just got up," Bella says. "Krista made breakfast. Blueberry muffins."

From the living room, Krista calls out; "They're out of a pack. You want some, just heat 'em up."

"Did you go out?" Bella says.

McConnell nods.

"How come?"

"Had something to do."

"Like what?"

"Just something. Don't worry about it."

His daughter looks at him, her face resentful.

"Finish breakfast. Alright?" McConnell keeps his voice low. "We'll be moving on soon."

"Today?"

"Maybe today."

Bella makes a different face. "I want to go ride with Krista again, she's not working till later, she said she'd take me."

From an adjoining hallway along the side of the house Finn Ackerman approaches—dressed in jeans and boots and a black vest.

He slouches into the kitchen. Runs a hand through his beard. "Yo, man."

"How's it going?" McConnell says.

Finn shrugs, rolls a muscled shoulder. "I don't know. You want to take a walk?"

McConnell glances at his daughter, tells her, "Go ahead, eat up."

He follows Ackerman into the mudroom—on outside, across the yard to the barn.

Ackerman turns around, stands four-square, his arms out at his sides.

"You alright?" McConnell says.

"No, man. I can't reach him. I still can't reach him. Nobody's seen him. I called everybody I know to call."

McConnell says nothing, only watches.

Ackerman's eyes are narrow, tension rippling through him. "So where is he? I'm serious man, where is he?"

"I know, I know."

"Where were you? Just now? Where did you go?"

"I had to go out. Make a call."

"You made a call?"

"With a burner," McConnell says. "I couldn't do it from here. In case the call gets pinged, you know? Traced here. I was making sure. Staying safe."

"Traced by who?"

"Law enforcement, man."

Ackerman stares. "So? Who you call?"

"Karyn."

"Uh?"

"Karyn," McConnell says. "A cousin of mine. Jessy moved out to Texas, to make a new start—because of her being there."

"Why call her?"

"To tell her—to tell Karyn to tell Jessica—that there's no more time. She's got to move, she's got to get her ass out of there. Get here. But Karyn told me she already left."

Ackerman regards him, face dark.

"She's coming, man," McConnell says. "She's coming, she could be here anytime."

"If she left," Ackerman says, "what the hell happened to Erv? Where the hell is he?"

"Listen," McConnell says. He blows out his cheeks. Stares off down the slope of the paddock, takes in the sweep of the farm. Childhood memories coming back. Of teenage years. Drinking and girls and small-time stealing—the path to what would later come. "I think, maybe she's with a guy," he says. "I think maybe she's with him."

"What the hell are you talking about?"

"Karyn told me Jessy's been seeing some son of a bitch. And I tell you, man," McConnell says. "I didn't want to think this, but maybe, just maybe, if Erv ain't around—if he really ain't around—if he's dropped off of the face of the earth, like it seems. Like if nobody's seen him, and I mean nobody. If nobody's even talked to him. Or heard from him. Since he went down in Texas…"

Finn Ackerman only stares.

"I tell you, man." McConnell shakes his head. "I think this guy she got with. I think maybe he might've done something. You know?"

Ackerman's voice is choked back tight. "Spit it out. What the hell you mean?"

"I think maybe he might've killed him." McConnell swallows. "I think someone might've killed your brother, man. I can't figure this out another way."

⁂

Whicher slows the rented Ford, checks the street sign—*Buffalo Highway.*

Jessica McConnell leans forward in the passenger seat.

"This something?" the marshal says.

"I think," she says. "I think it is, yes."

An hour of driving, cutting left and right among the Ridgway streets—back and forth to half-remembered places.

She points to a two-story frame house at the side of the highway.

Whicher takes in the galleries across the fronts of both floors—brown paint peeling from the window frames, A/C units mounted haphazard on the walls.

An outdoor timber staircase in back leads to the second floor—the house divided into twin apartments. Faded bath towels drape the upper floor gallery.

"You want to stop?"

"Yes," she says. "Pull over."

Whicher steers off of the highway, brings the sedan to a halt.

"We came here," Jessica says. "One of his friends lived here."

"You sure?"

"He lived downstairs. There was a family on top."

"What was his name?"

"Johnny."

"Johnny?"

"I don't remember. I remember being here." Jessica pops the door, steps quickly from the car.

Whicher cuts the motor, unhooks his seat belt, climbs out.

The smell from an overflowing dumpster is in the air. TV sounding from an open window.

No vehicles are parked.

No lights show in any of the windows.

Jessica stops at the front door. Looks at Whicher.

The marshal takes out his badge and ID.

She presses on a buzzer held in place with tape.

A muffled shout comes from inside the house.

"US Marshal," Whicher says. "Open up, please."

A minute passes.

The door opens.

An older man answers the door. His eyes bright, jittery.

Whicher holds out his ID.

"What's going on?" the man says.

"Sir, I'm with the US Marshals office. Looking for a missing minor. And a fugitive, an escaped felon."

The man screws up his face.

"Sir, if I could ask you a couple of questions?"

"A felon? What're you talking about? What minor?"

Jessica cuts in, "Sir, do you know Johnny? Is he still living here? Do you know him?"

The man's face is blank. "Johnny who?"

"He used to live here?"

"When?"

"Three, four years ago."

"Don't know him. Never heard of him. I've been here a year."

Whicher looks at the man. "Do you know the name of the last person living here?"

"No. Why should I?"

"You ever get mail?"

"No. If I do I throw it out. Throw it in the trash."

"You never heard of anybody named Johnny?"

The man stares silently, his eyes bright.

"How about the neighbor?" Jessica says. "Upstairs?"

"How should I know?"

"Alright, sir," Whicher touches a finger to his hat. "Thank you for your time." He steps from the door, walks along the side of the house.

At the foot of the timber staircase he checks for Jessica—saying something to the man—then stepping away.

The marshal grabs the hand rail, pulls himself up the stairs.

At the top is a screen door—he calls through; "US Marshal. Anyone home?"

Jessica climbs the stairs behind him.

The door opens. An emaciated woman in a sagging sweater stares out.

Whicher shows his badge. "Ma'am, I'm with the Marshal's Service—looking for a missing minor."

The woman looks him up and down, the suit, the hat.

"Do you know a man who used to live in the apartment downstairs? Name of Johnny?"

"What did he do?"

"Ma'am do you remember him, do you know him?"

"Johnny? Yeah."

"You know his surname?" Whicher says.

"Barber," the woman answers.

"Johnny Barber?"

"Yeah. But he left a long time back."

Jessica asks the woman; "Do you know where he went?"

The woman holds up her hands. "Why would I know?"

"Did you know him?"

"He was just the neighbor." The woman shakes her head. "He was young. He was noisy. He was a pain in the ass."

"You know a man name of Travis McConnell?" Whicher asks her.

The woman stares back, face inanimate. "I never heard of him."

"So, Johnny Barber? But no Travis McConnell?"

"I don't know anything about either of 'em."

The woman puts a hand to the door, swings it shut.

⋏

Bella McConnell fastens the chin strap on the ATV helmet. She swings a leg over a silver-gray Can-Am Outlander, presses on the starter button. The motor barks into life.

Krista, beside her, fires up an army-green Polaris Sportsman.

They circle out from in front of the house toward a dirt trail up the side of a wooded hill.

Travis McConnell watches his daughter disappearing. Listens to the noise of the ATV motors start to fade.

He walks across to the big barn, its doors wide open.

Inside, Finn Ackerman kneels at the front forks of the Big Twin Harley.

"They're gone," McConnell says.

Ackerman grunts.

"I guess they'll be a while," McConnell says.

Ackerman works the front brake caliper onto the bracket. "So they're gone." He picks up a ratchet from the top of a toolbox, starts to tighten a sliding pin. "So, let's hear it."

McConnell stands by the barn's open doors, lets his gaze run out across the old farm. "Alright," he says. "So, two years ago I get sentenced to sixty years for aggravated robbery."

Ackerman nods.

"Sixty years, man. Just like that." McConnell snaps his fingers. Stares into the gloom of the trees beyond the house. "Jessica moved to Texas. She took Bella out of school, took her out of the neighborhood she grew up in. Away from Nashville, away from everything. To start over. Get away from a living nightmare—a sixty-year living nightmare."

"She went to Texas," Ackerman says. "You had your cousin there?"

"Just a half-assed idea, she didn't know what the hell she was doing," McConnell says. "She just wanted to run, you know? Get away from the nightmare. She wouldn't come visit me in prison in Memphis, she wouldn't bring Bella. She said she couldn't stand it."

"Guess you never should've got your ass caught."

"Yeah?" McConnell glances at the man. "So, anyhow, she found God."

Ackerman only stares at him. Picks out another wrench from the toolbox.

"In Texas," McConnell says. "She started going to church regular, the church helped her out, with food, with whatever. She found God. She went all in."

"You know this how?"

"I heard. Little by little. From Karyn," McConnell says. "They never got along. But at the start, when she was first there, they'd see each other. After a while Jessica was always at the church, according to Karyn. And Bella started running wild. With nobody around to stop her, her mother always out, praying, finding herself, finding God."

Ackerman ratchets the pin in the caliper.

"Anyhow," McConnell says, "I got word about this guy. This other guy."

"This guy she started seeing?"

"Right," McConnell says. "This guy from the church."

"If she's all religious and whatever, into God, all of that, how come she starts seeing someone?"

McConnell looks at Ackerman. "I know. That's what I thought. I thought it was just some friend."

Raising up from the forks of the Harley, Ackerman grabs a rag, wipes off his hands.

"But Karyn told me," McConnell says. "She told me the rumors. Around town, around the church. The talk, the rumors in the congregation. That this guy was more than some 'friend.' And then I heard Bella was living in a hostel, a juvenile hostel. Like, a hundred miles away. By order of a court, some juvenile court. The whole thing was just a goddamn disaster, man, start to finish."

"So you decided to get out?"

McConnell nods. "I'd been working on it, for months, man. Already working on it. I can't do a sixty-year stretch. I knew that, day one."

Ackerman turns the wrench in his hand. Takes a step closer. "So that's the deal your end. But how about my brother? How about Erv?"

McConnell eyes the yard, the black Mazda, tucked in behind the blue Ford Raptor and the Camaro. He listens to the sound of the ATVs, faint sound on the wind. "We kept in touch," he says. "We kept in touch from the start. Later on, I got my hack to get him messages."

"This hack you were foolin'?"

"Carlene," McConnell says. "Little Carlene. But she was foolin' herself. She didn't need any help from me."

Ackerman only sniffs, wipes his arm beneath his nose.

"Erv found me a boat," McConnell says. "I asked him.

He set it up so I could use it."

"He knew you were getting out?"

"Carlene let him know. He knew I had the money to make it worth his while—man, I think he'd have done it anyway. We always helped each other out, no matter what."

"And?"

"So then he went down to Texas—to tell her."

"He drove down there?"

"He was working in Pittsburgh, sometimes he'd be over in Cleveland, or up in Erie, that's how he is, you know Erv."

"Right."

"So, he went down to tell her—tell her I was getting out. And bring her, bring Bella. Bring 'em back to Tennessee. When the time was right, he was bringing them up. Up here, to Pennsylvania."

"He went down when?"

"Ten days gone."

Ackerman looks at him. "And nobody's heard from him since."

"If something happened to him, man, if this guy did something. If he killed him. This guy that's with her now…" McConnell pauses. "I tell you, man…"

"Karyn told you they're coming here?" Ackerman says.

"That's what she said. This morning."

"Why come? Why would they come?"

"For Bella." McConnell looks at Finn Ackerman. "For Bella, man, not for me."

Ackerman breathes out. Lets his arm loose at his side, lets the wrench swing. "Shit…"

"If he's with her," McConnell says. "If he's really with her. I tell you, man—I hope for his sake he's not. With Jessica. I hope for his sake he doesn't come…"

※

On the tree-lined avenue, the gas station and mini-mart is quiet. From a parking bay out front Whicher watches the door to the store.

Jessica McConnell is inside, using the restroom.

The marshal stares at the street beyond the twin pumps, wondering what more of use there is to find.

Since the house on Buffalo, one more address—a brick-faced one-floor, the occupants a young family—the stay-at-home mom with zero knowledge of the occupants of Jessica's memory; a biker and a blond woman in their thirties.

The marshal takes his phone from his jacket, finds the number for Evelyn Cruz in Memphis.

He sends the call, stares out along the deserted suburban road.

Cruz answers. "Your boss says you're up in Pennsylvania. Tell me you found something?"

"We're going door to door," Whicher says.

"How's that working?"

"So far, it's not." The marshal shifts his gaze back onto the door of the mini-mart. "There's been no sightings, no reports of anything. State Patrol here are on alert, plus the local law enforcement."

"We've had no reports either," Cruz says. "He's either laying low…"

"Or he's driving something else," Whicher cuts in.

"In which case we have to wait for something—a sighting, anything."

"I got one lead," Whicher says. "A name, a Johnny Barber—a friend of McConnell's. Jessica found the place he was living, the guy's since moved on. I called the local PD—they say they'll run a search on the name. If we could find him, talk to him, maybe we could get an idea where to look."

"I'm writing that down," Cruz says, "I'll get on it, you have the address?"

"His old address is Buffalo Highway, out of Ridgway."

"What do you plan on doing now?"

"There's a couple more places we can check," Whicher says. "After that, if we still have nothing, I guess we're done. We can stick around here, gamble. Or head on back to Texas."

"I don't think he'll be there," Cruz says, "for what it's worth. He could be anywhere, him and the girl—out west would be my guess."

"If you come up with anything on that lead…" Whicher says.

"Got it," Cruz says, "I'll let you know."

⽊

Staring into the restroom mirror, Jessica McConnell smooths her pale skin taut across her cheekbones. She gazes into luminescent eyes beneath the harsh strip lighting. Trying to clear her head, to keep a hold, to think.

She pictures the marshal, outside waiting.

A swirl of violent energy spins inside—quickening in her veins at each new thought.

Outside, he waits.

Immovable. A rock in the river.

Holding fast.

She stands alone in the restroom at a chipped white sink. Breathing slow. Trying to clear the static in her head. To calm the surge, the sick feeling at her stomach.

The phone in her bag starts to ring.

She breaks off staring at her own reflection.

Swallows. Shoves a hand down into the bag, pulls out the phone.

The number on screen has no name listed.

A sequence of numbers is all—numbers scrolled across a backlit screen.

She presses to receive.

"Hello?" a voice says.

Jessica locks out her legs against the jolt of electricity inside.

"Mom?"

Her breath escapes her. She forces a sound from somewhere within. "Yes…"

"Are you coming?"

Jessica's eyes swim, the image in the mirrored glass little more than a blur.

"Dad says you're coming. Are you coming here?"

She glances at the restroom door—still locked.

"Mom, are you?" The note in her daughter's voice rising to a panicked pitch. "Mom? Are you coming?"

Jessica nods to the mirror.
Steadies herself. Grips the phone.
Exhales.

Chapter Forty-Five

Bella McConnell stares at the burner phone in her open hand. Still warm. Still warm from the call.

She breaks off, eyes locking on the mess of clothes and socks spread out over the floor in the box-like room at the back of the house.

Thoughts running. Spinning, tumbling in her mind—flashes of panic inside, heart racing.

She pulls on sneakers, grabs at the array of clothing, scrabbling everything into a bag.

Part of her unable to believe it.

Still unable.

Even though her father had told her.

Don't believe it, she'd told herself.

But she was here.

All the way back—all the way since running from the hostel—since that first night, the crib in Fort Stockton, the derelict house.

She'd told herself.

On the journey home. *Real* home, to Nashville. She'd blanked it all out.

Leaving Texas with the guy.

The *guy*.

She couldn't even bring herself to say his name.

But they'd made it—all the way to Nashville.

At the bar, Aunt Ursula's bar, she could barely believe it.

They'd done it.

He'd done it. He was there—her father—he was really there. At the back of the room. So good-looking. So much better-looking than any other man there.

He'd broken out—right out of prison.

He was *there*, just the same as she remembered him.

Everything after was a blur, all one long dream.

The journey north.

The other man, Barbone.

And the cabin, the horrible cabin, the deep woods.

The cold, the black nights. Hating it.

And then leaving.

Leaving the man, Barbone, leaving him behind.

Driving out through trees, creeks. Down backroads, miles and miles.

Till they were gone. Just the two of them. Driving the big roads, the interstates, the world rushing by, the whole big world. Everything good, so good, so happy inside, happier than she could believe. Free, totally free. With her dad, her real dad, nobody telling her what to do.

Free to live.

The thought of mom then like some ghost-thought—gone the moment she tried to reach to it. Just gone, she couldn't do it. She couldn't really believe.

But she was *here*.

Bella steps to the window, stares out.

Tell him.

Tell him to get ready.

She sees him at the barn—outside talking with the man, Finn.

Finn saying something to him.

The pair of them moving fast.

Disappearing, now.

Disappearing inside the barn.

⚔

The Browning Hi-Power is too big for the pocket of his jacket—Travis places it on the driver seat of the half-ton Sierra pickup.

In the gym bag is ammunition, along with the money from the sporting goods store.

Finn Ackerman watches from the side of the barn, arms folded, his small eyes dark.

"We get across," McConnell says, "I'll send back word, I'll get word to you. You know I'm good for this."

Ackerman scowls. "Hell, I don't care about the damn truck."

"I got money. I'll get it to you. You know I will." McConnell eyes a fender of the SUV, now hidden in place of the pickup in the barn. "You'll get rid of the Mazda?"

"I can get rid of it."

"Be careful, you know?"

Ackerman nods.

"Don't let anybody trace it back to here. To you. To me."

"They won't," Ackerman says. "Listen, I can get you up to Lake Erie, to the boatyard."

"No need."

Ackerman gestures at the pickup. "I got a hard-top for that thing. I can fix it on, you can ride in back, you and your kid. If you're driving it, anybody sees you, you got trouble."

"Nobody's going to see me."

"You don't know that."

McConnell reaches into the cab, stuffs the gym bag down behind the seat. He stashes an extra magazine in the door pocket.

"I know why you don't want me to come," Ackerman says.

McConnell looks at him.

"You think I'll shoot him. If he shows up."

"Yeah?" McConnell leaves the keys in the ignition, swings the door of the truck closed. "You'd have to get past me…"

"You need to make that crossing."

"We'll make it."

"You need to get there first," Ackerman says. "Get to the boat, man, get to the yard."

"We'll make it."

"You know I'm never going to let this go?" Ackerman says.

"I know."

"I'm never going to drop it. If you make it over, cross the border, first thing I'm going to do is find this bastard. I'll go down there, I'll go down to Texas—I'll find him."

McConnell meets Ackerman's eye. "I know you will."

"But if he comes here, I won't wait."

"We just need to get out," McConnell says. "Right now we have to get out."

"There'll be an accounting," Ackerman says. "One way or the other."

"I know." McConnell takes the Browning, puts the barrel of the pistol into his waistband. "I know what's to come."

⁂

Whicher steers the rental car down the Spring Creek Road—a narrow strip, sunlight strobing through the winter trees and saplings.

In his mind's eye he thinks of the Michigan deer camp—northern forest, not unlike the Allegheny, not unlike the feeling among the trees.

He pictures the camp. Pictures approaching it with the sheriff's team—slow at first, then manic. Storming the shooter's cabin. The close assault—the blood on the cabin wall.

And the body of the man—Barbone. With the blow to the back of his head.

The force to cause the wound, the broken flesh and scalp and the blood.

McConnell had done it.

He must have done it.

What kind of man was that?

Ruthless.

Brutal.

He must have seen them coming, somehow, Whicher tells himself. Seen them coming through the woods—or on the road. And struck down the man that helped him break out of a prison—the cell-mate that helped him get out, helped him run.

The marshal scans the road ahead where the woods give out to thin pasture. A ditch running alongside the road, filled with cattails. A timber house in a mown, grass square.

Nothing. So far, nothing.

Nothing bringing them any nearer. No closer to finding him, or to finding the girl.

He turns to Jessica. "This all look familiar?"

"We came here," she says, "I remember. I remember driving out—down the road out of town. That big pond we passed? The park with kids playing baseball? I remember it."

"So, down here somewhere?"

She nods, distant. Gaze unfocused out of the windshield.

"This farm?" Whicher says, patience thinning. "This place y'all came to? You're sure about it? That your memory's good?"

She says, "My memory is strong."

Whicher adjusts his grip on the wheel. "You miss that? Those days? Back then—before this?"

He cuts a look at her.

Her eyes are hooded, face guarded. "I miss my daughter," she says. "I miss Jacob."

"Jacob Harwood?"

She nods.

"How come Harwood has blood in the back of his truck?"

She doesn't answer.

"How come he has Bella's hair in his car?"

"I wanted to run away with him," Jessica says, her voice tight in her throat. "The minute I heard. The minute I heard that Travis had broken out of prison."

She stares dead ahead, her body rigid.

The marshal lets the words sit, turning them over, letting them run through his mind. "You heard he broke out; you thought to run away?"

She nods slowly. Eyes welded to the road.

"Why run away? Why run, when you already got away—down in Texas?"

"Because I'm pregnant," she says. "By Jacob. Because I'm pregnant by him. I have to get away."

⊥

Travis McConnell turns to his daughter standing at the side of the half-ton truck. "Make sure you got everything."

She stares at him. "I already did."

"We won't be coming back."

"I already checked out of ten motels," she says, "I didn't leave a thing behind."

"You got yourself spread out here…" McConnell watches Finn Ackerman at the barn. Carrying a five-gallon canister of gasoline.

"She's *here*," Bella says. "We have to be ready to *leave*."

"Go back inside," McConnell points to the house. "Check a last time, anything you see, get it, bring it out."

Her face colors, she turns from the truck, disappears into the house.

Ackerman wheels the Harley from the barn. Sets the motorcycle on its jiffy stand.

McConnell looks at him. "What's going on?"

"Thinking to ride shotgun," Ackerman answers.

"What?"

"On up to Erie."

"You don't need to do that."

"No?"

"I mean, what for?" McConnell says. "I don't need you to do that, man."

Ackerman unscrews the gas cap on the tank. "Maybe it ain't for you."

Flipping the truck keys over in his hand, McConnell's eyes cut to the house. "I appreciate you helping us out, man. You know that. But coming with us…I don't know."

"I want to ride to Erie, I'll ride there." Ackerman pours gas from the canister into the tank. "Whether you want me to or not. I want to see this boat, I want to see it, see what Erv left."

"Why, man?"

"I want to see for myself."

McConnell stares. Takes in the man's expression beneath the ball cap. "See what?"

"See," Ackerman says, his face darkened. "See if the son of a bitch shows up."

By a cattle guard at the head of a grit road is a posted sign—Whicher reads the name—*Ackerman*.

"This is the place," Jessica says.

Whicher studies the descent of the track, leading down through pasture and scant trees toward thick woodland—a private track, a dozen miles from the town of Ridgway. Sloping meadow, light moving in the trees beyond it.

"We came here," she says. "I came here with Travis."

A cold breeze blows into the open window of the car.

Birdsong is the only sound above the motor idling beneath the hood.

But some sense is stirring in him—the sixth sense, ticking in his gut.

Instinct.

At the presence of unseen danger.

The name on the post feels somehow familiar. As if somewhere he's heard it.

He scans back and forth through the windshield.

Stay alert, he tells himself.

His phone starts to ring.

He reaches for it, picks up, holds the phone against his ear.

Sheriff Ingram is on the line—from Hudspeth County.

"You still out in Pennsylvania?"

"I am," the marshal says.

"You still have Jessica McConnell with you?"

"Yes, I do."

"Well, now, you need to hear this..." Sheriff Ingram pauses.

"What's going on?"

"We just got done searching land belonging to Jacob Harwood—land belonging to him here, to the north of town."

Whicher hears the note in the sheriff's voice.

"You may need to arrest Mrs McConnell, marshal."

"Say again?"

"We just found a body. The burnt remains of a body. Beneath a fire here, a brush fire. There's a dead man buried out here. On her boyfriend Jacob Harwood's land."

⁂

Driving down through the last of the trees, Whicher sees the stretch of open pasture before him. A wooden house at its end—built on stone foundations. By the house is a red barn. In front of the house a black Camaro, a blue Ford truck.

Sheriff Ingram's words are in his head, the sound of his voice.

All the way down the track she's said nothing, asked nothing.

He'd kept the phone tight against his ear.

His mind races.

A body.

He thinks of the blood spatter—inside her house.

By the barn is an olive green Sierra pickup. A motorcycle over on its stand.

He drives toward the buildings. Sees nobody in view, looks for any sign of life.

Search this one last place, he tells himself.

Then pull it.

Stop.

Arrest her.

Pregnant. Not pregnant.

Have it done.

Take her back.

No more wasted time.

Take her back and find the girl.

⋏

The sedan slows as it approaches down the track. From inside the house Travis McConnell stares. The sound of the vehicle just enough; through the trees. Just enough to give him time to run inside.

Enough for Finn to step out of sight—into the barn.

But Bella is nowhere—nowhere in the house, he can't see her, she doesn't answer his calls.

The sedan draws level with the Sierra pickup—passes it.

Approaches the Camaro and the Ford in front of the house.

McConnell eases the Browning semi-auto from his waistband. Moves up by the outer mudroom door.

The windshield of the car reflects a cloud-streaked sky.

He can make out a man driving—in a Western hat.

In the seat beside him, a woman.

He stares at her outline, picks out the color of her hair, the set of the shoulders.

Knowing her.

From a place within himself.

No doubting.

That it's her.

✥

Whicher stares through the windshield as a dark-haired figure runs along the side of the house.

Small.

Slight.

The marshal stops the car, unhooks his seat belt.

He pushes open the door.

Jessica, beside him, scrambles out.

Whicher stares at the girl now standing stock-still at the corner of the house.

A girl he's only seen in photographs.

She stares back.

He steps from the car.

The girl's eyes cut to Jessica—starting to run around the side of the hood.

Electricity ripples in him—her presence will mean *his* presence.

His hand moves toward the Glock.

A man appears in the doorway at the house—pistol held out. Eyes agitated, intense.

Travis McConnell holds the barrel dead in line with Whicher's chest.

✥

Finn Ackerman sees the man through the barn's open doorway—stepping from the car to stare at Travis's daughter.

He sees Travis in the door to the house.

Travis with his gun out.

On the other side of the car, Jessica McConnell.

But his eyes snap back onto the man.

Anger flares inside him, a red mist, consuming. Reaching for the gun beneath the T-shirt, he thinks of Erv, his brother, Ervin.

Raises the pistol—stares at the back of the man's suit.

At a point between his shoulders.

⚔

McConnell's eyes flick from Jessica back to Whicher.

He takes a pace out of the house. "Back up. Move…"

"I'm a US Marshal…" Whicher eyes the pistol.

McConnell stops, glares, tendons rising beneath the skin of his neck. "Take out your gun," he barks, "lose it."

Whicher keeps his eyes locked on the man, McConnell—cranked, hyped, nothing to lose, the black barrel of the pistol swaying at the end of his arm.

He puts a thumb and finger to the butt of the Glock, eases it from its holster.

"Toss it," McConnell says, "lose it…"

Whicher pitches the gun out sideways, away from the house, away from the girl, Bella, now inching toward her father.

⚔

At the mouth of the barn, Finn Ackerman squeezes on the trigger—starts to fire over and over—sees the big man drop.

He starts to walk—out of the barn, teeth bared, still firing.

※

Whicher scrabbles to the back of the rental car—behind the wheel—rips the large-frame Ruger from the shoulder holster.

He takes aim at the man walking toward him.

Fires twice.

The man stops, darts back inside the barn.

The marshal ducks around the car—sees McConnell, with Bella, running toward the pickup truck.

Shots crack out from the barn—a round shatters the rear windshield, cascading glass. Whicher gets low—takes aim—the man sees him, steps inside out of sight.

A motor fires into life, Whicher twists around—sees McConnell at the wheel of the pickup, Bella climbing in.

Jessica McConnell crouches by the Ford truck—a look of panic in her face.

The marshal turns back to the barn, sees the man standing in the entrance.

He thumbs back the hammer, takes aim, center-mass—high for the distance. Holds the gun steady, squeezes.

The shot cracks out.

The man spins sideways, clutches at his ribs, doubles over.

The pickup is moving.

Jessica McConnell struggles to her feet, starts to run.

The shooter at the barn fires, wild now—rounds striking

the ground, striking the car as the pickup accelerates away.

Whicher kneels, takes aim, fires on the shooter. Sees him flinch, stagger.

And now a woman is in the doorway of the house—a blond woman—with a shotgun.

Jessica runs on toward the pickup truck.

"*Hold it,*" the blond woman shouts, "*you hold it…*"

"*US Marshal,*" Whicher shouts back, "*drop your weapon.*"

The woman's eyes are frantic as she stares at him.

Jessica stumbles, falls, gets up, her arms flail at her sides.

McConnell guns the motor, the pickup lurches forward—starts to speed away.

The woman fires from the house toward it.

Jessica crouches, covers both ears.

At the barn, the shooter is on the ground—he snaps off more rounds, arm outstretched at his side.

Whicher fires at the man—spins around, levels the revolver on the woman in the door. "Put down your weapon."

She points the barrel directly at him.

"I'm a US Marshal, *drop it now…*"

Chapter Forty-Six

The man at the barn lies bleeding—barely conscious, Whicher takes the gun from out of his hand.

Jessica McConnell stares up the track toward the woodland.

The pickup truck is already gone.

The blond woman runs from the house, shotgun abandoned at the threshold.

She kneels at the shooter's side.

"Call an ambulance," Whicher tells her.

He steps to the house, picks up the shotgun, moves to the rental car, whips open the trunk. Puts the shotgun and the shooter's pistol inside. Runs to retrieve the Glock from its place in the long grass.

He takes out his phone, dials 9-1-1.

A female dispatcher comes on the line.

"I have a gunshot victim, condition critical, I need an ambulance at…" he looks to the blond woman.

She stares at him, frozen.

"What address?"

"Sycamore," she says. "The Sycamore Farm. Off of Spring Creek Road."

Whicher repeats the address. "I'm a US Marshal," he says, "in pursuit of an escaped felon and a missing minor. My name is Whicher. I'm hanging up, I'm calling local law enforcement." He shuts off the call, looks at Jessica. "Get in the car."

The blond woman shouts, "*What did you do? What did you do to him?*"

"Stay with him. An ambulance is on its way."

Jessica stumbles to the passenger side of the car.

Whicher snatches open the door, gets in behind the wheel.

⁂

The single lane road is lined with dense woods.

Fifteen minutes—no sign.

The marshal eyes the road ahead.

The call to Ridgway PD is already made—alerts to the sheriff's office, plus state patrol.

No sign.

No sign of the Sierra pickup.

No way to know which way it went.

No seeing past the next bend in the road.

Jessica sits in stunned silence.

Whicher pictures her at the farm—running. Running for the pickup.

Running toward him. McConnell.

Running to get away.

Her daughter had been in that truck—but was she running to McConnell? Running to her husband?

Had she set it up?

Had him deliver her there?

A man was waiting—a man unseen in the barn.

He'd started firing just moments after they'd arrived.

The road ahead drops steep downhill.

Whicher sees a clearing, a gravel parking place—a broad river beyond it. He brakes, pulls in, brings the sedan to a halt.

He cuts the motor, elbows open the door.

Jessica looks at him.

"Get out," he says.

She steps slowly from the car.

Whicher eyes her.

She only stares back, mute.

Cold wind blows from the surface of the water.

"Did you know?" he says. "Did you know he'd be there?"

She makes no reply.

"Did you know Bella would be there? With him?"

Jessica shakes her head.

"The phone call I took—before we went in there?" Whicher says. "Sheriff Ingram. They just found burnt remains of a body—on your boyfriend Harwood's land."

She only stares at him, says nothing.

"There's blood in your house," the marshal says. "There's blood in your boyfriend's truck. Whose is it?"

"That man's brother," she says.

Whicher stares at her.

"Finn's brother. That man back there. The man you shot, the man shooting at you."

"What the hell are you talking about?"

"He came to Texas. Travis sent him. That man's brother. He came after me. To bring me back. It wasn't supposed to be like this…none of it was supposed to be like this…" Jessica McConnell puts her hands to her face.

"Like what?" Whicher says. "Did Harwood shoot him?"

Tears well in her eyes.

"Somebody came down to Texas?" Whicher says. "To take you back?"

Jessica nods, sobs silently.

"Did Harwood kill him?"

"None of it was supposed to be like this…"

The marshal breaks off looking at her, stares into the light on the surface of the river. "Where is he? McConnell? Where will he go?"

"I don't know…"

Whicher steps to her, takes hold of her arm, pins her with a look. "You came here—you came here before with him—where will he go?"

"I don't know…"

"What about this man, Finn? What about his brother?"

"They had boats," she says, "that's all I know. They had boats, they fixed up boats. They bought and sold them."

"At a river, a lake?"

"Travis took me out to a marine yard."

"Where?"

"Erie," she says.

"Lake Erie?" The marshal stands, mind hunting, a new thought forming.

Erie.

Lake Erie. A thin strip of water.

Thirty miles? Forty, north to south?

Half way across it, the border.

The border.

Canada beyond.

⚓

Pushing eighty on the highway north from Titusville, a name lights up on Whicher's phone.

He keys to answer.

Marshal Evelyn Cruz comes on the speaker.

"He's in a half-ton Sierra pickup," Whicher says.

"Where are you?"

"Headed for Erie. Best guess, he's headed somewhere up on the lake—he could be running for the border."

"We have people standing by," she says.

Whicher nods, grim-faced at the wheel.

"A lot of people are looking for him," Cruz says. "We just need a sighting."

Whicher's voice is cold; "They better know he has a minor with him—this can't end the way it did last time."

In Memphis, Cruz is silent on the line.

Chapter Forty-Seven

Ten miles out, the lights of Erie glowing against the dusk sky—traffic building, the evening commute already on the road.

Whicher switches lanes on the highway, stares along a line of tail lights, squeezes down on the gas.

"They're not in there..."

Whicher looks at Jessica in the passenger seat.

"They're not in Erie," she says.

The marshal holds the car in lane—looks at her again, trying to read her. "Do you *know*?"

"I won't have a hundred cops there..."

"Do you know where they *are*?"

"I won't tell you," she says. "I don't care what you do."

Whicher turns back to the traffic ahead on the road. "Tell me..."

"I won't have police there, I won't have them shot up."

"How do you know where they are?"

She points through the windshield at a road panel. "There. Head west. There—on Six."

"How do you know this?"

"Bella called me. We stopped at a gas station—this morning. I was inside. You were outside in the car."

The marshal thinks of it, doesn't respond.

"I spoke to her."

"You never told me…"

"I didn't know what to do."

Whicher cuts a look at her.

"Only you can know," Jessica says.

The marshal checks the rear-view, switches lanes. "What did she say?"

"She said they had a boat. She told me I knew the place. Travis told her. He picked the place because I knew it."

"Do you?"

Jessica nods.

Whicher asks himself again; could she be trying to escape?

Run with Travis?

"Did you know Bella would be there?" he says. "At that farm, with her father?"

"I didn't know."

Whicher thinks of the corpse on Jacob Harwood's land; of the head wound to Reed Barbone.

Used people.

Expendable people.

Used up.

Dispatched.

Jessica's face is a mask, her hands clenched at her sides.

"Are they waiting?" he says.

She won't reply.

"Are they waiting for you?"

"I don't know…"

He grips the wheel, passes two cars. "How far is this?"

"I don't know," Jessica answers, "fifteen minutes…"

No time.

"Call her."

Jessica eyes him, her face fills with fear.

"Call Bella."

She sits frozen.

"Do it," Whicher says.

Taking the phone from her pocket, she presses on a key to dial.

"Put it on speaker," the marshal says.

The number rings over and over.

A scratch of stretched-out sound.

No reply.

⭑

The lane through the state game lands is pitch dark—the headlamps of the rental car a rolling wash through the forest.

No lights, no sign of life since the highway, five miles back.

Jessica McConnell sits silent in the glow of the dash.

Whicher steers the car through the curtain of black trees.

In the headlamp beams the lane is ending in an empty dirt and gravel lot.

Beyond is nothing but ink-dark water; Lake Erie—black sky above it.

Whicher slows.

Sees no sign of McConnell, no sign of any boat.

He brakes to a dead stop.

Looks at Jessica in the passenger seat.

"It's along the shoreline," she says.

"Where?"

"There's a boathouse. And a cabin, we used to come here, Travis and me."

The marshal stares at dense forest butting up to the edge of the water. He picks up his phone.

"What're you doing?"

Whicher keys a number from the captain at the Ridgway PD.

A male dispatcher answers; "State Patrol, Troop E. Control center."

"This is Deputy US Marshal Whicher—in pursuit of the felony escapee out of Elk County—Travis McConnell—believed traveling with a minor."

"Yes, sir, marshal. Go ahead."

"I'm out at Lake Erie, acting on information he might be here."

Jessica McConnell stares from the passenger seat.

"Can you give me your whereabouts, marshal?"

"I'm on state game lands, off of Elmwood Lane, right at the end—I'm down on the shore. I'm at the water."

"You have visual contact with the suspect, marshal?"

"Negative," Whicher says. "I'm acting on information he might be here."

"You need backup?"

"I'm calling to let you know, is all—I'll check it out, I'll get back if I find something."

"I can check for nearest unit?"

"Y'all have marine assets on the water?"

"We have boats standing by. We have a helicopter airborne."

"He may already be crossing the lake, headed for the border," Whicher says.

"Copy that, marshal."

"I'll check here, I'll let you know what I find."

Whicher shuts off the call.

Jessica's face is hard in the dim light. "I thought you said you would protect my daughter?"

He pushes open the driver door, steps out. "I'll protect her."

Jessica follows, stares over the roof of the car.

"Which way?" He looks at her.

She points off along the eastern shore.

The marshal strains his eyes into the jet-black—picks out nothing. Slips the Glock from its holster.

⁂

McConnell sees the headlights through the trees, runs the forest path, heart in his mouth. He sees the car come to a halt in the gravel turnaround. The car.

The same car.

The same car, from the farm.

The man steps from it, the same man, the marshal with the hat.

Jessica is there—he sees her.

Just as Bella had said.

Edging forward, he raises the Browning.

Aims the pistol.

Grips.

Starts to squeeze.

⁂

The muzzle flash and the sound fill his senses—whiplash cutting through the branches, rounds striking trees. Whicher drops—a rush in his blood, his chest tight.

Arms extended he fires back into the dark, scans the black woods, looks for movement.

More shots—muzzle flare scribed against the night—breaking left, toward the water line.

He sees a figure, a running figure—Jessica—silhouetted, through the trees.

Rising to a crouch Whicher runs, jinks through the pitch-dark.

Against the sheen of lake, extending into the water is a line—a shape—a jetty, a boathouse.

Exploding from the forest, four more shots are points of bright fire.

Whicher feels a lick of fear, rounds rip and smack into timber.

Adrenaline surging he runs, crashes onward.

In the edge of his vision is a flicker—a flicker of light from the lake.

He sprints, tries to cut off the jetty—cut it off from the woods.

Something is to his right, he levels the Glock, searching out the slightest sign.

Then holds fire, conceals position.

Turning around, the shape of a boat forms in the dim light.

A boat in the water—far out along the jetty.

Voices reach him—Jessica, Bella. Urgent, panicked.

Backing through the trees, he edges to the shoreline—hears Bella calling out. Calling out to her father.

A crash of sound follows, an object hitting water.

A scream.

Jessica screaming.

Whicher sees something in the lake now—far out—off the jetty—an arm, a thin arm raised.

A face, a head.

Disappearing. Below the surface.

McConnell is moving—somewhere, he hears it, feels it.

Out in the lake the pale dot is sinking, floundering, between Jessica's screams.

Turning, twisting, he runs for the water—breaks from the trees to sand and rock and air and open sky.

Shots crack out in the forest behind him.

Pitching into the lake Whicher fights for breath, fights the cold shock, reaches out with both arms—swimming. Glock still gripped in his hand. Swallowing water, the weight of body and limbs and clothes pulling him down, dragging him under. Reaching, hand over hand, through the black lake. Primal fear inside, fighting now, fighting for air, for life, for the point still yards out ahead—to reach the face dipping beneath the surface.

A man's voice is somewhere far behind.

Shouting.

The mass of water pulls him under.

Waves cover his face, leave him gasping, an image in his mind, from nowhere, the Brazos River, Texas, being baptized, as a boy.

The sound of firing is somewhere. Shots firing.

From the shore, the jetty.

Jessica's cries; strangled, caught in her throat.

The dark sky closes with the water.

Whicher pushes on into the lake.

The white skin of fingers, of a hand is out in front of him—he lurches, rises up, sees her. Grabs at Bella's arm, pulls her to him. Drags her upwards, up into air.

Wrapping an arm beneath her, he holds her to him.

Choking, sobbing, she writhes in the water, clings on.

Turning for the shore he feels his legs, his back, his arms burning, his lungs on fire. Shutting out pain, shutting out all thought, only dragging himself, now, dragging them both through the water. Holding the girl clear, keeping hold.

As a motor fires into life, an outboard motor.

Reaching over and over, legs kicking, pulling at the water. In the cold, numb, dread-filled black.

Minutes or seconds pass. Time stretched, compressing.

The boat moving, now, moving from the jetty—out into open water.

The marshal hauling the girl back, animal fear inside.

Fear and cold and raw exhaustion.

Now striking something—something hard below.

AN AMERICAN RECKONING

Mud. Stone. The solid bank of the lake.

Feet on the ground, pushing for the shore, breaking clear of the water. Stumbling to his knees. Holding up Bella.

Bella crawling for safety.

The boat on the water, leaving.

Whicher staring after it, fighting for breath, spent, only staring.

As it disappears.

Reappears—turning.

Dragging himself to the shore.

Bella retching, on all fours.

Frozen, shaking, he watches the boat come on.

A small figure—Jessica at its helm.

McConnell holding a gun in his hand.

Bella sitting on her haunches in the water—watching the boat, watching her father, her mother.

McConnell pointing the gun at his wife.

Approaching the shore, the boat slows.

Bella stands up, starts to move toward it.

McConnell calls out, calls her name.

And Jessica is out now, out from behind the wheel.

She rushes McConnell, knocks him sideways, shouting out.

McConnell, turns, fires on her.

Jessica spins sideways, collapses, falls from sight.

As Bella stops in her tracks, hands at her face, hands up, raised in horror.

The marshal holds the Glock still—barrel down, he drains the water.

Then levels it.

Stares along its iron sights—fires.

Travis McConnell staggers backward.

Whicher crashes through the water arms extended.

But the man goes down.

Diving forward, he catches hold of the boat.

As lights begin to flash along the shore—blue light, red light. On the glistening black. And the white cone of a searchlight skims the water. Beneath the whump and chop and draft of the helo's approach.

Epilogue

*Texas Department of Criminal Justice Hospital,
Galveston, Tx*

Five days later.

At the northern end of Galveston Island, gulls wheel above the lot on Harborside Drive. Whicher parks the airport rental car by the horseshoe ramp of a helicopter landing port. Across the street from the lot, adjoining an emergency room, the fort-like prison hospital building looms high above the road.

Stepping from the car, the marshal takes in the blue-green waters of the Galveston channel. The surface of the bay splintered with light beneath the late fall sun.

He takes a leather briefcase from the passenger seat. Fits his hat, buttons the jacket of his suit.

Cloud moves brisk in the wind, the tang of salt is in the Gulf coast air. Ragged sabal palms frame container ships on the opposite bank of the channel. He eyes the Texas Department of Criminal Justice Hospital—eight floors of pale brick. Slit-like windows.

Not the first time he's visited. Not likely to be the last.

He crosses the sand-blown street behind a TDCJ bus filled with outpatients. Glancing up at the fifth floor, he thinks of Jessica McConnell, inside. Three days since delivering her. Stabilized first in Erie, before she could be moved down to Texas. With a gunshot wound to her side, plus injuries sustained from a fall on the boat.

He thinks of Travis McConnell—back in Tennessee, now. At secure medical facilities there. With a bullet wound to the leg. State Patrol marine assets had pulled him out of Lake Erie, half-drowned, not far from the boat.

The marshal clips across a bright plaza. Grass squares and live oak around the walkways.

Security inspection is ahead on the ground floor.

At the entrance to the building, corrections officers look him up and down—the big man in the suit and hat, moving brisk.

Whicher pulls out his badge and ID.

Joins a line at the smoked glass doors.

Prepares himself for the wait.

⭑

Alone in an ante room on the fifth floor, the marshal reads a transcript of collected interview notes with Jessica McConnell. Statements given in the Pennsylvania hospital before leaving. An on-call duty lawyer present. Jessica looking to co-operate, she said, for the sake of her daughter.

Whicher skim-reads, leafs through the pages. In his mind

drawing out the time-line of events.

The man named Ervin Ackerman had visited Jessica the day that Bella first went missing.

Twenty-four hours before Whicher's first trip to Hudspeth County.

Ackerman, the younger brother of the shooter at the Ridgway farm.

A childhood friend. A one-time partner of McConnell in his Nashville days.

He'd visited before Whicher's first interview—with Jessica and the juvenile officer, Georgia Eastman, at the house.

The Memphis prison guard had gotten messages to him, Carlene Jimerson.

Ackerman had driven down to Texas.

Told Jessica that Travis would be breaking out.

He told her he'd come to take her north, to take her and Bella—to Pennsylvania. To flee with Travis, cross the border into Canada.

Whicher sets down the transcript papers. He steps across the room to a water cooler.

Takes a plastic cup, fills it.

Stepping to a narrow window in the wall he gazes out beyond the rooftops of the medical center to the Gulf glistening in the distance. Vast. Calm now. But full of latent energy in its depths.

He drains the cup.

Returns to his seat.

Bella was at the hostel in Fort Stockton—so Ackerman

insisted he'd return. That Jessica find some way they could leave together with her daughter.

After he'd left, she'd driven to Fort Stockton. Waited on Bella. Waited for her to come out on break. She knew the places she liked to go. She'd found her. She told her they were leaving—leaving Texas, leaving everything behind. That Jacob Harwood would pick her up in the morning; that he'd drive her back east to Nashville, that she could go back home.

Bella hadn't needed any reasons. Running was second-nature, she could barely wait. She could overnight in Fort Stockton, she said. Harwood could be there the next day.

The marshal thinks of his own movements—the first full day of the investigation. Unable to find Jessica, he'd interviewed Karyn Dennison. Then driven back to Fort Stockton, to interview the supervisor there.

But Ackerman had returned. He'd gone to Jessica's house, just as he'd said he would.

Things had turned bad, he'd threatened her. Became aggressive, according to what Jessica said. Insisted she leave with him, insisted on taking Bella.

In blind panic, she'd hit him.

She'd been afraid.

She'd snatched a picture from the living room wall, hit him in the side of the head with its frame. Hard as she could. With its heavy wooden edge.

She hadn't known her own strength.

He'd gone down. Hit the wall, and then the floor.

Lain there.

While she ran from the room.

Thinking to get out, run from the house, run anywhere.

But he hadn't come out.

When she finally went back, when she looked in the room, he hadn't got up.

He was no longer breathing.

His tongue was blocked in his throat.

She'd dragged him to her bedroom, terrified.

Terrified somebody might come.

Sat holding her stomach on the bed, wondering if the baby inside was still alive. If God would snuff out the life of her unborn child for the life she had taken, somehow taken. Unable to fathom what she had done. Unable to move, barely able to breathe.

Whicher tallies it; the fine blood spatter, the bedroom carpet stains.

She said she'd forced herself to move Ervin Ackerman's truck, the vehicle he came in—a dark blue Toyota pickup.

The marshal thinks of the neighbor, standing with the dog, telling him he'd seen the truck outside of her place.

She'd dumped it across town. Prayed that nobody would find it, prayed that nobody would come.

Whicher glances at a report added into the case papers from the Hudspeth Sheriff's office—locating the abandoned vehicle.

Ackerman was dead, now. Dead in her room, in her rented house.

She'd checked into a motel in Van Horn, thirty minutes away.

Whicher nods to himself. He'd been unable to find her. He'd waited alone outside her house.

A male nurse appears at the doorway to the ante room. "Marshal? You can see Ms McConnell now. And the doctor says she'll be along just as soon as she can."

⊥

The single-occupancy room is overheated, Jessica McConnell sitting up in bed. A cannula sticks from one wrist, taped in place, no drip line attached. A silvered chain slinks from the bed to a cuff secured at her other wrist. A sheen is on her pale face, skin lightly swollen. Her blue-gray eyes are restless, intense.

Against the back wall, the marshal sits on a steel-framed chair. Resistol hat on a cabinet in the corner. Briefcase open on the floor.

A female nurse enters, checks a note on a clipboard. Opens up a locked cabinet on the wall.

She takes out a medicine cup, dispenses pills into it. Puts the cup into Jessica's hand. "Two pills," she says. "Drink plenty of water with them." She fills a glass from a jug by the bed.

The nurse glances at Whicher, writes on the clipboard. Locks the cabinet again, exits the room.

Jessica looks across to him. "When can I speak to my daughter?"

"Juvenile Service is responsible for her, now," the marshal says.

"Have you heard anything?" Her voice is parched. Frail in her throat.

"I know she's safe," Whicher says. "I know nothing's going to happen to her."

"All she wants to do is just go home…"

The marshal nods. Thumbs a page of his notes.

He checks his watch. No sign yet of any doctor.

He sits straight-backed in the chair, ill at ease—hospital time an unwelcome feature; from army days through long years in law enforcement.

Jessica sits up an inch in the bed. "What about Jacob?"

Whicher looks at her.

"Is he still under arrest?"

The marshal nods. Thinks of phone calls between USMS and the Hudspeth Sheriff's office. "He's talking," he says. "He has a body on his land. Doesn't leave him with much of a choice." He shifts his weight on the chair. Leans back. Holds up his notes. "Couple of things I was wanting to ask you?"

She lies inert.

"About the sequence of events following Ervin Ackerman's death?"

Jessica's eyes snap into focus.

A pulse beats in the skin at her throat.

"About what you've already said on record?" the marshal says. "You're not obliged to talk if you don't want to."

She puts a pill from the medicine cup into her mouth, reaches for the water glass. Takes a sip.

"After you hit Ervin Ackerman?" Whicher says. "You said you drove to Van Horn, checked into a motel?"

Jessica swallows the pill, takes the second. Puts down the

glass. "I couldn't bear to be in the house…"

The marshal looks at his notes. "But you left the motel, you went back."

She closes her eyes. Rests her head against the pillow. "That night," she says. "To see if he was still there. I knew he would be. But I went back. And then I knew I'd have to move him."

The marshal re-reads the section outlining her actions on the night. She'd dragged Ackerman from the bedroom to her kitchen—displacing furniture, the table. Realized she wasn't strong enough to get a man's body into her car.

"You tried to move Ackerman," he says, "but then you couldn't do it. So you drove out to Jacob Harwood's place?"

"Jacob's truck had a winch in the bed, I'd seen him use it."

"You drove to Cammack Avenue? Knowing Harwood wouldn't be there?"

"I have a set of keys to his house. I knew he was out of town," Jessica says. "I let myself in. I found the keys to his truck, I took them."

"You never called him? You never spoke to him?"

She shakes her head.

"You stand by that statement?"

"Because it's true."

"You took Harwood's pickup," Whicher says. "You drove it over to your place. Drove it around the side of your house, to the yard in back, to your kitchen." The marshal looks at her. "Nobody saw this? Nobody saw you move the body? Not even your neighbor?"

Her voice is flat when she answers, her eyes unfocused at the ceiling. "Nobody was home. Only the dog saw. That dog. Snarling, barking…growling at me the whole time…"

"And you got Ackerman's body into the back of the pickup?"

"The winch has a hook. I tied his hands together." She mimes the action. "I used the belt from his jeans. I dropped the gate on the truck…" Her face blanches. "I winched him into the truck bed, you know all this…" Her voice trails off.

Outside in the corridor the marshal hears the sound of people talking, sees movement through a glass panel in the door.

The face of the female nurse appears. Then goes again. Moments pass, the talk recedes. The sound in the corridor fades.

Whicher turns back to the transcript and notes. "You took Ackerman's body out to ranch land belonging to Jacob Harwood? To a barn there. To conceal it."

"Yes."

"You saw nobody? And then you took back the Ram?"

"I took it back to Jacob's house," she says. "I drove back to my house in my car. I tried to straighten things out, straighten out the kitchen, clean the blood from the bedroom floor."

Whicher thinks of the search of Harwood's house, of his truck. He'd never known she'd used it. That she'd used it to transport a body that night. "After you got done in your house, you drove back to Van Horn?" the marshal says. "You stayed the night there, at the motel?"

"I was too scared to stay at the house."

"And then you flew to Nashville. The next morning. The early flight."

"You know I did."

A rap sounds at the door, a female doctor enters. Asian. In her thirties, a slim woman with quick, dark eyes.

Whicher holds up a security pass on a lanyard. "US Marshals Service."

The doctor nods. Looks across at Jessica.

"My office called earlier?" Whicher says. "About Ms McConnell. To see if she can be signed out?"

The doctor checks a sheaf of notes in her hand. "She's going out to Mountainview?"

"Awaiting trial, yes, ma'am."

The woman looks up, shakes her head. "That's a long trip. By road."

"We can fly her out."

"She can't fly," the doctor says, "not yet. We want to be completely sure there's no infection. She's not well enough to be transferred. Or held in regular prison facilities. Material and debris can get pulled into a wound like this. The white blood cell count is still a little high. There's no question of her leaving yet, marshal. Not for another day or so. I can't authorize it. I'm afraid she's going to have to stay."

᛭

Outside in the corridor, Whicher finishes up a phone call to Chief Marshal Fairbanks in the Pecos office. A return tomorrow or the next day the only option; medical consent required to transport a detainee awaiting trial.

He watches hospital staff and COs at a desk at the end of the corridor. Talking fast. Pressed-looking. Three hundred-plus inmate patients to manage. To treat, to keep secure.

He breaks off, knocks at the door to Jessica McConnell's room. Enters.

Her eyes are on him, listless, from the bed.

"I'll be leaving," Whicher tells her. "Maybe back tomorrow. Maybe the day after that."

She nods. Anxious-looking. Lost.

"Tell me something?"

Her eyes come up on his.

"Why Nashville?"

She only stares, silent.

"Why run?"

"It was home," she says, finally. "Ursula was there. It was the only place I thought we'd be safe."

The marshal looks at her.

"I went to the house, that first day, Ursula's house. I didn't go in. I couldn't face it."

"You stayed to wait for Harwood."

"I waited. I stayed in Luna Heights. I have a receipt somewhere, some place off of Harding. I saw Ursula at the bar the next day. She told me you went to see her, that you were looking for me."

Whicher thinks of Travis McConnell. Robbing a sporting goods store fifty miles away. Then running to Nashville, that same day—Barbone already shot. Drawn back, like Jessica.

Drawn to refuge; the place that once had worked.

"They didn't come," Jessica says, "and they didn't come. It took them so long… And Jacob tried to be so careful."

"And so you called me?"

"Ursula persuaded me. I called. I waited, hoping they'd arrive. And then I met with you. To try to buy time." She reaches for the water glass, takes a sip. "But you took me to that interview. With that marshal, Cruz…" She puts down the glass.

"And your husband arrived at your sister's bar?"

She gives the slightest nod.

"Thinking what?" Whicher says.

"I don't know."

"That she'd help him?"

Jessica's eyes track the ceiling. "Maybe he was like me; just desperate. Just looking for anything. Some kind of lifeline. Hope…"

"Bella was at the bar by then?" the marshal says.

She stares blank at the light. "I asked Jacob to leave her there. Leave her there with my sister. I was going to meet with him, alone. Decide what to do, where to go. It was all crazy…you arrested me. You took me back to Texas." Her voice trails off. "Finally he had to leave. When I never came, when I never called…"

"Because I'd arrested you? Put you in the jail."

She slips down in the hospital bed. Exhales a long breath. "He left. And Travis found Bella…"

Whicher stares at the length of chain attaching Jessica McConnell to the frame of the bed. Everybody gravitated to a place they thought of as shelter. Jessica. The man, McConnell. What had he hoped for? What had he hoped to gain?

He'd left with Bella.

The marshal thinks it over.

In McConnell's shoes, his flesh and blood right there before him, would he have done the same?

⭑

A CO waits in place outside the hospital room, now—Whicher sees the gray-uniformed woman through the glass insert in the door.

The transcript and notes are all ordered, everything arranged back in the leather briefcase. The marshal fits his hat, takes the rental car keys from the pocket of his suit.

"What do you think will happen to Jacob?"

Whicher thinks it over.

She says, "Do you know?"

"He's guilty of destroying the body of a man unlawfully killed," the marshal says. "He has a lawyer looking to keep it state, not federal. Work with the sheriff, cut an early plea."

He studies Jessica.

Weight seems to pin her to the bed.

"They'll charge him. With destruction of evidence. If he co-operates, he'll get a lighter sentence. Serve time in a state jail. Believe me, that's better."

On the bed she breathes shallow, closes her eyes.

"He drove Bella to Nashville to protect your daughter—because he loves you, he says. You're the mother of his unborn child. He never knew you'd killed a man. The church are vouching for him. It's a first offense. I'd think he'd serve six months."

Tears run from the edges of her eyes down the sides of her face.

"They're vouching for you, too."

She turns, looks at him.

He rests his briefcase on the seat. "Your sister called. Chief Marshal Fairbanks told me."

Her voice is small in her throat. "What for?"

"To make a formal application to the Juvenile Protection Service. To be the caregiver for Bella." He searches for the right words. "And for your child. When it's time."

Jessica lies rigid, scarcely breathing.

The marshal softens his voice. "Foster care or adoption are your other options…"

Her voice is barely a whisper; "What do you think will happen to me?"

"I think you'll spend some time in prison," Whicher says. "A year, maybe. Maybe less."

"I never meant to kill that man."

The marshal nods.

"I was scared for my daughter. I didn't know what to do. I was just scared. Of everything. I was terrified. Of Bella getting taken away…"

Whicher picks up the briefcase, pauses a moment at the door.

Jessica lies on the bed, eyes searching his face.

"Harwood could be awarded custody of your child.

When he gets out." He looks at Jessica a long moment. "If that's what you want?"

Words rush from her; "He'd be a good father, he'd take good care…"

The marshal lets his eyes rest on hers.

"He brought me to God. I want to be with him. And with my children…"

"Your sister can give Bella a home," Whicher says, "for as long as she needs it." He fits his hat. "She can take care of your newborn. Till Harwood gets out. I'll call Georgia Eastman," he tells her. "As lead on your case. Tell her I'd recommend it. For what it's worth."

⋏

On Seawall Boulevard at the top end of the island, Whicher takes the old sidewalk along a ten-mile stretch of pale beach. Wind freshening. A light chop on the water. A mass of dark-edged clouds blowing in.

Out in the ocean, a pilot boat heads for the open waters of the Gulf.

He watches it. Moving past the shrimpers, the sailboats. Toward the tankers standing out in the deep.

He thinks of Jessica. Alone in the hospital room. A guard at her door. Thinks of the charges against her. Involuntary manslaughter, at a minimum. Destruction of evidence; concealing and burning a corpse.

Travis McConnell would be back inside, just as soon as he was healed from his injuries. With time added to his sentence for robbery, for felony escape.

He thinks of Bella. Just a child. An image of her in his mind; at the lake—watching her father gun down her mother on the boat.

He walks on down the wide boulevard, cars and trucks rolling by beachwear and souvenir stores. Past seafood restaurants and out-of-season motels. The names on their signs exotic-sounding. Colors bloomed with salt, streaked with rust.

Sand twists along the road in the wind. The marshal thinks briefly of Finn Ackerman, the shooter at the barn. Dead at the scene in Pennsylvania. By the time an ambulance arrived. Ready to shoot him down on sight, shoot him in the back, whatever his reasoning. Whicher lets it sit a moment, watching the waves roll in. No feeling of remorse is in his heart.

In the distance, along the beach, the old-time pier stands silhouetted—its rollercoaster ride and Ferris wheel strange shapes above the graying waters and the sky.

The marshal thinks of returning home. An hour or more to kill before heading to the mainland, for the flight from Houston.

He walks on. Along the ocean's edge. The pull of the tide churning waves on the sand. Thinking of change, consequence, of the speed, how fast a life could turn, could founder.

Jessica. Never seeing things as they really were, with McConnell.

Harwood. Through some flaw; naivety.

Turning toward the water he watches the pilot boat reach

a tanker. A man to place on board. A man of skill and judgement. Charged with the vessel's conduct. Course and speed. To bring it safely in, bring it in to port. To find the way in, the right way. Avoiding all danger. Tide and wind and the shifting sands beneath.

He stands, watches it a long moment. Till conscious thoughts drift from his mind.

An image of home and family stirs him, finally.

He moves along.

Resolved inside.

Keeps on.

Keeps his course.

Printed in Great Britain
by Amazon